# RETURN BY AIR

## TRACEY JERALD

# RETURN BY AIR

Copyright © 2020 by Tracey Jerald

ISBN: 978-1-7330861-6-5 (eBook)

ISBN: 978-1-7330861-7-2 (Paperback)

Editor: One Love Editing (http://oneloveediting.com)

Proof Edits: Holly Malgieri (https://www.facebook.com/HollysRedHotReviews/)

Cover Design by Tugboat Design (https://www.tugboatdesign.net/)

*For Tara, who made the decision to go it alone and still found true love in the end.*

# PROLOGUE

## Kara

"How far along are you again, dear?"

I let out a sigh of relief at my mother's banal reaction over my overwhelming news. I've known since just before I left Alaska to come back to Florida, but this is the first time my parents and I have had a moment to reconnect.

"Just over twelve weeks," I reply, modulating my voice carefully. I smooth my hand over my navy blue shirtwaist dress, my grandmother's bracelet glittering at my wrist. I dressed the perfect part of the daughter my parents always wanted today—demure, not the woman I grew into being.

Most of the way to a doctoral degree in physics at the age of twenty-three, there was nothing I wanted more than to experience science tactically. That was until I met *him.*

Then all I wanted was more of his words.

My soul needed more of his kisses.

And I lost myself in his touch.

"Kara, are you listening?" my mother snaps.

"I apologize, Mother. You were saying?"

"I asked what your plans were?"

"Well, based on my calculations, the baby should be due around mid-March."

"You haven't seen a doctor yet?"

"No, not yet. I wanted to resolve matters at school as I don't feel it would be appropriate for me to attend next semester."

"No, that wouldn't do at all. Would it?" My mother sniffs before taking a delicate sip of her tea. "Chip? What are your thoughts? You're too quiet over there." She tips her head imperceptibly in my father's direction.

My father's so detached, he might as well be in another room. He was on the phone for some time, scribbling hastily in his journal. When my mother's voice calls him to attention, he replies, "Hmm?"

"I said, it wouldn't do for Kara to attend school next semester. Do you agree?"

"Certainly not. After all, how will she pay for it?"

"Well, I understand babies are expensive, however, once grandfather's trust comes in..." I carefully outline my—our—plans.

My parents stare at me blankly, as if I'm speaking a foreign language. Then my father chuckles warmly.

I relax my posture slightly. It will be all right. All that fear for nothing.

Then he opens his mouth and shows me why I was terrified to come here—back to where they ruined so many memories, why I escaped into the land of fact over emotion. I wish I could whisk myself back to the land that matched his eyes for just a moment. Because even though I was less prepared for the consequences of lying in his arms than I am for this conversation, I felt safe there.

Even if it was only for a short while. Here? I don't know if I ever felt truly at rest.

Addressing my mother, he says, "Pat, excuse me for my terribly rude behavior earlier, love. That was what the call was about. Kara's trust can be blocked, just as it was for Dean."

"Excuse me?" I whisper. My older brother came out a few years before. And while we've maintained a close relationship, he was disowned by my parents. Or as disowned as a man of twenty-five could be. Thumbing his nose at the Malone heritage, he continued living exactly as he was as a fireman just outside the city limits.

I've loved my brother my whole life, and who he chooses to spend the rest of his life with means exactly one thing to me—Dean's happiness. But to my parents, it posed an image issue.

So, they dealt with the image. Much like I suspect, to my queasy stomach, my father's doing right now.

Ignoring my presence, my mother beams at him. "Oh, that's delightful, darling. I knew you could do it."

He smiles shyly at her praise for his abominable behavior. "They said it was trickier this time since Kara is over eighteen, however, I was able to convince the board she showed poor judgment by not only delaying her studies but by becoming sexually compromised. They agreed that if she was unable or unwilling to terminate the pregnancy, they would vote to revert her portion of the trust to the main fund." Barely sparing me a glance, he bites down on his lower lip. "I don't suppose you would consider—"

"How dare you!" I leap out of the settee I'm perched on, outraged. "This is your grandchild."

"That—" My mother cringes. "—is an abomination. One we could still see about resolving if you'd use that logic you're notorious for flaunting at inopportune times. Dear, Chip, did we apologize to the Fitzgeralds for the snub Kara gave their son the other night at the club?"

"I don't believe we did. Let me make a note to—"

"You want me to murder my child!" I shout.

"And you're asking me to give up mine," Mother interjects smoothly.

Even as I press my hand firmly against my lower stomach, I hiss, "No one is forcing you to do anything except abide by your own worthless credo." Storming to the door, I'm halted by my father's voice. "Yes?" I spin to face them.

"Before you leave, we expect you to return everything on your person that belongs to us."

Confused, I hitch my shoulders. "What do you mean?" I ask.

"Your credit cards, your cell phone. I'd ask for your car, but frankly, it's too annoying to deal with selling for the value. Oh, and that." He nods at the bracelet I'm rubbing back and forth across my wrist.

"No, Grandmother left this to me." I clasp my hand over it tightly. It's memories of laughter between me and Dean as children running up and down the beach at her home on Amelia Island, free from rules and etiquette. Free from the worry of disappointing my parents again.

"Your grandmother left it to the estate. We gave it to you," my mother counters. Turning to my father, she wonders aloud, "I know I asked before with the other one, but is it possible to disown your grown children?"

"I looked into it before, darling. I can see if anything different has arisen since then if you like?"

"Do, please," Mother encourages. "In the meanwhile, Kara—if you please?"

Almost like a robot, I pull out the few items they can lay claim to on my person, knowing with it I lose one of two ways I have to contact Jennings about the baby.

God, I hope he checks the email I sent him.

Dropping everything with a clatter onto their Chippendale pedestal table by the door, I reach for the clasp on my grandmother's bracelet. Without breaking eye contact, I stride right to my mother and whisper, "Grandmother wanted me to wear this. She wanted it for me."

"She didn't want this for you," my mother sneers, making a circle with her fingers.

"Maybe not. But she still would have loved me." Dropping the bracelet in her lap, I announce, "I'll wear it again one day."

Without a word, without a sound, I turn and walk away from my family's compound.

GROANING, I flush the toilet of Dean's bathroom. "I'm so glad I stayed with you when I got home."

Sitting on the edge of his tub, he rubs a hand up and down my back. "And this is where you're going to stay, Kara."

"I don't think your social life is ready for your sister to be curled up on your sofa bed—"

"We're moving this weekend," he states firmly.

"What?" I shriek, but that only sets off the nausea that seems to come whenever my emotions are out of whack. In other words, I don't feel like I've kept a meal down since before Jennings broke things off in Juneau. And I didn't even suspect I was pregnant then.

"Shh. Let me put this on your neck. It will help with the nausea." I hear the rush of water in the sink before a cold rag is dripping down my already ruined dress. "Goddamn bastards." Dean rubs his fingers over my wrist where I've chafed it raw in the hours since I managed to make it back to his apartment.

I let out a choked sob. "Mom and Dad?"

"Among others." He lets go for just a moment before I hear the opening and closing of a medicine cabinet. "Let's get some cream on and bandage you up. You don't need a scar."

"Dean, what you said—"

"We're moving, Kara. There's a two-bedroom unit open on the other side of the complex. Some of the guys are going to come help us move. All we need to get you is a bed and a dresser." He tells me our plans as he gently wraps my chafed wrist. "Think you can deal with your brother as a roommate?"

"I'll get a job as soon as I can. I'll keep our home clean. I'll..." My litany is stopped by Dean lifting my tearstained face to his.

"You'll take care of my future niece or nephew first. I love you, Kara. No matter who comes and goes in our life, you were the first person I loved."

I throw my arms around my brother and hold him tight in the cramped space. "You were too, Dean."

I don't know how long we sit there just holding on to one another until all the fight leaves my body.

When I wake up the next day, I wake up in Dean's bed. There's a small can of cold ginger ale next to me with a key and a note. Reaching for it, I read aloud, "Get out for some air. It will do you some good. See you when I get home from my shift tomorrow."

I put the note back and murmur, "I think I'll stay right where I am. I'm pretty certain falling from the air is what landed me here."

# JENNINGS

There's a light knock on my door. Not turning my head from my computer, I call out, "Come in, Lou," knowing only one person would dare to interrupt me while I'm reviewing the payroll she banished me to my office to complete two hours ago.

After all, as Lou informed me while nudging me in the middle of my back, "People like to get paid, Jennings, so why don't you get on that and make it happen before they all walk out on you? Better yet, maybe they'll steal your planes and just fly away to a better job. One with a boss who pays them on time."

I paused at the threshold of the door to glare down at the retired military drill sergeant who's the operations manager of Northern Star Flights. "Why do I keep you around anyway?"

"Because you're too scared of me to fire me?" she joked.

I opened and closed my mouth a few times before I entered my office and slammed the door behind me in response, refusing to admit she's right.

Now, for Lou to be interrupting me, either something's gone wrong down at the airstrip, or there's a phone call I have to be on. The door creaks open to reveal her trembling. I immediately jump to my feet in concern. "What happened?" Nothing shakes Lou's composure except an utter catastrophe. Despite her diminutive stature, the woman frankly scares the crap out of every arrogant flight jockey who comes through my office.

I'm now bracing myself as she makes her way toward me holding a large manila envelope. "What's in there?" I nod toward it.

Lou doesn't stop at the front of my desk. Instead she walks around the side of it. Twisting myself around, my body locks solid when tears leak out of her eyes. "Just tell me," I demand.

"It's from a probate firm in Juneau," she rasps out. "I hate to be the one to tell you, but Jed's—"

"Stop," I rasp out harshly.

"Jennings, I'm so sor—"

"No!" I cut her off, my mind already anticipating what she's about to say. But if the words come out, then it will be real. And that's impossible. She can't be standing in front of me telling me I've lost one of the brothers of my heart. Somehow, I'd have known. Right?

But even as my mind's denying it, I'm reaching for Lou. Harsh sobs rack my body as I realize I'll never see his wild brown hair standing up at every angle at one of our reunions ever again. I'll never hear his crazy stories about the locals at his bar in Florida. And the only time I'll likely get to meet his family—the man he married, his sister-in-law, and nephew—will be at his funeral.

"Just hold on, Jennings," Lou tries to soothe me.

I swallow and open and close my mouth as I try to speak, but no words come out, only an agonized moan. For once, I do what Lou says without argument and just grab tight.

After getting myself under control, I ask for a few moments alone. Dropping back into my desk chair, I wipe my eyes with a shaking hand before I reach for the offensive envelope. Pulling out the sheet of paper, I read the formal notification from Isler, Litchfield, Garrish, and Knight that Jed is truly gone.

A quick glance at the contents offers a briefly worded apology for my loss as well as instructional information about "where a memorial and burial service will be held for the remains of Jedidiah Jonas Smith," I read aloud in the empty office. "God, he didn't even have a chance to change his name with the fucking attorneys." Crumpling the paper in my hands, I press my fists up to my mouth to subdue the whimpering sounds of pain that try to escape.

Jed's gone forever. The best one of all of us. How? Why?

And unable to find the answers in the carefully worded letter, I sink down into my chair, lay my head down on my desk, and let the pain swamp over me as planes take off and land behind me, for once without my notice or caring.

All I feel is numb.

MUCH LATER WHEN I'm again able to form coherent sentences, I pick up the phone to call another one of our "brothers," Kody. "Did you—"

I can't even get the full sentence out of my mouth when he's breaking in with a subdued "I won't insult you by asking if you're going."

"Absolutely. Do you want me to fly down to Portland and pick you up?"

"Jesus, Jennings." His laugh is riddled with tears. "When we first met, did you ever think you would actually be saying that to me?"

A sharp pain stabs into me when my eye lands on the other item that was included in the envelope that came with the notification of Jed's demise. A second envelope had a copy of a photo of the five of us from the last summer we were all in the Ketchikan Lumberjack Show together. Our arms are all thrown around each other, and we're completely hamming it up for the camera dressed in suspenders and plaid flannel shirts—standard attire we wore for every show. Jed looks like a hillbilly in between us all wearing a pair of half-done-up overalls.

I gruffly reply, "Jed did. He believed in all of us." My mind drifts back to the nights we spent on break at the Smiths' family home those summers we worked together. We'd stay up talking about what our futures entailed. For me, all it meant was being in the air, no matter what that took. Or whose heart it meant breaking to do it.

We all did it. We found the will to find our dreams, all of us. Brad's got his family and his boat. Kody's building homes like they're Lincoln Logs. Nick achieved his dream years ago by becoming the MMA heavyweight title holder and is now helping create them. I'm in the air or directing people to get there. And Jed? "He found love and marriage, something he never believed he'd be able to do legally in his lifetime. How fucking heartless is life that it took him from it?" I wonder.

Kody lets out a rough sound in my ear. "That he did. Call me when you've figured out when we're heading up. I'll drive up to you and store my car at your place, cut down on time."

"Right." We both disconnect, each of us lost in a brotherhood of friendship that began close to twenty years ago.

And suffered a devastating blow tonight I only hope we can recover from.

BACK IN MY CONDO, I sit in the dark drinking straight from the bottle of locally brewed gin Jed sent me for my last birthday. "Listen, buddy, as a bar owner, I might not be able to afford as much as you can, but I can get you a direct line to the best-tasting liquor in the world," he joked.

He wasn't wrong about much, including the fact the Florida-made gin whispers down the back of my throat as smooth as water.

Lou came into my office not long after I got off the phone with Kody. She took one look at the devastation on my face and asked only, "What do you need me to do?"

"Payroll's done," I responded dully. "Find pilots for my flights."

"On it."

"If I haven't said it before, Lou, I appreciate what you do keeping everything in line here." My words are sincere even if my voice is flat.

"I know, boss. Now, get out of here." She squeezed my shoulder before she left my office. I left not long after. I only wish the rest of my night permitted such liberties.

The phone call I endured when I broke a date for a charity event frayed my temper to the very threads. "Jesus, it's not like we were an item," I snapped before I ended the call. And now I'm more glad than ever over my unwilling celibacy in the last several months due to the business taking on more work and keeping me away from home. "If this is what dating is like..." I leave the rest of my sentence unsaid as I take another swig of gin. Unfortunately, the lack of compassion from the woman in question reminds me vividly of a conversation I had with Jed years ago.

"Don't you want to settle down one day?" he'd asked me a few years ago. "Find the one woman who you'd give up anything to have, who could give you everything you ever wanted?"

"She doesn't exist, buddy."

Jed bellowed our a hollow laugh. "Jennings, one day, you're going to realize everything you ever wanted has been waiting right there in front of you and you never realized you could have had it all."

"If that's the case, I give you permission to slap me upside the head to wake me up."

Now, he'll never have the chance.

Stumbling to my feet, I go to the closet where I know I've kept photos of me and the guys over the years. Sliding the hefty box labeled "Lumberjacks" into my arms, I carry it over to the couch and yank out a bunch of pictures.

Kody's bright hair which looks almost neon orange in the Alaskan sun.

Brad's arms scooping his then girlfriend, now wife, into his arms as he threatens to dump her into the hot tub behind the Smiths' family home.

Nick, brooding, and flicking off the camera. Tossing the picture on the desk, I find one where there's actual laughter on Nick's face when he's pointing at Jed, who stripped his hair from its dark brown to bleach white. "God, look at Jed parading around without a care in the world," I wonder. My lips curve even as I set that one aside to put in a frame later.

The next picture has me blinking rapidly. "How did this one end up in here?" The slim brunette with glasses is laughing with Jed's sister, Maris, while Jed has them both in a headlock. He's grinning madly at the camera.

But even after all these years, my heart still twinges at the quiet beauty of Kara Malone. After all, it's not every day you realize you might actually be in love and then quickly shove the woman out of your life knowing that trusting someone with that much of your heart could lead to nothing but broken dreams and heartbreak.

After all, hadn't life taught me that from an early age?

Leaning back, I hold up the picture, which shows Kara smiling up at Jed. "I wonder what she's up to. Knowing Kara, she's probably slowed down global warming or she's sprouted palm trees in Antarctica," I mumble. But the truth is, she was just that brilliant.

By the time I met her, Kara had already attained dual masters in physics and ecology by the age of twenty-three and was on a fast track to get her PhD. And I was what? Petrified, I can admit with so many years in between. Lifting the bottle of clear liquid to my lips to take a drink, I sigh with regret at the way we ended. "She didn't deserve the way I dicked her over," I admit aloud, not for the first time. Then again, the only other person I've ever admitted that to is gone. Jed listened when I told him a few years ago the reason I let her go was because "I couldn't bear to watch her walk away like everyone else did."

Jed clapped me on the shoulder, before telling me, "Look around, my friend. None of us ever walked away," before heading back into the cabin we rented for that particular reunion in Montana.

Memories come rushing through my system the longer I hold on to Kara's photo. Staying up overnight in order to take the ferry to Juneau so I could string a few days together with her. Teasing her about trying to save the world as we lay in bed, when she'd very seriously explain, "No, just trying to make my part of it safer." I remember repeatedly chastising her for rubbing her wrist raw with her grandmother's bracelet over her delicate skin whenever she got nervous or upset.

"I wonder if she's coming to the service." Knowing how close she and Jed's sister were, it wouldn't surprise me. As much as Jed, Brad, Nick, Kody, and I are brothers, those two women were born sisters on opposites sides of the country.

And now we'll all be reunited because of Jed's death? It's abhorrent to me. My temper boils over at the injustice of it all. Swiveling in my chair, I hurl the bottle against the wall, and the glass shatters into a thousand pieces. "Damn you, Jed. Why the fuck did you go and die on us? What are we going to do without you?"

Dropping the picture, all thoughts of anything beyond the crazy-wild man who loved life and everyone in it, including a woman who's likely long forgotten I exist, disappear. I shove the box aside and cut loose.

It's like all the air has been sucked out of the room until I'm in nothing but a void of pain and emotion weeping near the tangible evidence of the past that showed at one time there were five of us who considered each other brothers.

Now, there are only four.

What are we supposed to do?

# KARA

D*ear Dean.*

    *Well, we're on our way back to Alaska. For so many years, I tried to tell you about my time there, and now that you're gone, it's funny how the words just want to pour out of me.*

    *Unless you've been there, it's almost impossible to understand her beauty and her savageness because they're intertwined so brilliantly they can't be separated. You have to love both to love the whole. Alaska isn't merely a piece of land to be lived upon; she breathes and embeds herself into your heart and soul mere minutes after you bow in her presence.*

    *She's demanding and regal, temperamental and savage. She's unconquerable. And humans are foolish to think they can.*

    *There are so many pieces that make up Alaska. She provides rare but distinct praise for those few dynamic souls who sustain their lives there. You know there was a time when I believed I could be one of them. Almost sixteen years ago, to be exact. Now, between all the years in between and everything that's happened, it seems like those years belong to a story that should begin with the words "once upon a time." Back then, I thought I had the mettle to build my dreams conquering sweeps of ice while breaking down walls built around a man's heart. I had my chance at the first.*

*It took a long time for me to realize I was blessed by her when I left; that Alaska gave me a gift to make up for my original one being lost.*

Pausing in my letter, I sigh. It doesn't matter how long it takes me to write it. Dean's gone. He's never going to receive it anyway. I glance to my right at the tall figure in the seat next to me. His dark hair flops over his forehead as he frowns down at his iPad. Slowly, I reach over and brush the hair away from my son's forehead.

His head turns toward me before he pulls the noise-canceling earbuds from his ears. With a frown, he asks, "Are you okay, Mom?"

Mom. Alaska made me a mother to a son whose heart is easily the size of her landscape. Well, technically, that's not correct. Jennings did, I think with a touch of lingering anxiety I shove aside knowing what's going to happen the moment Jed's will is read. After ignoring all of my attempts to contact him over the years, he's finally going to be forced to admit he's a father.

My breathing accelerates. I acquiesced to Jed adding in the codicil to his will because he accepted my conditions. It still doesn't mean what's about to be set in motion isn't affecting me because I know it's just going to add another level of emotional upheaval to the person I love more than anyone else in this world—my son.

Kevin frowns again when I don't respond fast enough. Quickly, I pull myself from my thoughts and answer, "Yes, sweetheart. I'm just woolgathering. Go back to your movie."

"Are you..." He doesn't finish his sentence before he shoves in his buds again.

I wish he would just tell me what's on his mind, talk to me about what's bothering him. Because if there's anyone in the world who understands what he's feeling, it's me. There's so much pain locked inside of him since he lost both of his uncles a few short weeks ago in an accident that's left the three of us devastated and floundering.

And here we are—heading right back to the place where it all started. After ensuring Kevin's attention is back on the movie, I close my laptop and tuck it into the seat back in front of me. Looking out the window, there's nothing but clouds from our current vantage point.

I know from my conversation with Maris the letters from the lawyers were going out today, as was the notice of Jed's death to the local Juneau paper. But that's not how he was known for the decades he lived in Alaska before taking a vacation to Florida and never returning. It's why, despite the local media coverage that invaded our lives for weeks in Florida with the death of the "Misters Malone," we haven't been faced with Jed's closest friends.

Yet. That's going to change the minute we touch down, and I know it.

We're about to endure a second viewing and funeral. Then, the second will reading. And a second chance for John Jennings to turn my world upside down.

We hit a pocket of turbulence that has Kevin's hand shooting out to grab mine. God, I want to laugh and then let silent tears fall, much like I've been doing late at night when I know Kevin's barricaded himself in his room. Our worlds have drastically changed. And they're about to be shaken more; he just doesn't know it.

But I do.

And I'll do everything possible to protect my son from the pain I've endured each time an email I sent to his father and it was ignored.

What I won't do is feel shame for the decisions I made, starting with the one where I walked out of my parents' life, moved in with my brother, and never looked back. Not once.

Not ever.

EIGHTEEN HOURS after we left Jacksonville, we're waiting for Maris to pick us up at the Juneau International Airport when Kevin takes a deep breath of the cool mountain air and sighs contently. "Mom, I thought you said Alaska was cold?"

Wrapping my arm around his waist, I wonder how time went by so fast that I now have to look up into his eyes to answer. "This is a warm day." My lips curve faintly at the shock on his face. "This sixty degrees you're basking in is almost sweltering for a native Alaskan."

"But—"

"Yes?" I answer distractedly as I scan for Maris's SUV in the darkness.

"But that's like our winter!" he sputters.

The words are out of my mouth before I can censor them. "Why do you think your uncle Jed loved our winter so much?" I tease. Then I curse myself a million times a fool as Kevin's body goes rigid beneath my arm. "I'm sorry, sweetheart." My voice is as cracked as my heart.

My son, my baby, is learning lessons he should never understand. He's been taught too early the agonizing loss of those you love. It's then I spot the vehicle Maris described over the phone. "There's Maris." I give his waist one more squeeze before I step away to pick up my carry-on, using my other hand to wave.

My best friend, and sister-in-law through marriage, pulls to a stop next to us. As she jumps from the driver's seat, her head of mahogany hair gleams in the fluorescent lights. Running around the front of the car, she opens her arms wide to wrap us both in the one thing we need more than anything.

Strength.

Leaning my head down on her shoulder, I take just a moment of it. Because it's not just the memorial service that has me on edge. It's what I know I have to do after.

And to honor the two of the three men I love beyond anything, I agreed, which is why it looks like I have enough luggage to last a lifetime when the reality is Kevin and I are only moving to Alaska for the rest of the summer.

Juneau, Alaska, is only accessible to an outsider by air or by sea. But for some indescribable months many years before, I never cared if I left once I stepped foot on her shores. I easily pictured myself living permanently in the state capital that drew me because of one love, introduced me to another, and finally, gave me the one I cherish above all others.

Driving from the airport to Maris's family home on the outskirts of downtown keeps me quiet despite the catching up between my son and my best friend. Reaching over the back of the seat, I grab Kevin's hand. "Are you sure you want to stay here this summer?" It's not that the reunion between father and son I agreed to leaves me much choice, but I'd be willing to fight unlike the way my parents did for me, but very much like the way my brother did for me every single day. Including the ways he often went against his husband when it came to matters of my son.

My son. I'd do anything for this child. Despite the resentment when year over year, I never heard a peep from his birth father, including a bounce-back message, I persisted in trying to contact Jennings to let him know he had a son. Shoving that thought aside, I give Kevin's hand a firm squeeze for the millionth time since we got the knock on the door telling us about the accident.

He nods. "I need to be away from everything back there. Everywhere I go, I'm reminded of what happened. I don't know why, but somehow I think I feel close to them because this is something they would do."

*You have no idea.* The thought passes through my mind as my eyes collide with Maris's as I shoot her a sidelong glance. "You're right, Kevin. It is something they'd do," I reassure him.

Something infinitesimally wound up behind Kevin's green eyes relaxes. "So, what's there to eat at the house? Airplane food sucks."

Maris jumps into our conversation at this point. "Honey, you know it's late. So, when we get back to the house, I think a light snack is in order—"

Kevin groans. I just smile, waiting.

Maris continues. "— because tomorrow we're going to have the best lobster chowder anywhere in the world. Tomorrow. Tonight, it's close to midnight our time, which is 4:00 a.m. for your body. Too late for anything heavy. You and your mom must be exhausted."

Kevin perks up. "Are we having lobster to go with it?"

I rebuke him gently. "Did Maris say that?"

"No, ma'am." I have to stifle my giggles when I twist back around in my seat and catch the wink Maris aims at me.

"Likely cause she wanted it to be a surprise," I murmur but obviously not quiet enough when Kevin lets out a rebel yell from the back.

Hearing that, a small stitch helps pieces of my desecrated heart seal itself back together. It's temporary, I know, trying to repair weeks of anger and devastation, and the fear waiting for me.

Pulling up to the home that holds so many memories, I begin to hyperventilate. My vision darkens at the edges as the clock spins wildly back to the last time I stood in front of this two-story home over fifteen years ago.

"Kara? Jesus, you're scaring the hell out of me." Maris shakes me hard.

"Mom?" In a faraway part of my mind, I hear my son's anxiety. It drags me from my nightmare the way nothing else can.

"I'm fine." Or I will be if I could erase the memories of John Jennings out of my head each time I see images of the home where my son was likely conceived. I give them a weak smile. "I'm just tired. And I'm ready to find a bed."

"Then let's get your stuff inside. Oh, I figured Kevin would want the basement," Maris says casually.

"Like a man cave?" Kevin says excitedly.

"Indeed. There's an open room down there with a bed, closet, gaming setup—" Maris doesn't get to finish before Kevin's holding out his hand for a high five, which Maris doesn't hesitate to give him.

"You didn't need to give up your space," I rebuke her gently. "Though for the sake of the smell of your house, it was probably a wise move."

"Hey!" Kevin protests.

"Is the teenager starting to resemble that remark?" Maris snarks before sliding out of the car. I'm not far behind. I pause when I take in the night sky. It shows me every star I ever made a wish on before I gave up on wishes and dreaming and went back to what I know best—analytical thinking. Shaking my head, I suggest, "Why don't we just take in the carry-ons tonight? Then we can deal with the larger bags in the morning."

"That works for me," Kevin agrees, patting his roller-board carry-on. My shoulders shake knowing his priorities mean it contains his gaming system as well as a change of clothes and his Dopp kit.

"Sounds like a plan," Maris says. "Hey, Malone?" Both of us turn. She pitches a set of keys in my direction which I catch easily. "Welcome back. I just wish it was under better circumstances." Her beautiful face has aged with the tragedy we've all suffered through.

I nod, but I mentally can't go there or I'll just crumble in the front yard. Jed and Dean are both gone; it's incomprehensible. We've lived through so much in the six weeks since their death. And yet, that has nothing on what we're about to face.

Nothing.

Because four men who loved Jed like a brother are about to find out the secrets that kept Jed from them.

And they're all because of me.

THE NEXT DAY, Maris and I are groggily sitting around the Smith family kitchen around 9:00 a.m. Juneau time when an actual landline rings. My brow quirks before I ask, "You have a real phone?"

"Oh yeah. With the winters up here, it'd be crazy...crap." Maris's checks the caller ID. "It's Brad."

Brad. Bradley Meyers. One of Jed's closest friends. A wash of nausea I decide to attribute to jet lag hits. Calmly, I pick up my coffee and take a sip before saying, "Shouldn't you get that?"

"I..." Maris stammers. "Shit." Snatching up the phone, she answers, "Brad." There's a pause. "No, everything is handled. All arrangements are made; thank you for offering." Her eyes drift over to me. "Dean's family made it in late." Another pause. "I appreciate the thought, but they're really not in a condition to meet anyone right now."

I mouth, "Thank you," to her, because while I know the cocoon around us won't last longer than the reading of the will, having this time to acclimate is critical for the mental well-being of my son. Jennings's son. The son I tried for years to contact him about.

Well, there's nothing I want or need from Jennings any longer, I tell myself firmly. It was a struggle, but in the end, we made it with more than most single-parent families. We live comfortably in a two-bedroom apartment not far from where I work, and Kevin is well adapted due to the two incredible male role models in his life. And if I secretly wonder if I'm going to be enough to get him through this next stage of growing to become everything I knew he could be from the moment he was laid in my arms, well, that's on me.

In many ways, I came to peace with the fact Jennings never wanted anything to do with his son long ago because he gave me something much better than a man's love. Jed believed his friend's life would be shaken by the news about his son. I have my doubts, but I guess we'll all know soon enough. I just wish my son wasn't old enough to be witness if it doesn't go the way Jed predicted it would. Whereas I'll leave with the love that grew out of my body and soul, I want Kevin's heart just as intact—if not more so—than we arrived. Is that going to be possible?

Just then, as I half listen to Maris wrap up her call with Brad, Kevin stumbles into the kitchen.

Everything comes second place to my son: ambitions, goals, dreams. They fade under the glow of Kevin's eyes when he spies me sitting at the counter. These are the moments every parent lives for—sharing everyday love and aches with a person connected to your soul. Jennings doesn't know that by his own choices.

Kevin comes directly to me, giving me a brush of his cheek before he goes to snatch my coffee. Shaking my head, I hand it over. "I'll just go get another one," I tease, brushing my hand along his jaw.

"Thanks, Mom." He yawns, mumbling his appreciation.

Maris wraps up her call. "Well, I staved off the welcoming committee," she announces before turning around and spotting Kevin. "Oh, hey, kid. I didn't see you there."

"Welcoming committee?" he asks.

"Some people who knew Uncle Jed wanted to come by. I'm not ready to be social. For the next few days, I'd like to get acclimated to being here, to the time change, to everything." I tell my son the truth without explaining it all. Not yet. I'll have to do that soon enough. I'm doing my best to protect him from anything ugly at the moment while his emotions are all over the place.

"Right." The one word he bites off says a million of them.

Maris and I exchange concerned looks. I open my mouth, but Kevin's words come out first. "Mom, when are you going to let me take care of you now that I'm the last man of our family?" He puts his mug down with a snap much the way Dean did his entire life.

"Kevin," I manage. The wound in my heart I thought was healing the tiniest bit gapes wide open. I'm surprised the blood pouring from it isn't seeping into Maris's kitchen floor.

"Got no one else to take care of you now." His head twists to Maris. "And I want to meet your friends. I need to get a read on them to make certain they're good people."

I have to clutch the counter in front of me. I can't breathe. "Baby, you're just fifteen," I murmur. "You have years…"

But Kevin doesn't agree. "I'm the only man left!" he shouts. "The only one. Dean's gone; Jed's gone. It's just me." The mug falls from his hands, spilling the remaining coffee on the floor. He jumps back, hissing at the heat touching his bare feet. But his green eyes, so like his father's, don't speak of anything but agony. He mutters, "I'll be right back."

Kevin stalks off toward the basement.

Maris and I stand there quietly for a few moments before she breaks the silence. "Is this normal since—"

"The anger? The outbursts? Yes," I admit sadly. "The 'man of the house' bit? No, that's new. I'll have to give his therapist a heads-up."

"I know I was surprised you put him in therapy right away, but I'll be the first one to admit I was wrong. God, Kara. What happened killed more than our brothers, didn't it?"

I nod. "Yes. That wreck also managed to steal the remaining childhood from my son. And you know what's terrible?"

"What?"

"Should I be more angry two men I adored are dead or that my son is about to deal with more than he's ready for as a result of it?" I shake my head. "Anyway, if there's one thing I learned from all of this it's that I'm not the only one whose love story ended abruptly. I guess being resentful is better than being dead."

And on that note, I grab a dish towel to wipe up the spilled coffee before excusing myself to prepare for another day of heartbreak.

# JENNINGS

Six days after we heard the news, Kody and I are landing in Juneau. But even as the wheels make that sexy screech on a perfect landing, the tension that normally releases in my body after a flight doesn't let go.

It's because we're here.

Juneau has been where Jed's family has owned a bar for generations. So, it's no surprise it's here he wants to be laid to rest. About five years ago, Jed left the day-to-day operations to his sister after he went on a vacation to Florida, met his now widowed husband, and decided to open a second place there where they planned on spending the rest of their days. The bitter taste in my mouth that those days were cut short has me lengthening my stride as Kody and I leave the tarmac and cross into the terminal.

Feeling like I'm a first-time visitor instead of someone who spent four summers here, I pause outside the terminal to ask, "Shit, I didn't think—does our cell coverage work here?"

Kody's blank expression tells me he has no clue.

I'm about to open my mouth to ask someone when a navy SUV pulls up. The door opens and Brad slides out of the driver's side. "Let me guess? Trying to figure out if you can make a call? Newbie mistake," he drawls.

"Got it in one," I admit sheepishly. I step forward to give him a hug. What would normally be a quick slap-and-go lasts longer and has more punch to my soul. "Wrong reason to be back," I choke out.

"Agree completely." We separate and he embraces Kody in much the same fashion.

"How did you get here so fast?" Kody wants to know.

Brad shrugs. "I drove."

"Smart-ass." A small grin tips my lips as I shake my head at him.

Brad continues, unperturbed. "I checked into the B&B already. They said neither of you had made it yet, so I called Rainey's cousin, who works in the tower. I asked if he minded texting me when you contacted them to approach. This one"—he nods at me—"got a green light, so I headed down. Now, throw your bags in the back. I'll catch you up on all I know along the way."

We do, Kody jumping in the middle just like he used to if Jed and Nick were on either side of him. "Rainey isn't with you?" I ask.

Brad shakes his head as he puts the car in gear and heads south. "No, she's going to keep the kids at home. This way, we have time for just us. She said to remind you both neither of you had better think about leaving this state without coming for dinner." He pauses. "I'll apologize in advance for the behavior of my hellions. They're thawing from winter hibernation."

We all chuckle. Kody asks, "Have you heard from Nick?"

Brad nods as we reach a stop sign. "He took the ferry from Ketchikan, so he won't get here until 2:30 or so."

"Why the hell wouldn't he just ask me to..." I halt my own words.

Brad takes his eyes from the road as he accelerates. "Because at heart, Nick is a good guy despite being a prick to, oh, the entire world. He went to lay a wreath at the show."

"I wish I'd thought of that," I mumble. Kody agrees.

"Well, since Jed's the one who kept him from ending up being arrested, it's the only reason he's even back in this state. He made it his personal mission to give thanks at the scene of the crime." Brad lets out a hollow laugh.

We all get lost in memories, good and bad, for a few moments before Kody bursts out with, "If it's that bad, then why did he go through Ketchikan?"

We pull up to a red light. "If I had to make a guess, Kody, I'd say it was to thank Jed a final time for his life." Brad eases the car through the light. "But if you want to ask the moody bastard..."

Kody flops back against the seat. "No, thanks. I like my jaw exactly the way it is. I know firsthand how he earned his belt. Remember?"

And with that light-hearted comment, we start swapping stories about those long-ago summers, wishing for time to miraculously shift back so we'd be as carefree as we were then. And so Jed would be with us one more time.

Just once.

Silence descends upon us as Brad pulls up outside the B&B we're all staying in outside of town. "Here we are." We all slide out. Kody and I grab our bags from the back.

"What do we need to do first?"

Breathing in the cool Alaskan spring air, I feel the one-two punch to my heart move more viciously than anything Nick could land with his powerful blows. "Drink. That's what I need to do before tonight."

"Maybe I'll arrange for Rainey to get Nick," Brad mutters, glancing at his watch. It's only a little after eleven in the morning.

Kody slaps him on the shoulder. "I've never known you guys not to be able to catch up. Jed's the only one who can't..." The rest of the words are left unsaid.

"Text Nick and tell him you'll send a taxi to pick him up," I order as we climb the steps to the pretty blue inn. "Also, tell him the driver might need to make a detour to get us more booze by then."

The last is said as the proprietor comes to greet us. A warm look is exchanged for one of alarm. Brad quickly jumps in to save us from being thrown out before we're checked in. "Ron, these are two of my three friends here for Jed's funeral."

The wariness is replaced by a look of abject sympathy so strong I have to avert my eyes. "I'm sorry for your loss."

Kody's voice is shredded when he says, "It was so unexpected."

"Yet as awful as it may seem, the quick and unexpected sometimes seems easier to those of us who have lived through the prolonged and suffering. It's all a matter of perspective." His face contorts as if speaking from his own experience. Holding out his hand, he says, "Ron Hotchkiss."

"John Jennings." We shake briskly.

He does the same to Kody. "Don't worry about bothering your friend with taxis and the like. If you all are too imbibed to pick him up, I can get him for you."

I turn to Brad. "How did you find this place?"

His smile is laced with all the pain we're all feeling. "I didn't. The package from Jed's lawyers included instructions on everything I was supposed to do, including contact Ron. I just followed them. What about you?"

I remember the picture in my bag. "I only received a photograph and a note from the attorney there would be a will reading after tomorrow's service."

We turn toward Kody, who shrugs. "Same here."

"I wonder about Nick?" Yet even as I say the words, a wave of pain over Jed planning all of this out in anticipation of a death that he never could have predicted was coming practically brings me to my knees. Turning toward Ron, I lift my bag. "Can we...?"

"Of course. Let's get you settled."

I'm not certain anything is going to be settled ever again, but I'm more than ready to get started with the drinking portion of today's events.

WHEN NICK ARRIVES, we're three bottles in, which is a fairly slow pace considering all we want to do is forget Jed won't be able to berate us for our childish behavior in the morning. Or ever again.

Dropping his bags at his feet, he gives his thanks to Ron before folding his weary body into the last arm chair in front of the fire. "Tell me you saved a bottle for me."

Brad passes him an unopened bottle of Jed's favorite scotch. Nick unscrews the top and lifts it to his lips.

I raise a brow. "You aren't in training?"

Tearing his lips away, Nick barks out a bitter laugh. "When am I not in training? Someone has to teach those young punks how to fight. But this only happens once." Pinning us with the glare he used to give his opponents in the ring, he tacks on, "At least it better."

Kody mutters, "I'm not the one with a suicide wish getting my ass beat by guys half my age on a regular basis."

As if that pleases him, Nick sits back and resumes drinking.

We catch up before I bring us back around to a topic I'm curious about. "Did anyone else get anything resembling the letter from the attorney like Brad did?"

Heads shake around the small space. "I called and asked Maris about it," Brad admits.

"What did she say?" I take another pull.

"Just that she was the executor of his estate and everything would be explained then. Rainey wanted to see if we could drop anything by, a casserole or something, but Maris shut us down. She said Dean's family is in too much shock. She was polite but firm. Said she'd see all of us at the viewing."

We all spend a moment digesting that because that doesn't sound like the outrageously outgoing Maris Smith who's as much our little sister as she was Jed's. I'm about to ask more about it when Nick pipes up. "I'm surprised his husband isn't the executor."

Brad shrugs. "Grief maybe? Who knows?" He takes a sip from his second glass. After all, one of us needs to remain sober enough to drive to the wake. Later I'm absolutely certain he plans on catching up.

Kody shudders. "I just hope it's not one of those open-casket things."

"Why?" Brad demands. "It's respectful."

"It's kinda creepy," Kody counters. "All that makeup and crap they use to make the person look like they're still alive when all they end up looking like is a wax figure out of some museum that's preparing to scare the fuck out of you."

We're all stunned by the vehemence of Kody's words when Nick yells, "Boo!"

Kody fumbles with his bottle, spilling it all over himself. "You're such an asshole," he fumes.

"Yeah." Nick smiles lazily. "But you know damn good and well if you said that shit if Jed was still alive, he'd have done the same thing—if not worse."

Kody looks away, but not before I catch the glint of tears the firelight illuminates. "You're right."

"Want to repeat that?"

"Fuck you, Nick."

"Nah, I hear that often enough." He pauses for a moment before he says, "Though it's normally, 'Fuck me, Nick.'"

We all laugh, but my mind is stuck back on something Nick said earlier. "I still can't believe he got married without us there." Jed had married his husband less than two years before at a destination wedding in the Caribbean Islands.

Nick nods. "Even when he was with us, he never spoke much about Dean. But I know he loved him, man. From the moment they met on that vacation, he was gone for the man."

"Wonder why we never met him. I mean, that trip was a couple of years ago now?" I muse aloud.

Brad snickers. "Would you introduce a respectable man to the group of us?"

"You did," I counter. "Many, many years ago."

"Much to her lament," Brad laughs.

"To Brad's point, I wouldn't introduce a woman I was serious about to you assholes on a good day," Nick agrees. "Which is why it's going to suck meeting him on the worst one imaginable."

I lift my bottle in acknowledgment. But I'm just grateful Jed had a few good years with someone who made him happy. "He must have been something special though. Jed wouldn't have fallen for just anyone."

There's general agreement around the group of us after which we lapse into our own memories and regrets of time passed.

Finally, Brad stands. "We have to get ready if we're going to be on time."

"Right." Shoving to my feet, I place the mostly empty bottle in front of me with some regret. I wish I could bring the rest of it with me to numb what I'm about to endure.

But Jed deserves better.

With that in my mind, I climb the stairs to put on one of the two suits I brought with me.

# KARA

"Mom, why are we being stared at?" Kevin slides an arm protectively around my shoulder after he returns from the restroom. Every parent wonders at some point what kind of person their child is going to be. Not me—mine is going to be a protector. Even at fifteen, I can tell that, as he tucks me tighter against his side to guard me from everyone in the room.

Including his father.

Not that he knows John Jennings is his biological father, and if there's a god watching down on me as the three of us endure the second service to pay tribute to Jed, and in our hearts Dean as well, he'll pay his respects and never be the wiser.

But there's not a chance in hell I'll be that lucky, and I damn well know it. Soon, everything is going to be exposed—the past I've tried to move on from as much as possible. Resentment slithers through me, burning away the pain, when I see the picture of Jed's smiling face. *I know I agreed to it, Jed, but why do I have to do this now?* I think harshly. *Why did I let you talk me into this?*

But none of that shows on my face when I reply to my son. "These people are all friends of Jed's, sweetheart." I reach up to grab Kevin's hand, squeezing it reassuringly. "They're probably trying to figure out who we are."

Maris sniffs into her handkerchief. I reach over and pull her closer. She lays her head on my shoulder, her perfectly tamed, glossy hair, in such a contrast to Jed's wild mane, cascading over the stark black of my funeral attire. We stand there, two women who loved two brothers who still had so much to give the world with so little time, when Kevin's arm tenses around me. Maris's head lifts. "Shit. Jacks up," she says, using the poker vernacular we adapted years ago to refer to when Jennings, Kody, Brad, Nick, or Jed would be about to intrude on our private conversations—more often than not about them.

The old shorthand hurls me back to the day I met all of them sixteen years ago, all ego, all gorgeous, up for a visit where they worked for the Lumberjack Show in Ketchikan. I felt lost among the over-whelming emotions in what was obviously an established family—that was, until Jennings set his sights on me. And I fell for it. And him.

"Would it be completely inappropriate to start a brawl at Jed's wake?" I mutter as Brad makes an approach with a pale face.

Maris shrugs. "If you can live with that for the summer, then I can."

Turning, I ignore Brad, who's almost on top of us. "Whose idea was that, again?"

"Your brother-in-law's," Maris says firmly. I'm about to remind her Jed was her brother first, but she holds out her hand saying, "Brad, thank you for coming."

I move slightly ahead of Kevin, who squawks in protest. Let him be pissed. No one gets to approach my son except through me.

Meanwhile, Brad uses Maris's extended hand to yank her close. I hear him murmur, "Mar, how...it was out of nowhere."

A rush of the bonds of the brotherhood Jed would talk about flow through me. It pains me to know they're hurting in much the same way I am. We're all on this same path together, but I still have to guard my reactions carefully because I learned there were only a handful of people I could trust my heart to. And the only ones left are Maris and Kevin.

And it's my duty to allow them to grieve.

Since the night the police showed up at our home to let us know about the crash, I've been numb inside. I've forced myself to be for Kevin, for Maris, to give them the time to heal. Frankly, it's amazing I've got this far without a complete breakdown. I can't imagine what's going to happen after the service tomorrow when... No, I tell myself firmly. It was all Jed asked for, pleaded for.

I can practically hear his voice in my ear whispering, "Give Jennings a chance."

And I'll honor his final wishes. Just like I'll honor the fact that some of the ashes in the urns are Dean's. After all, Jed was a beloved part of my life. *Our lives*, I amend silently. If Dean was the only dad figure Kevin's ever known, then Jed stepped into his role as favorite uncle without a hitch.

As if the cord that once bound his life to mine is transmitting a message, Kevin tugs me closer. With a sigh, I silently wonder when did the little boy who used to fit cradled in one of my arms shoot up to the six-foot boy-man trying to shelter me from the unknown?

Raising my hand, I give his a quick squeeze. "We don't have to stay much longer, sweetheart."

"Okay, Mom." Beneath his stoic demeanor, his determination to be strong for me, there's still the little boy who's lost.

But Kevin's voice snaps Brad's attention away from whatever he was saying to my sister-in-law. "Kara, I can't believe it's you." The shock in his voice confirms to me Jed kept his promise about us. Jed never told the Jacks about Dean beyond the fact he got married. I know he did that to protect Kevin and me, but now it just seems so useless, such a waste.

With his life cut far too short, I bitterly regret never allowing the Jacks to meet my brother. What would they have thought about the fun-loving man who was a perfect counterpoint to Jed's wild craziness? Now, I'll never know.

"Brad," I acknowledge him with a tip of my head. There's a reservation in my voice that's hard to miss, and it causes him to flinch. His devastated eyes drift to Kevin, and they widen almost comically. I want to grab my son and run under the intense perusal.

"You hardly look a day older than when we were all at that last barbecue at the Smiths' together." He turns and looks at the urn. "It's like no time's passed."

I make a noise, neither agreeing or disagreeing with him. Above all, I'm not encouraging Brad because to do that means opening the door to everything tonight. And I absolutely can't do that without preparing my son. Remembering the warnings from Kevin's therapist about keeping the funeral separate from the impending news of his father, I just pray to God no one makes a scene tonight. This need to prepare him is pressing urgently on me as I'm standing half a room away from the man who changed my life in so many ways.

But Brad chooses to engage Kevin. Holding out a hand, he introduces himself. "Bradley Myers. Jed was one of my best friends. More like brothers, actually."

Kevin imperceptibly relaxes against me whereas I tense beneath his arm. *Don't, baby!* I want to yell. But before I manage to open my mouth, Kevin does exactly what Dean and Jed taught him to.

He politely introduces himself.

"Kevin Malone, sir." He holds out a hand, waiting for Brad to take it, which he does, astonished.

"Nice to meet you. I swear you remind me of someone I know." Brad's eyes dart over to Maris, who's studiously avoiding his gaze. He turns blue eyes on me to skew me in place even as he shakes my son's hand before letting it go.

I'm not ashamed by my decisions. For fifteen years, every beat of my heart was for him. And despite knowing I was going to raise Kevin on my own, I tried, for many years, to reach the father of my child before giving up. But Maris, the only living person who knows the truth about every detail, presses up against me to offer her support.

"Kara?" Brad whispers, anger replacing the pain in his voice as he stares at the boy who in a few years I imagine will be the spitting image of his father.

Jerking my hand away, I turn to Maris and answer Brad's question indirectly. "What time did the pastor want family at the cemetery tomorrow?"

Maris catches on immediately. "The three of us have to be there at nine, so we need to be in the limousine by eight thirty."

"The three of you," Brad echoes. His eyes dart back to Kevin, and with that, my nurturing instincts come out in full force.

"Yes, Brad, the three of us," I clarify brusquely. "My sister-in-law, my son, and me. Dean, Jed's husband, was my brother."

The look on Brad's face would be comical under any other circumstance. But not now, not when we're so devastated by loss and trying to maintain a composure none of us truly feel in front of people who just don't understand.

Including a man standing half a room away and likely drawing conclusions with his friends. I clench my fists so hard my nails dig into my palms.

Brad's mind finally clears enough to reach out and tug me forward in what looks like an embrace to an observer. Stumbling, I barely manage to catch myself in time to hear him growl in my ear, "There's no way in hell you're going to convince me he's not Jennings's son. Not when he's the spitting image of him," before releasing me and stalking away without waiting for a response.

Not that one's needed.

I wobble dangerously on my feet. Maris and Kevin both reach for me. "Mom?" Kevin's face holds too much fear for someone his age. He's scared by what just transpired and doesn't have the skills to hide it.

"I'm fine, baby. I just got a bit light-headed." Stepping back, I turn to Maris to find her shooting glares toward the backs of the Jacks, who are leaving en masse. I touch her arm to get her attention. "Brad guessed?" she surmises as her attention returns to me.

"Oh yeah," I confirm.

Squishing me tightly to her side, she whispers, "Only a few more minutes, then I'm throwing everyone out." Muttering to herself, she asks, "I don't know what Jed was thinking."

I tell her honestly, "Some days, neither do I."

Maris pulls me tighter to her, if that's even possible. "We're almost done, babe. Then it's just you and me."

"And Kevin," I remind her.

"Think he's too young for a glass of wine?" she muses aloud.

"Yes!" I say too emphatically, drawing the attention of people around me. I smile weakly to assure them everything is as fine as it can be.

But just then, my eyes catch sight of John Jennings as he's about to walk out. He looks overwhelmed—more so than when he first walked in. And his eyes aren't on any of the photos of Jed placed tastefully around the room.

They're on me.

And they're devastated. Part of me feels an urge to go to Jennings, to explain, but Nick drags him to the door before I can give into the urge.

*Later*, I remind myself firmly. *Kevin is your priority right now. Let the will be read, and deal with Jennings later.*

HOURS LATER, Kevin's engrossed on his iPad in the basement. I hear a distinctive pop that heralded so many nights Maris and I spent together while I lived here for five of the most life-altering months of my life. When she slides the glass in front of me, I lift it to my lips with a grateful "Thanks."

She then proceeds to plunk the rest of the open bottle next to my arm. "I'm opening my own," she declares.

And on a day when I suspect neither of us expected to feel nothing but anger and bitterness, my lips curve. "Talking to you just isn't the same as being with you."

Maris lifts her glass and touches it to mine. "I feel the same way. How's Kevin holding together?"

Knowing he'll be engrossed for a while, I answer honestly. "As best as he can."

"He won't miss his friends while here?"

I wave my hand toward the basement door. "He'll catch up with them. If he wasn't, then I'd be worried."

"You raised an amazing young man, Kara," Maris compliments me.

I just shake my head. "I had a lot of help, my friend. Especially in the beginning." My mind flashes back to the days after I first realized I was pregnant, calling my parents, being cut off, then talking to Dean and knowing I always would have my brother. Then there was Jennings and coming to terms with the emotions I had as both a parent and a woman.

As the months, then the years, passed, Kevin and I had nothing but the world before us. Who knew then how life would work out?

"Does being here bring back the memories?" Maris asks.

"How could it not?" Taking a fortifying drink, I think back to the girl I was then. "I had stars in my eyes, literally."

"You still could have…"

"No," I say firmly. "Once I knew Kevin was on the way, it was up to me to make a life for us, Maris. I wasn't about to be separated from my son for months on end while I aspired to do scientific research on Mendenhall." Taking a sip, I remind her, "Being an intern at the gift shop is a lot different than camping out in a tent with a Coleman as a heat source on top on the far reaches of the glacier for months on end, taking measurements of annual snowfall and looking in a makeshift lab whether the snow crystalized right." After another drink, I tack on, "I don't think they deliver Huggies as often as I would have needed them."

"It was your dream," she remembers softly.

"I did better than a dream; I grabbed hold of my reality the moment I heard Kevin's heart beat for the first time," I whisper fiercely. Staring into the depth of the full-bodied red, I murmur, "In the end, I got to see my brother fall in love. Knowing he had that at the end helps somehow."

Her hand reaches over and grips my free one. "Knowing Jed had those last few years with Dean, Kevin, you…"

"Maybe it was better they were together when…"

"Yeah, but it doesn't stop us from missing them."

"Only every second I allow myself to think of it. What about you?"

Maris shakes her head. "Same. Which is why I don't allow myself the luxury of thinking. Are you ready for tomorrow?"

"Were we ready the first time?" I ask meaningfully.

"No. But this time, we won't have a fucking media circus outside the door," she counters.

"Some parts of it were beautiful," I whisper. "All of the bar employees, the honor guard from Dean's coworkers, my former students coming to the memorial."

"I was floored by how many showed up," Maris remarks before taking a drink.

"I think every person the three of us ever knew showed up." I dash tears from my eyes as I recall the line of people who stood in line to pay their respects.

"And Kevin?"

My heart cracks wide open as do the floodgates that I'm sure will open during the service for Jed tomorrow. "I'm glad we arranged something separate for his friends to come pay their respects. I was not about to put those children through…"

"God, I hate this," Maris spits out. "I'm grateful you're going to be here for months, that I get this time with you, but I hate why. Their lives were over way too soon."

"You're not telling me something I don't say to myself a million times a day since it happened. But Maris?" Her eyes connect with mine. "After having a front-row seat to a love that beautiful, I'll never settle for less than what they had."

Still clinging onto my hand, she lifts her glass. "To finding a love that extraordinary."

And in the still-freezing air, in a part of the world so beautiful it makes the vow sacred, I touch my glass to hers. "To love."

# JENNINGS

My guts are tied in knots as we pull up to the funeral home. "A thousand dollars if you turn us toward the airport," I only half joke.

Brad parks before reprimanding me. "None of us want to be here, Jennings."

"It's not that I don't want to say goodbye to him. It's just..." I take a deep breath before admitting, "It's the end of us. The end of the us that we were."

From the distance, I see a couple of women and a tall boy pull open the glass outer doors. I squint, because the boy reminds me of someone, but I quickly dismiss it before trying again to explain. "Jed was our glue. Next to him, the only thing that keeps me close to being sane is the air. And I have to face the loss of one without the other? You're asking the impossible."

Understanding crosses Brad's face, wiping away the disapproval. But it's Nick who says, "He's always going to hold us together. He's always going to be our glue. No matter what, we'll never leave him behind because to do so is to forget everything about the crazy bastard we loved."

Kody's voice is rough when he says, "The ache we're feeling is a measure of the love we have for him, for each other. We need to remember that."

Brad gives a bark of a laugh. "Did you guys get what I left in your rooms?"

Nick reaches over and whacks him upside the head. "You're such a dick. If anyone ever caught me in Canadian boxers, can you imagine what that would do for my image? My publicist would kill me."

"So don't make a spectacle of yourself by dropping trou at the wake?" I suggest. I reach down and slide my dress slacks down a bit to show off my red-and-white waistband.

Kody groans before he pulls his pants down to show the stars on his.

Brad does the same before he says to all of us, but his words pierce my heart. "We'll never forget Jed because he was the best parts of each of us. So, let's go honor him by meeting his family."

"Then let's get shitfaced," I mutter, shoving open the door.

IF I COULD HAVE LOOKED at anyone's picture a week ago and brought them back into my life, it would have been Jed, not Kara Malone. But there she is standing next to Maris. And with both of them huddled in the corner of the room near Jed's ashes, I'm finding it difficult to make my approach to offer my condolences to Jed's baby sister.

The years have been more than kind to Kara, I can't help but notice. Despite her obvious grief, she's more attractive now than when we dated years ago. Her long, light brown hair which used to flap in the windy Alaskan breeze has been cut to a chin-length bob. Instead of making her look older, it highlights her full lips and enormous eyes, which are no longer covered by large frames, begging a man to ferret out their secrets. Shaking my head, I turn my back toward the duo and ask Kody, "Are we being rude?"

"Not going to Maris, you mean?"

"Yeah. It's just with Kara there, I don't know; I feel kind of odd."

He claps me on the shoulder. "Jennings, if you feel that way, then I can go over and..." His sentence trails off. "No."

Brad and Nick step up next to us. Kody immediately demands, "Brad? Did you have a clue, you asshole?"

"A clue about what?" I ask. I start to turn around to get a bead on what they're seeing that I can't.

They all hiss, "Don't!" simultaneously.

A small part of me wishes I hadn't. Not then. Not when I was supposed to be grieving Jed.

I must be seeing things because a tall boy steps out of the hallway and moves immediately into the arms of my ex-girlfriend. Kara's face trembles for an instant before it firms up as her head tips back when she lifts her hand to cup the cheek of the handsome kid. She strokes his cheek and jaw tenderly before pulling him down as she raises up to brush a kiss on his cheek.

Like she did to me a million times.

I can't make out what they're saying, but the love that's there is obvious.

So is the fact that if I were to fly home to Seattle and pull my high school yearbook out of storage, he'd be my damn spitting image.

I feel hot fury and cold rage all at the same time. "How?" is all I manage to get out.

Brad steps in front of me. "I swear to you on my life, on Rainey's life, I had no clue, Jennings. I don't know—"

"There's not a doubt in my mind." Is that my voice that's so flat, so lifeless?

"What I was going to say is, I have no idea if Jed knew," Brad says carefully.

Time freezes much as I imagine my body is. "No," I immediately deny. "There's no way he would have known and..." I watch another set of well-wishers approach the two women.

Nick growls, "It's pretty obvious to me Maris knew."

"I'll be back." Brad leaves us to approach. I turn back to face Nick and Kody, both of whom are pale.

The three of us stand in our small circle. The room is too warm, and my legs are quivering. I'm about to excuse myself when Brad comes back over. The perspiration on his brow needs to be wiped off.

"Well?" Kody demands whispering.

Brad claps me on the shoulder. "Let's get out of here."

Nick, ever the smart-ass, fires off, "You mean we're not going to pay our respects?"

"I think our friend here is going to have plenty to think about by the time we get back to the B&B without you deliberately baiting someone in grief," Brad says diplomatically.

I hold up a hand. "Just tell me this. Is that boy my son or not?"

Brad solidifies the night as one I know I'll never forget. "She never confirmed either way. But she admitted he's her son."

"What did you find out?" I demand. This time, I turn and look over my shoulder. The young man is devastated. His hand is clamped down on his mother's shoulder. He has my dark hair, my nose. Hell, from this distance, I can even see he has my jaw.

I'd bet every plane in my fleet he's mine.

Kody and Nick lean in.

Brad hesitates before admitting, "I found out the reason why Kara's glued to Maris. She's not just anyone. She's Jed's sister-in-law; his husband, Dean, is Kara's brother."

And the overly warm room spins as the implications of all the secrets Jed's been holding starts to sink in.

And at that moment, Kara's eyes and mine lock across the room full of grief-stricken people. Her chin lifts with something else I can't name. Daring me to come at her, her son, to what? To cause more pain and destruction when there's already so much occurring? There's only one way I know I can avoid that. Turning to the men I'd do anything for, I beg, "Get me the hell out of here before I lose it."

"You got it." Nick grabs me under the elbow and drags me for the nearest exit, Brad and Kody bringing up the rear.

The minute we're all safely in the car, I turn on Brad. "Is. He. Mine?" I demand.

He clutches the steering wheel for a moment before he faces me, disclosing, "She didn't deny it."

I thought I came to Alaska to pay my final respects to one of my closest friends. I didn't think I'd end up so angry my throat feels too tight to speak, and there's an ache in my chest worse than when I found out Jed was gone. I barely manage to get out, "Let's go," before I lapse into a silence.

I don't hear anything being discussed around me. All I can think is, *Jed, you bastard. Why didn't you tell me?*

# JENNINGS

I should be paying attention to the words of the minister, who's talking about the life enriched by love Jed led, but I can't. Because my mind is still reeling with the words of condolences he offered to the members of Jed's family spoken a few moments ago.

First to his last relative by blood, his sister, Maris—a long-standing member of the Juneau community.

Then he went on to give his condolences to Kara Malone and her son, Kevin of Ponte Vedra, Florida, nephew of Jedidiah Jonas Smith Malone.

*How the fuck didn't I know? How could he not tell me?*

Kara's head is dropped, so all I see is the arch of her slender neck. The new cut exposes a neck I remember spending hours kissing. When during one of the many times I made love to her that summer did we make him? Did her amber-colored eyes blink up at me like an adorable owl after we made him? God, Owl. I called her that so many times. How did I forget?

What else did I forget? Protection? I frantically try to remember, but damnit, it was close to sixteen years ago. I feel myself overheating in the small sanctuary. I want to howl in frustration, grab her by her slender arm, and drag her out to demand all of the answers. But I can't.

Her shoulders are shaking with silent despair as the minister says prayers over the urn. She turns her head and lifts her hand to wipe under her eyes. As she does, the light streaming through the church windows glints off her tears. After her fingers brush back and forth, she wraps her arm around the boy sitting next to her, who is sobbing so openly, it echoes in all parts of the vestibule. His dark, mahogany hair stands wildly on end, as if no amount of hair product can tame it. *Only a good haircut will, son.* My heart burning, I force myself to look at him again.

Kara's son. My son. No matter how much she may try to protest, there's little doubt in my mind.

The conflicting feelings inside my chest are threatening to cause me to collapse. I want to howl in pain over Jed's loss and somehow breathe life back into those ashes so I can kill him all over again for not telling me.

But a tiny voice whispers in my mind, *Did he try to?*

*I guess I'll never know*, I think brutally, tuning back in to the minister's words.

And then I'm stunned for a second time. "The life Jed shared with his husband was vital to him. He wrote these words to be read: 'I was a man whose heart was bound by promises in two very different worlds.' He hoped everyone understood that no matter what, he loves them. Now, for all of eternity, he and Dean will be together, as they were in life."

My lips part in shock when I hear the minister's words. Jed's husband, Kara's brother, is gone too? My heart softens a bit, remembering the look she shot me across the room last night, as Kara slips her other arm around Maris and pulls her tightly against her as well. I can barely hold on—how is she standing?

Brad leans over to hiss in my ear, "What do you think—"

I cut him off with, "No idea," before Nick punches me in the arm to shut me up. What's supposed to be a light tap will likely leave a bruise.

I don't get pissed. It's the first real thing I've felt since seeing Kara and her—our—son last night.

✳

THEIR COMBINED ashes have been buried under a tombstone with simple words. *Beloved husband, son, brother, and uncle. Loyal and loving until his last breath.*

As the ashes are placed, both Kara and Maris, who had regained their composure, use handkerchiefs to dab at their faces again. The boy, Kevin, hasn't stopped crying once. It's a tribute to how much love he has for my friend, for his uncle, and it makes my heart ache. At the same time, I'm infuriated by the fact I want to run up behind my ex-girlfriend and our son, tug them into my arms, and assure them things will eventually get better. But how can I when I'm so pissed I can barely speak to the men who have had my back for fifteen years.

Fuck.

A stream of light lands between Kara and me, right across Jed's grave. And just like the funeral home last night, our eyes connect as we're both drawn by it.

Hers hold a depth of pain that almost throws me backward by the force of it. It's so naked and raw, it intensifies my own tenfold. If grief is the price to pay for love, then Kara loved Jed and her brother with everything she had.

Then her face changes. Her lashes lower briefly before they open and meet mine again. The pain is temporarily masked. Instead, I see determination and pride. There's no anxiety, no fear. Nothing from a woman who deliberately kept her child away from the man who fathered it.

The little voice growls, *Maybe he isn't yours.*

The hell he isn't. Even if he didn't look like a replica of me when I was at that age, there's something drawing me to him. Shoving the thought aside as I jam my hands into my jacket pockets, I try to tune in to the final blessings. Encountering the folded letter from the attorney requesting my presence at the will reading, I control my breathing. Maybe I'll have answers later.

Because I sure as hell can't leap across a dead man's grave to demand them, no matter how much I want to.

I'M stunned not to find Kara waiting at the attorney's office later that afternoon. Maris, whose coloring is so reminiscent of Jed's, is conferring with the attorney when we enter the conference room. Her head twists in our direction. She gives us a brief nod before taking a seat. "Brad, Kody, Nick." It may be my imagination, but her lips curl a bit when she says my name. "Jennings."

We all murmur, "Maris," before sitting down.

The attorney opens a file and slips out a thick document along with two sealed envelopes next to a box.

"Denise, if you could please get the door on your way out?" The attorney jerks his chin toward the front of the room. "Ng and I have it from here."

"Yes, Mr. Isler." The young woman quietly exits the room, closing the conference room doors behind her.

Kody speaks my thoughts aloud. "Are we not waiting for Kara?"

The attorney and Maris exchange a speaking glance. "Ms. Malone was in consultation with her brother and brother-in-law at the time their wills were made. She is aware she is not a beneficiary of Mr. Smith's will. Subsequently, there is no need for her presence."

"What the actual fuck?" I breathe. A million thoughts go crashing through my brain. What does Kara do now? Does she have enough money to raise my son? I immediately think of the changes I'll need to make to my own estate planning when Isler's voice breaks into my thoughts.

"If that is unacceptable, we can delay the reading until a later time."

"That's not necessary," Nick pipes up.

I'm stunned silent, unable to speak to give my assent. *What did you do, Jed?* The thought whispers through my head as the lawyer nods before beginning. After a brief introduction to the paralegal in the room, the lawyer begins.

We all shift uncomfortably when the lawyer declares, "And so, I leave the following."

"All properties previously divided in fifty/fifty ownership between myself and Maris Ione Smith become hers solely. This includes Smith's

Brewhouse in Juneau, Alaska, and our childhood home our parents left us upon their passing. This does not include Hook and Ladder Beachside in Jacksonville Beach, Florida, as ownership will revert to my investors with the proceeds going into my irrevocable trust. My sister should know she was the light of my life, and should she precede me in death, my world has been a dimmer place for not having you in it until the end, Little Mari Sunshine."

Maris sniffles as she nods, likely none of the lawyer's bequests coming as a surprise but her brother's words grabbing her beyond the grave.

"To my husband, Dean Kevin Malone, I want you to know words can't capture the miracle of the love I found with you. To you, I leave my irrevocable trust with the understandings associated with it. Should he precede me in death, the trust is to be split evenly between my sister and my nephew by marriage, Kevin Jennings Malone, with the understanding the trust is not to be touched for any reason until his twenty-fifth birthday except furthering his education, medical necessity, or as agreed upon by the executor of the estate as necessary to maintain his current standard of living."

My fists clench and unlock upon hearing my son's full name. Kara named him after her brother and me. I'm not given much time to process that as the lawyer continues.

"To my sister-in-law, Kara Malone, I leave my eternal gratitude in sharing the Malone love. I just wanted you to know, you will never know what it meant for you to open up to me when you had every right to keep yourself closed off. From now into eternity, know I had a special place in my heart for you. Even in death, I have to try one last time for both of your sakes. If it doesn't work out the way I think it will, don't think ill of me in your memories years from now." The lawyer pauses. "A copy of this will be provided to Ms. Malone, per Mr. Smith's wishes, which is why her presence was not required here today."

Maris whispers, "God, Jed," before her entire body shudders. Since I'm the closest to the tissues, I slide them across the table. But I'm stunned speechless when instead of sadness, I find anger sparking in her eyes.

"Maris?" I ask hesitantly.

"Be quiet, Jennings," she hisses, her voice awash with bitterness. "This isn't over yet."

With a twisted feeling in my stomach, I face the lawyer.

"To Bradley Meyers, I leave my boat in Florida and a two-year fully paid tender. Take Rainey and the kids on a vacation out of the cold, my friend." Brad gives a watery chuckle.

"To Kody Laurence, I leave my travel journals, sketch books, and drawing kit. There's also an open-ended monthlong trip paid for at the retreat we went to in Montana. Inside one of the journals, you'll find a drawing of a tree house I thought would be perfect there. Make that happen, will you? Sorry, Kody, the sketches suck. My skills were never up to yours. If I could wish anything for you, it's to see there's more than houses that needs your magic touch." Kody scrubs his head in his hands as he nods up and down. Ng, the paralegal, comes up behind Kody and hands him a box which Kody accepts.

"To Nicholas Cain, I leave my gold cross and chain. There was never a day I didn't wear it. Faith was important to me. You need to believe something, my friend. It wasn't me who saved you. It's time for you to accept that as you look in the mirror. Maybe if you're wearing this, you will." Nick looks away, a tic in his jaw. The lawyer clears his throat. "Mr. Cain, this is for you." The lawyer stands and walks around the table. When he reaches him, he presses a small box in Nick's trembling hands. "Thank you" is choked out, but it's not the lawyer he's addressing. It's Maris. Because Jed told it true: he was never without that necklace, and he has to know what Jed leaving that to someone else must do to her.

She shrugs as if it doesn't make a difference to her while Isler reseats himself and gets his bearings.

Resuming his location in the will, he continues. "And finally, to John Jennings, I leave the contents of these two envelopes. It's my ever-loving hope you understand the meaning of them before you do something beyond forgiveness." The lawyer slides both envelopes toward me, the first small, the second much larger.

The first one says READ ME NOW in Jed's distinctive scrawl.

I immediately tear open the back.

*Jennings,*

*Before you fly out of control, a few things to think about.*

*Kara tried to contact you about Kevin; yes, you asshole, if you didn't pick it up from the service—that's your son's name. She has evidence to prove she did which surprises me considering she was perfectly content raising him alone. As much as it frustrated the hell out of me when I found out, I understood why Kara made me promise not to tell you. To her, the bonds of family are sacred— with good reason.*

*If you use your brain, you'll remember I tried every possible way to get you to come visit me in Florida. I figured once you ended up in my sphere, there would be no way you wouldn't end up seeing her and all of this would be unnecessary. Remember me practically begging you to fly down to Florida—that I had something amazing I wanted to show you where I lived?*

*Consider this the slap upside the head you said I could give you one day.*

*Welcome to the best parts of life.*

*Friendship.*

*Fatherhood.*

*Love.*

*I've made some arrangements (and you'd better figure out a way to make this work, company or not). If Kevin is under 21, Kara has agreed to stay in Alaska with him for the summer after my death (if he's of age, he'll be asked to spend equal time with you at his convenience).*

*You have a clear sky. Unlimited visibility. It's all on you to fly or fall now that you're in the air.*

*I'll just be watching from much higher.*

*I love you, man.*

*Jed*

I can't say a word as I read the letter a second, a third time. Swallowing is difficult. Finally, I fold it, tuck it back into the envelope, and lay it on top of the other which is much thicker.

It's also stamped PRIVATE. Beneath it Jed printed "OPEN ALONE."

"Thank you," I manage to choke out. Maris lets out a growling noise. My head swivels to meet her devastated face. "I'm sorry," I whisper. I don't just owe her those words; I owe them to Kara.

And so does my son.

Maris blinks rapidly before her mouth firms. "Are we finished?" she asks Mr. Isler haughtily. "I'd like to check on my family."

"For now, Maris," he tells her gently. "There will be papers..."

"But not today?" Her voice breaks on the last word. Nick tenses next to me.

"No, not today," the lawyer concurs.

Maris barely acknowledges the lawyer with a nod before dashing from the room.

"I apologize..." Mr. Isler starts.

"Save it," Nick snaps. Shoving to his feet, he quickly makes his way toward the door, shoving the box in his suit pocket.

"It's not that we don't appreciate everything your firm has done." Ever the negotiator among us, Brad stands and holds out his hand. "It's just been a trying day."

"I'm sorry for your loss." Isler shakes Brad's hand before moving down around the table. Reaching me, he gives a quick shake of his head. "I hope you find what's in those envelopes valuable, Mr. Jennings. When I sat down with Mr. Smith—sorry. Mr. Malone. Since Jed never changed his name legally, it's difficult to think of him that way."

I grunt, not caring how he refers to my lost friend. Isler continues. "When Mr. Malone sat down to develop his will, he and Ms. Malone had a disagreement over the phone whether you would find it so."

"Did they?" That tidbit of information is like losing Jed all over again.

The lawyer emits a low noise. "It was intriguing to listen to them debate the issue. Ms. Malone was skeptical you'd appreciate the gift."

My brows raise, but I don't reply.

After offering his final condolences and leaving us alone in the room, Brad, Kody, and I are left standing there. Kody asks, "What did the letter say?"

I let out a slow burst of air. "That if I wasn't so stubborn, I'd have known about my son a long time ago. But that Kara's committed to staying with Kevin for the summer for him to get to know me."

"Holy shit; he is yours?" Kody breathes. I nod.

"I don't know what to say," Brad admits.

"I...I need some time alone to read this." I hold the other envelope aloft. "Then..."

"Then?" Kody asks.

"Then I think it's long past time to contact Kara." My head twisting to the window, I see an SUV roar out of the parking lot. Nick's standing outside, hands on his hips. "And I have a fairly good idea where to start."

# JENNINGS

The ability to fly has long provided me with an unparalleled sense of freedom I've extended into all areas of my life. Beyond the brotherhood with the men I worked with summer after summer, I never gave a damn about anyone or anything other than growing my wings.

But at what cost?

The fondest memories I have about growing up on the farm were riding a tractor and hearing the whoosh of a jet fly overhead. I dreamed of a day where nothing would hold me hostage to a place where I didn't want to be, so when I inherited that farm, I used it to fund my purchase of Northern Star Flights about eight years ago.

I first came to Alaska because I heard it was possible to make more money than I'd ever dreamed of in comparison to working on the damn farm. I fell into my job working at the Lumberjack Show for a great wage and tips making close to four times what I would have back home. When I found out it was possible to work on my dreams simultaneously with the limitless sky, nothing held me back from returning summer after summer. Then, that final summer, I met Kara. I fell into a lazy kind of infatuation with her. It was impossible not to after I got to know the real heart that beat beneath the brilliant mind. Days off became about touching her smooth skin, watching her eyes glow as I made her body burn under the cool air.

And then, she began to mean more. And that terrified me.

The future wasn't thoughts of blue skies, but amber crystals. So, I ended us because nothing was going to hold me back. I couldn't be tied down, physically or emotionally, to feeling trapped again. The idea of flight was the only thing that ever gave me hope freedom existed.

Kara being out of my life would ease the ache of not having her, I told myself back then. After all, flying was supposed to be my everything. It wasn't supposed to be a woman, unless that woman vibrated beneath me with at least 160 horsepower. Flying was supposed to fill all the holes left inside of me. It was supposed to take me beyond feelings and pain and doubt.

Clutching Jed's letter, I admit to myself it failed.

"Did he know?" I whisper aloud.

"Know what, buddy?" Brad asks. We're all back at the B&B huddled around the fireplace.

"That if I knew about my son, I'd have given it all up? I never would have left him the way—"

"The way your parents left you?" Kody finishes grimly.

"Yeah." I tip my head back against the chair. My mother got tired of being, well, a mother. And my father got tired of trying to raise a son alone, so he dumped me at his sister's—whose best was slightly above marginal when it came to feelings. "And yet, I ended up doing exactly that to Kara." Guilt overwhelms me, and I still haven't opened the other envelope.

Nick speaks up. "Did you, Jennings? You didn't know."

We're sitting around the fire after having changed into warm sweaters and jeans. I'm trying to work up enough courage to go find a private space to read Jed's final words to me because I'm afraid of what they're going to say. The envelope on my lap has some weight to it.

"No," I agree. "But would that ease your feelings of guilt if you were the ones holding these?" I hold up the letters.

Brad looks away, unable to agree. Kody shakes his head. Nick just remains silent and stoic as always. I go on. "If what Jed said in his first letter is right, Kara has irrefutable proof she tried to reach out to me. I have nothing to be angry about, and yet a part of me..."

It's Brad who finishes my thought. "Is."

I nod. "I am. I missed out on everything."

"That sounds like you're hurt," Kody pipes in.

"I'm that too," I acknowledge.

"Then maybe it's time for you to go read what's in there," he suggests.

Sighing, I drag my legs from the ottoman they'd been resting on. "I guess it is." I head toward the door, stopping only when Kody calls out, "Where are you going?"

"Outside. I need to be as close to the sky as I can be right now." Without another word, I head toward the back door where I can read Jed's last words to me.

The spring air whips through my hair and sends a chill through me. "Should have grabbed my coat," I mutter to myself. Dropping down onto a bench, heart pounding, I slip my finger beneath the envelope's seal and pull out a folder. Flipping it open, there's a letter on top. It's dated a little less than two years earlier.

*Jennings,*

*It's late as I write this. Dean went to bed long ago. We're all exhausted. He and I are in Alaska. Since the bar is here, I wanted an Alaskan firm to represent my estate in the event something ever happens. So, he's already irritated we're discussing these sort of things so early into our marriage. But I have to take care of Maris, and now Dean.*

*All day, Dean and I have been at the lawyer's office. And we had to call Kara over the one thing I wanted to add to my will. The battle she and I had while I was standing in front of Isler was explosive.*

*Heads up in case you forgot — that woman has a temper. Don't take it lightly.*

*But I won for you. At least I hope you look at it that way. I received Kara's agreement to tell you about Kevin under certain circumstances: if he was termi-nally ill and needed medical assistance, if Kara decided to re-marry and that individual wanted to adopt Kevin, if I died (so I could tell you my part of the story), or Kevin asked for the name of his birth father, specifically, so he could find him.*

*If you're reading this letter, well, you know what happened. My attorney has had strict instructions on what to do in the event I passed — who to contact and all that bullshit. But if you found out before I passed, I think I was going to give you an antique airplane propeller that's in Dean's and my home in Florida. If you're not a dick to Kara, maybe she'll be nice and still give it to you.*

I chuckle a little even as I wipe my eyes with the back of my hand. "It's like I can hear you right next to me, Jed," I whisper into the cold air. I keep reading.

*Maris knew from the moment Kara found out she was pregnant, though she didn't tell me. I met Dean through Kara on my vacation to Florida. Falling for him wasn't in my plans. But while meeting Kevin was a joy, it was the biggest shock of my life. Remember, all of this was just a few years ago. I'm still not entirely clear on what happened to Kara specifically, but I know their parents are no longer in their lives. It's a very sore subject for both of them. And when Kara left Alaska, she and Dean moved in together.*

*I breezed into town to look at some real estate for a winter bar and met up with Kara. I ended up buying the place and met her brother. Honestly, it was love at first sight. I'm in awe when I think about how a vacation, falling in love with a place, and deciding to stay can change your life. But I won't say it wasn't a shock for us all.*

*Family hasn't been good for her, Jennings. Think about that when you talk with Kara. She came to Alaska and the world changed for her, not all of it in a good way.*

*I refuse to tell you anything about what I* know *versus what I* lived. *That's Kara's story to share when she's ready. I'll just say she's a strong woman, Jennings. Decisions were made, right or wrong. I understand her reasoning, I feel your pain.*

*So many times over the years I've been torn between the brotherhood I had with all of you and the love I fell into with Dean.*

*I apologize, Jennings. Kara was never one to trust easily, but now? There's few people she has absolute faith in.*

*My own temper's flaring a bit because I wish you had just come visit. I wish you had checked your junk mail once over the last thirteen years, but there are too many maybes. Maybe I could have broken a promise to the man I love...no, I couldn't do that.*

*This is one secret I had to keep, as much as it burned my soul day after day.*

*I wish there was something else I could have done to have cleared the way for you. I know you, brother. I knew how you would feel if you truly* knew.

*Hence our agreement.*

*You have a single chance at the greatest gift a man could ever have —
fatherhood.*

*Fuck, it kills me that you're reading this and I can't tell you this to your face.
I can't wait for you to find out how much your son is like you without having
ever met you. Kevin's been a comfort to me living so far away because I feel like
I have a piece of you with me every day.*

*Then again, I do: your son.*

*I hope in time you can forgive me, my friend. As the Alaskan rain and the
Florida sun lifts me to my reward, I would like to think you already have. But I
suspect it will take getting to know the best part of you that will ease the resentment inside you for that to occur. That's okay. I understand.*

*I love you, brother. Always.*

*Jed.*

*PS Here are some of my favorite pictures of Kevin since I've known him.
I'm in some, you'll see Kara and Dean in some others. Meet my family, brother.
And do me a favor? Take care of them for me. I know you can do it.*

I have to set the folder aside. "Jesus, Jed," I croak out. Pressing the
heels of my hands against my burning, wet cheeks, I breathe in the
evening air. Inhale, exhale, over and over until I can get myself under
control.

Regaining my composure, I scrub my hands against my jeans before
I pick the folder up again to flip through the small stack of 5x7s Jed
included. A picture of Kevin kicking around a soccer ball with a man
who looks so much like Kara, he must be Dean. Another one of Jed
and my son fishing out on Jed's boat in the middle of the ocean. One of
the small family out to dinner on Kevin's—I count the candles—thir-
teenth birthday. There's one of Kevin in the swimming pool with Dean
during what must be another birthday party. In this one, Kara's off to
the side laughing as they're both splashing water at her.

And finally, there's a copy of all of them two years ago when Jed
and Dean got married. Jed and Dean are dressed in matching blue
shirts and rolled-up khakis. They look calm and happy. Jed's arm is
wrapped around Maris, Dean's around Kara. And the women each have

their hands on Kevin's shoulder, who's wearing a miniature version of his uncle's attire.

Without thinking, I pull out my phone and find Jed's contact. It hurts when I press Jed Home Alaska knowing he won't answer. One ring. Two, before Maris picks up. "Hello?"

"Hi. It's Jennings. Is Kara there?"

Silence before Maris hisses, "Do you think today's the right time for this?"

Wearily, I scrub my hand over my face. "I just want to talk with her, Maris. That's all."

"Hold on." I can't hear anything, so I assume Maris put me on mute. A few moments pass before I hear a shaken "Hello?"

A tingle of awareness travels up my spine hearing her voice for the first time in over fifteen years. "Hello, Kara. It's Jennings. Do you think maybe we should talk?"

I hear her breath catch. After she releases it, she cautiously says, "Not tonight. I need to keep an eye on my son."

As much as I want to burst out with "our son," I rein that in. "All right. Do you need a few days?"

"Can you meet me at Jed's gravesite Wednesday at ten?" That's three days away but not unreasonable.

"Of course." I'm stunned and thrilled simultaneously at her capitulation.

"I'll see you then." I'm still holding my phone to my ear as she disconnects.

# JENNINGS

At Jed's gravesite Wednesday, I'm unable to comprehend the magnitude of the way my life has changed. I've lost a friend who I thought I knew better than just about anyone, but I gained a son I knew not at all.

"Why didn't you tell me, Jed?" I whisper achingly.

"Because I refused to let him." I whirl around when I hear Kara's voice behind me. Dressed in jeans, boots, and a shirt, she barely looks older than the girl I knew all those years ago. "Thank you for agreeing to meet me," she says quietly. "It may seem unconventional, but I didn't want Kevin to overhear everything I need to say."

"Or anything I might want to," I reply.

She acknowledges my words with a slight tip of her head. "In a thousand years, I never would have predicted things to have occurred this way. I hope you appreciate that." Her chest heaves up and down. "The last few weeks have been incredibly difficult. I'll ask for your patience while I explain my side of the story. Then I'll be bold enough to ask for a few more days of your patience while I speak to my son."

"Our son," I correct her, unable to hold back.

Her head turns in my direction. She acknowledges, "Yes, Jennings. Our son."

My breath hitches. Kara scuffs the grass near the recently over-turned earth with the toe of her boot back and forth, over and over, while we stand in silence in the brisk morning air. She doesn't say anything, and neither do I because she said she needs to start. Well, frankly, I need her to as well.

When she does, her voice drags me away from the cars driving over the nearby Juneau-Douglas Bridge. "Meeting you when you came home with Jed that weekend? Our connection? Those months we spent together were like nothing I'd ever experienced before in my life, and not because they gave me my son." She studies my face, and her mouth twists. "I certainly don't expect you to reciprocate that emotion."

I nod, unable to speak. I was twenty-one to her twenty-three the summer we were together. Over the last few days, I've spent a lot of time trying to remember everything about Kara's and my time together. Little bits and pieces are starting to come back as she stands before me. Beyond that, the biggest things I remember are how incredibly smart she was and how much we burned up the sheets when we were alone. Maybe that's because I can't get beyond the idea we made a child long enough to remember much else.

But her next words chase all thought from my mind.

"I flew home not long after I found out I was carrying Kevin." All of her movement stills as those words settle between us.

I swallow, remembering words to that effect from Jed's letter. "Okay."

Bracing her feet apart, she lifts her chin to stare directly into my eyes. "To say things went poorly is probably an understatement. I learned very quickly how to stand on my own two feet."

"What did you do?" I ask.

"Not much at first," she admits wryly. I feel my lips curve slightly at the self-deprecating tone. "If it weren't for Dean..." Her words drift off into the air as pain rushes back into her voice. "God, I hate why we're here." Turning, she paces back and forth.

"Why did you wait to tell me?" I ask the question without preamble. I might draw her anger, but anything is better than witnessing her agony.

"I did try to tell you. I tried calling you before I left Alaska, and then I tried to email you."

"What email did you use?" Kara rattles it off, and I wince upon hearing my old internet email address I use when I want access to an internet public login or need a food coupon.

"I take it you don't check it often?" she concludes.

"How do you know I check it at all?" I ask perversely because I have to be angry at something, and right now, that's Kara.

"I knew people from school. Back when Kevin was young, I asked them to see if it was a valid address. They did a bit of research on your email address—where it had been accessed from. The problem was it's been accessed from so many places, all of whom have a John Jennings, I couldn't just pick up the phone and dial 1-800-You-Got-Baby," she snaps before resuming her more placid demeanor. I don't say anything, but just wait.

"I think when I was pregnant was the most nerve-racking. I had no idea what to expect. Maris and Dean were my lifelines. Maris was also sworn to absolute secrecy. She couldn't tell Jed because I knew that would mean you would be told."

"That's ridiculous," I snap, letting the leash on my anger slip.

Kara holds my gaze evenly. "I wasn't exactly logical then, Jennings. Back then, I wasn't bringing a single person into my son's life who I didn't trust wholeheartedly, who didn't want to be there. Right or wrong, it was the decision I made and back then, the support I—we— needed was absolute. And I did keep trying, Jennings. Even after I made that decision." Reaching into her jacket pocket, she pulls out a folded stack of papers. I'm startled by how thick it is. She pushes the papers toward me when I hesitate. "Go ahead. I tried for months to reach you before I ever gave birth."

Taking them, I scan the first one. My heart cracks when I see the line asking me to call her as soon as possible about something important.

"How far along were you when you sent this?" I hold up the first letter.

"About fourteen weeks." Her eyes gloss over with memories I'll never have. "I sent that to you after I spoke with my parents to let them know."

Anger bubbles up when another memory of our time together pops up in my brain. Kara Malone grew up pampered and wealthy, and resentment fills me. "Would using some of Mommy and Daddy's money to hire a private investigator have been too much for your pride?" I lash back.

"Yes, since they disowned me for being pregnant. I didn't have much starting out as they revoked my trust." All the air stills between us. Kara immediately looks contrite. "I apologize, that's not your burden to bear."

A wave of nausea almost crushes me. "Christ, Kara. All this was happening while you carried our son?" My voice is faint.

She shrugs. "What is there to say, Jennings? I did the best I could. But I resigned myself to the fact I was going to raise Kevin by myself a long while ago. Certainly, I never expected Fate to bring my brother and Jed together. Yes, I raised our child alone, but I didn't do it to be cruel."

No. "You're just a woman who survived."

"After going through stages of grief, yes. Coming to acceptance was the hardest. And, I'll be honest, I relived every one of those emotions every time Jed tried to convince me to let him contact you."

"Why didn't you?" This might be the hardest thing to accept.

"Because trust doesn't come easily to me any longer."

"I can appreciate that," I murmur. "Would you be willing to tell me more?"

"About what?"

"Anything. Throw me a lifeline, Kara. What was your pregnancy like?"

"Well, once I was well enough to travel—"

I interrupt her. "There were problems?" I ask anxiously. It's fifteen years too late, but there's a crater in my chest that's aching from where my heart's been ripped out. I rub my hand across it. I never recognized what pain would be involved when it was torn away.

"Nothing more than the average mother deals with, Jennings. I had a god-awful time with morning sickness. But sick or not, I had to leave

Alaska." Her lips curve up slightly before they drop. "I was mortified for my fellow passengers."

"It was a rough trip?"

"I got home." She ducks the question. Her hand starts rubbing her wrist back and forth. It's an endearingly nervous habit I suddenly remember Kara used to have because Jed would joke she'd rub the sapphires from her grandmother's bracelet into her skin by doing it.

But she's not wearing it now. "Where's your grandmother's bracelet?" I manage to get out around the lump in my throat.

Kara blinks at me in shock, before lowering her head to where she's chafed her wrist rubbing her shirt back and forth. She pulls down her sleeve before she bites out, "My parents took it back."

"What do you mean?" My voice is so low that if a hard wind were to come off the water, the question would be lost.

"The day I went to tell them I was pregnant," she admits.

It might be sacrilegious, but I'm shouting, "Goddamnit!" Turning, I pace a few feet away from Jed's fresh gravesite. Linking my hands behind my head, crushing the papers, I swear ripely.

After a few moments, I turn to find Kara looking down at Jed's grave with such despair, it slashes into my chest. She brushes the tips of her fingers under her eyes, not even hiding her love for the men buried there. Even though I didn't know her brother, and I feel like my head is spinning from the ways I didn't know my friend, I need to say something to ease her pain.

"I'm sorry for your loss," I choke out hoarsely. Her head swivels my way. "From everything you've said and Jed said, your brother sounds like he was a remarkable man."

"They were both such a part of our every day, I don't know what that looks like anymore for either me or Kevin." Kara hesitates before admitting, "Making friends was never easy for me growing up; that was Dean's gift. He was the bolder of the two of us, more outgoing." She shakes her head.

"I honestly don't remember that about you." Though admittedly, I think to myself, until the night I found the photo, I hadn't thought about Kara in forever. Now, standing with her facing me, my mind is zinging memories at me all at once.

"I can assure you, if it hadn't been for Dean's influence in my life, I never would have had the courage to have spoken with you that night at the Smiths'."

Before I can respond, she continues giving me a gift I dare not hope for—information about my son. "I find Kevin's the same way. If he had a choice, he'd lose himself in a book or playing some online computer game. Jed got him to try more physical sports like swimming and soccer." My chest aches as a soft smile crosses her face. The love for our child is evident by the way her posture relaxes and the softening of her tone as she speaks of him. In my mind, I pull up the image of her beaming in the photo Jed left me. Oh, crap. I wonder if she knows about them.

"Jed's letter included some pictures of him. He seems like a happy boy, Kara." Her head whips around toward me. "From what it looks like, you've done an amazing job raising him."

"He mentioned he was going to include a few, but I appreciate your candor." I nod as she continues. "And I appreciate your compliment, but I didn't do it alone. It really does take a village to raise a child," she admits wryly. She kicks at the grass in front of her again.

My heart is pounding in my chest when I stumble asking, "Are...are you both staying with Maris for the summer?"

Kara nods. "Why?" she asks, her movement stilling.

"If it's okay with you...if I can arrange...damnit, Kara. I know I don't deserve to ask for this." As much as I want it already even after knowing for only a few hours.

Panic flashes across her face. I want to reach out and touch her to ease the fears, but I think my touch would be less welcome than my request. "You want to spend time with Kevin." Her voice is devoid of all emotion.

"With your assistance. I understand this is a tough time, and I don't want to do anything to make it more difficult," I reassure her gently. "Kara, I know at this late in the game, I could put up a fuss. I could come in hot and do something stupid like talk to lawyers to see what legal course of action I have, but the reality is, Kevin is old enough to state his wishes. And these—" I shake the papers in my hand. "—are an obvious attempt by you to do what is right. Whatever high ground I had is gone. Please, I'm trying."

"It may not seem like it, but I appreciate that." Her body's still tense.

"Will you let me get to know our son?" I rumble in the misty morning air. Now, I take the chance and reach out to touch her arm to give it a quick squeeze. "Please," I plead.

She's stock-still for a moment before she steps back, breaking the connection between us. "Now that Jed and Dean are...gone, Kevin is trying to become the man of our house." I don't miss how she stumbles over the words. It reminds me I don't know how Jed and Dean died. And Maris never offered up the information. But that's not for now.

Kara's focus is on the freshly turned ground where the ashes of her brother and our friend are buried. "I need to prepare him first."

*Excuse me?* I don't realize I've spoken aloud until her head snaps around so fast the short strands of her hair smack her in the face. I stumble when I try to follow up my incredulousness. "He doesn't know about his father?"

"He knows plenty about the man who donated half of his cells. In fact we've had several discussions about genetic recessive traits since his eye color is yours," Kara haughtily informs me. Damn, now is absolutely the wrong time to remember how hot I found Kara when she got arrogant about her scientific knowledge. "What we haven't had a conversation about is the man who donated those genes would be in Alaska at the funeral of his beloved uncle Jed. He's suffered enough blows recently. And as you've already said, I'm the only parent he knows. So, I'll find the right time to talk to him about it."

I'm about to argue with her when she holds up her hand. "Enough, Jennings. I'll talk to Kevin and call you." She turns and walks away from Jed's gravesite without saying goodbye. Or letting me give her my new number. Damnit, how is all of this going to work out?

Left behind, I stare at a woman I was once intimate with. Memories bombard me as her long legs eat up the distance on the grassy knoll until she's out of sight.

But one thing burns at me.

I turn back to Jed's grave and ask the only man who could have answered the question but who can't give me the answer. "What the hell do I do now?"

Like I expected, there's no answer in the cool morning air. With a sigh, I turn and head back to the B&B to get a hold of Lou so I can start to strategize how I can manage to stay in Alaska for a prolonged visit.

Because there's no way I'm missing the opportunity to get to know my son.

# KARA

That didn't go as poorly as could be expected.

I pass the turnoff that would take me back to Maris's house and head straight on Mendenhall Loop Road. I had always intended on bringing Kevin with me when I came back here for the first time, but maybe it was meant to be like this.

Taking a chance, I drive up to see if there is parking in one of the two tiny parking lots. Someone is feeling benevolent as I turn down an aisle just as a family of four makes it to their vehicle. My heart pounds in anticipation. *Soon*, I tell myself. I'll have a moment of freedom I haven't in so long.

Shoving my wallet into the pocket of my jacket, I sprint to the Visitor Center. After impatiently waiting for them to process a season pass, I race back down the ramp toward the signs that will lead me to the Nugget Falls Trail.

I don't look up. I can't. I need to get to the spot, my spot, before I do.

Luckily the trails aren't busy midweek. The air by the glacier bites at me as I'm not dressed for the cooler temperatures as I approach her majestic beauty. Finally I stop, knowing in my head what I should see when I glance up. But the knot that's been in my stomach since last night expands as I'm unable to comprehend the difference between the glacier's magnificence since I last saw her sixteen years ago and now. "What's happened to you?" I whisper aloud. But for all intents and purposes, the question I just asked is one the snow and ice should have been shouting back at me after what happened to Dean and Jed.

Sinking down into a crouch, I wrap my arms around my legs and let loose the tears I held back. Remembering the call I had to make to Maris to let her know about the death of our brothers. Hearing in my head her screams which echoed the sentiments of my heart. The nights I'd rock Kevin against me as he'd sob his pain out.

And I'd be lying if I didn't cry a little because the last time I was crouched in this very spot, I was holding the early pregnancy test I sealed carefully in a ziplock. I'd just given up my dream of being a scientist who cared for this glacier.

Now, as I press my hand to my flat stomach that nurtured and held Kevin for almost ten months, I know I was destined for a new path.

Pushing to my feet, I ignore the chill permeating my skin, take the trail back, and head toward the water's edge. My eyes crinkle a bit when I see the interns are still putting out pieces of 200-year-old glacier ice strategically around the water's edge for the visitors to touch. Slowly, I make my way around to the farthest edge and take in the glory of the Tongass National Forest as it begins its short summer season.

"I needed to be here to resolve all of these feelings still bottled inside of me. I didn't realize how much seeing Jennings again would affect me," I murmur aloud. Looking skyward, I whisper, "I can't say I welcome him in my life, Jed, but thank you for ensuring Kevin has the chance to know his father."

As if he can hear me, a burst of sunlight breaks through a cloud and illuminates the lake. A second ray joins it. My heart gives a joyous leap. A hiccupping laugh escapes before a cluster of altocumulus clouds comes by and breaks up both rays like a prism.

*I will always love and miss both of you. I will never let Kevin go a single day without remembering you,* I vow to my brother and his husband silently. Staining the muscles of an already aching heart, I whisper, "I promise."

Hearing the rhythmic waves of the glacier water, I squat down and reach out to put my hand into the heart of the frigidity, realizing this is all that's left over from the cause and effect of others. I shudder inside when I whisper, "Kind of like what's left of me," I whisper, pushing myself up.

Slowly, I walk back to the parking lot knowing by the time I get back to Maris's, she'll be frantic wondering what happened during my meeting with Jennings. And then I have to figure out the best way to talk with my son without causing any more damage to an already devastated heart.

"Seriously?" Maris yells as she slams the kitchen cabinet, turning to face me with a stack of bowls in her hands. She's in the process of preparing a hearty lunch of stew and freshly baked biscuits which I'm just in time for since I called to let her know I would be home on my way back from Mendenhall.

"I'll ask you to keep your voice down. I prefer to have a discussion with Kevin, not have him find out by overhearing us." My voice is low but firm. I may not be the most outgoing woman, but prod me even just a little about my son and I'll turn as ferocious as a Kodiak bear seeking food after hibernation.

Maris sets the bowls down carefully. "I'll apologize, but really? Jed's barely in the ground and Jennings wants to become Mr. Dad? Now?" Her voice ends on a crack.

I glare at her even as I shift to comfort her. Before I can do either, she holds up her hands in surrender. "Sorry, sorry. But is this something you want to do?"

Leaning forward on the polished wood waterfall counter, I brace my elbows on it as my forehead falls into my hands. "Not particularly, no. But I don't think I have much choice." Softly, I finish giving Maris a quick recap of my conversation with Jennings at Jed's gravesite. I don't blame her for her outburst when Jennings using the term "legal course of action." It was what I felt like doing at the time as well.

"I'll never understand why Jed thought this was a good idea. You're all Kevin needs," she vows loyally.

My simmering anger reduces and immediately smooths out. "It's what Jed wanted," I remind her.

"And he's gone. Jed shouldn't get to dictate how you and *your* son live your life. You've done damn well without Jennings in it." Maris spins around to grab the stew off the stove.

"Jed believed his knowing would make a difference to all of us," I remind her. And why I'm defending her brother's arguments used on me, I have no idea.

"Jed's been wrong before," she snaps. My heart grows heavy, because I know what she's referring to. Unfortunately, Nick has never seen her as more than "Jed's little sister." And Maris has paid the price for that for years by loving a man who has never seen her and having a ringside seat as he roams the world with a new woman.

But— "Is it Jennings you have the issue with, Maris, or is it me?" I ask quietly.

That brings her up short, still holding the soup pot. "What do you mean?" she asks carefully.

"This anger is something completely different. I never noticed it before during our calls. What is it?"

She hesitates a moment too long before opening her mouth.

I slam my hand down on the sleek wood, causing a pain that has nothing to do with the one beginning to burn in my heart to shoot up my arm. "Tell me," I demand.

"Maybe if you weren't so stubborn, Jed wouldn't have felt the need to be tied to you, to Florida. I know he missed home. He told me so when we talked. If it weren't for you, maybe my brother would still be alive! Why wouldn't you listen? Now, he's dead and you're here."

"And if you believed that, why didn't you open your damn mouth? You knew twelve years before your brother did. Why am I just being persecuted for decisions you supposedly supported me about?" Cocking a hip, I mimic her huskier voice. "'I'm so proud of you, Kara, for doing this on your own.' You kept the secret from Jed, from the Jacks, just as long as I did. So why is it I'm the one who's taking the blame because life took something precious from both of us?"

"Because you should have been willing to accept help!" she shouts.

"Okay, so let's turn the tables. Why don't you tell me how you really feel about Jed leaving the cross to Nick?"

Maris clamps her lips shut, but her eyes speak volumes.

I point a shaky finger in her direction. "Do not stand there and judge me for the decisions I made. You weren't there. I made the best choices I could to provide stability for my son. Jed may not have liked my decision, you may have lied to me about your opinions on them, but none of you lived day in and day out with a child. I did. And as a mother..."

"Once Jed first offered, Kara, once you knew exactly how to get a hold of Jennings, you should have just..."

"Stop," I lash out. Maris could have slapped me; it would have been less painful. "You said you agreed with my choices."

"Kara—"

I stop her from speaking. "Once Dean and Jed fell in love, I refused to put Jed in the middle because Jed was Jennings's first. Their bond was supposed to be as sacred as yours and mine." Now, I'm the one shrieking as memories come flooding back. "I made the best decisions I could to provide for Kevin, to protect us. When Dean took me in, I was cut off, but he didn't think twice. Firemen of his rank back then didn't make a lot, but my Dean? He worked himself to the bone to help pay for my medical care. He took care of me until I could teach after Kevin." I'm talking to Maris, but I'm remembering those early days out loud.

"Kara, please don't," she begs me.

My eyes wander around, seeing everything and nothing. "I kept an accounting of every dime Dean spent, and every paycheck I earned after I became a teacher, I paid him back a little at a time. He hated that, did I ever tell you that? I must have. I told you everything."

"Stop, honey. Please."

My voice goes dreamy as I remember the early days back in Florida. "I didn't even have money to buy a cell phone after my parents disowned me. And he couldn't afford to get me one with the additional rent and food. God, do you remember? The hospital had to call Dean to tell him I went into labor. And then he called you so you could hear everything. But holding Kevin that first moment? It made all the suffering worth it. It made every moment of pain I've endured as a mother worth it." Then fury whips clean through me. "See, what you don't get, Maris, is that as a mother, you'll do anything for your child. And for the last fifteen years, I've made the best decisions I could with people around me I thought I could trust. People—" A sob escapes my throat. "—whose opinions I relied on. I raised my son on my own because he was mine. And until Jed began to work to change my mind on that, you agreed with that."

I ignore the tears falling down Maris face as I continue. "God, it all comes back to family, doesn't it? I was right all along. There are some things you just don't do to family. With the way Dean and I were, I believed right here—" I smack my hand into the center of my chest before continuing. "—there are some bonds you don't break. Some people you don't put in the middle or turn your back on. But your brother thought he knew better. He believed his brotherhood could withstand it—his with Jennings, and his with me. So, fine. Blame me. Blame me for his death and for everything beforehand."

"Please, Kara, stop," Maris beseeches me.

Ignoring her, I continue. "I let him convince me to put that codicil in the will *knowing* my son would ask before that because he's as inquisitive as I am. And I'd be in this *exact* same position. I fought Jed, but only because I didn't want to think about what it would mean to all of us. For better, for worse, I made a beautiful child with Jennings. And there are too many connections for us to avoid them forever."

Maris is silent as I regroup my thoughts. When I speak again, my voice is laced with a pain I haven't had the luxury of fully releasing. "I was almost at the point of breaking down and giving in about the whole damn thing when the wreck happened. Death took away the chance I had to tell Jed he was right about what he was willing to give up for my son. I didn't have the opportunity to ask him what he thought I should do. And now I never will."

Turning I ask, "What I don't understand is how *you* could lie to about me what you thought all these years."

"I didn't lie to you," she whispers.

I say without turning around, "Right now, I'm finding that hard to believe. If you'll excuse me, I'm going to lie down. I'll tell Kevin to come up when he's hungry," before I head to the stairs off the main room of the Smiths' family home toward the basement.

"Kara, wait!"

I pause with my hand on the doorknob. Emotions are choking me. *Keep it together,* I warn myself. I wait for Maris to speak.

"I'm so sorry. I don't know what I'm saying. You know that's not what I think. I don't know where my head's at. Please, please forgive me," she begs.

Our sisterhood bonds may be strained, but I answer immediately. "I will. I just need time." I pull the door open to the basement and call down. "Kevin? Maris made stew. I'm going to lie down for a bit."

"Okay, Mom! I'll be up in a few."

Without another word, I close the door on the conversation both physically and metaphorically before heading up to the guest room. I need some privacy to process everything that I just learned and how it factors into how I deal with Jennings.

Because I need to dig deep for the courage I lost a long time ago. And there's only one person I know who can give it to me.

Wearily, I make it up to my room and pull out my laptop. Opening up a new file, I start typing.

*Dear Dean...*

# JENNINGS

"How did it go with Kara?" Kody asks me when I get back.

I don't say anything, I just slap the folded stack of papers Kara handed to me in front of him.

"Tell me that bitch isn't going to try to sue for custody at this late date," Nick drawls.

I don't know whether to thank him or rip his head off, but he just gave me a target for all the emotions seething inside of me. Turning, I manage to coldcock Nick Cain. It probably helps he's sprawled across the couch with a tumbler of scotch in his hand, but I don't give a shit. "Never, ever, call the mother of my child a bitch again."

Nick surges to his feet with in seconds, the liquid falling forgotten to the floor. His fury is palpable, just like mine. Good, I need to do something to let out this impotent rage.

Unfortunately, Brad and Kody don't see it quite the same way. Brad shoves himself in front of Nick, while Kody grabs my arms from behind. "The hell with this. If Jennings gets a free shot, then so do I," Nick demands.

Brad growls, "Pretty certain you took yours first, man. Shitty thing to call Kara a bitch when Jennings hasn't had a chance to tell us jack."

Kody's arms slacken. I twist and jerk until I'm free of his hold. I'm still breathing hard, my rage a tangible thing. But not at Nick. "I'll take the hit; I deserve it." My eyes are steady as I hold his.

Everyone freezes before there's a cacophony of sound. "Are you insane?" "Did you get into a wreck on the way home?" And Nick, smug bastard he is: "They didn't give me the belt for nothing, Jennings. Certainly not for that pansy-ass tap you gave me."

"I was at the fight; I know what I'm asking for." And then, fuck, even Nick gets a concerned look on his face. My jaw tightens when I pick up the papers and smack them so they fly across the room like I'm making it rain money. "Every. Few. Months. For fucking years. She'd email me. Asking me to call her. Saying she had something important to talk with me about. Then Jed meets Dean what, three years ago? That's when the emails stop. I haven't figured out why. What I do know is her good-for-nothing family cut her off."

"Oh, God." Brad collapses back on the sofa.

"Then, Jed kept telling me I should come visit." Turning, I face a stunned Kody. "You were there one time when he asked. Do you remember? And what did I say?"

"'No way, man. The business is taking up too much time,'" Kody quotes me almost verbatim before his own legs give out and he collapses in the chair behind him.

"That." I throw my thumb back where Kody was standing and face a still-standing Nick. "That's what I said to the man who was likely bound by a vow to his husband, his sister-in-law, and the *mother of my child!*" I roar at Nick. "He kept trying to get me to come and see. And if it weren't for Jed *dying*, and a promise that he elicited from Kara, I may still never know I had a son." And I don't care if it's a sign of weakness, my knees give out beneath me. I fall right where I stand.

I'm rocking back and forth on my knees amid all of the "*Dear Jennings*" letters Kara sent to a freaking free email account I've barely glanced at for anything more than a coupon in more than sixteen years, when I feel a steel hand clamp down on my shoulder.

Nick's face is so close to mine, I can't see anything beyond it. His voice is a soft rumble when he says, "We'll help you however we can, Jennings. I swear, we will. Yeah?" He adds on the last the same way he did when we were both on Team Canada hamming it up for the crowds in the Lumberjack Show. Back before we had lives that kept us apart more than we were together. Back before we only saw each other once a year at a reunion, that Jed, I remember painfully, didn't attend the last year.

Dragging me off my knees, Nick waits for my response. I have to swallow to get the moisture back in my mouth before I can give it. "Yeah."

He slaps my back. I stumble forward, skidding on the printouts. When I turn to glare at Nick, all he does is tap his jaw and smirk.

I roll my eyes. "I still got the punch in, asshole."

"All right, children." Brad claps his hands together. "Before you do any more damage against each other, I think we need to bring reinforcements into this discussion."

"Who?" Kody asks.

But I already know. "Rainey?" I guess.

"Rainey," Brad confirms. Sliding his phone out of his pocket, he calls his wife. It takes a moment for the call to connect. "Honey, would it be a problem if I brought the guys home to eat? No? Good. Also, how hard would it be to find a sitter?" A longer pause. "Yeah, we're probably going to need more than a few drinks."

"Forget probably," I call out.

Brad laughs. "Yes, that was Jennings. No, I'm not telling you more over the phone. See you in a few hours. Love you too." Hanging up, he advises us, "You guys better brace, because Rainey said the kids are going to climb you like monkeys."

"It's too bad Jennings can't get practice for his with yours," Nick says. "But based on the size of his kid, I don't think there will be any daddy/son tree climbing going on."

I glare at my friend, who merely quirks a brow before asking, "What? Too soon?"

"Way, way too soon."

"Okay, before we go to Brad's, let's talk everything through. Because the minute Rainey knows, she's going to want to call Kara for a girls' night out. And we all know how well that's going to go over." God bless Kody for reminding us of everything practical because he's absolutely right.

"Yeah." I let out a sigh. "Let me tell you guys what happened."

After we pick up the letters, I proceed to tell the guys everything that happened when I met Kara at the cemetery. They ask a lot of questions, but at the end they come to the same conclusion I do.

I have nothing to do but wait.

LIFE AT THE MEYERSES' household is sheer chaos. Like Brad predicted, his kids began to use us as indoor jungle gyms the instant we stepped through the door. Rainey, on the other hand, merely grins.

"What do you have cooking?" I ask her as I lean down to brush a kiss on her smooth cheek.

She wraps her arms around me to give me a much-needed hug before she answers. "Chili, which I made mild so I can send some to my sister's. This way she can use it to feed her two kids plus ours so I can find out the scoop." Pulling out of my arms, she opens a small cabinet to the right of the stove which sports an impressive collection of sealed hot-sauce bottles. "Jed sent those to Brad over the years."

My heart trips at her words. "He used to send me newspaper clippings and online articles about the local economy along with real estate listings," I share. I would file them under a special folder titled "Jed's Craziness." Only he wasn't so crazy. He was trying to pull my head out of my ass.

Likely misinterpreting the look of pain on my face, Rainey is quick to continue. "There are at least a case of them in the basement, and that doesn't account for those in *both* of our refrigerators. Please." She turns sparkling blue eyes up at me which haven't changed since I first met her twenty years ago. "Help me by using some to doctor your food."

I understand what she's really asking is for help to get Brad over his grief by releasing some of the memories. "Honey, after tonight, I don't think he's going to have that problem," I reassure her.

"Really?" she says hopefully.

"I think he's going to be too focused on worrying about me," I mutter.

Rainey narrows her eyes. "What did you do, Jennings?"

Brad steps into the kitchen with a case of beer he pulled up from the basement, saving me from having to answer. "Kids to your sister's first, babe. Then, we'll talk while we're eating." Tearing open the box, he hands me a bottle.

"Opener?"

"Second drawer to your right," Rainey responds. "Honey?" she calls to Brad as I uncap my beer, pocketing the cap.

"Yeah? Jennings, toss it here." I underhand pitch it to him. He easily catches it before using it to open his bottle.

"Am I going to want to hurt Jennings?" Rainey asks sweetly.

Brad takes a long pull of his beer before answering honestly. "Maybe."

"Great. Just great. Luckily for you, Jennings, the tequila is already chilling." She stomps over to the pantry and scans it. "Now, do we have tomato juice..."

"Tomato juice?"

Without turning around, she hisses, "Lime after shots is...crap. I used the juice in the chili. I'll just have to pace myself by doing a shot and then eating a bite of food." Backing out, she slams the door closed. "You'd better talk fast."

Rainey's sister, Meadow, bursts through the door. "I'm sorry I'm late!" Kody's head snaps around. His face lights up at seeing her since they used to be close years ago, but she breezes past him. I don't miss his quick frown before he's distracted by Brad's son.

"Hold on, I have chili for you," Rainey calls to her sister.

"Thank God. I was wondering what I was going to feed the monsters. Hey, Brad." She gives her brother-in-law a quick hug. "Good to see you, Jennings."

I tip up my lips and hold out my hand. "Same. Thanks for helping out."

She shrugs. "Not a problem. We swap kids all the time." She hefts the bag.

"Can I help with that?" I ask immediately.

"Try a diaper bag sometime," she jokes.

I really would have liked to. Regret washes through me that I wasn't able to be there for Kevin's early years.

"All right, Meyers munchkins. Let's go! Get your coats and bags. I don't know about you, but I'm hungry!" Meadow calls out as she rushes out of the kitchen after exchanging a quick kiss with her sister. Within moments, after Meadow departs with the kids, calm descends on the house. Kody and Nick join us in the kitchen. Nick looks no worse for the wear, but Kody's shirt is untucked and he looks less than his usual pressed self. But the smile on his face can't be faked.

"Had fun?" I direct the question at him.

"Kids are great. Almost makes me want to look at settling down," he admits.

Brad's about to open his mouth, but Nick beats him to it. "Or you could just get them full grown like Jennings did. Then you can miss the whole diaper stage. You still have the fun of diving into the fun of teenage adolescence though."

Kody sighs. Brad shakes his head. I just wait, but I don't have to for long. Rainey's screech, of "What?" can likely be heard down the street at her sister's house.

Brad tries to placate her. "Now, honey..."

"Don't you 'now, honey' me, Bradley Meyers. What the hell is Nick talking about? No, wait." Before I can even answer, Rainey goes to the freezer and pulls out the tequila. Uncapping the bottle, she takes a swig. Slamming the bottle down, she races over to the warming chili and shoves a spoonful in her mouth to attempt to kill the burn of the alcohol down her throat. "Now I'm ready to hear about this."

I brace my hips against the island counter. "Do you remember Kara Malone? The woman I dated..."

"When you were all Lumberjacks? Of course I do."

"Brad said he told you Kara showed up at the viewing after you left with the kids."

"He did."

"Did he tell you who she showed up with?"

She cuts her eyes toward her husband, and Brad ducks his head. He knows he's in the shithouse for sure. "No, he failed to mention that," she bites out acidly. "Who did she bring? Her husband?"

I finish off my beer. As I put the empty on the counter next to me, Brad's already uncapping the next before handing it to me. "Thanks, man," I say gratefully.

"Jennings," Rainey snaps. "Who did Kara bring with her?" Her lips are compressed together as she waits for my answer.

"Her son."

"So, she had a little boy? So what?"

"Her fifteen-year-old son, Rainey," Brad interjects.

Rainey's jaw slackens. "Oh, my God. Is he..."

I exhale slowly. "Yes. He's mine."

Rainey doesn't respond. She turns to Brad. "There's another bottle of tequila in the basement. If you don't want to be divorced by morning, I suggest putting it in the freezer. Stat."

Brad, definitely not a stupid man, puts his beer on the counter and heads for the basement stairs. "On it."

Rainey points at me and says, "You're not leaving until I know everything."

I meet her eyes and say levelly, "I didn't think I was."

"This is...I can't believe...Oh, my God!" she yells.

"And right there sums up how I'm feeling," I tell her sadly. "I feel so much, too much, and I don't know what to do with all of it."

Then, Rainey smiles the smile that made Brad fall for her in high school. It illuminates her face, lighting her eyes. And her words? They warm my heart, making me realize this was why I needed to come here.

"Welcome to parenthood, Jennings. Now that you are one, those feelings will never, ever end."

# JENNINGS

"What did you feel when you saw Kara again?" Rainey asks me hours later. She passes me the second tequila bottle. Kody's passed out on the floor in front of us.

"What do you mean?" I take a pull before handing it back to her. I know I'm going to be sick as hell later, but numbing my brain and my heart may be worth the price.

"It's not a hard question, Jennings, and you're not a stupid man," she snorts. "What was it like to see Kara?"

"Why?"

"Do you always answer a question with a question?"

I finish up my beer. "When I don't want to answer it, yes."

Brad walks up from the basement with the last six-pack of beer, announcing, "I can't guarantee this hasn't gone skunk."

"Can you get him to answer a question?" Rainey asks.

"On occasion. Why?"

"I want to know what it was like for him to see Kara."

"Just don't call her any names," he warns his wife. "Jennings took a swing at Nick for daring to call her a—"

"And that's enough out of you," I declare. But Rainey's face twists as she starts to think. And drunk thinking is a bad thing with this woman.

"You took a swing at Nick," she concludes, breathless.

"It wasn't a big deal. He made a completely uncalled-for comment."

But Rainey sets her curls dancing by swinging her head back and forth. "Jennings, do you remember the last time you took a swing at Nick?"

Brad mutters, "Ah, crap. I forgot about that," before he falls onto the couch next to his wife.

"Who knew? It was likely—" But my body locks as the memory is plucked out of the recesses of my mind. "He hit on Kara first," I whisper.

"And you dragged him to the Smiths' backyard and began flailing at him because of it," Rainey reminds me. "I was there, remember? Kara had moved in, what, maybe two weeks earlier, honey?"

"Something like that," Brad confirms.

The room is spinning between the crazy amount of alcohol I've consumed and the realization that "I've maybe messed up my life to such a degree there may be no coming back," I groan.

A voice from the stairs startles all of us. "There's always redemption, Jennings. Didn't Jed teach all of us that?" Nick crosses over to where we're sitting before taking the bottle of tequila away from Rainey. Tipping it back, he pours the clear liquid down his throat like it's water. "The question is are you going to waste it?"

"I don't even know where to start. I need help," I admit.

Nick claps slowly. "It takes some of us longer to learn than others."

I throw him the middle finger before I turn to the one couple whose love I've been constantly exposed to that has lasted no matter what has come along to try to fuck it up. "What do I do?"

Brad goes to open his mouth, but before he can speak, Rainey reaches up and clamps his lips together. Holding them together like they're a duck, she speaks. "What does she want you to do?"

"Wait." Frustrated, I push myself to my feet and step over Kody to pace. "She wants me to wait until she talks to our son to explain everything. But I want to know everything about him."

Brad bats Rainey's hand away. "Where are the emails Kara sent you?"

"Hold on." Moving into the foyer, I grab my overnight duffle. I pull out the emails and hand them over. As Kody lights up the room with his snoring, Brad reads one, then passes it to Rainey, who passes it to Nick.

Finally, it's Nick who speaks. "How long are emails kept?"

"I don't know, why?' I answer.

He shoves a printout under my nose. "Because, you moron, Kara attached files to these. Maybe there's a way to get to know your son without having to wait."

Immediately, I turn to Brad. "Can I use your computer?"

"Up the stairs. Second door on the right. Password to my login is 'Lumb3rjack!'"

Nick snickers, but I don't waste any time until I hear Rainey call my name. "Yes?" I pause with my foot on the bottom step.

She bites her lip worriedly. "You're anxious. I get that; I would be too. But if I can be honest?"

"Always," I encourage her.

"Kara's not the same woman she was all those years ago. From an emotional standpoint, she's light-years ahead of you. It's part of motherhood. So, please listen. Focus on her words and what she's saying," Rainey pleads. "It was unintentional, but life hasn't been easy. The charm you won her with the first time isn't going to work now—either with her or her son."

"What will?" I ask starkly.

Rainey's expression is helpless. "I don't know. But if at the cornerstone isn't faith and trust, you'll never know what it really means to be a father."

Before I leave, I admit my true regret to all of them. "I wish I'd let Jed talk me down to Florida well before now."

"It's always easier to look back and wish time back," Nick says quietly. For the briefest moment, the demons that live deep within my friend surface. "But unfortunately we can't. All we can do is move on, however life lets us."

I nod before heading upstairs to be alone with Kara and, hopefully, my son.

THERE ARE WELL over forty thousand emails sitting in my webmail account. "I suppose I should be grateful it's not higher," I say with disgust as I delete another batch before moving on to another. Another click deletes hundreds of messages.

It takes me another hour until I'm left with twenty-nine messages from Kara's different email accounts spanning ten years. I'm so damn grateful this freaking free mail server keeps messages as long as your account is considered valid and that I kept up with all my required password changes that would hit my legitimate email address. I just wish I had bothered to scan the messages that were waiting, but I didn't think there was anything important waiting for me.

If I only knew.

My fist clenched at my side, I click on the first message I see from Kara in October almost sixteen years ago. It's simple and to the point.

*Jennings,*

*This is the second time I've tried to email you. I've also tried to call you, but I'm not certain if you recognize the number. To be honest, I don't know if I have the right number. I no longer have my cell phone. I've left messages, but I'm not certain if you're checking them. It's imperative you contact me as soon as you can.*

*Thank you,*

*Kara*

I grit my teeth, realizing the first message must have fallen off the server. "Hell, I should be grateful this many are still here." Scanning the message, I see she left me a number with a 904 area code and her address. Broodingly, I contemplate the screen. Would I have known? With Kara's direct, no-nonsense email, would I have understood? "I'd like to think so," I murmur before clicking on the second one.

It was sent Christmas Day.

*Jennings,*

*I don't know if you received my first two emails. I'm hoping you check your messages today due to the holiday; at least I hope so. Email isn't how I want to break this news, so please contact me as soon as you can. There are things you need to know and information I need to have.*

*Thank you,*

*Kara*

"How far along were you at that point, Kara?" My voice is jagged. I click on the next message dated March 28—a little over fifteen years ago. And it gives me the answer.

*Jennings,*

*God, I hope I'm writing the correct email, because this is the only way I have to contact you. The number I've been calling has been disconnected.*

*I do however believe it's your right to know about your child. He was born on March 25 at 9:03 AM after an eighteen hour labor.*

*I named him Kevin, after my paternal grandfather. I would have consulted with you, but I haven't heard from you. His full name is Kevin Jennings Malone. He weighs 8 pounds, 2 ounces.*

*My contact information remains the same for now. If it changes, I will let you know.*

*Kara*

This time, there's a .jpg attachment. With shaking fingers, I use the mouse to double-click on the file. And then he's there on Brad's enormous monitor.

I can only suspect it was her brother who took the picture, but there he is, my son being held by his mother in the first few hours after his birth. Kara's smiling weakly at the camera. "My baby," I croak. "My son."

"So there were pictures." Nick stands in the entrance to the door. He's holding two mugs, one which he hands to me, and I take it gratefully.

"Look at him," I whisper as I turn back to the monitor. "He's so tiny."

"Does Kara tell you how big he was?"

I nod dumbly, still entranced by the photo.

"What do you want to do?" he asks me quietly.

"I want to find some way to turn back the clock."

"Since that's not possible, what's your next option?"

I zoom in on the photo of Kara and Kevin. Even though there's a joy on Kara's beautiful face, I can still see the fear marring what should have been the most perfect moment of her life. "I hate that you were so afraid. I hate I wasn't there for you both. I'm so sorry," I say aloud.

"That's where you start," Nick shoves to his feet.

"What?" I'm too fascinated by the tiny bundle that became my son and the brave woman who carried him.

"By figuring out a way to say you're sorry." Nick's simple wisdom is exactly what I needed to hear. Absorbing that once again, I decide to press my luck and ask something that's been niggling at me.

"Hey, Nick? Can I ask you something?"

"Of course. My wisdom is always available for you." His condescending smirk makes an appearance.

But it falls from his face when I ask, "Why did Jed leave you his cross?"

For a moment I wonder if he's going to storm off without answering. Finally he responds, "You're not asking me something I haven't wondered a thousand times already. By rights, he should have left it to Maris. She found it with her grandfather when the three of them were on vacation together."

I let out a low whistle. It's my only response.

"Jed told me once his grandfather believed his luck changed after he wore it," Nick says absently.

"Did he?"

"Yeah." Nick lets out a rough sound. "I tried to convince Maris to take it back in the parking lot. That didn't go over well."

"No?" I can't imagine it would have since everyone except Nick has recognized Maris has been in love with him for twenty years.

"I would have thought she would want this part of her family back." He frowns, bewildered. "Anyway, I'll leave you to it. Holler if you want any more of that." He nods at my cup and leaves me to my email and my photos.

For the next several hours, I don't leave the computer. I open each of the messages Kara sent to me.

*Jennings, I know you wanted to fly. Well, I just gave Kevin his first airplane today.* She attached a photo of a dark-haired toddler holding a stuffed airplane.

*Jennings, There are too many of you in the US for me to track you down in any other way. And I can't afford to hire a private detective. I'm so sorry...* I curse loudly when I read her apology on Kevin's third birthday along with a picture of him blowing out the candles.

*Jennings, At first I wasn't sure who he looked like, but by now it's obvious it's you.* With a picture of Kevin all dressed up for his first day of school as a kindergartner.

*Jennings, Jennings, Jennings...* All of the emails have the same polite informative tone.

Until the last one.

*Jennings,*

*Tonight I have to let you go. I have to move on. I just want to say thank you for this gift, this miracle.*

*Science tries to explain the miracle of parenthood, but they can't. Until I had Kevin, I thought I could, but I never knew. And I feel so terribly sorry you don't have that.*

*Maybe someday you'll understand the beauty of a simple hug from someone who's very heart exists because yours does. I hope you do because there's nothing quite like what I'm feeling right now. Kevin knows something's not quite right and his only aim is to make it better.*

*It won't make any sense to you, but I'm confused and upset because I'm preparing to do something I'm not quite ready to do, Dean's excited by it for me, but I'm not sure I'm ready.*

*Is there a time I ever will be?*

*I hope you understand this will be my last email. I have to let you go. I have to move on. I suspect our lives will intersect someday in the future when Kevin asks me more about his father. But I need a shot at finding out who Kara Malone is.*

*Since I know you're not reading these, this makes no sense to you. And that's okay. Your email account has been a good place for me to talk to all these years.*

*If you eventually find these and want to get to know Kevin, all I ask is for you to please do me the kindness of reaching out to me first.*

*Kara*

"How do I go about winning back the trust of a good woman?" I whisper to the room as dawn seeps into the sky. "How do I show my son I'm someone worth knowing when right now I'm not even sure about that myself?"

I forward all of the emails to my work account before closing out of the mail application. Then I shut down and make my way downstairs to get a few hours' rest.

Rainey was right. The next part isn't up to me. It's up to the mother of my son. All I have the right to do is wait.

# KARA

"Mom?" Kevin knocks on the door to my bedroom hours after my confrontation with Maris. "Are you okay in there? I brought you some stew."

*God, my son is such a good kid*, I think as I sit up beneath the blanket I've been curled under since I finished my latest letter to my brother. "Come on in, baby," I call out.

"I'm not exactly a baby," he teases as he pushes the door open with a tray in one hand.

"No, you're not, are you?" My heart aches as I study him.

Having just seen Jennings, I'm struck more than ever by how much Kevin has inherited from him: his hair, his eyes, his height, the cut of his jaw. I push up to a sitting position so he can set the tray across my lap before he does something that reminds me he'll always be my little boy—he climbs into the bed next to me.

"It's going to get better, right?" Hearing the anguish in his voice over a nightmare few experience at his age slays me.

How is one little man supposed to endure this much pain? Especially with the addition of what I'll have to tell him? "It will. Somewhere down the road, maybe."

He tucks his head into the curve of my shoulder. "Are you glad to be here?" His voice trembles as he asks a question aloud that's obviously been preying on his mind when there's already too much there.

"Yes and no. I wish it was by choice," I answer truthfully. After Dean and Jed's death, Kevin's anxiety spiked—something I'm truly concerned about with the addition of adding Jennings into his life. *At what point is all of this going to be too much for him to handle?* I wonder desperately.

Kevin relaxes fully against me. His arm snakes around my stomach, and I stroke his hair. "You used to do this when you were a little boy," I murmur, before pressing a kiss to the top of his head. Wrinkling my nose, I add, "Did you shower today?"

He shrugs. "Why bother? It's not like I'm planning on going anywhere."

"Except for the fact that you and your teenage boy stench are now fouling up my sheets?" I tease.

He tips his head back and he grins, popping out a small dimple he also inherited from his father. Then a white-hot rush of panic floods through me. Mine—he's always been mine.

Analytically, I know Kevin has an equal number of chromosomes from both his father and me, but it's hard to reconcile that emotionally, especially after speaking with Jennings. If it weren't for the small spray of freckles across Kevin's nose both Dean and I had, Kevin would be Jennings's mirror image when it comes to his looks.

But his heart? What will finding this out do to the precious heart I nurtured for fifteen years? I squeeze him closer to me, whispering, "Why couldn't you stay a little baby?"

"Mom?" His confusion is evident.

"Just feeling emotional, sweetheart." Fumbling for a reason, I remind him, "Soon, you're going to be off to college. What am I going to do then?"

"I'll always be with you, Mom," Kevin vows, laying his head back down.

Hugging him tighter, I raise my eyes to the popcorn ceiling that's been in this room since I first rented it from the Smiths. Again pressing a kiss to the top of his slightly greasy hair, I relish the moment, even as I cringe a little. "How many more chances will I have to do this?"

"As many as you want," Kevin assures me.

We lie in comfortable silence until Kevin asks, "Is everything okay with you and Maris?"

"Yes and no." I refuse to lie. There are times when I'll delay telling him the truth, but if I do, I'm honest about why.

"It will be okay," he reassures me.

"What makes you so certain?"

"Because Maris is family," he says simply. "The last family we have. Nothing she did can be worse than losing her forever. Right?" He blinks up at me questioningly.

Hearing those words from Kevin puts a lid on the cauldron of seething emotions that have been swirling around in my head. Because he's right. Nothing is worse than death. "You know what, Kevin? I forget sometimes you might not look a lot like me, but you're smarter than I could ever dream of being." I squeeze him tightly. "Let's go find Maris before she heads to the bar, then how about you and I plan a day together tomorrow. There's someplace special I want to show you." *And something important I need to tell you*, I add silently.

Kevin rolls off the bed and holds out his hand. "Sounds great. But I wouldn't say I don't look like you, Mom," he counters.

"Oh?" I squeeze his hand as we leave my now cold stew sitting on the bed to make our way down to the main living area.

"After all, wasn't it you who once said me, you, and Uncle Dean all got these silly freckles because our brains must be too big to contain in our heads?" His beautiful green eyes turn like polished jade with the memory. He quickly turns his head away to hide his emotions.

I said that when he was what, four, five? I recall struggling to explain why we didn't look alike because some jerky kid in his preschool asked where his daddy was. It was the quickest thing I could think of years before a young boy who had plenty of love consciously understood people's misconceptions about what was "normal."

It was the first time he ever asked me about his father, but it wasn't the last. That was this past fall during the genetics portion of his AP Biology class. God, that conversation was much easier to tolerate as I could discuss recessive traits and draw charts to make Kevin understand his parentage. Now, I only can hope he's open to hearing what I have to say tomorrow when I bring up the man himself. For a moment, fear assails me, causing my feet to stumble.

But my tall, and still growing, son catches me. "Better watch out, Mom," he warns. "You don't want to take a fall. It could be nasty."

Moving ahead of me, he doesn't hear me whisper, "I already did, but I got you out of it. So, I'd do it over again in a heartbeat."

Getting my bearings, I walk back into the kitchen to find the sister of my heart eyeing me warily. I barely open my arms before she's crashing into them. "I'm sorry," we both cry simultaneously. We both laugh even as we pull back an arm's length.

Kevin makes a disgusted snort. "Women," he says before walking past us to the television.

"I don't think so, mister," I yell after him. I didn't raise my son to make a comment like that. Though thinking about it, it's something my brother would say when Maris and I would be together, so I can't prevent the ends of my lips curving.

"You ain't seen nothing yet, bucko!" Maris yells after him. But her own tip up as well.

It takes everything to hold back our laughter at his "Whatever, Mar!"

She sighs, dropping an arm around my shoulder and resting her head on mine. "I love that kid."

"I know you do."

"And I love you, Kara. I lashed out because life without Jed…"

"I know. You're the only person I know who is there for me, no matter what."

"And I always will be." A darkness settles between us as those words hold such a heavier meaning now than when she used to say them before. Her voice is pitched low so Kevin won't overhear. "I'm sorry, Kara. You were right."

"And so were you." I know my quietly spoken words shock her. "But I can't look back. I can only move forward." Facing my best friend, I push a strand of her hair away from her face. "But right now, there's only one person who I'm terrified for."

"Kevin," Maris whispers.

I nod, before telling her, "I'm taking him out to the glacier tomorrow. I'll tell him about his father. I've never lied to him, and I won't now."

"Remember what I said before?"

I hold her gaze as I reply, "All of it."

She swallows audibly before whispering, "You made the right decisions. You created a life full of love, and that boy in there has wanted for nothing. And no matter what happens tomorrow, Kevin knows, the same way that I do, that he can be angry, disappointed, sad, and you will always be by his side through it all." She leans over and kisses my temple. "I'm the one who wasted her life waiting for love." Maris lets me go abruptly as she races for the door.

I'm gaping like a fish behind her, trying to find the right words when she calls out, "Night, Kevin!"

"Night, Maris!"

"Be sure to eat, Kara," she admonishes. But the light in her eye isn't because she got in the last word. It's because we're okay. And we always will be.

"I will," I call back, finding my voice. She gives me a wink, her shields firmly in place.

I'm rooted where I stand, worrying about her, about tomorrow. That is until the sound of the TV penetrates, and I demand, "Kevin, what are you watching on that TV?" I yell.

"Oh, come on, Mom," he whines.

"I don't let you watch that garbage at home. What makes you think I'm going to let you watch it here?"

"But it's not blocked out on Maris's TV," he says hopefully.

"Because she's an adult who's allowed to watch whatever she wants," I counter.

"Can't I just watch one episode?"

"No."

"Please?"

"Do you want all of your television privileges revoked?"

"You're no fun, Mom," Kevin pouts before changing the channel.

"No. But I love you very much." Then I dash upstairs to retrieve my food.

For the rest of the night, we play tug-o-remote until we both call it a night. Reminding Kevin I'm going to wake him up early in the morning so we can go hiking, I hug him. "Dress warm. Night, sweetheart."

"Night, Mom. Sleep well."

*I doubt I'll sleep at all*, I think as I watch him head down the stairs. *But I'll be thinking of you.*

And that's all that matters.

# KARA

"So, what's so special about this place we're going to?" Kevin asks on a huge yawn.

My left leg is bouncing up and down. "Hmm?" I answer distractedly, as I lift my to-go cup of coffee to my lips.

"Why are you getting me up at the crack of dawn to go hiking. I mean, jeez, Mom. It's not like we're not going to be here all summer." Kevin reaches for his coffee. "Why did you get the bigger mug?" he grumbles.

I scoff as I take another drink. "Because I'm the mom? That's why."

"That's your answer to a lot of things."

"It's worked so far." I turn left onto Mendenhall Loop and wait for Kevin to put his coffee back down. "I wasn't much older than you when I realized what I wanted to do with my life."

"Be a teacher?"

I shake my head as I pull into the visitor parking lot. I park before telling my son, "Drink up. We'll hit the Visitor Center to get you a pass. You can't bring anything but water on the trails. It's bear safety, and it's serious here, son. Remember that."

"Bear safety? Like..." he starts to joke.

"Like the kind that are more frequently attacking humans globally.

While it's still uncommon, Kevin, we must be cognizant of what we can do to prevent it," I advise him seriously. He puts his mug down. "While we're on the trails, we're encroaching on their territory. The Tongass National Forest has strict rules about food and no flavored drinks on the trails. Water only." I turn off the car and open my door.

Just as I do, Kevin asks, "I know you're a science teacher, Mom, but how do you know so much about—"

*Our story starts now.* "Because I used to work here a little over sixteen years ago," I tell him gently.

His gasp echoes in the car. "Mom?" Kevin asks warily.

"Come on, son. We have a long walk ahead of us." And with legs barely supporting me, I grab the bottle of water I remembered to bring and turn to close the door. Kevin hasn't moved. His fingers are interlocked on his lap, his breath labored. Finally, he flings off his seat belt and gets out.

I live and die in those first seconds when his eyes meet mine across the roof of the car. It's like seeing Jennings all over again at the funeral. The exact same eyes, from the color, to the shape, to the emotion riddled with pain and accusation, questioning me without saying a word.

Turning, I hunch my shoulders against the wind and the misty rain that's decided to accompany us. A plane passes by overhead, preparing to land, reminding me of Jennings. How appropriate, I think sardonically. I look over and see Kevin waiting on the sidewalk. "This way." I gesture.

Less than half a dozen words are exchanged until after we get his pass. Finally, I brush my fingers against his arms gently. He jerks slightly. "Follow me," I urge him.

Without waiting to see if he's following, I start walking down Nugget Falls Trail. His long stride has him catching up quickly. I take a deep breath and start talking. "I was twenty-two, about to turn twenty-three, when I started working here. I answered an ad in the paper for a room at the Smiths' because living in the housing offered for interns was driving me completely batty."

Even though he doesn't respond verbally, I can tell by the clenching and unclenching of his fists Kevin's listening, so I continue. "I also got

Maris out of the deal. Your uncle Dean used to joke I should have asked her family for a refund."

Despite his obvious anger, he admits, "That's something I can totally imagine him saying."

"Ask Maris about it. She used to come back with 'I should go back in time and charge her double.'" I mimic Maris's voice perfectly.

Both Kevin and I chuckle, easing some of the tension between us. "Did you meet my father here? While working?" he tentatively asks.

"I'll answer that question, but let's get a little further ahead in the trail. There's a special spot I want to get to."

"Okay, Mom."

We keep walking a ways. While we do, I fill Kevin in on the parts of my history he may have overheard over the years but never fully understood. Bashfully, I remind him, "You know I was an accelerated student. I had already finished up both of my master's degrees from UF, was well into my doctorate, when I was offered the internship. I had to work with my professors to end my spring coursework early, but they were thrilled because it would look remarkable on my resume."

"Is that what you did?"

"Yes."

"Wow." Kevin sounds impressed.

I say proudly, "It was amazing. I thought it was my job to be able to talk all parts of the Tongass National Forest. I studied for months so I could answer questions about the glacier, be able to give a presentation at a moment's notice." Catching the highly impressed look on his face, I laugh. "Then I found out I would be working in the gift shop."

Kevin chokes on his laughter. "The...the gift shop?"

A smile breaks out across my face. "I kid you not, sweetheart. Trust me, you will learn more about patience by working in some field of customer service than any other job. I swear it."

"You used those hard-earned science degrees to sell postcards?" I welcome his wise-ass remark.

"And to point people in the right direction of the bathroom; let's not forget that," I add haughtily.

At this point we've reached the spot where I always loved sitting when my shift was over at the Visitor Center. "Coming to work every day was a challenge, but I knew that if I persevered, it would lead me right where I was meant to be."

"And then you had me," Kevin says flatly.

"And then I celebrated the fact I was pregnant with you," I correct him gently.

"What?" he asks, confused.

"Kevin, I was in love with your father," I say softly, admitting something I never told Jennings. Because at twenty-three, who knew what love was? I certainly didn't until I held his son in my arms.

"You were?"

I curse myself having never told him this sooner, like when Dean and Jed were alive, to help me with some of the questions I'm not going to be able to answer easily. I'm terrified I'm going to have to rely on Jennings to help me navigate the emotions of a teenage boy which, to me, is like jumping out of a plane with no parachute. I swallow all of that fear back and sit down. Patting the spot beside me, I tell him, "Yes, I was. Here, sit down."

"Am I going to get eaten?" he asks half-jokingly as he drops beside me.

"You run faster than me. You'll be just fine," I remind him.

"Mom, after everything we've been through, there isn't anything I wouldn't do for you. There isn't a chance I wouldn't try to take on a bear for you. I hope you know how much I love you." His voice cracks.

"Baby, I love you too." I can't not hold him anymore. I rise up on my knees and pull him to my breast, rocking back and forth, just like I did when he used to have nightmares. Just like I did a few weeks ago when nightmares came true and we were told Dean and Jed were killed.

God, I hope he doesn't associate this story with that. Pulling back, my heart aches more than it already has been with the naked longing on his face. "What's my father's name?"

"John Jennings."

Kevin frowns. "My middle name. Why does that name sound familiar?"

I take in a deep breath and let it out halfway before admitting, "Because you may have overheard Uncle Jed talking about him. He was one of Uncle Jed's best friends. In fact, he was at the funeral the other night." I wait for the explosion.

Only it doesn't come. What does is much worse.

Kevin's face crumbles. "He was a friend of Uncle Jed's?"

"Yes. That's how I met him. When Uncle Jed came home from working as a..." But I don't get to finish my sentence because Kevin's scrambling to his feet.

"Uncle Jed knew? Uncle Dean knew? Who else knows? Maris?" His face is set in stone, closed off.

"All of them knew he was your biological father, yes," I answer cautiously.

Kevin's face twists into something ugly, but he doesn't say anything. I give him a few moments before I whisper, "Kevin..."

There's no way to brace myself internally when he asks me, "So, was it you he didn't want, or was it me?"

"Baby." My voice crumbles. "It's not quite that easy. He didn't know until Uncle Jed died."

"How? And I told you, I'm not a baby!" he shouts. The sound seems to permeate the air around us.

"Don't you realize you'll always be my baby? You could be two, seven, fifteen, or forty-seven and you'll always be my baby. One day, you'll have your family surrounding you, I'll be old, and..." Suddenly Kevin's swooping me up in his strong arms, squeezing the living breath out of me. "Whoa, what did I say?" I manage to get out.

"You were talking about growing old. You're never going to get old." From angry to panic in one breath to the next. The psychologist warned me he'll feel the threat of losing his loved ones more severely for some time. "Don't be surprised if he clings to you. It's a defense mechanism, Ms. Malone."

I understand because we're just two people equally scared by the past, the present, and the future for the exact same reasons.

I hold my son for a long time until he asks, "So, you met my father at Uncle Jed's?"

Pulling back slightly, I touch his face to smooth out the scrunched-up V in his brow. "You know. You can take the time to think about all your questions if you want," I offer.

"I want to know as much as you're willing to tell me," his says gruffly.

I release his body but not his hand. "I met John Jennings when he and Uncle Jed were visiting Uncle Jed's family. They were Lumberjacks down in Ketchikan—"

"They worked for a lumbering company?" he interrupts.

"No, Kevin." A small smile breaks out across my face because although Kevin understands I knew Maris and Jed from working in Alaska once upon a time, this part was never made quite clear. Suddenly, I'm oh so glad I'm the one who gets to be the one who explains it. Uncapping the bottle of water, I take a drink before handing it over. Kevin had just taken a large guzzle when I deadpan, "They were star athletes in the world champion Great Alaskan Lumberjack Show."

Kevin's water flies out of his mouth. "Jesus, Mom. You timed that."

I smirk. "Of course I did, honey. Payback's tough to swallow. Literally."

"What does a 'Lumberjack' actually do?" he demands.

"Oh, honey." I smooth a lock of overlong hair away from his face. "I feel like that's a question you should ask your father. But for the love of all things, please ask it while I'm sitting there. And if you have a care for Maris, do it while she's around as well."

Our eyes collide and we both laugh before Kevin says, "You got it. By the way, you know who would have appreciated your little revenge?"

And together we say, "Uncle Dean."

Kevin's burst of happiness crumbles like the therapist warned me it would. "I miss him so much, Mom."

My hand smooths up and down over my son's back. "Of course you do. But you know what your therapist said?"

"Not talking about them isn't honoring them," he quotes. "I know. I just get this funny feeling when I do."

"Grief?"

"No, it's like I expect them to come drop down on either side of me. Then the pain comes back so fast, it's like I can't breathe." He shakes his head. "Honesty, Mom?"

"Always."

"I'd begun to think about asking you about my father before this happened," he admits. I wish I could say I'm surprised, but I'm not. He's growing up to be a man; of course he'd want to know about the one who helped make him. "One of the guys at Scouts was asking why Uncle Dean always came with me. Now, it feels like I'm betraying him —Uncle Dean, that is—to be talking about this John Jennings guy when in so many ways, Uncle Dean was my dad. Does that make sense?"

"More than you can possibly know," I assure him. "But you know what Dean would have said?"

Kevin shakes his head.

"It's the same thing he said to me." Closing my eyes, I can picture my brother holding Kevin on his lap. "Know I'll always be behind you, but take a chance on what could be in front of you."

Kevin nods. "Were you scared?"

Realizing Kevin's switched topics as he's wont to do, I follow along easily. "About having you?

"Yes."

"Oh, yeah." Drawing my knees up, I rest my arms on them as I recount a truthful, but edited, version of my summer in Alaska. How I met Jennings, how I fell in love, and how I left to go home. "I flew home, scared. I had to go. And, Kevin? I needed to tell your grandparents..."

"For all that helped," Kevin mutters.

I cede his bitterness without comment. Ignoring the slight, I continue. "Uncle Dean and I had you, sweetheart. We didn't need that toxicity in our lives."

"That's the truth."

This is where it gets sticky. "But it left scars on me, sweetie."

"What do you mean?" His hand reaches for mine.

"For years, I contacted Jennings to tell him about you through an old email account. Eventually, I stopped trying."

"Why?"

"Because I had to move on, Kevin. I needed to focus on you in our then." I take a huge breath. "And then Uncle Jed came to visit one day. Dean came to pick me up, and I swear to God, it was love at first sight." I remember the chill that chased through me when they met.

Kevin picks up a rock and throws it. "When you saw Uncle Jed again, why didn't you ask him to call him?"

A good question and one I was expecting. I try to explain it as best as I can. "Imagine if Brooks," I say, naming Kevin's best friend, "did something you didn't agree with."

"I'd like to think I'd do the right thing," Kevin persists.

"You'd sell him out for the last chicken strip," I mutter.

"Only if it's Zaxby's, Mom," Kevin's quick to assure me. "But deep down..."

"We all like to think we'd do something one way until we're in a situation," I inform him quietly. "And looking back, maybe we'd like to do things differently. But there's too many people to change one thing to come up with a different answer: Jennings, Jed, Maris, me. For me to make this different for you, I'd have to go back in time." I stare out over the water.

"Do you think he would have wanted me?"

Letting out a sigh, I admit, "Uncle Dean thought so."

"I wish he was still here."

"We all do, honey."

"What else can you tell me about this Jennings?" There's a faint resentment when he speaks Jennings's name. I don't press for now.

"I honestly don't know a lot about him now. I know he didn't have a great childhood. I'm frankly shocked he let in the Jacks enough to maintain the friendship he has over the years."

"The Jacks?" Kevin asks, confused.

"It's what Maris and I called your Uncle Jed, Jennings, and their friends Kody, Nick, and Brad. They're closer than most brothers are. So, when Uncle Jed met you, it put him in a very difficult position."

Kevin pulls away to face the glacier. "I'm sorry for that."

"He never was," I say confidently. Kevin whips around. "Time and again, he said he knew his brother well enough to bet on Jennings loving you; it was my fears over him losing that part of his family the way Dean and I lost our family that held me back. If it went wrong, I knew a part of his heart would hurt without them."

"So, what made Uncle Jed change his mind?" Kevin chews on his lower lip.

"Remember when Uncle Dean and Uncle Jed came back to Alaska?" He nods, and I continue. "They came to rewrite Uncle Jed's will and to see Maris." Kevin's body jerks next to me. "I know. It was something I never thought we would need. There were four circumstances under which we'd be having this exact conversation. I have to be honest, sweetheart, the one I expected was you'd simply ask me about him." As an aside, I whisper, "God, do I wish it was that one."

Kevin pushes to his feet and holds out a hand. I reach up and grab it. He wraps his arms around me, and the warmth of the sun beams down on both of us. As completely unrealistic as it is, I want to believe it's Dean and Jed telling me it's going to be all right—that we'll be all right.

After a few minutes, I feel Kevin's stomach rumble against me. "Hungry?" I reach up to cup his face.

"I don't suppose we could continue this over food?" he asks hopefully.

"Fortunately, there's a diner not that far away," I tell him. "How about you and I get something to eat?"

He nods, and I let out a breath. If Kevin had turned down food, then I'd be worried. "I can't promise I'll have all the answers," I warn him as we make our way back.

"That's okay, Mom. You always were willing to listen to my questions. That's the most important thing."

And as we hike back, I have to surreptitiously wipe my fingers under my eyes. I have survived too much as of late to not appreciate the fact that my son held on to me with all of his might instead of pushing me away.

Like my own parents did.

# KARA

I wait until after eleven to dial the number left in the papers Jed's left me which were brought to the house after the will reading.

One ring. Two.

His dark voice answers, "Hello?"

I'm caught off guard, and my voice comes out shaky. "Jennings?"

"Yes?"

"It's Kara Malone. I hope I'm not disturbing you?"

It's Jennings's turn to stutter. "No, I was just... Not at all. I'm just surprised to hear from you. I didn't expect to so soon." Silence descends between us.

Maris is outside with Kevin keeping him occupied. She's pointing at a burned-out tree, likely telling the story of how I got hammered and thought it was a bear. He's amused while she's running behind it showing him how she jumped out and scared the piss out of me. Literally. I still have to figure out how to get back at her for that. Unfortunately for her, I have all summer to figure it out.

Jennings still hasn't said a word, so I know it's up to me to speak. Without beating around the bush, I tell him, "I spoke with Kevin."

"Christ, how did it go?" The immediate leap to concern in his voice makes cold parts of me want to warm.

I've never been answerable to anyone about Kevin before, so I grit my teeth before articulating each word. "Most of it is private between me and Kevin. If he chooses to share with you at a later date, that's between the two of you."

There's a weary "Right." Then his magnetism leaps through the phone. "You said 'if he chooses to share with you at a later date.' Does this mean...?"

Pain tears through me. I know what I have to do. It doesn't mean the pulsating ache in my heart that's being caused out of devastation and regret is any easier to bear. I simply say, "How about joining us for breakfast tomorrow morning? Your son would like the opportunity to meet you."

His voice is gruff when he replies, "Just let me know when and where, and I'll be there. I promise."

My voice is neutral when I remind him, "Please remember, you're promising your son, Jennings, not me. I assume this is your cell phone number?"

"It is." A pause. "How did you get it?"

"Jed left a letter for me to open in the event..."

"Right. Yes, Kara, this is my cell," he confirms. "Would you mind sending me a message with your contact information? I don't know if the information from your last email is current."

I hold my tongue about him finally reading them and instead reply, "Of course." Quickly, I slide my phone from my pocket and send him a text. "You should have received a text from a 904 number?"

"Just got...Jesus. You didn't need to tell me it was Kara Malone." He sounds aggravated.

"Just making certain you knew it was me," I say with forced lightness. "After I let Kevin know we've confirmed tomorrow, I'll text you when and where."

There's a long pause before I hear Jennings's broken voice mutter, "I know it was what Jed wanted, but this was your decision—yours and our son's. I can't begin to tell you what it means."

My head falls forward against the glass. Memories of how I once loved this man fill me. Maybe it's that knowledge that precludes me from the natural wariness I normally maintain. "Just...do right by him,

Jennings," I whisper before I hang up the phone without saying goodbye.

Sliding my cell into my pocket, I walk over to the back door, lean on the rail, and yell, "Who wants me to cook for lunch?"

Kevin calls back, "Do they have fast food here?"

I nod and his face lights up. "McDonald's or Subway." I name the top choices, thinking that naming the local salmon spot wouldn't be high on his list.

His lip curls a little. "There's not a Zaxby's?" he says, naming a popular chicken chain near our apartment in Florida.

Shaking my head, I school him not only about food choices but about life. "Sometimes, my darling boy, you're going to find out that you have to make do with what you have because what you want isn't available."

He grumbles something I can't hear, but Maris does. She laughs and slings an arm around his waist, pulling him closer to the stairs. "Come on, kid. You can decide on the way."

"If we go to Subway, I can pile on all the fixings for a monster sub," he jokes.

"That is if they have the same fixings as home," Maris tells him seriously.

"Oh, come on," Kevin whines. And while that would normally grate at my nerves, it sounds so beautiful to hear him act like a normal teenager, I let it slide. Because for this moment, we're not thinking about the terrible things that have happened to our family, nor are we thinking about what the future is about to bring.

All I have on my mind is the exquisite Alaskan day for us to spend with each other. Tomorrow, and breakfast with Jennings, seems a long way off.

KEVIN IS WAITING PATIENTLY to have an attendant refill his drink when Maris tells me, "I haven't slept well remembering what I said to you," she admits.

I reach for Maris's hand. Keeping one eye on my son, I murmur, "I should have told him sooner."

"Maybe. But you were hurting for a long time."

I nod. "Yes, I was. But I grew up. Shouldn't I have figured your brother was right and Jennings did too?"

"Maybe," she concludes sadly. "God, now I have to feel guilty about how I treated him the other day."

"When?"

"At the reading. I was less than kind." But her blue eyes raise to mine. There's a spark of the Maris I know and love hiding in the depths of them.

"Do I want to know?" I ask, seeing Kevin weave his way back over to us.

"I was perhaps a bit more peckish than I was with the others."

"Including Nick?" I ask incredulously.

When she nods, I giggle. "Oh, God, I love you. I almost—*almost*—wish I'd been there to witness you there being your badass self. Thinking of that is almost as good as all the times I imagined him landing on his dick during the log roll when I pushed out Kevin," I manage to wheeze out, making Maris screech in hysterics just as Kevin sits back down.

"What's so funny?" he demands

"Maris just reminded me of something funny your father once did."

"What was it?" he asks curiously.

"Oh, it was one of the acting things he did as a Lumberjack with Uncle Jed. Be sure to ask him," I say with a hint of a wicked smile.

"That reminds me." Kevin reaches for something in his back pocket. He pulls out a folded-over piece of paper and a pen. "I started to make a list of things to ask him," he declares.

Maris lifts her head long enough to gasp, "He may look like Jennings, but he is completely your child through and through," before she chortles.

Kevin frowns. I throw part of my sandwich roll at her. Ignoring Maris, I address my son. "I think you've done a great job, honey. How many questions do you have so far?"

"Forty-seven," he announces.

"Can I be there when he interrogates him? Can I?" Maris makes it sound like it's her fondest wish.

"No," I tell her firmly. To, Kevin, I say, "Keep in mind, this is probably going to take some time. Your father wants to know about you too. As you think of things, keep adding questions to your list. Then, over time to get to know him. I'm sure there will be times when you may not know what to say, and if you get stuck, you can always ask a question?"

"Good idea, Mom. I'll just keep adding more." He thinks for a moment and writes some more.

While Kevin's distracted, Maris lifts her head. She points at Kevin, then uses both hands to make the heart symbol, and then points at me.

I mouth back, "I know." Because I do. No matter what, I know how much my son loves me. It's just, what will the additional burden of having a father bring to him?

But sitting there with my son and my best friend, I can't help but be tickled when I imagine what John Jennings would do if I did let his son interrogate him. And I have to stifle my laughter when Kevin keeps diligently writing.

# JENNINGS

I arrived so early, I'm on my fourth cup of coffee while waiting for Kara and Kevin to show up at the crowded restaurant in downtown Juneau. I eye my cup warily; it wouldn't surprise me if my server spit in my last refill. The last time he pressed me to order, I lost my temper and snapped, "How can I make it any clearer I'm waiting for someone?"

"Sure you weren't stood up?" The lanky server is standing there holding a fresh pot.

"She would have called," I say confidently, but my voice sounds jittery. Is that nerves or the copious amounts of caffeine infiltrating my veins?

"Hmm." The waiter shrugs while cavalierly pouring, causing him to spill some on my paper placement.

Even as I'm mentally deducting another percentage from this guy's tip, the door opens. My son steps inside and holds the door open for his mother. She smiles up at him as she passes by. I wonder who taught him such exquisite manners. Fiercely, I think, it should have been me, but quickly I deflate. *What do I have left to teach him, Jed?* I wonder.

The burly guy who seated me makes his way over to them. Kara tips her head way back and smiles, gesturing with her hands. He leans against the host stand and smiles down at her. Instead of bringing her my way, they start chatting. She motions for Kevin to join them.

My eyes narrow as the young man holds out his hand, lips moving. After taking it to shake, burly guy says something to Kara. She gestures in front of her, gesturing what? How large she got with our son while she was carrying him? Kevin pats Kara on the head; she elbows him in retaliation.

The man yanks her forward and gives her what appears to be a welcome hug.

Maybe it's too much coffee, but there's a churning in my gut as she returns it. Pulling back, she pats him on the chest before motioning in the direction of the dining room. But even as the moment I've been anticipating for days is about to unfold, I can't hear anything over the roar between my own ears.

Kara's still a beautiful woman, I try to tell myself dispassionately, but failing miserably. Did I ever notice the way the light catches the gold woven through her hair, or is that as new as the cut that swings when she turns her head from side to side? Annoyed at my thoughts, I'm sure if I'm noticing anything new, it's probably just because I haven't seen her in so long. *Right*, the voice inside my head mocks, *keep telling yourself that.*

When they reach the table, I notice the smile Kara's wearing doesn't illuminate the room the way I remember it could, but that's most likely due to the circumstances of why we're all here. It's subdued, despite being friendly to the behemoth next to her.

Surging to my feet, I experience doubt so swift it almost sends me back into my chair. How do I introduce myself to my son?

Kara isn't as flustered. "Thank you, Wenzel. It was great to see you after so many years," she concludes warmly.

"You too, Kara. I wish it was under better circumstances. Nice to meet you, Kevin."

"Thank you, sir," my son acknowledges respectfully before his body shifts in my direction. All manners drop from his demeanor when he whispers, "Whoa."

Kara lays a hand on his arm as she greets me. "Hello, Jennings. I appreciate you being able to join us on such short notice." She holds out her hand for me to shake.

"Kara. It's good to see you again." I immediately take her hand, trying to help her demonstrate to our son there's no animosity between his parents. I'm not surprised by the delicate bones beneath my fingers. What I'm shocked by is the dance of awareness I only feel when I'm sitting behind the stick to flutter up my arm.

She yanks hers away. Her eyes grow large which is what earned her the nickname "Owl" so many years ago. She felt it too; I just know it. Before I can say anything, she covers her response by smiling up at the younger version of me. "And this is Kevin Jennings Malone."

There's no air. Someone stole it all because the room's spinning crazily around me. I'm still reeling over the fact she named her son after me despite everything.

My son narrows his eyes down at his mother. "Who," she continues, unperturbed by the insolent face, "has a number of questions he'd like to ask you. I hope you understand."

"Of course. Kevin, it's my absolute pleasure to meet you." I don't expect him to say the same, so I'm not surprised when he doesn't. He does take my extended hand in a firm grip. More regrets pile up when I realize it was likely Jed or Dean who taught him to maintain eye contact until he releases the grip.

"Please sit," I encourage them both. "If you'd like the booth side, I'm happy to switch."

Kara waves her hand to hold me in place. "You're settled; don't be silly."

"As you may remember, I'm rarely that." My voice is low. Where is this need to tease her coming from? I wonder even as Kara's head jerks in response.

Her lips part in shock, but before she can react, Kevin pipes up, "Mom, can I have coffee?" There's almost despair in his voice.

"More?" Kara says incredulously. "You polished off half the pot at Maris's this morning."

I want to call the waiter over, I want to slide my own drink across the table that Kevin's sending covetous glances at, but I don't have the right to intervene.

Not yet.

"I didn't sleep well," he reminds her.

Her face softens. "Kevin, I also want you to sleep tonight. I'll compromise; you can have a soda, okay?"

He leans over and rubs his temple against hers, clearly not afraid of the hit it will give his image to show affection to his mother. My chest aches from being in his presence all of a few minutes. Surreptitiously, I rub my hand over it.

Demonstrating he may be my visual image but he's as observant as his mother, Kevin remarks, "Are you all right, sir?"

Dropping my hand back to the table, I reply, "I drank too much coffee," to cover the fact I want to burst into tears my teenage son is asking about my welfare. "And if it's all right with your mom, calling me Jennings is fine," I hesitate a breath before tacking on quietly, "Son."

Kevin's head swivels to Kara, who's already nodding, much to my relief. He relaxes before he acknowledges, "I was wondering what I should call you. Mom's kinda strict about addressing people properly as 'Mr. This' or 'Ms. That.' That would have been a bit awkward with my birth father if you ask me." I blink in astonishment when my own dimple flashes for a brief moment in a much younger face.

Fortunately, I'm saved from responding when the waiter appears to ask Kara and Kevin their drink orders. Inside I'm relaxing a little. My first act of parenthood and I didn't screw it up. Or would this be my second, I think glumly. If so, that would mean I fucked up the first, which would be showing up.

"So, Jennings? I have a lot of questions for you." Kevin's seems to be calm, but something must alert Kara. She sits up straighter and narrows her eyes on our son.

"Kevin," she warns.

"Mom says you didn't know about me, but I'm not so sure. Maybe you can clarify if you just didn't want me?" His voice is as calm as if he asked if I take cream or sugar in my coffee.

I freeze even as Kara moans, "God, Kevin. We talked about this.

Jennings didn't know." Her head is in her hands, rocking back and forth. She looks like she's ready to burst into tears any moment.

Leaning forward, I drop my voice. "I won't ask for an apology for me. You don't know me at all. But I will absolutely demand one for your mother."

"Excuse me?" Kevin's chair squeaks a bit as he leans forward himself.

"You just flagrantly disrespected your mother by asking that. Ask me anything about my history, my life; I'll answer it. But it's obvious by her reaction you upset your mother the first time you asked, and yet you asked it again. That shows a lack of respect for the woman who gave up everything to raise you. Consider her and where we're at when you ask your questions." Finished making my point, I sit back, leaving my son seething.

The waiter walks up just then to take our orders, and I snap, "Not now. Come back."

Kevin smirks in a way that's disturbingly familiar. I'm horrified when I realize I likely gave every person of authority the same attitude at some point in my teenage years.

Kara takes compassion on me because she issues out a warning "Kevin," which is heeded immediately.

He sits back in his chair and braces his arms on the table just as his soda is placed in front of him. Twisting his head to the side, he says, "Thank you," politely to the server I was so rude to earlier.

"You're welcome," the waiter says before scurrying away. Of course. Just when I need him to throw me a lifeline by asking if we're ready to order, I think darkly. I take a drink of my coffee to cover my discomfort.

I'm bracing myself for anything, so I have to blink when Kevin asks, "Tell me, Jennings, what do you like to do?"

"I feel like I'm being interviewed," I feebly joke.

Kara winces.

"Well, if you don't mind." Kevin reaches into his back pocket and pulls out a folded sheet of college-ruled paper. I stare. "Mom says I should always make lists of questions about things I'm interested in," he explains. "That way if I have the opportunity to get them answered, I can."

I gape at Kara, whose face holds no apology, merely acceptance. "He was an inquisitive child, Jennings. From the moment he could cogitate, I was answering a million questions about a million topics I had no answers to." For a moment the dark that's been carefully hidden on her face escapes. "It made us a formidable team at Trivial Pursuit against Jed and Dean, didn't it?" Her hand runs along his arm.

Kevin swallows hard, the death of his beloved uncles obviously not something he's easily comfortable with discussing. But, as much as it hurts to think of Jed being gone, I like Kara's idea of not letting their memories die. Especially for our son.

"Flying," I blurt out, shifting the focus away from Kevin's discomfort and back to his questions.

"Really? Like, what kind of planes?" His eyes narrow.

Yep, definitely an interview. I sit up straighter and fold my hands around my cup. "Well, I'm qualified to fly everything up to and including a Gulfstream, but the plane I fly most often for work is a Pilatus PC-12 Turbo-Prop. My personal plane is a Cessna 172."

"I get a Gulfstream is big; what's the difference between the other two?" The hostility slips slightly as curiosity takes over. So, without pandering to his age, I explain the difference between the different types of planes, what they can do, and why I use them. Because I keep the explanation straightforward, I estimate that takes me all of five minutes. I prepare myself for my next question, so it's almost a relief when he asks like a typical teenager, "You own them all?"

I'm about to answer, when Kara frowns before saying, "Kevin." It's a rebuke but a gentle one.

He mumbles, "Sorry, Mom," before explaining, "It's just the only people I can think of who own their own planes are celebrities. You didn't tell me my father was like that."

Shame is making my heart beat erratically. "I'm not, Kevin. I should have explained I own an air charter service in Seattle where I live."

A myriad of expressions fly across his face before confusion finally lands. "I don't know what that is," he admits.

"There are a number of small islands around Washington state people live on. So, boats and planes are used to get everything onto and off of the islands."

"Like what?" His inquisitive nature is making this easier than I expected.

I don't realize I've spoken aloud until Kara's calm facade drops. She tosses her head back, laughing. "You say that now, Jennings, but I would have loved for you to have been the one to answer his questions about why Elmo is red."

"My answer would likely not have been anywhere as good as yours, Kara. I would have probably said something about the creators liking a bold color for their craziest character," I jest.

There's no way I could have predicted what happened next.

Kevin starts coughing while Kara's mouth hangs open in stunned silence. "What? Was it something I said?" I'm bewildered.

Kara shakes her head to get her bearings. "I apologize, it's just—"

"Yes?"

Kevin answers for her. "That's pretty close to what she said, Jennings." With a private smile, he picks up the pen he placed next to his list and scratches off a question near the bottom of the list. I feel a crazy burst of pride I survived another question without trying. "Now, back to flying. Are you like FedEx with overnight delivery?"

Deadpan, I tell him, "Does FedEx transport bodies?"

I lift my coffee to hide my smile when Kevin screeches, "Bodies?"

Just then our waiter comes back. His words wipe the smile right off my face when he asks, "Before you ask where he hid the dead ones, would you like to place your order?"

Being interrupted erases the ease off Kevin's face. My muscles bunch as my temper slips. Kara quickly leans across the table, places her hand on mine, before saying, "Let me."

Breathing hard, I settle back. Over time, I hope Kara learns to trust me enough to protect our son. And maybe when we're all together, her. But right now, I have to let her handle this.

"What's your name?" Kara asks with false sweetness. This must be her teacher-to-student face. Suddenly intrigued, I sit back to watch her work.

"Um, Patrick," the kid, not much older than Kevin, stammers.

"Well, Patrick, let me take a moment to explain something I was taught by Henry James."

"Do I care?" he snarks.

I'm about to jerk Kara and Kevin out of there when Kara quotes the literary genius. "Three things in human life are important: the first is to be kind; the second is to be kind; and the third is to be kind." Her smile fades before her next words come out. "You work in an industry where you rely on the benevolence of strangers for your livelihood. It behooves you to behave in a manner accordingly."

Instead of addressing Kara, he bumps Kevin's arm. "Does she talk to you like this a lot?"

Kevin doesn't hesitate before answering. "Yeah."

"Then maybe you can translate, because I have no idea what the hell she just said."

And much to my immense satisfaction, my son snarls, "Stop being a rude dick and listening in on all your customer's conversations. Maybe then your tips will pick up. Otherwise"—he gives a negligent shrug—"I suspect more people than my mother and father will be complaining to your management. Oh, and for the record, I'd like pancakes."

If I'm bursting with pride, I can only imagine what Kara's feeling. This boy/man she raised from the time he was mere cells in her body didn't hide he wasn't down with what was going on. He also, with a few words, showed his mother she had his support and love.

Less than a half hour in his presence, and I'm already falling for him.

Then Kara pipes in with, "I'd like waffles with blueberries on the side." She leans forward and hands her menu to the waiter, who hasn't made a move to take it.

I lift it from her hands, not letting her hold on to any more burden than she has to, not anymore. "And I'll take the manager's special. Plus I'll take the manager," I tack on.

That seems to startle the kid out of his trance. Quickly he pulls out his pad, writes everything down, snatches the menus from my hands, and darts toward the kitchen.

Kevin painstakingly draws a line through another question on his list. Then he asks me, "So, are the bodies dead?"

And despite the fact I know I'll continue to be interrogated for the rest of the meal, Kevin's question snaps the tension between all of us. Somehow we all manage to stop laughing before the manager arrives at our table to profusely apologize before we have to say a word.

# JENNINGS

"So, what happens now," Kevin asks after we make our way out of the cafe. "Is this 'see you until I graduate' or something? Or do we make plans for actually getting to know one another?"

I'm exhausted and exhilarated at the same time. I don't know if I've ever talked so much about myself as I was answering the list of questions my son threw at me.

Except maybe when I was getting to know his mother.

Knowing he's part Kara's, I should have expected he'd ask anything that came to mind. But his questions took me all over the place. But when the simple "What's your favorite color?" which I easily answered, "Blue," segued to, "Do you believe using a nuclear energy—the kind that makes bombs—could propel a spaceship faster than chemical rockets, thereby accelerating the space program into a new generation of exploration?" I thought I was going to need the Heimlich maneuver.

Fortunately, while I recovered, Kara intervened. "Stop trying to interview people for your AP Physics project without giving them any context. We've talked about that. You need to give them an introduction and ask their permission to use the question in the results, otherwise it doesn't count."

"I wasn't going to use his answer," Kevin argued.

Kara just raised a brow.

"Well, unless it was a really good one. I mean, come on, Mom. Jennings is a pilot. He might have some insight into the topic."

"Maybe if I understood half of what you asked, I might have an opinion on it," I muttered.

Kevin's dimple popped out before he presented an explanation about the kind of energy it takes to launch a rocket into space. During that time, I sipped coffee and openly admired the young man, while secretly admiring the woman who raised him.

How did she do it? I want to ask her, but it obviously wasn't the time.

Now, we're outside awkwardly blocking the narrow sidewalk. And I have to explain what happens in the immediate future. I have no idea how it's going to be received. "Well, I have to fly back," I start.

Kevin's face closes up, and Kara's face pales even as her lips compress together. I hurriedly continue. "I only packed enough clothes for the weekend. I need to get enough stuff to last me for the summer, a work computer, things like that. I can run my business from here, but I need time to prepare." Seeing the relief Kevin's trying to hide, I dare to lift a hand to his shoulder and squeeze. "I'll only be gone three days tops."

"Oh...okay. Sorry, it was just... Sorry."

"We're all dealing with something new here, Kevin. And I think I've proven there's nothing you can't ask me." I hold his eyes as I speak the truth. I don't look at Kara because right now, this is about regaining the altitude I might have lost with my son. It's not about her. At least, it shouldn't be.

Or, it isn't until I hear her soft voice chime in, "I never gave that much thought, Jennings. I'm sorry." And when I do look at her, her face is contrite.

And standing on a sidewalk, with my hand on our son's shoulder, the final barrier between the memories of me and Kara gives way. Oh, God. The last time she said that to me was the night I called her to break up with her. *"You're right, Jennings. I never gave that much thought. I'm sorry you want it to end because I feel so much for you. Just know you'll always have a special place in my heart."*

Right before she hung up.

My fingers tighten around Kevin's shoulder.

"Jennings, it's okay. Really," Kevin reassures me. "I get it. None of us were prepared for this, were we?" His laugh is hollow.

"No, but I'll be back. I promise." My voice is hoarse. "Just a couple of days." Then I flinch when I recall how many times I said that too. My mind conjures up memories of saying that to Kara with her long hair draped over my arm as we lay on the grass in the Smiths' backyard. She'd nod and say...

"I know, Jennings. Don't worry. Just...travel safe." Suddenly, she takes a tiny step back as if she too was thrown back into a time vortex sixteen years ago. Because she said that.

Every fucking time I had to leave.

"I'll call you when I land," I tell them both.

Kevin tilts his head. "I'm assuming you didn't fly commercial."

I bark out a laugh. "No. I flew up one of my planes."

"How long..." Kara starts, and then she stops herself from asking as if she doesn't have a right to know when other than the boy who's my mirror image, she probably has the right to know more about me than any other person in the world. Lifting her face to the misting rain that started while we were having breakfast, Kara prompts Kevin, "Is there something you'd like to ask your father?"

"Oh, yeah! Mom said it was all right to ask if you wanted to come to dinner tomorrow."

I want to say yes with everything that's in me, but I know if I don't leave to go back to Seattle now, today, I won't go. "Can I take a rain check on it? If I leave today, I can be back in time for dinner, say Tuesday?"

Even as Kevin's nodding, my heart's pounding while I wait for Kara to respond. I'm trying to not let anyone down. I'm trying to not screw up this opportunity. I'm trying to behave responsibly, but part of that is taking care of the people who work for me.

Kara nods. "That's fine. Let me know if there's something special you want otherwise we tend to feed in bulk to accommodate the hollow leg in the house."

Kevin puffs out his chest. "I proudly resemble that remark."

"So does our food bill, darling, but that's okay." They both laugh when Kara pats him on his flat stomach. But my heart clenches not only at the byplay, but with worry. Kara and I need to have a conversation right after I have one with my attorneys.

"So, Tuesday?" I bring them back around to the original topic at hand.

"That sounds good, Jennings." Kevin holds out his hand. I take it and shake it firmly. "Thank you for joining us today." God, his manners are beyond reproach. Now, I wish I'd pushed harder to meet Jed's husband while he was alive so I could say thank you for being the parent I should have been. But it's too late. And it's way too soon for me to grab my son and hug him.

Instead I turn to Kara and pray all of the emotion in two simple words conveys when I say, "Thank you."

Her "Of course. It's what Kevin wanted" tells me so much about the kind of mother she is. "We'll see you Tuesday." Turning, the two of them make their way down the street to the public parking garage.

While I wait until they become specks, I call Lou, telling her I'll be in the office tomorrow. I contact the airfield to fuel up the Cessna. And I call my attorneys to arrange for a late-evening meeting. "No, I don't give a damn how much it costs. These changes are urgent. I have to have them signed before I fly out Monday," I snarl, before I press End on the phone.

Then, I stalk off in the direction of the same public parking garage to head to the B&B. Once there, I slam right into Ron, which is a good thing as I was going to hunt him out anyway. "Ron, do you have availability to rent me my room for the summer?"

Ron smiles before walking behind the desk. Pulling up his computer, he murmurs, "It would be my pleasure, Mr. Jennings."

"I'm grateful." And I truly am. Because even this small act will allow me to get to know my son better.

And the time to get on my knees thanking his mother for the chance.

❄

NINE EXHAUSTING HOURS LATER, I've left my lawyer's office in down-town Seattle. I'm running on fumes and a residual anger at the people who persisted in trying to "present you with the best advice on how to protect yourself, Mr. Jennings. Ms. Malone could..."

I slammed my hand down on the conference room table. "Just do it," I snarled.

"Ms. Malone raised your son with next to nothing, and should she choose, she could slap you with a financial request which would bleed you dry," another associate tried to explain.

"That's not the type of woman she is," I argued.

Even as I pressed them to make changes to change my estate, they urged me to take documents up to her to have her sign them, relin-quishing all rights against Northern Star Flights. "We understand she's asked for nothing, but she still can," one of the associates pressed.

But by that point, my patience had snapped. "She doesn't even know I'm here!" I yelled, before the room got quiet. "Kara just lost her brother and her brother-in-law. It was because of them I even know I have a son. This woman single-handedly raised my son into a strong, intelligent young man. Screw liability; this is something I need to do." I dropped back in my seat.

"Everyone out," Reginald Silas, partner of the firm, barked. "Let me talk with Jennings privately."

The rest of the people scurried. Finally, it was just the two of us before he asked, "How did it feel to see Kara again?" Reg was a first-year Lumberjack the summer I dated Kara.

"She's just as smart as she was when we knew her. And she's an amazing mother." I admitted. "Then to add Kevin to the mix—"

"That's his name? Kevin?"

I nodded. "Named after her paternal grandfather."

He toyed with his pen before asking, "Why do I sense there's something else you're not telling me?"

"What do you mean?"

"Why did her brother and brother-in-law dying mean you finding out about your son?"

"Because Jed was her brother-in-law."

Reg's pen went skidding across the table. "Are you kidding me?" he rumbled as he tries to regain his composure. "How long did he know?"

"A few years from what the letters he left me indicate," I admitted.

"And you had no clue?" he pressed.

"None," I said firmly.

"Jesus, Jennings. This means Jed's gone?" Reg's face was paper white.

"Yeah, man." We were both silent for a moment thinking of our own memories. "If you don't mind wrapping up these changes to my estate, I'd like to head back to my place so I can meet with Lou tomorrow to deal with work crap. I really want to spend every possible minute in Alaska."

"Don't worry. I'll have everything ready for you to sign by Sunday or you can forget the bill." He waved his hand dismissively. "But back to my original question—"

"There have been so many tonight, I'm not sure which one you're referring to," I told him in all honesty.

"How was it to see Kara again?"

This time, I handed him the answer I knew he was waiting for. "Every memory slammed into me like it was yesterday. She's barely aged a day."

Standing, he gave me a similar truth to the one Rainey did only a few days before. "She was a good woman."

Pushing myself to my feet, I rounded the table and headed for the door. "She's a good mother," I concede. I'm not willing to admit more than that.

"Don't let this chance pass you by," he offered.

Stilling, I whirled to face him as he gathered notepads and pens left by his terrified employees. "Are you saying I should hit on the mother of my child?" I demanded.

He paused before dropping the stack of notepads in front of him. "No, I'm saying you should see if there's a spark there. She's a rare woman, Jennings, and she's always going to be in your life now. You figure out the rest."

I opened and closed my mouth before slipping from the conference room. Without a word, I hurried past Reg's loitering and made my way to the elevator. But Reg's words sounded so much like something Jed would say to me, they reverberated over and over in my head long after I made my way back to my condo.

Pulling into the underground parking, I see Kody's car is long gone since he and I parted ways at the airfield. Soon, it will be me who's gone. Two more days.

Then I'll be back in the air, back to Alaska. And getting a shot at the family I never expected to have.

# JENNINGS

I step outside Warm Up with a large Red Eye in one hand, a scone in the other, desperate to find a place to sit in the back courtyard for a few moments to gather my thoughts.

It's been an intense few days between seeing Kara again, meeting Kevin, and flying back to Alaska with a very different outlook than I did when I landed just last week.

After putting in hours of work this morning, I needed to get away from the B&B for a while. I wanted alone time to drive around and experience Juneau without anything interfering with my thoughts. Over and over, I kept thinking so much had changed, but here and there would be something that would remind me of Kara. Despite how much has changed, I easily recognize different places Kara and I went on dates and got lost in each other. We'd laugh for hours over silly things when she didn't do silly. She pulled out the serious in me, when I swore I wasn't going to do serious.

And then, I went out to her glacier. Standing there, it took everything in me not to howl at the sky in agony. "She gave up her dreams of you." Unable to tolerate being in her sacred place, I hiked back. Shivering in the car, I found myself in desperate need of caffeine and a moment to regroup.

Just as I step off the rickety back steps, I freeze in place. It's like some mysterious longing reached out to her because there's a familiar ash-brown head bowed over a laptop as she frantically types. One I didn't expect to see until our prearranged dinner tonight with our son.

Slowly, so I don't startle her, I ask Kara, "Is this seat available?"

Her head nods toward it without looking up. Amused, I straddle the picnic bench. She's still hammering away, absorbed in whatever has her attention. Unwrapping my scone, still warm from the oven, I break off a piece and place it on a napkin. I slide it across the table to see what she'll do.

I wonder if her response to me will be as instinctive as mine is to her, I think fleetingly.

Absentmindedly, Kara reaches over and grabs a bite with a muttered "Thanks, Ace," shoving the chunk in her mouth before she comes of her stupor to comprehend what she said. "Uh, hi" is mumbled around a bite of chunky scone. She flushes before offering me a tentative smile.

"Hey," I say before taking my own bite. "Fancy meeting you here."

"Yeah. I just needed some time away without bombs exploding or phones ringing." There's a subtle bruising beneath Kara's eyes I would wish away if I could. "Are you getting acclimated?" she asks conversationally.

I nod down to her laptop, both answering her question and teeing up my own. "I went out to the glacier today." I couldn't be more stunned by her response when she lifts a fist to her mouth and presses it there. I go on, unable to pull the words back, but not entirely certain why I should. "I remember when you'd get lost for hours writing down theories about climate change and how it would affect the glacier. Have you been out there yet?"

"Twice," she whispers, her eyes lowering to her laptop screen. "I was just telling someone all about it."

Shit. "I'm sorry, Kara. If you're talking to a friend, I didn't mean to interrupt." Well, I did, but not like this.

Her face takes on a look of tremendous pain. "I was typing an email to a man who will never get it, Jennings." I freeze, wondering if she means me, when she whispers, "I just can't bear to close down his email address. Not now, maybe not ever."

"Your brother?" I guess.

She nods. Her fingers run over the top of her laptop. "He's the only one I've ever been able to talk with about anything." Her voice is modulated, but beneath it, I detect a wealth of hurt she hasn't let go of.

"I didn't have brothers or sisters. Well, other than the guys. So, I can only partially understand what you're feeling."

"I remember you talking about growing up with your aunt and uncle. You're not close with them?"

I shake my head. "They passed several years ago." And the only good thing they did for me was leave me the farm so I could sell it off to fulfill my dreams, but I don't mention that. I'm not certain Kara would understand the ease with which I was able to do that when she's sitting here mourning.

Kara opens her mouth, a perplexed expression on her face. It's one I'm familiar with as in the past it was a precursor to a question being asked, but she must change her mind. Instead, she volunteers, "Dean, he was everything to me. It's funny how people come and go in your life, but I never missed anyone since I had Dean. And now, I miss everything." She looks away.

I want to ask her if she missed me, but I gave up that right a long time ago. I spent all weekend remembering our discussions about the things we wanted from our lives. I cursed myself over and over for thinking she was just a woman meant to pass through my life as I packed to return to Alaska. Now, it's too damn bad we're in no place where I can explain what I've been thinking. I hold my words in, instead urging her to unburden herself with my silence.

"We used to talk every day. I'm not ready to let that go yet because ..."

"Because?" I probe softly.

She hesitates before the corner of her lip quirks. "How do you let go of the person who read you bedtime stories? Who read them to your son? Who would have sacrificed anything for you?"

"I don't think you can," I tell her honestly.

"So, you don't think I'm crazy for writing to my dead brother, telling him all about the emotional intensity of introducing my son to his father?" she challenges.

I rub my fingers back and forth over my beard, gently pulling. "People journal. They write letters and burn them. Both things are cathartic; why is this any different?" I respond.

A less tense silence falls between us. So, I try to change the topic away from her grief. "How's Kevin?"

And that's when I realize my tactical mistake. Because while Kara has aged beautifully, motherhood has made her stunning. Her lips curve slowly. Her eyes, shimmering with tears, become as bright as the sun. And as she passes a hand through her hair, her high cheekbones stand out.

I shift in my seat, uncomfortable at the instantaneous reaction I have to her. "Jed's probably howling," I mutter.

"Why do you say that?" An adorable V brings her brows together.

I scramble for an answer that won't have the dregs of whatever she's drinking thrown in my face but still isn't a lie. "Because we're acting like strangers, Kara," I say diplomatically.

"In many ways, we are, Jennings," she returns. "But I get your point. What do you want to know?"

*Are you dating anyone?* immediately comes to mind, but I suppress asking that. Instead, I take us to more neutral ground. "What grades do you teach?"

"Tenth through twelfth. That includes most physics and AP Physics classes. Well, other than the one Kevin will take next year. His is a college course that we got special permission from the county for him to take," she brags.

I sit back stunned. "That must be hundreds of students."

"About two hundred." She shrugs as if it's not a big deal, when it clearly is. "I enjoy it."

"More than you would have enjoyed being up here at Mendenhall? You were all I could think of when I was at the glacier," I blurt out stupidly.

Our eyes collide and the noise from the other patrons disappear. We could be anywhere or nowhere. I know exactly what Kara's thinking because the thoughts are going through my head as well. We're in this precarious situation where we're far from trust, but there's a bond between us we can't eliminate. We're going to be in each other's lives, for better or worse.

I retract my question. "I'm sorry, Kara. You don't have to answer that."

"There's still a long way for us to go before I'll be comfortable sharing those kinds of feelings." She rubs her wrist, and I ache for everything she gave up.

*If you'd only been there*, I beat myself up again. Instead all I say is, "I understand."

"How can you, Jennings?" she snaps. Rubbing her hand across her forehead, she apologizes. "I'm sorry. I'm not myself these days. That wasn't fair. There's still so much you can do for Kevin, needs I can't meet for him emotionally."

"It seems to me, Kara, you've given him everything."

"Thank you, but he was beginning to change even before...all of this. Now, I'm petrified everything that's happened at such a crucial time—when he's about to become a man—is going to mark him." Her frustration is evident in every word.

Propping my chin on my hand, I lean forward. "And that, right there, is how I know you've given our son everything, because you love him. There are children who aren't quite so lucky in this world."

Her eyes flare at my words. "Jennings..."

I lean back and pick up my coffee and the remainder of my scone. Standing, I nod down to her computer. "I'll see you tonight for dinner?"

"I...yes."

"Is there anything I can bring?"

"If you don't want to listen to your son whine about being hungry, feel free to bring anything to shove in his mouth while I finish up cooking," Kara replies drolly, her composure completely restored which is a shame. I rather like when I can shake it up and find my Kara beneath this calm demeanor.

Wait. My Kara? Where is this coming from? I crumble up the paper before stuffing it into the disposable cup. "Then I'll see you later.

Oh, and Kara?" She freezes in the act of opening her laptop lid. "I suspect somehow, some way, your brother is actually reading those letters. Would you mind passing along my gratitude to both him and Jed?"

Her lower lip trembles, so she bites it to prevent the emotions coursing through her from letting loose. Instead of responding, she nods.

"I'll see you tonight." With a side wave, I start to head back through Warm Up to where my rental is parked. Now, I just have to figure out where a grocery store is.

But when I pause at the threshold to make certain Kara's okay, she's already typing again. This time, there's a small smile playing about her lips. I wonder what she's telling her brother about me, I think fleetingly.

Really, it doesn't matter. What matters is knowing that for a moment I helped chase away the void of despair that was threatening to overwhelm her. Feeling something unusual in the region of my chest, I weave my way through the throng of people waiting for their custom-made coffee and out the front door.

# KARA

"Is it possible for you two to behave yourselves? I feel like the two of you have regressed in age," I say exasperatedly to Maris. Jennings just texted me to let me know he was on his way.

His reply text of *I told you I'll be on time; I keep my promises.* pleased me. For Kevin, I told myself firmly.

Meanwhile as I'm pulling chicken casserole out of the oven, Maris bats her eyelashes. "Mommy, I'll be good. I swear."

Kevin chooses that moment to return to the kitchen. He snorts. "You look like you're hunting your prey like on that show we watched on National Geographic. Remember? It was the one where the female ripped the male's head right off." I stumble with the heavy pan because of the outrage on Maris's face. "Honestly, Jennings seems decent."

Indignation replaces the false sweetness on my best friend's face. "Did your son just tell me—"

"Mom, Maris is being—"

Dropping the two-ton casserole onto waiting trivets, I wipe my hand across my sweaty brow before glaring at the two individuals who have somehow morphed into toddlers within moments because of a man who has been back in our lives for what seems like a nanosecond.

"Stop it right now, or I swear I'm not frying up neflies to go with these," I warn.

That shuts the two of them up simultaneously. "That's—" Maris starts before she wisely shuts her mouth.

My son is less diplomatic. "Mean. Cruel. You can't promise a man heaven of bacon-fried dough and then rip that glory from him," he declares dramatically.

"Then you and Maris had better watch yourselves. Here's the ground rules for tonight," I announce just as the doorbell rings. "Crap," I mutter.

Maris and Kevin look at each other before shrugging. "I guess it's whatever happens, happens," Maris calls over her shoulder as she leaves the room.

"I haven't begun heating the pig fat yet!" I shout after her. "You have to earn it!"

A second later, she's bringing a confused Jennings after her. "I have to earn pig fat. I have to say, I don't know how to do that. Does it involve singing or dancing because you might remember I'm not really that great at either of those," he reminds me.

I don't know who starts laughing first, but within seconds, Kevin's back is against the fridge to hold him up and Maris is leaning against the doorjamb for support. And I put my hand down to brace myself, not realizing my arm's about to brush against the heating electric skillet. "Ouch!" I yelp, jumping back.

Jennings drops the bag he's holding and is at my side in seconds. "Let me see," he urges as he cradles my arm against his chest.

"It's nothing," I stammer, despite the nagging ache beginning to spread.

"Kara, let me take a look. Please? If it's something serious, I want to be able to get you help." Jennings's face is pale.

Despite the annoying throb which will likely linger for days, I want to reassure Jennings I'll be fine and have him let me go. Him holding me is causing more issues than the annoying burn. "Fine." There's a part of me that wants to shake him off and just finish cooking dinner, but the blood pounding through my head is making me a little light-headed.

Maybe it wouldn't hurt for him to look at it.

Dragging me over to the sink, Jennings bends my arm at the elbow. He winces. I panic a little. "Is it that bad?" I demand truculently.

His thumb rubs on the side of where the skin feels the most tender. "It just looks a little red. Maris, do you have any ice?"

"Righty-ho, Jennings," she drawls. Soon a paper towel is wrapped around my arm, and a plastic bag filled with ice is put into Jennings's hand.

He frowns before opening it a little and sucking the air out. "That's better. It will mold better to your arm."

"Jennings, it's just a minor burn," I protest, but he frowns down at me.

"You have to take care of these things, Kara," he admonishes me. As if I don't know as a mother.

I feel dizzy and it has nothing to do with the minor cooking mishap I'm so used to dealing with on my own. Hazarding a glance over at Maris, she answers my unanswered question with a swirl of her finger near her right ear. Great, she thinks Jennings is acting loco as well.

Dinner's going to go great between Kevin deliberately baiting his father, Maris being Maris, and Jennings acting like a mother hen. I debate whether to start drinking now.

"I think it's feeling better now," I tell him gently, pulling my arm away. "But thank you. Normally, I'm the one handling all the scrapes and cuts around the house."

For some reason, that makes Jennings look inordinately pleased. "Oh, crap." He looks around. Dropping my arm as quickly as he picked it up, he darts over to where he dropped the bag he was holding. "I just hope nothing broke."

"Broke?" I repeat.

Jennings produces a large greasy bag, which he hands to Kevin. "Those are from Pike's Place. They're usually better fresh."

"Are those the little donuts?" Maris demands just as Kevin shoves his hand inside to investigate.

"They are," Jennings confirms.

"Gimme." Maris chases Kevin around the kitchen.

"No! It was Jennings's gift to me!"

My only response is to take the ice pack, lift it across my eyes, and fervently wish I hadn't been so generous to make this offer in the first place. "What did I do to deserve this?" I mutter aloud.

Jennings lets out a piercing whistle that causes me to drop the ice bag on the floor. He reaches down to hand it back to me. "Maris, Kevin, they're to share. Later. Now, Kara, you asked me to bring a predinner snack; I hope this works." Jennings produces a few bottles of wine, olives, a selection of cheese, and meat, and a loaf of crusty bread. "Is there something I can put this on?"

I can't respond. I'm too busy gawking at the edible bouquet in front of me. "Is that brie?" I say almost dreamily.

Jennings confirms, "It is. Do you want some?"

"Gourmet cheese is a serious weakness for me, right up with seafood. Dean used to take me to this little specialty cheese store on the north side of Jacksonville for my birthday each year," I reminisce. Then I turn away so I don't get emotional. Because the last thing we need is to add that to tonight's menu.

Jennings doesn't say anything. His jaw just tightens as he plucks at the brie wrapper.

Maris heads into the pantry and comes out with a tray. "I'll get a knife. Kara, if we have this, I'm certain we don't need neflies. Why don't we save them for when we have kielbasa? Kevin, does that work for you?"

"Totally. Mom, can I go call Brooks?"

"Sure, sweetheart," I say absentmindedly. "Don't be too long since your father is here."

"Right. I just wanted to before it got too late back home. I haven't told him I have a father yet." Kevin takes off toward the basement at a fast clip.

"And I need to get dressed for work so I can head out right after we're done eating," Maris declares. "Will dinner hold for twenty? Jennings was a little early anyway."

Jennings flushes as he chops the bread into wedges of varying sizes.

"Absolutely," I confirm.

"Great. Back in a few." Maris heads toward the stairs.

"Thank you, Lord." I send my thanks upward when the kitchen has resumed its normal level of peacefulness. I enjoy the silence as I unplug the skillet to let it cool before I put away the five pounds of bacon I would have had to fry up to get the necessary amount of grease. When I turn around, Jennings is handing me a piece of bread laden with brie and a slice of prosciutto on a napkin.

Right now, it makes me want to launch myself in his arms and kiss him all over his handsome face. Curbing that, I murmur an appreciative "Thank you" before I take a healthy bite and moaning. "Let me find the corkscrew."

Jennings chuckles. "Have they been like that all day?" he asks as he continues to slaughter the bread.

Turning from the gadget drawers triumphant, I admit, "It's always like that between them. It got worse when I started cooking. The meal is one of their favorites."

Jennings nods, adding the last of the bread lumps to the platter. "So, what are neflies?" Jennings asks, putting down the knife.

"A very thin dough boiled in water you then have to fry in bacon grease. It's an utter pain in my ass to make, but Kevin begged for it." I shrug like it's no big deal.

"Are you going to put me in the same category as our son and your friend if I tell you that sounds fucking fantastic? I've been living off of fast food all weekend."

"Yes, but I'll forgive you because it really does taste as good as it looks."

"Is there any chance I'll get to have it?"

"Maybe. It depends."

"On what?"

*On if you don't disappoint our son. On if we can get along well enough for you to be around.* But I don't say that aloud. "On whether a growing boy can withstand the temptation to not eat the bacon that's in the refrigerator," I say lightly.

"Kara?"

"Yes?"

"I'd really like to talk with you about..." But Jennings is interrupted by Kevin's footsteps on the stairs.

"Brooks says hi, Mom. Oh, cool. Snacks." And I leave whatever Jennings was going to say unsaid. Instead, I enjoy Kevin hoovering through half of the tray before Maris makes her way down the stairs while making small talk with his father.

Not long after, we sit down to eat. Conversation flows smoothly with Jennings asking Kevin what he's seen in Juneau. I fear he's going to choke on his meal trying not to laugh as Kevin brings out evidence of his argument that Juneau has a distinct ratio of fast-food restaurants to residents because "—before we left, Mom was researching the builders for our first home, Jennings. In the neighborhood we're looking in, there are at least seven, not counting our local grocery store. And if you drive just a few minutes," he exclaims, as he shoves a bite of casserole into his mouth, "there's at least twenty more." The look he sends Maris is filled with horror. "I feel like we need to send you boxes of TGI Fridays on dry ice."

"You do realize I can buy that at Walmart?" she says dryly as she stands. "It's actually more of a treat to have you and your mother here to cook and have a conversation with."

"I get you, Maris," Jennings agrees. He takes another bite and swallows. "This is about twenty times more delicious than most things I eat out."

"Oh? Do that a lot?" Maris asks innocently.

Suddenly, the heavy casserole doesn't want to go down. I decide I've had enough. I lay my fork on top of my plate, readying myself to stand, when I feel pressure on my wrist.

Damn, why is it now I remember his fingers used to touch me all over my body, anywhere, everywhere. They're stronger now than what I remember in my memory, but I still just the same at the feeling of Jennings's hand on my skin. It sends chills skirting up my spine, and I can't have that.

Fortunately, Kevin misses the byplay in his attempt to see how much food he can consume. Jennings doesn't move even as he addresses Maris's veiled question. "Yes, Maris. I do. Most of the nights I'd talk with Jed would be when I was in the office chowing down with my pilots or my operations manager and her partner."

"Oh." Maris doesn't say anything else. But it's like a pall has been cast over what was a lovely evening.

Right now, I want to strangle her. Clearing my throat, I gently remind her, "You said you were working tonight?"

Lifting her wrist, she groans. "I was supposed to leave like ten minutes ago. I wish I could stay and help clean up, but..."

I lift a hand and wave her off. "Go. I've got this." Maybe with her gone, some of the tension will dissipate.

There's a quick flurry of activity where I sit stoically at the table until Maris is running out, calling, "Bye, everyone!" as she makes her way out the door. Finally, a little calm. *Or maybe,* the little voice in my head says, *it's just going to get worse.*

"Hush," I mutter.

"I didn't say anything," Jennings pipes up, amused.

I groan and drop my head to the table. Unfortunately, since I didn't move the plate out of the way, the edges of my hair catch in the chicken casserole. "Great, just what I needed to cap off tonight," I gripe as I use my napkin to pluck the soup, sour cream, and chicken mixture out of my hair

Both Kevin and Jennings are laughing. "That was better than the time I got you with birthday cake, Mom."

Jennings is impressed. "Hers or yours?"

"Hers. How old were you that year?"

This time when I attempt to stand, Jennings doesn't protest. I scrape off the scraps in the disposal before quickly running it. "It was three years ago, so thirty-five. And thank you for reminding me how old I am."

"You're not old, Mom." Kevin's face takes on a frightened look. I have to figure out some way of easing that.

I grab the plate holding the brownies I baked earlier and the tiny donuts Jennings brought and carry both over to the table. "True." Then, like it just hit me, I snap my fingers. "Just think. Next year, when you get your license, you'll be able to run to the store for me."

"Yep. We agreed that was part of you paying for gas money," Kevin responds quickly, the tension easing from his shoulders.

"You realize that means getting everything on the list? Right?" I prod.

"Yes, Mom."

"Everything?"

"Of course," he replies indignantly, as he shoves a donut in his mouth.

"Including feminine products," I say calmly. Jennings barks out a laugh as Kevin coughs. I continue. "Of course, one of the benefits of a woman getting older is..."

"Jennings, I think I'm going to see what's on TV for a while. I'm sure you and Mom have a lot to catch up on." Kevin grabs a brownie, plus another donut, and dashes from the table.

Once he's out of earshot, I start giggling. "Well, that worked nicely. I'll have to tell his therapist about that." I reach over and grab a brownie.

"You're a terrific mom." Jennings's voice jolts me away from my personal celebration.

"Um, thank you?" I lift the brownie to my lips and take a small nibble before putting it on the napkin in front of me.

His voice lowers. "He's in therapy?"

Because Jennings has a right to know, I nod. "He took Dean and Jed's deaths hard. I wanted him to have someone to talk with."

"Is it covered through your insurance?"

I snort. "Physical therapy, yes. Emotional therapy? They covered four sessions—as if you can build the trust with your therapist in just four sessions."

"So, you're paying for this out of pocket?" he asks incredulously.

I shrug. "I'd do anything for him, Jennings. Making sure his mental and emotional health are okay..."

"Is something you can ask for help with, Kara." His eyes are steady on mine. He reaches over and places his hand over mine. "Please. He's my son and..."

"And what?" My heart is pounding as he squeezes my fingers tightly before answering.

"And I'm already falling for him."

I give Jennings a truth he may not be ready for, but it's the truth nonetheless. "Then you know exactly how I feel since I fell in love with him about two minutes after I found out I was carrying him. So I know exactly what it's like to take the fall."

"Will you let me help him? Help you?"

"Why don't we see where this goes?" I suggest, not saying yes or no. I stand, take my wineglass, and go to refill it.

As I turn to grab the bottle, I don't know whether to be anxious or concerned when I hear him mutter, "I already know where this is headed."

*Dean, Jed, are you listening? Please don't let this be something that ends up hurting Kevin,* I plead to the heavens. Taking my drink, I go back to the table to continue my conversation with Jennings until Kevin's emotionally stable enough from my teasing him about women's sanitary products to join us again.

# JENNINGS

Kara has been gracious with the making a conscious effort to bring me into Kevin's life. So far it's only been a meal a day, and I'm starving for more, but at least she called me and explained why.

"I know you've missed out on so much, Jennings," she told me when she was inviting me over for dinner two days ago. "But I spoke with Kevin's therapist. She feels it's best to take care as there have been enough emotional turmoils in his life recently. Together, we have to ease him into this in a way that can be monitored."

So, while I want to whisk Kara and my son off to some remote cabin where the three of us can learn every nuance about each other, I'm putting my own wants on the back burner. Kevin's welfare is the most important thing to both Kara and me. But, even as Kara and I both admit the bond between Kevin and me seems to be growing each time I visit, with her making excuses to leave the room for longer periods of time, there's a complication.

It's getting harder to ignore the fact the air seems to disappear every time Kara gets near me.

I groan aloud at the desk in my room at the B&B. "Little Owl," I say aloud in the empty room. The term of endearment suits her even more now than it did back when I first knew her. Between those unblinking golden eyes and the layers of color in her brown hair, the uncanny ability she has of sitting perfectly still before darting off to tackle something critical in that moment, the moniker I dubbed her with sixteen years ago is even more apt now.

That and the fact she makes this adorable hissing noise when there's something scientifically inaccurate on TV.

I almost fell out of the chair the other night when the noise came out of her mouth. First her face scrunched up, and then the sound came out right before she yelled, "That's not right! The science is off!"

Kevin, obviously used to it, merely patted his mother's arm consolingly while he offered some advice. "Word of warning, Jennings. We try to never let her watch anything with science involved unless it's on NatGeo."

"Good to know," I chuckled, even as the screeching sound emerged from her mouth as a small-town sheriff stumbled across a town in California as he uncovers a secret laboratory of scientists responsible for all mankind's scientific breakthroughs.

I can't remember the last time I had a better night before then. Until the next night I was with them. And when I'm not there, Kara and our son constantly consume my thoughts. I go to sleep thinking about them with a smile on my face and wake thinking about them first thing in the morning.

And in my dreams, Kara chases me there. The floodgates of my memories now open, my brain has spent the last several weeks superimposing the woman she is today with her touch from the past. And I'm slowly dying every time I'm with her. "I finally get it, Jed," I say aloud. Kara Malone is an incredible woman, one I never should have let go. And I'd give up just about anything to have a second chance with her, to be able to hold her while touching her soft body. Anything, that is, except our son.

*But what about next week, next year? And who's to say they're going to want you around?* my inner voice inside challenges me. My stomach churns remembering the feelings from my own childhood. Before we move forward in any capacity, I need to have a private conversation with Kara, one that has nothing but everything to do with our son.

With that thought in my mind, I grab my phone. Instead of texting, I dial and wait.

One ring. Two. Then a breathless "Hello?"

My heart twists a little just hearing her voice. "Hey, Kara," I say casually.

"Oh, hi, Jennings. I was just going to text you about dinner." There's a lag in our conversation I need to fill. Fast.

"I actually think we should talk." Even as the words come out of my mouth, I wince. Did that sound as ominous to her as it did to me?

"What? Is something wrong?" God, it must have. I can feel her anxiety through the phone.

"Everything's fine," I soothe. "I just think there's some things we should talk about without Kevin overhearing, and now that we've established a good foundation"—at least I hope so—"it might be good to get some things out."

"Oh. Right. Of course." I can almost picture her organizing her thoughts into lists. "Maris is off tonight, and frankly I'd feel more comfortable with her being here for Kevin. Even though he's old enough I'd normally leave him home alone, this is a new place, and with everything that's happening..." She's babbling, so I jump in.

"I understand," I interject smoothly. "We both understand why you're being cautious. So why don't you check with Maris, and if that works, I'll pick you up about six? Restaurants close early around here."

"That's fine."

"Either way, I'll see you then."

"Bye, Jennings." And I hear her disconnect.

I'm about to try to force myself to go back to work when suddenly I grumble, "Crap," and pick up my phone again. Dialing a different number, I wait. A different female voice answers. Without any preamble, I say, "I'm taking Kara out to talk tonight. Where can I take her without it seeming like it's too much of a date?"

A millisecond later, I have to pull my phone away from my ear as Rainey screams her excitement. I can't blame her though.

I feel the same way.

❉

KARA'S MOANING around a spoonful of soup. The sound hits me low in the gut as I try to swallow the poached pear and gorgonzola salad I ordered. "Good?" I manage to grate out.

"Delicious. The way they combined the Thai flavor is incredible." Without thinking, she holds out her spoon. "Here, you have to try this."

Unwilling and unable to pass up the opportunity to place my lips where hers have been, I lean forward across the small table and capture the spoon she's just dunked into the savory broth. Without losing her eyes, I guide her hand toward my mouth so I can I wrap my lips around the oval. "Delicious," I agree.

She's trembling slightly when she pulls back. The spoon clatters against the side of the saucer as she drops it. "I'll just wait for my main if you want any more."

Oh, there's a lot I want, but I keep that to myself. Shaking my head, I dive back into my salad which could comfortably feed a family of four. "I'm just glad there's a refrigerator in my room. I forget the size some restaurants give as portions," I admit sheepishly.

Kara laughs, her countenance relaxing. "I know; it's a complete crapshoot. Either you're getting a portion the size of a quarter—"

"Or one to feed a small family?"

"Exactly! And the prices are the exact same either way. Despite the fact I love finding new places, there's something to be said for chain restaurants when you're on a budget."

I put down my fork. "Will you promise to be honest with me about something?"

Her face takes on a wary cast. "I could lie and say yes, but I don't think you want that, Jennings. So, ask your question."

"Will you let me help with Kevin financially?" Her mouth opens, but I hold up my hand. "There are some very large-ticket items coming up in your future, Kara: cars, college, not to mention feeding our child, who seems to be a bottomless pit. Please, will you consider it."

She opens her mouth to answer, but someone comes by to refill our water. I hate we're having this conversation in a restaurant, but where else could we go? We can't have a talk about our son at Maris's, nor did I think she'd be open to having it where I'm staying. But— "I want to grab the servers by their apron strings and tell them to go away unless I throw rolls at them," I grumble.

Kara chuckles. "I don't think they'd appreciate a food fight, Jennings."

"I think this is why I went into business for myself. I've never really had a lot of patience."

"I—" Kara's interrupted by our server coming by to ask how we're faring, increasing my frustration level.

"I'm finished," Kara says pleasantly.

I scowl and voice, "Same. Also, can you give us a few minutes before you bring us our main."

"Certainly." The server disappears with our dishes, leaving us alone.

"You were saying?" I ask.

Kara twiddles with her napkin before laying it down smoothly. "Kevin and I lead a modest life, but we're happy. What he needs is a solid male role model who's going to be there for him."

"I hope I'm beginning to show him I can be that man for him." I'm probing for an acknowledgement of that from her, and I know it. It's foolish, yet I need to hear from her she thinks this is going well.

Looking thoughtful, Kara picks up her wine and takes a sip before placing the glass back on the table. "I knew one day, I'd need to be emotionally ready in the event you never came into our child's life. I mean, I believe in being prepared."

"That sounds more like a Boy Scout than a student," I tease lightly, but my stomach is in knots uncertain of where she's going.

I'm rewarded with faint lift of her lips. "I guess that's Dean's influence on me. And on our son since he's the same way. Why do you think he had that list of questions for you the other morning?"

My own lips curve wryly. "How many are left on there?"

"I'll never tell."

"I hope he never runs out," I tell her truthfully.

Her finger runs lightly around the base of the glass. "Maybe this is going to work out," she murmurs to herself.

"You thought it wouldn't." I reiterate the concerns Jed brought up in his letter. I try not to let the fact the man she's supposed to have been getting to know over the last several weeks has been making little impression.

Kara looks distressed but squares her shoulders. "It's not you, Jennings. It's me. And that's not an excuse. Trust comes hard. And that's hard for me as I get to know the man you are today. The man sitting across from me appears to be a good man. But this isn't sixteen years ago; this isn't a first date. We're parents discussing our son. And after everything with my parents and..."

I'm breathing hard as Kara continues. "Not only am I working through getting to know you again, but I'm battling my own regrets that Jed was right. And I'll apologize now for not trusting him, for not giving you a chance to know Kevin long ago." The words appear to be torn from her.

My hand reaches across the table for hers. "Kara, there's no need to apologize. You made the best decisions you could. You tried. I promise, I'm not going to let you down." I will all the emotion I can through my fingers as I squeeze her hand before she pulls hers away.

"I truly believe you're trying. Can you understand that right now, for me, that's a lot?" she pleads.

I'm about to say more when our server arrives with our main entrees. Placing the dish in front of Kara, she offers a demure "Thank you."

I gruffly say the same.

We're both eating in silence when Rainey's words come back to me. Kara's emotionally light-years ahead of me due to circumstances she had no control over. She gave over her life, her heart, and soul to raise our son. Whereas I'm stepping in at the eleventh hour to fall in love with him.

I can't be shocked she's cautious. I would be too. All I can do is my damnedest to support them, emotionally, financially, however they'll let me.

"You didn't answer the question I asked about helping you with Kevin," I murmur, cutting a bite of steak.

She hums. "That's because I'm still thinking about it. Why don't you give me a little time to mull it over?"

"How long do you think you'll need?"

"I don't know. Maybe another fifteen years? It takes me a while to make decisions, you know."

My eyes jerk upward. My mouth is already open to snap out a retort when I see her face.

Her eyes are golden circles in the dim candlelight. They're dancing with mirth. And her lips are twitching.

I burst out laughing.

A small grin crosses her face. "A very good sign for parenthood, Jennings."

"What's that?" I pop the bite of steak in my mouth.

"A sense of humor. And our son has an excellent one, though you've only seen glimpses of it. I honestly believe you'll do just fine," she informs me serenely.

"And what about his mother? What does she have?"

"A lot of patience. I've been dealing with a smaller version of you for almost twenty years" is her immediate retort. "Jed used to say being near Kevin was like having you around 24/7."

I laugh again. "He said practically the same thing to me in his letter."

Kara puts her fork down. "Maybe one day, you'll tell me what he said?" she asks hesitantly.

"Maybe one day I will," I agree amicably.

*Like the day I know you're seeing just me with the eyes of the woman you are today*, I think silently as I cut into my steak.

# JENNINGS

We spend the rest of the meal discussing all things Kevin. It's one step forward and two steps back because I'm thrilled to know every minute detail about my son, but now I have a bigger problem.

I want to know every tidbit about his mother as well.

Paying the bill, I slip my card back in my wallet while Kara finishes her coffee. Her fingers trail over the rim of the cup, the nails unpainted but perfectly shaped. I blurt out without thinking, "You still don't wear polish on your nails."

It's as if all the clinking and muted sounds around us cease to exist, and Kara stills. "What did you say?" she asks.

Feeling the heat hit my cheeks, I ignore her question and instead focus on her cup, which is now empty. "Would you like any more?" I ask politely.

"No, thank you." Standing, she reaches for her jacket, but I'm there to take it from her. Holding it by the collar, I stand there patiently while she slips in one arm, then the other. As she belts it, I lean over her shoulder and whisper, "You'd be surprised at the things I remember, Owl. I've got nothing to lose by admitting there's been no relationship since you that's meant as much to me."

As Kara whirls around to face me, I lean closer and murmur, "And it hurts to realize the boy had a chance to have it all, and as a man all I have are memories." Holding out my arm, I gesture for her to precede me out of the restaurant.

If I didn't see the flutter of her pulse at the base of her throat where her coat gapes, I wouldn't be certain of the reaction she had to what I said. But my words affected her, maybe more than she's ready for.

But it's enough to keep the hope I have for her alive.

Without acknowledging a thing I said, she passes in front of me. I get a whiff of the perfume she wears. It wafts through the air full of feminine power and refinement.

It's Kara.

And I can't stop myself from wanting her.

Placing my hand at the small of her back, I guide us between the tables and out the door into the cool night.

A SHORT WHILE LATER, we're back at the house—a car ride made in silence. Kara makes to open her door the minute we stop when I lay my hand on her arm. "I'll be right around," I advise her, before jumping out.

She doesn't say a word. Rounding the front of the car, I open it for her, something I know I've done a million times but in another life, by another me. Regret swamps me when I realize so many things have been tainted by an immature boy who didn't realize the precious woman he held then.

We stand in silence in the gravel driveway. "Thank you," I say suddenly.

"For what? Saying things during dinner that might have offended you? No problem."

It never occurred to me Kara might be beating herself up for telling me the truth. "You didn't."

"I was hoping I hadn't, but..."

"But what?" I prod.

"I don't know you anymore, Jennings. I don't know if you're being polite or sincere. I don't have all the facts, and I hate that." Her frustration is palpable. She tries to duck under my arm to head to the house, but I hold her firm.

"Finally, we're getting around to talking about the last topic of conversation for tonight. Us."

Kara slaps her hand on my chest. "Don't confuse things for Kevin, Jennings," she warns me.

"For Kevin, or you and me?" I counter.

While she's trying to come back with a retort to that, I tug her body just a little closer to mine. "I really want to kiss you, Kara," I tell her honestly.

Her whole body jerks at the idea before she tries to wave off my confession. "Proximity, nothing more."

"So, you're saying what we're both starting to feel again is because we're handy to one another?" I ask incredulously.

A flash of confusion crosses her face. "What else could it be?"

"You just said you need facts; maybe you need proof," I rumble before my head drops down to shadow her face from the car light glowing on either side of her.

"This isn't a good idea," she says breathlessly. "We're trying to work things out for our son, not trying to resurrect something that's—"

"No, I think it's because you're the one I was meant to find."

"How can you say that when years ago you let me go?" The hurt in her voice can't be hidden.

"I don't have a good answer, Kara. God, I wish to fuck I did. I only know what I'm starting to feel now." My head lowers more.

"Jennings." Despite the wary hunger I can see lighting her face, her voice is a plea for mercy, something she's fearful to express.

My nose glides against hers gently. The breath escapes from our mouths in little puffs of air, swirling between us like smoke before it disappears in between more harsh, heated exhales. "I won't take it from you, Kara." My lips are brushing against hers with every movement. "You have to be willing to meet me halfway."

"Haven't I already?" she sighs in resignation before pressing her lips tentatively against mine.

It's all the invitation I need.

Giving her all the freedom to break away, I leave my arm on the door, just sliding my fingers over to grab the end for purchase. My other hand threads under the strands of her silky-smooth hair to cradle her head as our lips touch for the first time in what feels like an eternity.

And the minute they do, I realize I'm not just in trouble; I've just lost control.

As my tongue slips past her parting lips, I'm slammed with memories colliding the past with the present. Back then, right now, Kara tastes of the cinnamon flavor she adored in anything—gum, coffee, mints. I'm thrilled with the memory as much as with the kiss that brought it to me. I want to howl in elation as I dip in to taste her over and over.

But at the same time, the raging beast of jealousy inside me rears its ugly head. Unlike then, the woman in my arms knows how to kiss me back. Her tongue flicks at mine. She pulls back enough to nip and suck at my lower lip before I seize control of our kiss again, trying to obliterate the thought of the men, any man, who had his lips on her in between our then and now.

It's completely irrational, but I don't care. There's nothing Kara will be able to say that scientifically proves it, but down to the bottom of my soul, I know she's mine. And in the fragmented darkness, this kiss is our first step back to becoming an us.

We're so enveloped in each other's arms, we've forgotten where we are. My body is trembling as it holds the door shielding her from view. A low moan emits from her throat just as I hear called out, "Mom, is that you? Are you back from dinner with Jennings?"

And it's like a cold bucket of water being thrown over both of us. Kara jerks out of my arms with a squeak. Her trembling hand lifts to cover her mouth. "What the hell am I doing?"

"No. Don't regret what just happened," I plead. Not seconds after it did anyway. But judging by the walls already being slammed up behind her eyes, I know it's too late. I want to howl in frustration, but that will do me no good. Not when I'm trying to prove to all of us, including myself, I'm in this for the long haul.

"I'm sorry." I step away, giving her some space. "You're right."

She blinks at me as if she's never seen me before, let alone been so intimate with me, the results of which are likely upstairs watching TV. "Excuse me?" Kara's thrown off guard at my 360.

"We need to factor in everything, especially our son, before we move forward. Together." I put an emphasis on the word just to get a reaction. Inside, I'm soaring as her little shoulders square off against me.

"We can't change our past," she reminds me.

"No," I agree. "But maybe the present isn't as locked as you think it is. Nothing is set except the stars."

She hesitates before her precious science forces her to give me hope. "And even they're ever changing."

I hold out my arm to escort her to the door instead of doing what I really want to, which is fist pumping the air. When we reach the stoop, Kara turns away to open the door, before saying, "Good night, Jennings."

I wait until the door's almost closed in my face before I slap my forearm up against it. "Tomorrow? Let me take you and Kevin up in the air?" I ask, bringing us back to the original reason we went out to dinner alone in the first place—our son.

Her fear is palpable. "Jennings, I'm scared."

And if I'm reading her correctly, not just about going up in my plane. My free hand reaches for her small one gripping the doorjamb. "I know I haven't earned it, but let me show you what it's like up there. Get to know another part of me Jed knew. Please."

After what seems like an interminable wait, she nods. "What time should we be ready?"

Without betraying my heart pounding inside my chest, I smile down at her. "That depends. Are you going to be better if you eat something before or after?"

Her face takes on a decidedly green cast in the porch light. "After," she says quickly.

"Then I'll pick you up at five."

"In the morning?" she repeats as if I've lost my mind.

"Well, yes."

Her head falls back when she laughs, exposing the creamy skin of her neck. I want to bury my face there, absorbing the sounds against my lips as she's emitting them. But it's too soon. Instead, I satisfy myself with the joy coursing through me when she swings the door wide open and says, "That's fine, but you can come in and tell your son the plans."

"I'd love to," I say honestly. As I pass by her, I whisper a finger down her cheek, delighted when she shivers in reaction. "Thank you, Kara."

"For what?" she manages to get out. Her pupils are dilated, the black obliterating everything but a ring of amber.

"For giving me the chance to show you all of me."

She shakes her head, as if trying to right it. "I wonder if this is going to end up being a mistake," she tells me honestly, right before she steps in behind me. Passing me, she calls out, "Kevin, your father has something to tell you!" A thundering of footsteps just overhead tells me I was right; Kevin was in the family room watching TV.

"But you're too intrigued not to investigate what's still there between us," I whisper so softly she can't hear it as she climbs the few stairs to the main living area. "And I'm counting on that."

After I've told my son what time I'll be by to pick them up in the morning, he reacts as if I've betrayed unwritten vacation rules. "I'm sorry, Jennings. In the morning?" Kevin's voice is horrified.

I nonchalantly say, "That's the best time to see the sunrise from the plane."

Turning to his mother, he begs, "All I ask for is coffee."

Kara's laughter will follow me into my dreams. As will so much about this evening: Kevin's excitement about the flight, my emotions over what she said over dinner, and that kiss. God, that kiss.

After saying good night, I jog down to the car. Casting my eyes upward, I can practically hear Jed's voice in my head saying, *I could say I told you so, but...*

"And you'd have every right." Opening the car, I slide behind the wheel. A quick glance back at the house has my heart quickening when

I see the curtains drop back in place. Kevin? Or—my pulse thrums madly—Kara?

Starting the engine, I pull away from the curb. I need to get some rest so I can show the two people who are becoming my heart where my soul lives.

In the sky.

# KARA

"Did you ever really get over what you felt for Jennings?" Maris asks me.

I just told her about the kiss and my reaction to it. I feel my cheeks warm again when I recall how I lost myself in Jennings's arms. "I tried," I defend myself.

"Tried," Maris scoffs, before she pours more wine in my glass. "Care to elaborate?"

"Well"—I draw out the word—"there was Linus."

"Ah, Jed's bartender." Maris shakes her head. "I knew he wouldn't last."

I glug back some wine. "Why not?" I demand. The hot former Navy cook made for some interesting nights after shifts I'd picked up during summers to put money toward Kevin's college education.

"You kept saying he didn't smell right. Too much grease from the restaurant. Next?"

"Quincy." But even I cringe a little saying his name, knowing what's coming.

And Maris doesn't disappoint me. "I still don't understand how you said his name in bed. Did you ever shorten it? 'Oh, Quince, Quince,'" she gasps.

"Jesus," I sputter. "That's new."

A wicked smile crosses her face before she takes a sip of her own drink. Putting it aside, she reaches across the counter to grip my hand. "Honestly, honey, of all the men you half-heartedly dated over the years, I truly only think you gave one a chance. What truly happened?"

I think back to the eighteen months I was together with Tony. And, yes, he could have made me happy if I was just a me. But— "He didn't want Kevin. And the longer we went on, the more obvious it became," I admit as I twiddle with the stem of my glass.

Maris rears back. "You never told me that. I mean, didn't he propose?"

I nod. "That was the night I ended it." My face takes on a faraway look in the dim light shining from the family area. "He'd taken me to his place to do it. There were flowers strewn everywhere, but God, Maris, all these years later, I still can't forget the look on his face. Before I gave him my answer, I mentioned changing the guest bedroom into Kevin's room. He recoiled, like I'd just said he had two heads."

"Or told the truth about how small his dick was," Maris growls.

"Or that," I agree. "It was like all the blinders slid off. It was clear on paper we worked—two teachers with promising careers. But I had a stigma attached to me that he wanted nothing to do with. He stood up in what should have been this romantic moment and explained he thought I would transfer custody of my son to my brother, who was 'doing the job anyway.'" I air quote the last, disgust lacing every word.

Maris slides her wine farther away and reaches for the tequila she keeps in a decanter. Pouring us each a shot, she mutters, "I can't believe you didn't tell me this."

I shrug. "Why would I? I'm the one who ended it. Besides, your dad passed not long after. You had other things to be concerned with."

"So you carried this load of crap for all these years?"

"It wasn't so much a burden as it was a slap in the face," I admit. I take my shot and shake my head at the quiver that floods my body from the burn hitting my stomach as it spirals out through my veins. "I never realized what scars I carried from what my parents did to me and Dean, Mar. I mean, how could you virtually disown your children for being human? For being gay? For having a baby out of wedlock? It took me close to ten years for me to trust that side of myself again to accept a date, and that was a single night out with one of Dean's friends."

"I remember you calling me in tears that night," she murmurs. "You'd just come back from the salon and cut your hair."

"You have no idea how much I cried before I made that call," I confess. "I kept trying to make lists of ways to back out."

"Why?"

"Because I was terrified. All I could think of was I was opening myself—and potentially Kevin—to someone who would let us down in the same manner my parents did. And maybe my judgment was right after all." Pausing, I take another drink. "Putting Kevin first in my life was never in doubt, so I don't regret turning down Tony two years ago. What it leaves me with is maybe I should have listened to your brother, knowing I owe Jennings an apology, but damnit." I dash tears from my eyes. "I had reasons to be concerned about opening myself up too easily. I still do. Should I throw them all away? Where would we be now if I didn't?"

Maris downs her shot. "I don't know. I can't answer that. All I can do is ask you this: What did kissing John Jennings make you feel again?" She pours another into my glass.

I stare at the clear liquid before I lift it to my lips. "You're a mean friend," I tell her.

"Why?"

"Because you know this shit is like a truth serum," I accuse before downing it. I wipe the back of my mouth with my hand. "Ugh, tell me you have Tums."

"Loads."

"Thank Christ for that."

"You realize you're avoiding the question," she nudges gently.

"I'm not avoiding it as much as I'm looking for an alternative theory to solve the problem," I declare as I plunk the shot glass down on the shiny wood grain.

Maris tilts her head. "What problem?"

"The fact feeling anything for this man could fling me as high as the sky before sending me crashing to the ground."

"So, you did feel something," she says slowly.

"He noticed I wasn't wearing my grandmother's bracelet, Maris. The first time we spoke," I whisper. "He was infuriated by it. Ever since, he's been worried, anxious, interesting, and intriguing. I think what I'm feeling is terrified."

Maris's head drops. "God, Kara."

"I know. So much has changed about him; I don't know how to process it despite the feelings I had for him then." I inhale sharply. Then I admit to her something I've only told Dean in letters late at night. "Would we have made it past that summer? God, we were so young. It was a hard truth I came to accept before I was able to put Jennings aside to move on with my life. And I can't say my life hasn't been a good one. It's just been unexpected."

Maris doesn't say anything, she just lets me continue. "Logically, my mind is telling me it would be a potential tragedy to feel something for Jennings again so quickly," I admit. "Even after tonight, spending time with just him, I'm setting up the perfect scenario for an epic disaster."

"So, it's better to have nothing when you have the possibility of everything?"

"I could be devastated and be left alone to cope. Again," I emphasize before Maris can argue.

"Or you can be the explorer you shut down inside years ago," she counters.

I'm startled into a reply. "What?"

"I agreed with your decision all these years, kept promises because I understood your pain and your logic. I lived through the fear you endured by your side, and look what you have—a son you raised brilliantly." Tears well in my eyes at her words. Maris goes on. "All the stories I heard from Jed's reunions with the guys indicated the John Jennings I knew from before was the man he was today. I suspect now, that was just guy talk because after listening to all of this?" She lifts the bottle and drinks quickly. Wiping her mouth after swallowing, she whispers, "He remembered your bracelet."

A sting hits my eyes, but I'm exhausted of emotions right now. "I know. And it's sweet, but..."

"But think on this," she interrupts. "Do you ever remember Jennings being sweet? Patient? Considerate?"

I close my eyes before admitting, "He's been nothing but since the day by Jed's graveside."

Maris smacks her hand on the countertop to emphasize her point.

"But that could just be because of Kevin," I protest weakly.

Maris pours herself another shot and tosses it back before an edgy smile tips up her lips. "When you're lying in bed overanalyzing this tonight, ask yourself if he was thinking about his son when he kissed you." Then she turns and walks away.

"Rude!" I yell after her.

"But you love me anyway" is her only reply as she climbs the stairs. Soon she's out of sight, and I'm left with nothing but my own thoughts.

And due to the tequila truth serum, there is nothing blocking them.

# JENNINGS

We taxi down the runway in the early morning light. I pull back on the wheel in front of me, Kara's gasp almost drowned out by Kevin's war whoop, and my insides settle for the first time since I saw them both standing at Jed's service. "Are you ready?"

"Isn't it a little late to ask that?" Kara squeaks.

Checking the panel, I see everything is perfect. Holding the stick with one hand, I reach over and cover Kara's balled hands. "Everything is going to be fine," I assure her.

"Christ, Jennings! Put both hands back on the wheel!"

Kevin laughs from the back. "I hear that a lot too, Jennings."

Not wanting to antagonize Kara further, I comply. "Oh?" I direct the question to my son.

"Yep. Mom decided I was mature enough to start learning to drive," Kevin explains. "Only around the parking lot in our complex though."

"And what do I have to say all the time?" Before Kevin can answer, Kara moans, "Ten and two. That's where you put your hands, honey."

If Kara is up to razzing our son, then she's definitely up for some teasing of her own. Flipping a switch so Kevin can't hear us, I ask, "But Kara, this isn't a traditional wheel. Where should I keep mine?"

Forcing her to pry open her eyes, she uses them to shoot daggers at me. "You know where they're supposed to be, John Jennings." My smirk turns into a full-blown smile when she tacks on softly, "And where they shouldn't be."

Casually, I remind her, "And aren't you very glad I know exactly what to do with my hands, Kara?" Darting a quick glance over my shoulder to make certain Kevin's occupied, I tease, "Otherwise we might not have a chaperone on this little adventure."

But Kara Malone is many things, and lightning quick is one of them. "Jennings, if it wasn't for that 'chaperone,' what reason would I have for being in this plane?" Satisfied by her response, she crosses her arms and looks out the windows.

Fury with myself for pushing her too fast keeps me silent as we soar higher into the lightening sky. But I know I have to address her comment. "A number of them," I manage to get out in between clenched teeth.

A snort is her only response. It makes my lips twitch. "God, Kara, how can a man look at you and not be utterly beguiled?"

"Beguiled is an interesting choice of word," she muses. "One I never listed when I tried to think of what you thought of me."

Thinking we might be getting somewhere, I ask, "What words did you list?"

"Namely, that I was contrary and boring." Shocked, I whip my head around to find hers pressed hard back against the seat while I struggle with the need to put the plane on autopilot to show her how wrong she is about her own self-assessment. "In the end, what matters is respect, Jennings. We have to build the foundation of co-parenting for Kevin based on that."

Focusing on turning the plane, I contemplate her words for long moments. Nothing but the faint hum of the propellers and the static through our headsets can be heard.

Finally, just as she inhales to speak, I hiss, "Other than the last thing you said, the rest was utter and complete crap. Even the Kara I knew back in the day valued herself more than to spout such nonsense from her mouth. So tell me, what asshole did you date after me who made you feel less than the confident, brilliant woman I know you are?"

Her "Excuse me?" comes through the headset faintly, and I know it has nothing to do with the gear.

"You heard me."

"I did, I just can't believe you said it."

"Why?" I'm genuinely confused.

Her head rolls my way. On her face, I find fatigue and tolerance. "You look like you're about to give me a teacher-to-student lecture." I smile.

Her lips don't even twitch. "Maybe because I am?"

"About?"

"About restraint," she says seriously. "Jennings, I'm not going to lie to you and say I'm not flattered by the fact you're attracted to me after all these years."

But before I can interrupt her, she continues on. "But I've been thinking about it most of the night. What I won't have is Kevin confused by his parents' relationship. He has the rest of the summer with both of us to understand mistakes were made on both sides and we're working to make them right for him. For him, Jennings. I'm not looking for an affair."

I'm breathing hard when Kara finishes. "Is that what you think this is?" I demand.

"What else could it be? I'm just me—a single mother who's on the brink of losing the one thing she gave up everything for."

"You're not going to lose Kevin to me," I say roughly.

"I know. But time isn't as kind as you are being," she reminds me gently. "Soon he'll be leaving home and—"

And before she can say another word, Kevin's frantically tapping me on the shoulder. Flipping the controls so I can hear him, I say, "What is it, son?" relishing the emotion of using that word.

That's when it hits me. I'm feeling all of these emotions for the first time, and Kara's starting to go through the process of letting him become the man she raised, not only to allow me into his life but to leave her behind. But excitement overtakes the man arising inside the boy when he points out the window and calls through his headset, "Mom, have you ever seen anything so beautiful?"

The mix of sun and clouds leaves the morning sunrise a blend of orange breaking through the lilac sky. Plenty of artists have tried to capture the beauty in paint and photographs. Many have even tried in words. Amazing how it's the woman beside me who does it justice when she shifts slightly, reaches her hand out to our son, and says, "Just once. The minute they laid you in my arms for the first time."

And it's in that moment, in the early-morning air where everything is still but the pounding of my heart, I realize Jed didn't just give me a wake-up call by dying. He saved my life by putting it right in front of the woman who's trying to deny she needs me in hers.

Keeping silent, I listen to Kevin and Kara discuss what it takes to form a sunrise so beautiful. I'm amused when Kara whispers reverently about scattering. "It's when particles too tiny to see change the direction light travels, sweetheart. Look at what happens."

"Have you ever seen it before?" Kevin's voice is solemn.

"Never from a vantage point like this." Shifting in her seat, Kara's face is filled with astonishment. "Is this what you feel every time you're in the sky?"

"No." Her brows draw down to a V before I continue. "Each flight shows me there's more to be found in the air. Just when I thought I experienced it all, I find something else. I thought before I had it all, but I was wrong." Adjusting our course slightly so the sun doesn't blast us directly through the windshield, I murmur, "And I'm just glad Jed realized it."

Kara's prevented from saying anything when Kevin yells, "Mom! Look! Isn't that the glacier?"

"No, it's a glacier, but it's not Mendenhall. At least I don't think so? Ask your father; he's the one whose second home is up here in the air." Kara's smile and words offer me a tentative truce, but I don't want one.

I want the passion and power I know live in her so I have a shot at her heart. I follow the river for a moment before answering, "No, that's not Mendenhall, Kevin." I hope he doesn't ask me to fly there. I have other plans for visiting the glacier in the air. Instead, I turn us farther west.

I may seem like I'm just flying, being in the air, but the reality is I'm putting my soul on display for the two people who are quickly becoming everything. I need for them to understand who I am while I'm up here. So, for the next hour, I answer question after question about the plane and about flying.

And not just from Kevin.

# KARA

"That landing reminds me of when Kevin used to when he'd play flight simulator: smooth and easy," I admit bashfully. "Not like me; I'd just crash the thing into the ground for the fun of it."

Kevin guffaws loudly in my ear. "One thing I'll say about you, Mom. You don't lie."

Jennings flashes me a crooked smile but doesn't say anything as he's talking with the tower. A moment later he responds as we taxi toward the hangar. "I'm glad that went smoothly. I've got precious cargo on board."

"Kevin is absolutely that," I agree.

"I wasn't just talking about him," Jennings says mildly.

I want to punch him for flirting so openly while our son is listening in, but I don't. I tell myself it's because he's still navigating something that costs the price of my dream home into a ridiculously tight parking space at the direction of a ground crew member.

I stubbornly refuse to acknowledge the warmth his words cause inside me because I'm terrified of what happens when I'm let down again. Lying in bed last night, I replayed my conversation with Maris. I recalled everything about the men I dated, especially my almost engagement. And I realized Maris was right; I've been holding back on living not only because of what my parents did, but because of the man next to me. I held back on living because no one else could make me feel what he did.

Now that he's here, I'm holding back because of my own fears. And still, he's a part of every molecule of my being. How could he not be when I held a part of him next to my heart for ten months?

I have no idea what to do, I think wearily. And right now, I wish with every fiber of my being I could pick up the phone and call my brother instead of typing him another letter I know I'll never get a reply to. I can just see how this one's going to go. *Dear Dean, What should I do? Jennings is in our life again and I don't know how to feel. What kind of big brother tests would you run him through to make certain he's not going to crush my heart the way he did before?* Frantically, I try to imagine his voice in my head, but all I get is the impression of me, Kevin, and Dean laughing on a Sunday watching football while I prepared something in the Crock-Pot. My heart aches when I remember how we used to have so little, but the reality is we had everything.

Jennings turns off the engines. I'm lost in my memories as I remember Dean cursing over Jacksonville losing another game because we couldn't get a decent quarterback to throw a pass. Suddenly, the headset that permitted us all to hear one another in the air is being lifted from my ears. Startled, I meet Jennings's compassionate eyes as he pulls it away. "Did we lose you there, Mom?" he teases gently.

"Maybe for just a moment," I admit sheepishly.

"All we need to do is get you unstrapped, and then we can get out of here," Jennings assures me.

Refusing to acknowledge the disappointment his words cause, I nod before turning to tease Kevin. "Are you ready to crawl back into bed?"

"Yes, but it was so worth it," he yawns. "Thanks, Jennings."

"Anytime. I mean that. And it doesn't have to just be at dawn."

"Why did we go up, then?" Kevin asks as we climb out of the plane.

Jennings doesn't reply until we're all standing next to the plane. "There's something magical in the air when the night shifts between night and day."

"Do you take your planes up at that time a lot?" The question pops out of my mouth unbidden.

Jennings shakes his head. "The last time I went up that early, I took Jed. He was in Seattle for a quick trip and spent the entire flight telling me about the man he'd fallen in love with."

"Dean," I choke out. God, from my own thoughts of him to hearing this, it's almost more than I can bear.

"Yes." We could be the only two people in the world as he telegraphs his heartfelt apologies with his eyes as the morning sun streams through the hangar. Clearing his throat, Jennings breaks our connection to finish answering. "Life got in the way, son. So, maybe it was fitting the next people I shared this magic with was you and your mom." He stares out at the morning sky. "Magic isn't in flight. It's returning to your wishes you made upon the stars by getting close to them in the air." Almost embarrassed, Jennings clears his throat. "Any-way, let's get you both back so you can get some rest."

I don't think before I make the offer; I just do it. "We're going to sleep, then we planned on just gorging on junk food all day and movies. You're welcome to join us."

I don't know who looks more excited about the invitation, Kevin or Jennings. But I know it's right when Jennings's voice catches as he asks, "What time?"

I don't answer. I'm not the teenager who will sleep until tomorrow unless I'm cattle prodded out of bed. So, my lips twitch when Kevin declares, "No earlier than four, Mom."

I turn to Jennings and rephrase Kevin's order more politely. "Is four okay?"

"Four can't come soon enough," he assures us.

And I hate how my heart skips because I feel the same way.

Even as we head back to Jennings's rental, I can't help but worry. We may have landed safely, but why do I feel like somehow I'm going to end up crashing and burning?

❄

I'M DANCING around the kitchen singing along with one of my all-time guilty pleasures. My hips are swaying as I'm tapping the wood spoon against the pot of simmering chili. Putting it on a paper towel, I jump to the side in time to the music, twisting my way across the expanse of the linoleum floor as I make my way over to the fridge. Flinging the door open, I shake my hips to another popular hit when the sour cream tumbles to the floor. "Crap," I curse aloud but sigh when I manage to catch the Tupperware of freshly shredded cheese before it meets the same fate. Glancing down, I heave a sigh of relief when I see there's not a gooey white mess to clean up. "At least I didn't manage to screw up snacks."

I'm so caught up in the music, I never heard the knock on the door, so I scream when I hear Jennings answer, "I think for another performance like that, it would have been worth it."

"Jesus, Jennings." I quickly turn to drop everything in my arms onto the counter before catching my breath. I call out to the speaker to lower the volume. "I thought I was alone." My cheeks are stained in embarrassment. Reaching for a towel, I wipe the chili splatters in earnest.

Before he can say anything, Kevin bounds into the kitchen. "Mom, how much longer until food? I'm starving." he says, accompanied by a pathetic look of a puppy deprived of a treat.

"It will go faster if you ask your father how hot he likes his nachos and if there is anything he doesn't like on them," I inform him sweetly.

"Jennings..."

"I'll eat everything you have on the counter with the exception of raw onions. As for the heat—" There's a slight pause. "—I prefer things hot."

"You and Mom," Kevin says in disgust. "I don't know how you do it. I'll go get the first movie ready."

Ignoring the pounding of my heart, I assemble the nachos and gooey cheesy sauce, liberally applying topping in between the layers. After laying on a sprinkle of shredded cheddar and cojito cheese, I take the tray in my arms and move over to the wall oven to slip the nachos in to broil. Before I can struggle balancing the pan and the door, Jennings is there, ready to assist.

*Don't get used to it*, the little voice inside of me silently warns. "Thanks." Closing the door, I wipe a hand across my brow. "I lost track of time," I admit.

His lips curve, causing his dimple to appear. "Would that be because you were too busy making what may be enough nachos to feed a family of twelve or because of the dancing."

I flush hotly.

"And singing," he says as he steps closer into my space, making my heart beat faster. I can smell the warm, woodsy cologne he put on, and I tremble inside.

Damn him, I'm not going to fall for those thick lashes that surround crystal-clear eyes. I refuse to be stripped of all my sensible reasons why becoming involved with John Jennings is a bad idea. The problem is the pull between us is stronger than ever. I'm so damn attracted to him, it's next to impossible to be this close to him and not feel the magnetism radiating off him.

Stepping back, I move over to the counter and pull out a chef's knife and a head of lettuce to get rid of the tension so I can hold a conversation with some semblance of calm. I don't want to feel this way with Jennings; I just can't prevent it.

Tension descends on the kitchen. I'd say Jennings feels it too, when he approaches me warily. "Correct me if I'm wrong, but you're attacking that lettuce like you'd prefer it to be my head. How could I have done something since I last saw you?"

The problem is, it's not anything he's done, per se. It's my anxiety flaring. There's shared moments between us as we show Kevin we don't hold animosity toward one another where I remember all the fun and the good times we shared, then...*wham!* Something reminds me of my fear. He's been gracious, accepting, and understanding. I have to figure out how to fully trust Jennings because every day I see the bonds between him and Kevin growing. I just don't know how to deal with them. I continue to chop my frustration out on the lettuce despite how my body yearns to lean forward and make him crazy with all the ways I know I could.

Jennings must decide with Kevin nearby he's smarter to leave confrontation alone, instead commenting, "I've rarely seen someone with knife skills that good unless they were trained."

Giving in to his waving of the white flag, I pick up a pepper and expertly deseed it as I tell him, "Jed taught me."

He smiles. "That explains it."

"He needed to if I wanted to pick up shifts at Hook & Ladder during the summer."

"Hold on," Jennings interrupts me. "You said you teach high school, right?"

"Yes," I reaffirm. I pull another pepper toward me, but Jennings's hand lands on mine just as I start to chop. "That was stupid! I could have chopped your finger off!"

"Screw that, Kara," he says, making me want to show him the damage a chef's knife can really do. "Why were you working shifts at Jed's bar?" he asks low, menacingly.

I answer unthinkingly. "Why, to make more money to put towards Kevin's college...Jennings!" Without warning, the knife is yanked from my hand and is skating across the cutting board. I'm being pulled into Jennings's arms, pressed tightly into his chest where I don't just smell his cologne, I'm devouring it. My "What is your problem?" is muffled against his sweatshirt.

He doesn't answer me anyway. Instead, he rocks me back and forth for long minutes before letting me go.

I feel the loss of his warm body against mine, but it's the look of painful agony on his face that has me whispering, "What's wrong?"

Trailing a finger down my face, his voice is so low, I can barely hear it when he says, "Everything," before he turns and calls out to Kevin, "So, what are we watching?"

Frozen, I stand there until the timer startles me. What was that all about? Having two hungry guys to feed, I shake myself out of my head and lift the nachos out of the oven.

Moving the large pan to the counter, I smile to myself as I hear Kevin and Jennings debating back and forth about which is better, Jimmy Fallon and the Roots singing along with classroom instruments or James Corden's carpool karaoke.

I add my own two cents when I call over, "Jimmy Fallon singing 'I Want It That Way' is embedded in my heart."

Father and son exchange a long look before bursting out into laughter at my expense. I just shrug before sprinkling on the final peppers onto the mounding tower. Grabbing a stack of plates, I make my way over to the television. But I freeze when my son haughtily informs his father, "Unless you like classic rock, we can't be friends."

Because it's not the teasing I care about at all. That's something Dean used to say to Kevin when he was little over and over as he schooled him on the Stones, CCR, and Lynyrd Skynyrd. "Can't live in Jacksonville and not know our native sons by heart," he'd tease my son with as he would cut his generic chicken patty with a dollar-store cookie cutter to make it look fancy.

I hold my breath, waiting to see what happens next.

"Who taught you that?" Jennings laughs. "Your mother and Maris used to listen to garbage. In fact, she kinda just confirmed she still did."

I stick my tongue out at Jennings as a reply but angle my head toward Kevin.

His face twists for a moment before he blurts out, "Uncle Dean. I remember he used to play all this great music when he'd pick me up from daycare."

"He sounds like someone I would have enjoyed getting to know," Jennings replies evenly, his tone not betraying anything beyond interest. I want to sag in relief, but that would be too obvious to our son. With a quick glance in my direction, he murmurs, "I wish I had the chance."

My son nods. "I'm certain you would have. He was great." Then his voice takes on a hesitancy. I wouldn't be the mother I am if I didn't pray with every fiber of my being my son would open up to someone, anyone. Even if that's his father he's known about a month. So, I hold my breath as Kevin asks, "Maybe I could tell you about him sometime?"

Jennings leans over to snatch the remote up from the coffee table. Flicking the television to Off, he casually says, "What's wrong with now? The movie can wait."

And Kevin starts to open up. I don't know if it's because Jennings has no preconceived notions about Dean or because he wants his father to understand him better, but my son finally releases some of the pressure that's been built up inside of him since Dean and Jed died.

Shifting so I'm out of Kevin's line of sight, I catch Jennings's eye and mouth, "Thank you."

The corner of his mouth tips up, the only sign acknowledging he saw me. Then his focus returns entirely to our son. Exactly the way I always dreamed it would.

Quickly, I deposit the plates on a side table, hurrying back to the kitchen to grab the nachos. My heart beats a rapid staccato in my chest. When I turn around, Kevin has leaned forward, his head dropped beneath his shoulders.

Jennings has shifted as well. He's braced his elbows on his knees. I hear him murmur, "Sounds like your uncle was a pretty good dad to you."

And my son agrees, "He was. He was a great dad. And then I had Uncle Jed. Most guys, they don't get it. But you don't mind if I say that, do you, Jennings? Mom said you talked about that."

Jennings's head snaps to mine, his light eyes intent. I feel frozen in my space. *Did I tell my son too much trying to ease this path? God, what if I was wrong?* I realize I didn't cross a boundary when Jennings turns his attention back to Kevin before decisively nodding. "Your mom is right. I've thought several times your uncle must have been an impressive man to have raised you to be the young man you are. And I feel honored you think I'd understand more than your friends."

Kevin's head bobs up and down.

The moment of silence extends. I'm afraid to move, afraid not to. But it's Jennings's words that free me at the same time they stagger me.

"Son, there are days when you're never going to believe this, but your mother is one of the smartest people in the world."

Kevin scoffs. "I already know that, Jennings."

But Jennings shakes his head. "I don't mean when it comes to science, though I bet she'd still give any lab rat a run for their money. I mean about her love for you. There isn't a thing she wouldn't do for you. She's brought nothing but good people into your life—starting with your uncle Dean. And when he couldn't be there anymore, she knew you would need someone to talk with because he was such an important part of your heart. I hope you know by now your grief is very appropriate for a boy who just lost his 'dad.' She's so smart she knew you'd need help and went to every length to get that for you."

"You think so, Jennings?"

"Yes. And let me tell you, to be loved like that is the goal for anyone, no matter their age." Jennings looks as troubled as Kevin for a moment before he schools his features. "Now, let's help your mom. And maybe while we're munching on nachos, you can tell me more?"

"That sounds like a deal." Kevin shoots to his feet. For just a second he seems undecided, but as quickly as he wraps his arm around Jennings, he lets him go. Jennings's arms immediately lift to wrap around him, but he doesn't get the chance.

I can't move for a moment because it's everything I ever wanted, my son reaching out to his father, but at the same time it's devastating to my heart because deep down, secretly, I'd always imagined I'd be a part of the equation. Squashing that, I celebrate the breakthrough Kevin's making by reaching for the platter of nachos. "Who's hungry?" I call out. Turning, I almost stumble into Jennings. "I've got this if you don't mind grabbing the trivets?" I ask.

A muscle ticks in his jaw. "You've done so much, Kara. More than you could possibly know." With that ambiguous statement, he grabs the trivets so we don't burn up Maris's coffee table.

After I lower the tray, Kevin exclaims, "Awesome! Uncle Jed's recipe for nachos."

I hand out plates. "Dig in," I encourage.

"Jed's recipe?" Jennings questions.

"For the restaurant. I made it so often, I memorized it." I laugh. "Like after the first thirty orders the first weekend."

"Right," Jennings clips out. Turning to Kevin, he says, "I'll let the expert show me how to dig in."

Kevin doesn't waste any precious time. Even with his plate filled high, he shoves a mouthful in as he sits back. "So good, Mom. Thanks."

I reach over and stroke my hand over his head. He bats it away like normal. I just grin. "Anything for you, sweetheart."

Jennings sits back with a plate full of cheesy deliciousness, and his eyes dart between the two of us. "You're a very lucky man, Kevin."

Kevin sits up straighter, the "man" comment startling him, I'm sure. "What makes you say that?"

"You have a mother who loves you beyond anything. She gave you the best and even then wanted to give you more." Jennings's eyes shift to my face which must be frozen in shock. "I'm coming to realize she's one of a kind."

"Yeah, she is." Kevin changes from little man to big boy by leaning over and giving me a quick kiss on the cheek. "Thanks, Mom."

"There's no need to thank me," I protest.

"I'd disagree," Jennings murmurs before shoving a large wedge of nachos into his mouth and letting out a small moan. "Christ, these are good."

My head and my heart are currently in a fight with one another, so I decide to ignore them both by answering another organ that's wading into the battle.

My stomach.

Taking my own bite, I'm not forced to answer him verbally. But sooner or later, Jennings is going to demand answers to the questions burning in the back of his eyes. Questions I'm just not ready to address for a second time in my life.

# JENNINGS

I'm driving back to the B&B doing nothing but hearing her words replay over and over.

*"Why, to make more money to put towards Kevin's college...Jennings!"*

"She wouldn't have had to do that if I'd have been there," I declare resolutely to no one but the cool air wafting through the car. But even as I say that, I wonder if anything will ever allow Kara to forget the man who forced those circumstances to become her reality.

The more time I spend around my son and his mother, the more I regret. Everything.

I always believed deep down I was unlovable because of the way my parents left, so I never gave my aunt and uncle a chance. Kara's words from dinner the other night play over and over in my mind.

*"It's not you, Jennings. It's me. And that's not an excuse. Trust comes hard. And that's hard for me as I get to know the man you are today. The man sitting across from me appears to be a good man."*

My life in Seattle is empty, save the business. I wonder if I did that deliberately so when it all abandoned me, I wouldn't fall apart. Then I hear Kevin's voice, his certainty.

*"But you don't mind if I say that, do you, Jennings? Mom said you talked about that."*

She's right; I didn't mind. It simply savaged me but not because my son had a role model like Dean Malone. Even if Kara had married and her husband had given him that, there's no way I could resent Kevin having that influence. It devastates me it wasn't me who gave him the tools to become a man. Someone else did. Why? "Can I accept the fact it wasn't me?" I ask. My voice is filled with bitterness.

Pulling up, I park my car and just sit there while it idles. I choke out a sob as I spew aloud at Jed. "Are you laughing up there? Christ, I'm going insane. It's killing me, Jed. You knew I'd fall in love with Kevin the minute I met him, and there's no way I could hate you for keeping a promise to her. I don't blame you; I never could. Kara doesn't either in case you're wondering. She freely admits that Kevin was likely going to ask soon. We all miss you so much."

God, I'm reduced to talking to Jed while the pouring rain traps me in my car. I keep babbling. "I'm falling for Kara all over again. Did you plan on that too? I feel every wretched piece of me pulled to the surface when I'm with her. Is this what you wanted, you crazy fool? Yes, I get it. Her family was a piece of shit." A crack of thunder rents the sky. I make a hiccupping, choked sound that tastes of the nachos I consumed earlier. "Okay. Other than your husband. She's Kara, but she's different. She's warm and funny, but she's still Owl buried beneath the fear. And how the hell can I resent her?" I'm breathing hard as I come to the state of forgiveness I needed to in my own heart. "I'm proud of her and so frustrated by her and wish I met Kevin sooner. And by the way, you dick? I want to kick your ass; how could you let her work for you?" I'm yelling in my car. If it wasn't raining, people passing by would be getting a hell of a show, but I don't care. I just got finished telling my son it was okay to let loose the emotions building up inside.

Now, it's my turn.

"Jed, you're the only one I can talk to. And I have no idea if what I'm doing is right or wrong. I just wish I could get some answers. Hell, I'm just an idiot talking to thin air anyway." My head crashes down on the steering wheel as pain overwhelms me.

I don't know how long I sit there before a text comes in. It's Kara.

*With the storm, I was worried about you driving. Can you let me know you got back to the B&B okay?*

My lips part in shock. "Maybe I was wrong, buddy. Maybe you are watching us all muck it up down here. If you are, tell Dean thanks for everything he's done for Kevin. He's missed by some people who loved him an awful lot."

Quickly, without thought, I grab my phone and send two texts to very different people. Without waiting for a response from either, I jump out into the storm and race inside to strip my now soaking clothes off. Then without much effort, I fall onto the bed and sleep.

THE NEXT MORNING, I find a response from Reg. *It will take a bit of time for us to confirm the accounts. Once sent, we can't retract an amount like that.*

I quickly type back, *That's fine. I don't want her paying taxes on the amount, Reg. Adjust the amount to compensate for anything she'll owe the IRS.*

*Understood, Jennings. Is Kara aware you're doing this?*

I hesitate before I type the truth. *We've discussed it.* Because that isn't a lie. We just haven't come to an agreement on any decisions about Kevin's financial support. But after last night, there will be no more working in shifts in a hot stuffy kitchen to cover any expenses for my son.

Not if I have anything to say about it.

Kara's not once asked about my financial situation. She has no idea of the state of my personal accounts, nor of my business accounts. All she wanted was a male role model for her son. *Well, sweetheart,* I think grimly. *You've got one.* And this man is determined to teach his son that no matter who he falls in love with, you take care of that person until your back breaks and your fingers bleed.

And while Kara may have already begun those lessons, she'd better be ready to show our son the one of graciousness when a windfall lands in her accounts. My fingers fly. *Just let me know when it's done.*

I see dots moving before, *And you want it to be that high? If we were to go based on your income back in the early days, you would owe significantly less.*

Furiously I type back, *And she paid medical bills out of pocket, Reg. You know what I want her to have.*

His *Understood. I'll get it done.* does little to soothe my frayed nerves. Throwing my legs to the side of the bed and my phone on the nightstand, I run my hands through my hair. "She's going to kill me," I say aloud. Then I soberly add, "But she deserves everything. She's given me so much more than this."

Reaching for my phone, I scroll to find the one I sent to Kara before the one I sent to my lawyer before I got out of the car.

*Come out for the day with me. It's time for us to have an honest conversation without impressionable ears, don't you think?*

Her reply came through as I was arguing with Reg just a few minutes ago. *If Maris can stay with Kevin. I really don't want him alone after last night. With all the talk of Dean, I want to know he's with family.*

Her concern for Kevin's well-being makes my heart twist in my chest. I had typed back, *If Maris can't, what about Brad and Rainey? Maybe he could hang with their family.* I know Rainey's been making some inroads with Kara and looking to set up time for all of them to get together.

I held my breath hoping she wouldn't be stubborn, hoping last night shook something loose inside of her the way it did in me.

And that's why my stomach muscles clenched when I got the text of *Okay. I'll talk to Maris when she wakes up, so I won't have an answer for a few hours. If not, then yes if Brad or Rainey can do it. Otherwise it has to be another day.*

Laying myself back on the bed, I close my eyes, still clutching the phone to my chest, cautiously hopeful. Because that's all I can be.

Then my eyes jerk open. It's only 6:00 a.m. here. Quickly I type, *Is everything okay? Why are you awake?*

I see the dots move. Then stop. Then they move again before a new text comes in.

*I waited up for Maris to tell her about Kevin's breakthrough tonight, but she didn't come home. That's nothing to worry about — she's at the apartment above the bar. Then I was thinking back about today, the laughter, the emotions.*

*Are they good ones?* I type back quickly, concerned she's not in a good spot with the way things are progressing with our son.

*Most of them, yes. Some are necessary. I'm handling them* is what comes back much more quickly.

I suspect she also sent a long letter to her brother. I wonder if that habit will end as time passes and her heart heals. I hesitate before making the offer, but damnit, I want her to start getting comfortable with the fact I'm here for her now too. *Do you want to talk about it? I'm here for you too, Kara.*

I wonder if I've overshot my moment when the dots move. With a swoosh, I receive, *Not now, but soon. You need to know anyway for Kevin.*

And I'm left intrigued and confused. I tell her as much.

What I get back is a bunch of emojis that make absolutely no sense. *Is that supposed to make it clearer?* I ask.

*No, I was just showing you what I was feeling.*

Suddenly, I feel like I'm studying a preflight checklist before take-off. I evaluate each and every emoji in detail, trying to discern what to say next when a new text comes in. *Get some rest Jennings. We'll talk more later.*

I want to tell her to wait, but the clock on my phone tells me it's almost six thirty in the morning. With a groan, I reach over and plug my phone back in.

I'll memorize Kara's self-study guide before I hopefully see her later. I'll show her I'm a superior student when it comes to handling the emotions of the Malone family.

# KARA

My fists are clenched tightly in my lap as Jennings lines up his Cessna for us to take off. "This is your idea of a good place to have a conversation?" I demand belligerently.

Jennings laughs through the headset. "What better place, Kara? Up in the air, we have plenty of time to just talk without interruption." Jennings speaks to the tower. I hear through my headset, "Cleared to take off, runway 1, Juliette Sierra Foxtrot 206." Slowly, the plane begins easing forward.

I have to admit, I'm impressed. "It's like you're speaking another language when you do that."

He laughs. "It reminds me of when you used to talk about the different kinds of soil topography here in Alaska. I was, and am, slightly in awe over how smart you are. Hold on, babe."

Immediately, my hands shoot to the armrests on either side. Jennings chuckles in amusement. "I didn't get the full effect of this yesterday when I took you both up. Why didn't you tell me you're afraid to fly?"

"I'm not afraid, per se." And as we lift off the ground, I open up. After writing to Dean last night, I talked with Maris this morning. "I've never been good at this," I admitted to my friend over coffee.

"What, being happy?" she countered.

Staring into the depths of my cup, I whisper, "Relationships. People. Feelings."

Then Maris blew my mind when she retorted, "You have a chance some of us don't have. Just see where this leads?"

Jennings picked me up later after I told Kevin I was spending the day with his father. "We have a lot of things to talk about" is all I said.

He shrugged before saying, "I think I got the better end of the deal. Maris says she's taking me to...where?"

Maris smoothly interrupted. "I'm going to take him on the ferry and spend the night in Ketchikan. We're going to see the Lumberjack Show."

I groaned. "Jennings is going to murder you," I warned her.

An impish smile crossed her face. "He'll think it's worth it."

Brought back to the present, I answer him. "It's just since we got the news about Dean and Jed, I'm terrified about something happening to me. Then, what happens to Kevin?"

Silence stretches between us. I joke, "That must seem silly to a pilot who's in the air every day..."

"Hush for just a minute," he interrupts me.

I'm about to take umbrage until Jennings speaks in a strained voice. "I keep wanting to bring you up here so maybe you'll get to see a side of me you haven't really met. But instead, you keep getting under my skin, reminding me of all the things I already know about you I can't get out of my head."

I reach over and place my hand on Jennings's bicep, which bunches beneath. "Then show me you," I say simply.

"Are you sure? We can turn back if you'd be more comfortable." His declaration immediately endears him to me more.

"Show me the air," I tease him lightly. But I don't miss the way his head whirls in my direction, a small smile playing about his lips. "But before you do, would you mind reminding me of how proficient you are at flying this thing, Ace? Despite my questions, I was too freaked-out yesterday to pay much attention," I confess.

Jennings's smile fades. "This means we're going to talk about the past."

I lift my hand from his arm and wave it to indicate the beautiful skies around us. "I can't go anywhere."

He lets out a sigh, faces forward to check the gauges, and then turns his head back to me. "I moved to Seattle when I left Juneau. It wasn't long after..."

"We broke up?" I conclude, turning to face the almost blinding sky. Reaching up, I slide my sunglasses up, telling myself they're to protect my eyes.

"Yes." Jennings clears his throat. "Every summer I was flying here. Every minute I wasn't on stage or in Juneau, I was working with a small charter to get in enough hours to graduate to larger planes."

"You must be thrilled. All your dreams came true, Ace," I tease gently.

"That's the funny thing about dreams. One minute you think you've attained them all, and then you wake up realizing there are more of them to be had." I open my mouth to speak, but he beats me to it. "It seemed like some days I was working round the clock, but logging flight time is ridiculous." He rattles off the flight hours needed for small-plane certifications.

"What about large jets? Like commercial pilots?" I yelp, suddenly terrified that someone like the boy Jennings was is going to be flying me and Kevin back to Florida at the end of the summer.

Jennings laughs. "The FAA has some serious requirements for commercial pilots, Kara. Relax."

I do, infinitesimally. I ask the question with the curiosity I was born with. "Why were you working so hard? You were young, Jennings; you had so much life ahead of you."

His response is swift. "If I wasn't going to allow my heart the chance to have what it craved, because I feared what might happen if I did, then I needed to give everything to what my soul needed to breathe."

"The air," I say firmly, expecting him to agree and us to continue to talk about flying.

His next words both soothe and scare me. "You didn't ask what I wouldn't allow myself, Kara." His tone is almost offhanded as he turns us again. The more banks and turns we take, the more he's keeping me off-balance. Much like this conversation is.

"What's that?"

"You."

"Please," I scoff. "Jennings, we were so young."

Jennings's face twists with an emotion I can't name. I go on in disbelief. "You said things were over because you didn't want a girlfriend on the other side of the country. Am I wrong?" I accuse.

"No. I spent a lot of time thinking about you as I studied the letters you sent to me."

"You read them?"

"Yes."

I don't know whether to be terrified or thrilled. Those letters were some of my most innermost fears as a young parent. "I'm sorry. There are so many things I should have said and things I probably shouldn't have."

Jennings hums through the headset. "I know you are—sorry, that is. Because despite the confident woman in front of me, there was a scared girl who made the best decisions she could. And despite all of that, she still tried." Jennings pushes the small plane faster.

I don't say anything, but there's no way he can't hear my accelerated breathing through the microphone.

"Kara, look out the window," Jennings urges me.

I do, and I gasp.

"I listened to you, Owl. All the nights I got to hold you. This was your dream." Jennings lowers us slightly so when we pass over the majestic beauty of the Mendenhall glacier, I can practically make out the crevices in her.

"All these years. She's still so strong, so beautiful."

"And she perfectly represents how I felt about you then and how I'm beginning to feel about you now." My head whips away from the window. My lips part in shock. "I can't go back in time and say what was between us would have made it. I was a terrified boy who didn't know much beyond escaping the past and finding his future. I cared for you, and we made something beautiful out of that. I think forgiveness—on both sides—is key for us to give what's still between us a chance." Jennings yanks off his glasses so I know my answer isn't just important to him; it means everything.

Shakily, words I didn't know I'd had buried deep inside come out. "I can live on my own. I can survive. But if I could go back and give myself one gift, it would be you answering one of my emails. Just one. Just so we had a chance." I take a deep breath, and my voice trembles. "Jennings, there was nothing to forgive you for. I just hope one day you can forgive me."

Heat and hope descend on his features. Then a rueful acknowledgement of our location. "Fuck, now I'm the one who wishes we weren't in this damn plane. I want to kiss you to show you I already have, but I won't take that chance."

Turning my face away from Jennings, I stare down at the glacier that always felt like it was tied to my soul. Then I murmur, "Even without our lips touching, I kinda think you just did."

My head swiveling back, I catch the surprised look turn to cocky arrogance. I burst out laughing. "Come on, Ace. Show me more before it's time to head back."

Turning us, he turns again so I get one more magnificent view before saying to me, "The sky's yours. Where do you want to go?"

"Where do you want to take me?"

The grin he gives me tightens my nipples and causes my thighs to clench together. "So many places, Kara. But for now?" He turns and heads us farther away from Juneau and the memories there.

And as we talk, I learn more about Jennings's life now. What I find is that it sounds terribly lonely despite the crazy business he seems to thrive on. My life, with all of the horrific events of late, the ups and downs over the years, still feels like it was more complete than Jennings's is.

And that makes me hurt for all of us.

WE TOUCH BACK DOWN at the airport in the late afternoon after spending hours in the air talking. I now know more about the man Jennings has become than I ever imagined. And, I think ruefully, he knows more about me than I would have shared under any other circumstance. But damn him, I want to choke him when he mutters, "Good thing we got the clearance to land; we were riding on fumes."

"Damn you, Jennings!" I screech, hauling off and punching him in his arm which has taken more than its fair share of abuse in the last four hours as the sky enveloped us and we got to know one another without anything between us.

He laughs, capturing my hand and bringing it to his lips while we're at a stop as a parcel delivery flight that makes Jennings's plane look like the one Kevin used to play with as a baby passes us by. "I need to get my computer out later," I murmur.

"Why?" He drops my hand to put both hands back on the wheel to cross the now clear tarmac. "Want to tell your brother about your day?" I don't feel upset about him bringing up Dean or the letters. It's a comfort to have someone know.

"I'll do that later, but Dean and Jed"—my voice softens—"were fanatics about backing up everything to the cloud. I have *everything* here, Jennings. All of Kevin's pictures, his videos from when he was a baby to just a few weeks ago." We pull into a hangar, and Jennings cuts the engine.

I don't know what to do next, so I just wait until two strong hands reach over and lift the headset I've been wearing for hours off my head. "What made you remember that?" he asks me gently. His fingers trail down my cheek.

I smile widely. Of all the hundreds of questions I've answered today, that's the easiest one. "Because your plane looked like a toy Kevin used to play with next to the UPS one when we were pulling in," I say with brutal honesty.

Jennings tosses his head back and laughs. His eyes are sparkling when they meet mine. "No one else has ever made me laugh quite the way you do."

And since today has been about honesty, I smile back and admit, "I'd be lying if I said I didn't enjoy today."

"Good," he murmurs. Unhitching his seat belt with ease, he leans across the console separating us. His face is getting closer. My heart is pounding.

But then again, so is something else.

I slam my hand against his chest and stop the kiss that I now want as much as Jennings because there's something much more pressing at hand. "Bathroom before your lips get anywhere near mine. I swear to God, Jennings, if you don't find me a restroom, I'm going to pee all over this seat. Having your child made it so I have little to no bladder control." He wants honesty, let him deal with that.

His head drops to my shoulder, and his body shakes with laughter. But his large hand moves perilously closer to where aches of a different sort have peaked throughout the day to push the release button to my harness. "I'll be right around to help you out, Owl."

"Thanks, Ace." My voice is a bit breathless. But I scramble to grab my purse so I'm ready when he reaches up to catch me as I scramble out of the cockpit of this plane, and he points me to the nearest restroom.

Because I want to see where the rest of this date heads.

## KARA

"This is so good," I moan around a bite of champagne-and-truffle fondue. "Where did you find this place? Maris has never mentioned it."

"If I told you I looked it up on the Food Network website, would you believe me?" Jennings tells me before he shoves his own crouton dripping with luscious cheese sauce into his mouth.

We're getting low on things to dip into the cheesy goodness, and I frown trying to come up with a solution. Jennings picks up on my displeasure immediately. "What's wrong?" he demands.

"The croutons are almost gone. Give me a moment; I'm thinking." Tapping my skewer against the side of the fondue pot, I drop it and reach for the bread basket. Tearing what's left into little bites, I give my dinner date a smug smile before declaring triumphantly, "There. Problem solved."

"We probably could have asked them for more, Kara," Jennings says logically, but I note he immediately stabs a bite of bread onto his skewer and dunks it in before I can pick mine back up.

"We can do that too. But this way we don't have to wait."

"Always so smart," he says admiringly, at least I think it is. But still my skewer clatters to the table as I'm reminded of something said by too many dates.

*Must you know everything?*

Picking up my glass of wine, I take a long drink, trying to shove the thought back into the box it came out of. I'm not with them, I remind myself. I'm with Jennings.

But after Jennings has shoved his third forkful of fondue into his mouth and I haven't reached for another bite, he frowns. "What's wrong?"

"Nothing," I say automatically.

"Bullshit. One minute we were fighting over the fondue like it was our last meal, and the next..." His eyes drift to the bread, to his own fork, and finally up to my face. "Something I said took you away from me," he growls. "What was it?"

"Nothing, Jennings. Really. It's fine." I put the wine down and pick up my fork. But before I can spear a piece of bread, Jennings grabs my wrist.

"And that's the first lie you've told me since the day began." His voice is frustrated. "I promised you no lies, and you said the same. Whatever it is isn't 'fine,' Kara. Tell me what I said."

I open my mouth and close it. "You said I was smart," I blurt out.

He looks confused. "And you are. You're one of the most brilliant people I've ever met—man or woman. That's not a compliment?"

"It hasn't always been," I confess. I tug a bit, and Jennings lets go of my wrist. Placing my fork down, I quickly apologize. "I'm sorry I didn't tell you the truth because I didn't want to bring other people here. Today was as close to a perfect date as I've had in a long time."

"And I've done little more than take you up in the air and feed you. Imagine what's going to happen when I actually start to woo you again," he says smoothly.

When I look up and meet Jennings's eyes, I feel scorched by what I see in them. My lips part, but no sound comes out. Heat that has nothing to do with the small flame beneath our melty cheese licks at my skin.

"Now, tell me what it was I said so we can work through it. I'm not leaving things unsaid between us, Kara. Too much is on the line."

"Men, at least some of the ones I've dated, haven't always been supportive of a smart woman," I blurt out. Jennings places his hand on top of mine and squeezes. "I'd do something like I just did, problem solve, and they'd ridicule me, make me feel small."

His thumb brushes back and forth over my knuckles. "I don't want to bring other women here, but I think I need to. Just for a moment. Not long ago, I felt like they were interchangeable. Jed used to ask me about when I'd get tired of it, and long before I met you, I realized I was. Now, I'm out for an evening with a woman who is self-sufficient, valiant, clever, and better yet, understands the meaning to all of those words."

I can't help it; I grin.

Jennings smiles, but it doesn't reach his eyes which are intense on mine. "She's brave, loyal, and loving. Remarkably, she's beautiful, and she has no idea about any of it. So if the men she dated are as foolish as the women I did, then I hope they all find happiness together." He lifts my fingers to his lips. "I have other plans."

My heart flips over in my chest, but before I can even think of a reply, our waitress, Cindy, appears. "Oh, I'm so terribly sorry. We just got a new batch of croutons out of the oven. Would you like some to finish your appetizer?"

Jennings and I exchange a quick glance before we both burst out laughing. Thank goodness he regains his composure enough to say, "Yes, thank you." Otherwise, I might have pulled the rest of the delicious cheese to my side of the table.

No matter if his words gave me chills in all the good ways.

And it's making me think I really don't want this night to end.

# JENNINGS

I don't want this night to end.

Kara and I are the last seated in the restaurant. In fact, I've way overtipped the waitstaff to make certain they knew I appreciated the extra time they've lingered over nothing while Kara's continued to tell me stories about her brother and Jed. And while I've cherished the insight I've gained into my friend's life in Florida, I relished every single moment I've spent with the woman who's shown me hopes and dreams don't just have to be found thousands of feet up in the air.

"And then there was the time Jed came to the bar wearing only a Speedo and a St. Patrick's Day hat." She's gasping as her head crashes into the table with a thud. Her giggles are infectious, even as the image she paints makes me want to bleach my brain, but I can't ignore the third time the manager passes us deliberately.

I run a hand over her hair. I guess I should have expected it when her head snaps up to mine, eyes blinking in rapid succession. "I think they're trying to tell us something," I say gently. "Let's head out and we can find somewhere to keep talking. I want to hear more." The truth is, I want to hear everything.

A light blush covers her cheeks. "God, Jennings. I haven't even checked in with Maris about Kevin." Quickly, Kara reaches for her purse, but I stay her hand.

"Why don't we head out? We can check from the car?" I suggest.

Relief crosses her face. Quickly we don our coats and thank the manager profusely. He grins. "Come back anytime."

I roll my eyes behind Kara's back, knowing that has as much to do with the outrageous tip I left as him being gracious. But within minutes, when we're tucked in the warmth of the vehicle, Kara starts in surprise.

"What is it?" I ask. Hooking an arm around the back of her chair, I lean over her shoulder.

She holds up her phone. "Kevin. He's having a blast." She holds up her phone to show me a picture of Kevin and Maris happily ensconced in the hotel with snacks spread out all around them.

I smile. "So, our son is happily tucked in for the night."

"It appears that way," she confirms, slipping her phone into her purse.

"Do you trust me?" I ask her. Inside, I'm quaking slightly as I wait for the answer. Even though today was as close to a perfect date as I could have imagined, the simple question could shatter that illusion into a million pieces.

Her head turns. Our mouths are a hairbreadth away from one another. We're physically closer than we have been since the night I kissed her, and yet the intimacy of this moment is greater than the other. So much rides on her answer. Her lips part, and I brace for an excuse. So it takes every ounce of willpower to not crush my mouth down on hers when she whispers, "Yes. Especially after today."

"My Owl." I massage the back of her neck. Her laughter stops, but she trembles.

"Then do you want me to stay with you tonight?" Before she can say a word, I hold up my hand. "You had just started telling me a story. Fair warning, I may need to drink heavily after listening to it, so be prepared for me to crash on your couch," I tell her with a touch of amusement, pressing a kiss on the crown of her head.

Her head shakes back and forth so fast, I can't say I'm not a little hurt. "Okay. I'll just drop you off, then." I go to turn on the ignition.

Kara's head snaps up so fast, she clips me on the edge of my jaw. Not that I'm complaining because she presses her lips to it on her way to my mouth. Her mouth then touches mine gently. Pulling back a bit, she studies my frozen features, before whispering, "I don't want to tell you the story if you're going to drink heavily, Ace. I want you to touch me, and I think you need your faculties about you when you do that." Her head arches away from mine, eyes lowering dreamily.

"Shit," I hiss out, before I capture her lips with mine.

As Kara's upper body softens against mine, one arm tightens at the base of my neck. The other cups my jaw.

And just like that, flashes of memories hit my mind.

Kara's breast cupped in the palm of my hand as I leaned over her. Her breathing heavy as I took the sweet dusky-tipped nipple in my mouth.

Kara's legs parted as I dragged my cock through her wetness, preparing to enter her for the first time.

Kara's hair flying as I rolled her over so she rode on top of me. Her giggles echoing throughout the room.

I want all of that again, I think ferociously. But it's the last I want more than anything. I want Kara's uninhibited laughter to penetrate my soul. Gently pulling back, I wait for her eyes to drift open before I rasp, "Come be with me."

Wide-eyed, her lips part, and there's a low pang in my stomach when I realize I'm suddenly terrified she's going to say no. Her soft "Yes" is more than a beautiful woman agreeing to a night in my bed. It's a chance to start over with a woman I realize I should have held on to almost a lifetime ago.

So, I'm not surprised my hands are shaking when I put the car in gear. What I am surprised by is when she reaches over and lays her hand on my leg.

Exactly the same way she used to do when we were dating.

And that, more than anything else, calms me down enough to put the car into gear and drive us to the B&B.

# KARA

The silence in the car intensifies the need between us. Occasionally, I feel Jennings glance over. I don't for fear I'll tell him to stop the car and crawl into his lap like days of old. Flashes of the stupid ways we'd find to make love are being superimposed with the sexiness that's uniquely him now.

It's causing the tingle beneath my skin, and the only thing I'm touching is his leg. If I do more than that, I'm afraid of what I'm going to do.

Then again, if the thumping of my heart is any indication, I'm terrified anyway.

After we park, Jennings grips the wheel for a moment before reaching down for my hand. Lifting it to his lips, he tells me, "I'll be right around. Wait for me," before sliding out of the car.

With nothing to do, I fold my hands around each other and just suck in air. It can't be more than a few seconds, but I feel like I'm hanging between two different realities, one in which I'm living in the past and the other where I'm living in some sort of fantasy. I haven't decided which I want to be in when my door flies open.

Jennings braces himself between the door and opening, effectively caging me in. I flick my gaze up and down his body, letting it linger

over certain parts of him before jerking it back up to his face. I feel the
warmth hit my cheeks when his lips curve. Damn him, he knows
exactly what he does to me. Taking his offered hand, I pull myself up
until I'm flush against him.

He grunts at the impact of our bodies but says nothing. The hand
not holding mine slides over the curve of my hip, tugging me tighter
against the long column growing behind his jeans. He arches a brow.
Lust and something more, something I can't name, crawls into his
eyes. We stand there with nothing but air between our bodies until
Jennings yanks me out of the door and slams it behind us. "Come with
me now, or I'll have you underneath the moon. And God, Kara, if your
memory of us is as good as mine is, you know that's not a threat."

"No, that's a promise," I murmur, remembering the night in question where Jennings drove us to a secluded spot and did just that.

Jennings drops my hand once we reach the back entrance of the
B&B long enough to whip out his key. "Thank God Ron has a back
door to this place," he mutters. Soon, the door is open and he reaches
for me again. This time he grabs a hold of my wrist and drags me up
the winding staircase to his room.

We make it there without another word passed between us. Soon
he stops in front of a door, but instead of letting me go, he traps my
body in between it and him. "I want your hands on me, but I'm not
sure if I have enough self-control," he admits.

Up until that moment, a part of my mind was still afraid. Both of
us have had other lovers before and after each other, but this was
Jennings. A part of me always knew he was something special. Relaxing, and heady with the power he just turned over to me, I slide my
hands under his open jacket, feeling each and every muscle. Rising up
on tiptoe, I nuzzle the soft hair of his jaw. Hearing him groan, I smile
against his jaw, before whispering, "Find some." Then I kiss him softly
before I turn him loose. "Open the door, Ace."

The door flies open behind me, and I stumble but don't fall
because Jennings's arms catch me. "Keep moving backward, Kara," he
growls.

I could have pulled away from him easily, but the arousal I hear in
his voice kicks up my own about ten notches. I tug the pull to my

jacket down slowly as Jennings kicks the door behind him closed. As I let go of him with one arm to shrug out of it, he reaches behind him to lock the door.

"Keep going. I want your skin vibrating beneath my fingers."

"You next." I push at his bomber jacket with eager fingers. He quickly complies, letting it drop to his feet with a loud thump.

Leaning back against the door, Jennings pulls me in between his legs for a kiss. His mouth descends over mine, his tongue licking at the seam of my lips until I groan, giving him the access he needs. Need, want, and that something else I can't quite name rise and fall like the plane did this morning. Only this time, I'm flying in Jennings's arms.

It's always been this way with him, even when we were so young, I think dazedly. There was so much I just liked about Jennings, and then there was this intense, white-hot chemistry between us. It brought us to a different plane where we both lived for those glorious summer months, where the air and land could touch without catastrophic consequence.

Soon, kissing isn't enough for either of us. My hands are frantically shoving under Jennings's shirt. His fingers are playing with the skin of my stomach where he's pulled my sweater away from my jeans. Tearing my mouth from his, I beg him, "Touch me."

His eyes promise me everything I want, but his mouth smiles even as he denies me. "I plan on savoring every inch of you."

I groan as I'm backed toward the bed. Well, Jennings may not be ready to touch me, but I'm more than ready to have my hands on him. Impatiently, I slide his shirt up until it's bunched beneath his arms. With a smile that's always hit me low in the gut, he lets me go with one hand to pull it off over the back of his head before tossing it aside. "Better?" he asks.

"Much," I reply tartly right before I slide my fingers through the hair sprinkling across his firm pecs. Honing in on his nipples, I tweak them between my finger and thumb, hearing him groan aloud. Leaning forward, I place my mouth on the center of his chest and brush kisses over him until I reach my target. I hear his ragged sigh as I twirl my tongue over his nipples before I latch on fully.

"Fuck, Kara. God, yes." Jennings's voice is broken as he grips the back of my head against his chest.

I'm scoring my nails up and down his back, fully intent on driving him insane, when he pulls me back to mutter, "My turn."

I'm about to protest, but I can't because Jennings is whipping my own shirt up and over my head. Then after my head clears, I don't have the desire to. He's letting out a long sigh as he traces his fingers over the delicate lace edging the cup of my bra. With each pass, his fingers dip lower and lower until finally they brush against my straining nipple.

I whimper when they finally make contact. Jennings's only response is to pull his hands away before reaching down and flicking open the clasp between my breasts. I shrug off the offending garment just in time for him to crush our naked torsos against one another.

"So much better," I manage to get out before he drugs my senses with another one of his kisses. Long moments later, I realize Jennings is bearing us down onto the bed. "Finally," I mutter.

I feel his smile against my neck. "Impatient little owl. Always so hungry for knowledge."

Sliding my fingers into his hair, I urge his face back. "You forget I've taken this course. I'm looking for a better grade."

His mumbled "Not sure if that's possible" sears through my soul in ways I can't explore right now. Instead I press a kiss to the side of his neck and then draw his head down.

Jennings doesn't miss the invitation.

Waves of pleasure course through me as Jennings's beard scrapes against my skin. God, this is new, I think to myself as I arch into his mouth every time his jaw caresses me. "Maybe I'm not the only one looking to improve his score in class," I say breathlessly as Jennings draws his chin over the side of my breast.

He just laughs darkly right before he takes my aching nipple in his mouth and sucks. Hard.

"Jennings," I moan. His eyes snap to mine as his tongue flicks over the tip. "Don't stop. Feels so good."

"Other side," he mutters, shifting to do just that. But his fingers play with the wet nipple he left open to the air. And the sensations have me practically levitating off the bed.

I'm writhing in his arms. My nails drag up his muscular arms, his shoulders, anything I can grab. "Let me touch you," I plead.

"Let me enjoy you this time," he counters. My heart trips when I realize he means for this to be more than once. "Let me taste you, Kara. God, I want to wake up with the scent of you on me."

In this moment, I know Maris was right. I never got over my feelings for John Jennings. Even if it's for one night, I want this—no, need this. "Then show me," I dare him.

His eyes glow before he slowly rakes his teeth down my neck, nipping along the way. Bypassing my aching breasts, his lips cruise through the valley between them. His beard is like an extra set of hands leaving fire in its wake as my body arches against him. "Touch me," I beg.

"Aren't I?" he taunts. His fingers make quick work of the button of my jeans, and he tugs them down. Slowly, oh so slowly over my belly until he also catches my panties along with them. I lift my hips to assist him.

I nearly come as the kiss of air touches the smooth skin of my pussy. "Please, Jennings," I moan.

"Damn boots," he mutters, twisting away to yank off one of the things impeding him from getting me completely naked. Glaring at the offending objects, he hurls them across the room. I hear a crash and giggle softly. Jennings pauses in the process of reaching for his own laces. "I love the sound of that," he whispers.

"What?" I ask, confused.

"Your laugh."

I contemplate him sitting at the edge of the bed. My pants are halfway down my thighs. His boots are about to meet the same fate as mine. "Is now when you want to talk about it?" I demand.

He shakes his head. Toeing off his own boots and socks, he stands and reaches for his wallet. Tossing it onto the nightstand, he mutters, "But we will," before he shucks his own jeans and boxers to the floor.

Thick and iron hard, his cock springs out at me, begging for my touch. Immediately I reach for it only to be denied when Jennings starts shaking me out of my jeans. "Damn you," I growl. As soon as I'm freed from the offending garments, I try to scramble to my knees.

He pushes me to my back. "I swear to God, if I don't taste you in the next minute..." He doesn't finish his sentence. Instead he presses my legs out and rubs his fingers in circles against my clit. He lets them dance for a few seconds before sliding them lower—and before his lips replace his fingers on the tight bud.

My fingers find his hair. "Oh, God." My head falls back. My hips arch against his mouth as his fingers slide into me simultaneously. "Jennings." I don't know if his name is a cry for mercy, for relief, or for more. It might be all three. My hips rock against his mouth over and over, juices dripping.

I'm on the verge of begging. His fingers plunge inside of me as his beard abrades me, leaving delicate scratches that only enhance my arousal.

I lift my head to find him watching me, and just then he curls his fingers, reaching for a spot that makes my neck snap back in rapture. "Jennings," I moan just as the walls of my vagina clamp down over and over.

He surges up until he's lying on top of me. His lips meet mine, and I taste myself on him. I smell the essence of what he did, and my heart trembles. Jennings isn't done as he lets me ride out the aftershocks with his long fingers still pulsating inside of me to drag out my orgasm.

Then he snarls a word that makes my body tremble from head to toe. "Mine."

Rolling off me for a moment, he fumbles for his wallet. Fishing out a condom, he makes quick work of rolling it on. In the meanwhile, I recover some of my wits about me to scramble to my knees, and just as he's done, I shove him to his back.

I straddle him, moving until he's pressed his cock against my opening. His hands are gripping my hips tightly, rubbing my hips back and forth over his cock, preparing us both for him to slide inside. After a few moments, I demand, "Now."

Jennings loosens his grip, and I slide down to take him. The feeling of being stretched by him in this position almost makes me come immediately. Only the knowledge I want to drag him over the edge with me keeps me from flying again on my own. Sliding my fingers up his stomach, I reach down and pinch his nipples, which makes him throw back his head against the pillows. His hands slide from my hips to cup my breasts, and I let out a long moan.

We're both panting when I start to rock my hips back and forth, each and every movement brushing my clit against his pelvic bone. His grunts and the tightness of his thighs beneath my ass telling me he's as affected by what we're doing as I am. I slowly pick up the pace. "Jennings." I can barely get his name out.

Our hips rock together frantically. He rears up to clasp my head as he captures my lips, still thrusting up into me hard even as his tongue licks and strokes inside my mouth. Tearing his mouth away, he snarls, "Kara, get there."

Bracing my hands on his shoulders, I churn my hips faster. Every movement causes my clit to rub against the hair springing out from around his cock. He grinds his heels into the bed and digs upward. My head falls forward onto his shoulder as I hear him grunt out his release as his hips pump in quick succession. Despite the condom between us, I can feel his heat as he spurts into me, which triggers my own shuddering pleasure.

I sag against him, unable to hold myself upright any longer. I barely notice when Jennings's arms tighten and he pulls us backward, spreading the misshapen covers over us both. I can't process anything through my brain. I don't want to think or analyze anything right now.

I just want to forget about everything except the feel of Jennings's arms around me.

Until I'm forced to leave this cocoon and remember everything that brought us here.

# JENNINGS

The next morning, I wake up to Kara dressing. "Where are you going?" I murmur. Patting the bed next to me, I reach out a hand. "Come here."

She stops what she's doing and pads over on bare feet. I trace the seam of her jeans up the inside of her legs. "There's nowhere to be. I doubt Kevin will be back for hours," I remind her.

"I was going to call an Uber," she admits. "I need to think, Jennings."

Those words after the way her body entwined with mine throughout the night causes my heart to sink. Instead of reacting first and regretting later, I continue with my ministrations. "What about?"

"This, us. How it affects everything."

"Then let me give you something else to think about," I offer, not entirely unselfishly.

Her soft moan reaches my ears right about the same time her hand lands on top of mine to push it away. "Jennings, I have so much jumbling up my head," she groans. "Stop distracting me. I have to go."

"Like hell you do," I growl. Hauling her over my body, I ignore her screech. "Haven't we wasted too much time apart?"

"And I've had to learn to handle my issues on my own," she retorts. But even as her words push me away, the look on her face pulls me in.

"Ouch," I tell her softly.

She flinches in response. "God, you don't deserve that. This is why I need to—"

"Talk to me, Owl," I urge her.

Capitulating, she nods.

I feel like last night solidified things between us, but in the light of day, was yesterday enough to make her understand I want more than just a moment out of time? Once I've urged her beneath the covers, the feeling of her jean-clad legs against my bare ones distracts me in a way that terrifies me because she almost left without a word.

Pushing a strand of hair back from her face, I open my mouth, but she beats me to it. "Maris called me stubborn; maybe she's right."

I'm stunned. This isn't where I expected our conversation to go at all. The leash I had over my emotions loosen as I tug her body so close, her face is pressed against my bare chest. "Why did she say that?"

"Because it took Jed to bring us here," she whispers, the touch of her lips reminding me not only of last night but of those long lazy days of our youth. But instead of bringing pain, after last night the memory is sweet.

Kara continues. "She said if it weren't for me, maybe my brother would still be alive." Wet hits my chest as Kara's voice breaks. "Maybe she's right. How can you not resent me for so much, Jennings?"

"Kara," I try to interrupt, but she keeps going, giving me a bird's-eye view into the way her mind works through a problem. I can only pray she reaches the right solution when she's done.

"It felt like a betrayal the first time I accepted a date after I had Kevin." My muscles tighten. I want to hear about other men about as much as I want to see her walk out of my life. God knows, I wasn't a damn monk, far from it, but I'm not the same man I was. And Kara? My feelings for her are already so much more intense than they were the first time around. My arms tighten as she continues. "Isn't that stupid? By then I'm sure you'd forgotten about me." Of course, now's the moment she lifts red-rimmed eyes to seek out the truth.

I don't lie, but I do break the truth gently. "I didn't have a living day-to-day reminder of us the way you did, baby. And I swear, I'm not saying that to hurt you, us. To be honest with you—" I settle onto my back and pull her up to rest her head against my shoulder. "—I came across an old picture of you, Jed, and Maris before the funeral. Amid all the grief I was feeling about Jed, I still wondered about your life," I muse.

"Whatever," she scoffs in disbelief.

"Not kidding. He had you both wrapped around your necks. Your hair was so long then. Both you and Maris were trying to punch him in the stomach to let him go. And he was wearing these obnoxious board shorts that—"

"Had pelicans all over them?"

My head dips down to find her hand over her mouth. "How did you know?"

"Because that picture is on a table in my family room, Jennings. It was one of my brother's favorites." Her lips press together as a lone tear falls down her cheek.

I run my hand over her shortened hair. "When did you cut your hair, Owl?"

The tears come faster. "Kevin was ten. Dean convinced me to go out with one of his friends. Why does this matter?"

"What made you do it?" I force myself to ask, though something inside me already knows the answer.

"I couldn't be the woman who looked the same in my memories if I was going to try to move past them," she whispers.

"Smart." I press a kiss on her lips. "Brave." Another one, this one lingering more. "And courageous. You built a life for our son he obviously cherishes. How many people have been in your same situation who have given up?"

"Plenty I'm sure, but I had help," she argues.

"Your heart is reflected in your eyes, Kara. Pure gold. You had options, and you chose the one that would always make you remember."

She traces my chest over my heart before confessing, "He was a part of both of us. To me, there was no other choice, and I've never regretted it once."

"And you say you're not courageous?" Rolling her over to her back, I frame her face in my hands. "When I saw you at the funeral home, my first thought was if I was going to look at anyone's picture and bring them back to life, it should be Jed, not an ex-girlfriend," I confess. "I missed him too much."

Kara doesn't take offense. Smoothing her hands over my shoulder, she nods. "I understand. I made a lot of similar declarations when I heard about their deaths."

"I was wrong."

Her wide eyes blink up at me. "Excuse me?"

"I loved him like a brother, I will always be grateful to him, but I was wrong. There's nothing I would trade that makes up for the time I've had with you and Kevin."

"I just wish they didn't have to die to bring us here." Her voice is tragic.

"Why has no one ever mentioned how they died," I wonder aloud.

Kara shifts in my arms. "It's not a secret, Jennings. It's just—difficult—to talk about."

"Will you tell me?" I ask quietly.

She shakes her head. "I don't want it in your head."

"But it should be in yours alone? Isn't pain shared pain halved?"

Shoving herself away from me, she yells, "What the hell are you now, a shrink on top of being a hotshot pilot, Ace?"

"No, but I—"

"Dated one? I'm sure of it," she lashes out.

I clench my jaw but don't say anything.

"None of you, not a single one of you, understand what it was like to get the knock on the door. The sheriff's office. At first, I thought it was Kevin." I suck in a harsh breath. "Yeah, that's what it means to be a parent, constant worry that someone is going to harm your child," she says desperately.

"Our child," I correct her.

"Whatever." She flicks her hand at me. My eyes narrow, but Kara doesn't retract her statement. She goes on. "They asked me if I was

Kara Malone. When I confirmed I was, they flashed their badges. There were three of them."

"What did they say, Kara?"

"I don't think they knew *what* to say. I kept begging them to tell me it wasn't Kevin. 'Please tell me it's not my son,' but I never called him by name, so they didn't confirm it. Finally, I grabbed my cell. One of them reached out and grabbed my wrist. 'No, Ms. Malone. It's better you hear it from us.'"

I stiffen. "They touched you?"

"That's the last thing to worry about, Jennings. They were trying to prevent me from seeing the million and one texts. They had no idea all I wanted to do was hear Kevin's voice. But then he ran through the door." If I feel a pervasive relief wash over me at her words months later, what must she have felt? "It wasn't him, that's all I could think. It wasn't my baby." I swallow hard as she rasps, "How could I have been so selfish?"

"Once I calmed down, they asked if I was the sister of Dean Malone. I tried to get Kevin to go to his room—he refused. Then they asked if I was also the emergency point of contact for Jed Malone. When I said yes, they told me we needed to hurry. I thought they were both alive. An accident. It wasn't until I was in the back of the officer's vehicle being taken to the hospital with Kevin that I heard the words 'mass pileup.'" Her eyes flicker up to meet my horrified ones. "And that's when Kevin completely lost his mind."

I stroke her hair as haunted amber eyes seek out mine. "The service was exquisite and a nightmare wrapped into one. Everywhere I turned there were colleagues of Jed's and Dean's, families who knew them both, all of whom came to pay their respects. And amidst it all was Kevin, who was so shell-shocked the only two male influences in his life were swept from him in what seemed like a heartbeat."

Beseechingly, she looks up at me. "Do you understand now why I email my dead brother? Do you understand why I can't let him go? Why our son needs to talk to someone? Do you understand why I need time to think?"

"I do, but I also know something else."

"What?" Her voice is shredded.

"Jed asked me to take care of his family," I tell her firmly. Rolling from the bed, I walk over to the dresser and pull the letters out he wrote to me. Walking back over to Kara, uncaring I'm as naked as the day I was born, I hand them to her. "Go ahead, Owl. It's time."

With a trembling hand, she reaches for them. As I'm sliding back into bed, she scooches back against the headboard to brace herself. "READ ME NOW?" Her watery voice laughs. "It's like some of the memos he'd leave his kitchen staff."

"Have I mentioned I despise you worked there?" I mutter as I tug her closer.

"No, why?"

"Because I would give up the world to take care of you," I admit honestly.

Her face softens, but she doesn't respond to my declaration. Instead she pulls out Jed's first letter. "God, I can hear him in my head as we argued that day. I'd give anything to have that time back," she whispers as she folds the letter back and hands it back to me.

I brush a light kiss on her mussed-up hair. "I wouldn't give up you or Kevin," I tell her seriously. She blinks up at me. "Just remember that. Now, read the second one."

Kara holds the larger envelope for a moment, before sliding the letter and the other contents out. "Oh, I remember this picture!" she exclaims.

"Kara, sweetheart, the letter," I remind her.

"Right." A few seconds in, she mutters adorably, "I do not have a temper."

Which just makes me smile.

When she finishes, she flips through the photos until she's clutching the one of them all at Jed and Dean's wedding. "It was such a happy day, and in the back of my mind, it was so wrong," Kara whispers.

I pluck the pictures from her hand and place them on the night-stand with the letter. "Why?"

"Because you all should have been there. And I knew it."

"Then, tell me all about it. Tell me about the men who helped raise my son," I encourage her.

So for the next few hours, in between convincing Kara I need to touch her body all over again, I hear all about the exploits of Jed and Dean Malone. And I laugh and hold her while she cries. And by the time she convinces me she needs to get back, I'm more assured than ever that not only did my son have an amazing life, but my friend did as well.

As did the woman I'm falling for all over again.

## KARA

I use my key to open the lock when I get home late in the afternoon. My body aches as much as my heart after everything that's happened since last night. Dropping my keys on the foyer table, I hop on one foot and then the other to slide off my ankle boots. Then I almost land on my ass when Maris drawls, "Is that how you got them off last night?"

I stumble back and thankfully the door catches me. "Jesus, you scared me."

She leans against the newel post negligently, her luscious curves wrapped in a T-shirt that proudly supports Kevin's swim team and flannel PJ bottoms. I smile faintly as I make my way toward her. "Nice shirt."

"I could say the same since I'm pretty certain you debated what to wear for your non-date for an hour." My cheeks turn the same color as the burgundy sweater as I pass by. Maris lets out a throaty laugh. "Come on, Kara. Did you really think you were going to come back and I wouldn't figure it out?"

"There was a chance of a miracle," I grouse, making my way straight to the coffeepot. Before I reach for a mug, I ask, "Where's Kevin?"

She shakes her head. "He's in the basement engrossed in some online game with Brooks." She waits until I take my first sip to tack on, "He asked where you were when we first got in; I told him you were napping. I told him not to disturb you because I didn't want him to figure out you weren't home from what his father's cock was doing to you. Again."

I spit the burning coffee in every direction. Including, I note with satisfaction, all over Maris's pristine shirt.

And what does she do? Laughs in my face. "So, tell me was it as good as your memories?"

I don't hesitate a second before responding, "No, it was better and more. He wants this to be a beginning. And I don't know what to do!" I shout, every fear of the past and present coalescing.

Immediately, Maris stops taunting me as she ushers me up the stairs. "Kara, we talked about this," she reminds me.

"There's research, and then there's fieldwork!" I shriek. "And John Jennings holding me, letting me cry all over him about Dean, and cuddling is more than I can bear!" I take a glug, not caring if I'm scalding my mouth.

Maybe it will prevent me from wanting to kiss my son's father, I think desperately.

"What's scaring you, Kara?" Maris slides her arm around me.

I open my mouth and the word, "Everything," pops out.

"Well, there's only one person who can help you with that," she reminds me.

I nod, staring down into the dark depths of my cup. "Jennings," I concede.

"No," she contradicts me, surprising me. "You. Jennings has made his play, a fairly spectacular one based on the amount of whisker burn on your skin." She grins cheekily at me as she pushes me into my room.

"Oh, God," I moan, wondering how I'm going to cover that from my impressionable child.

"But if it were me, and I wanted the chance to see where this goes, I'd be putting this guy out of his misery."

"How?" I ask plaintively.

"Sounds like a perfect night for another date—this time with a chaperone. Dad has to understand the rules of what it's like to date Mom, and that 'dating' doesn't mean going from an all-day discussion to an overnight sleepover. Just for the record though, since I love you, I love Kevin, and there's nothing I want more than to see you happy, when you're ready, I'll be happy to continue to expand his knowledge about Alaska by taking him on a few overnight trips." Maris winks, but God, her support means everything.

"After how things ended up the first time around, how can you think this is a good idea?" I ask her, not without some worry at her response.

Maris reaches over and tugs me against her side. "It's simple really. First, you've both grown up and matured, but you both still have this explosive chemistry when you're in a room together."

"I didn't realize that," I mumble against her shoulder.

"That's because you're predisposed to looking for facts when this is pure emotion," she says without rancor.

I accept her comment, because I know it's true. "What's the second?"

"Neither of you would do anything to hurt your son."

"Also very true."

"But I've got one more. And to me, it kind of tips the scales," she admits.

Leaning back, I look into her wild blue eyes to find them blinking rapidly. "Maris?"

"Jed loved both of you down to his soul, Kara. It took me seeing both of you together these last few weeks to put together the puzzle my brother already completed. He was so damn smart." Her voice breaks, and I squeeze her tighter. After swallowing a few times, she manages to whisper, "Jennings, the man I see now? The man my brother knew? Kara, he's different." She turns to face me fully. "Maybe it wouldn't have worked back then, but maybe this is your time."

"How do I *know*?" I place an emphasis on the last word.

She leans forward until our foreheads are touching. "You don't. Not until you try. Don't you teach this to your students?"

"I don't teach this," I moan.

"No, but you teach trial and error. Do you give up on your theory?"

"Hypothesis, and no. Not until all options are exhausted." And like that, it clicks inside me. I've been judging Jennings by the results of us from before, not us now. I squeeze Maris. "I think I finally get it."

"Good. Now send your text and go shower before your son comes up. You're making me all hot and bothered, and there's no one I want to jump other than my battery-operated blue friend."

I'm clutching my dresser to hold myself up from the laughter as Maris saunters out of the room chanting, "Buzz, buzz."

But, I still manage to reach in my pocket for my phone to text Jennings.

THE MINUTE KEVIN and I walk into PINZ later that night to meet Jennings, my nerves kick in. Jennings waves a hand to indicate where he's already reserved a lane. And every step we take closer toward him shows me the wicked smile on his face isn't about the game we're about to play, but the one we already started.

I shouldn't have worried. The second we're in earshot, Kevin bombards Jennings with the three most critical items necessary for a successful bowling experience. "Can I get soda, candy, and chips?"

"I, uh..." Frantically Jennings's cool facade drops, and he's back on the hot seat of parenthood once again. "Whatever your mom says, Kevin. We're going to grab some dinner after this. I wasn't sure if you wanted—"

"Can we get Subway again? Can we, Mom? Please? I'm seriously craving their Ultimate after being up half the night with Maris."

I shrug. "Works for me. What does your father think?"

Jennings appears gobsmacked that he's about to endure some of America's notorious fast food as part of a "date with his family," which is how I phrased it in my text to him earlier. But he recovers quickly, I'll give him that. "Whatever you want," he starts.

Kevin goes to pump a fist in the air.

"Within reason," Jennings concludes.

Kevin's face falls. "Now you sound like Mom. Are you sure you two aren't colluding against me?"

"Yes, because your father and I spend all our spare time talking about ways to torture you. Now, why don't you get your shoes while I chat with your father a bit," I remark drolly.

"Kevin, there's a card on file already for the lane."

"Got it!" We both watch as our son sprints off. I can smell the scent of Jennings's cologne as he comes closer. "So, would it be completely inappropriate for me to kiss you right now?" he asks casually.

"Yes!" I screech, drawing the attention of the bowlers in nearby lanes.

"I thought it might be. Would a hug be out of line?"

I open my mouth to protest because I don't know how Kevin will react, but Jennings slides an arm around my waist and tugs me toward him gently. My hands end up on his shoulders when my face hits his chest. "Iwasgoingtosaywait." My words come out all mushed against the flannel he's wearing.

Jennings just barks out a laugh. "Relax, Kara."

I manage to pull my face away enough to glare up at him. "Relax? I was relaxed."

He flicks a finger down my nose. "No, you're worried. I just haven't figured out if that's because your plot to keep this on a friendly basis isn't going to work out quite the way you were thinking or because I'm willing to respect that boundary." His brow raises before he tacks on, "To a point."

I sputter, "You are so damn full of yourself. Is this something they teach you as a pilot?"

He shrugs, as if Arrogance 101 is actually a course. "What they actually taught me was not to panic or something bad could happen."

"What else did they teach you, Jennings?" Kevin's voice pipes up behind me.

I groan out loud. "Just kill me now. Please?"

Jennings chuckles but doesn't say anything. His eyes aren't on me but over my shoulder. He also doesn't let me go. Instead, he spins me around until we face our son.

Kevin's eyes dart back and forth between us. "Are the two of you trying to tell me something?" His bowling shoes clatter to the floor.

I try to pull away from Jennings, but he holds me firm. "Damnit, Jennings, let me—"

"Kevin, you're the man of the house. I'd like to state my intentions," Jennings says, his voice unusually serious.

Before my eyes, I watch as Jennings's mini-me squares his shoulders and takes his father head-on. Part of me is so proud, and the other part of me wants to pull him back into the little boy who would come running to me for a skinned knee. "And they are?" he asks suspiciously.

"I care for your mother a great deal. I'd like to start dating her. That would mean spending time with her in addition to the time I spend with you. Hopefully, in the future when you and I get to know one another better, we will have the same opportunity to spend quality one-on-one time together too." Jennings no-nonsense talk startles Kevin at first, but then I watch my son's face settle.

"I appreciate you approaching me with your honesty. Above all, that's the most important thing Mom's taught me about relationships: honesty first."

"That's a good rule to abide by, son." Jennings's arms tighten briefly before they loosen. "Do you have any concerns you want to ask us about?" Jennings holds his breath. I feel him inhale at my back.

Kevin frowns thoughtfully. "I'd like to know if Mom is happy because right now she looks terrified."

"Apt," I mutter to myself. To my son, I say, "I don't know where this is going to go, Kevin. To me, the most important thing has been and always will be you. If you don't think this is a good idea or if you have concerns, then this goes no further."

Kevin's face crumbles. Jennings's arms open just as I'm about to demand he lets me go. I rush forward and grab a hold of Kevin. Wrapping my arms around him, I whisper, "You're worth everything to me, baby. First, last, and always."

"I know. That's why I want you to reach for your happy. It's what Uncle Dean and Uncle Jed would want you to do." His words are like a fist to my solar plexus.

"When did you become so wise?" I whisper as I pull back to push a lock of hair off his forehead.

"Let's see—somewhere between begging for a soda and getting my shoes? That's when I saw Jennings make his play." I'm now gaping. Kevin leans around me to hold out a hand to his father. "Slick move, by the way."

Jennings is stunned only for a second. Then he gets another bonus point from me when he says to my son, "You are way too young to be thinking about girls like that," he declares.

Kevin scoffs. "You two weren't much older before you had me."

"That's how we know!" Jennings and I both yell at the same time. I spin around to face him and find him frozen in shock. I grin. "Welcome to parenting, Jennings. I've had years to ease into the dating stage."

He glares at me before he passes by me to offer his hand to Kevin. "I promise, I'll do my best to cherish her." His eyes find mine, and the look in them warms me from the inside out.

Kevin shakes it and returns with, "Good. Otherwise I suspect there's going to be a ghost sighting in Alaska. Now, while Mom's getting her shoes, can I please get a Coke? A man can only handle so much drama without his daily allotment of caffeine."

"Oh, for God's sake. Go!" I banish him to the snack bar. Suddenly all boy, he races off, almost taking a header the moment his bowling shoes hit the carpet.

My shoulders shaking, I feel Jennings's arm wrap around my shoulders. "Thank you," I tell him sincerely.

"All I did was treat him the same way I wanted to be treated at his age—with respect."

Leaning up, I brush a kiss on the underside of his jaw. "Well, you did that. Now, Dad, are you ready to have your ass whipped?"

His brows wing up. "Are you thinking you can take me, Ms. Malone?"

I shrug. I learned a long time ago that for me, bowling is simply another scientific equation to be figured out. "I'm thinking you're about to find out."

Just as I'm about to walk away to get my shoes and find a ball, Jennings reaches out and grabs my elbow. "Side bet between you and me." His breath is hot against my ear.

"Deal," I answer immediately.

"Whoever wins gets to pick our next date." He nips my ear. "And that's a date without the amazing chaperone we created."

Just as I'm about to agree, Kevin comes back with a soda that will keep him up for days. I sigh and am about to admonish him when he speaks first. "Look, number one rule of this thing." He flicks his finger back and forth between us. "Check the PDA. My tender eyes can only handle so much," he announces haughtily, before he takes a slug of his drink. When he's done, he slams it down to emphasize his point. And belches.

It's then all three of us burst out laughing.

In the end I end up kicking Jennings's ass at bowling. I gloat all the way to Subway.

And the next day when the three of us hike around Mendenhall, I put all of my studying to good use when I educate both my son and his father all about the glacier. Later, they tease me that I sounded the most knowledgeable about where the bathroom was.

I ignored them as I stomped back to the car to the male laughter following me.

God, they're so alike.

I can't say I don't love it.

## KARA

"He's so different," I muse.

Maris is leaning against the picnic table next to me as we observe Jennings, Brad, and Kevin teach Frisbee to Brad and Meadow's kids.

Rainey comes up with Meadow and demands, "What did we miss?"

I laugh, because this reminds me of the good memories of my time here—of girlfriends and laughter. Things I never really had until I lived here because I never had anyone who cared enough about me to pull me from my books until Maris. "We were just admiring the view," I say blandly.

"Impressive, isn't it?" Maris remarks.

I shrug nonchalantly before giving up all pretense. "Why is it men get better-looking as they age?" I demand.

Maris snickers as Meadow chokes on the sip of beer she just swallowed. Rainey grins. "It's supremely annoying, isn't it? I mean, here we're the ones who push out their kids, and they're the ones who...Oh, God." Her eyes widen.

"What?" I demand. Turning in the direction of Rainey's gaze, I go stock-still.

"Sweet baby Jesus," Meadow wheezes out.

"Need help finding your voice?" Maris taunts me.

But I can't speak. Jennings has pulled his shirt off and is using it to wipe the sweat from his face. He's laughing openly at something Brad yelled which I can't hear. I doubt I'd be able to understand the words anyway, my every thought is so scrambled.

"You all right, Kara?" Rainey asks, concerned.

Just then, Kevin runs over to his father and tackles him, causing the Frisbee Brad flung carelessly in his direction to go sailing overhead. Jennings shouts, "Oh, so that's how you want to play it, son?"

"Bring it on, old man!" Kevin laughs. Rolling over, he reaches down for his father's hand to help him stand.

Jennings grabs him in a headlock and rubs his head with his knuckles until Kevin's laughter rings out with his surrender. "I give! I give!" Spotting me, he cries out, "Mom, come save me!"

I may be rooted to the spot, but I force my lips to work. "You got yourself into this predicament, sweetheart. Only one way out that I can see."

"How's that?" Kevin calls plaintively.

"By admitting age, treachery, and deceit will always overcome youth, skill, and ability," Jennings declares as he loosens his hold. Keeping an arm hooked over Kevin's shoulder, he tosses a wink at me over his shoulder before leading Kevin back toward the other kids.

I'm still motionless as the other women come up to huddle next to me. "Are you all right?" Maris semi-repeats Rainey's question.

Turning away from the sight of everything I've ever wanted, I shake my head even as I admit, "I don't think I'm going to be the same ever again."

Even as the perpetually strained expression lifts from Meadow's face, Rainey squeals in delight, and Maris tips her head back toward the cerulean blue sky, lips moving. Her expression is pained and so beautiful it makes my heart hurt in that same way when we're talking of our brothers. So, I gently prod, "What are you saying?"

But before she answers, she hauls me next into her arms for a powerful hug. "I'm thanking Jed for giving you this—the thing you've been missing for sixteen years."

"What's that?" I ask, confused because despite what I feel growing for Jennings, I wouldn't say my life's been lacking. Quite the contrary, I've had Kevin. I've been the one who's been blessed.

"You have a chance at a once-in-a-lifetime love that…" Maris starts before I interrupt.

"Technically, it would be twice," I correct her, much to Rainey and Meadow's amusement.

She rolls her eyes before gripping my shoulders. "Fine, Ms. Technicality, twice-in-a-lifetime love. Most people don't have the ability for the first; don't waste this gift on old fears, Kara."

"I agree," Meadow jumps in. "We've been hoping this would happen." I jerk my head in her direction, but not before hers ducks. There's something off with her, but Rainey just shakes her head. Mentally, I shrug. Maybe in time.

But that just reminds me of what I don't have. Time.

"I'm terrified," I admit to my friends. And I jerk against Maris when I realize, despite the years, Jed gave me this back too—a sisterhood of women who understand the call this wild land has on your soul. And the grip of the men whose hearts match it. Both are so compelling, it's impossible to separate one from the other, I think with a bit of sadness as I explain.

"Where can this go? We'll be going across the country from each other again at the end of the summer. I have a job; Kevin has school." And the weight of that wants to crush every moment of joy I feel with Jennings because it's what happened all those years ago being played out all over again. This time, though, I'm the one holding back and being practical in the face of love.

"You're not dead," Maris snaps. "He's alive and so are you. The rest are just excuses."

I gasp at the harshness of her words.

"While how Maris said it is brutal—" Rainey glares at her, but her voice softens. "—she's not wrong, Kara. You've both been existing— why not live?"

"Because living eventually leads to dying." The words are torn from me. Everyone around me freezes. "If I don't give in to this, if I don't love him, I don't have to worry about when it's going to…"

"Wind up in a twenty-two-car pileup? Even if that's only in your heart?" Maris wraps her arms around me immediately. "God, honey. I'm so sorry. I've been so selfish grieving, I just assumed you were too."

"I am. Jennings is helping." Knowing faces beam at me from different directions. They're all wearing different smiles from sweet to outright smirks when I clarify, "He's listened to me and Kevin talk about Dean and Jed; it's been good for all of us."

"And here I thought she was going to mention the fact the sleep-overs I was so generous to offer with Kevin were helping." Maris's lips twitch.

I punch her as Rainey and Meadow laugh. Then, why not? "No, that's not hurting by any stretch of the imagination, but honest to God?" They all nod, and I let out a sigh. "How am I going to deal with leaving a second time with his son?"

Rainey steps forward and puts her hand over my heart. "Can I offer you some advice?" Without waiting for a response, she goes on. "Let this guide you instead of your head. If you do, it will lead you wherever you're supposed to be. And that's especially true with Jennings."

I nod, too overwhelmed to speak.

But someone else isn't.

"Listen! If the cheering squad is going to put on a show like that, this match is going to end sooner rather than later!" Brad yells across the yard right before he flings the Frisbee into Jennings's chest.

Jennings doesn't bother to catch it. It plunks heedlessly to the ground because he's stalking toward me, a predatory look on his face.

*Listen to my heart,* Rainey said. Without thinking, I take off in his direction at a jog. He picks up his pace until soon we meet in the middle where he circles my waist with his arms and swings me around in a circle. I laugh, heedless of the cheers from the girls which are undoubtedly louder for this display than any the guys did while playing.

"Jennings? What are you doing? Get back here!" Brad yells as all of the kids swarm him from all directions chanting, "Forfeit! Forfeit!"

"Give it up!" Jennings yells back. For my ears only, he murmurs, "I've already got the things I need to make me feel like a man."

Reaching up, I quickly brush my lips against Jennings when I hear Kevin yell, "God, how do you deal with your parents kissing? I've lived fifteen years without being subject to this. Gross."

"Well, if we're going to be persecuted." Jennings's words come out as a statement, but they're really a question.

One I answer by rising up on my toes and tugging his mouth down to mine.

I feel like heaven is close. This kiss is perfect in every way imaginable.

The cool Alaskan air.

Jennings's beard leaving marks against my skin as he deepens the kiss.

Our son standing twenty feet away acting like nothing out of the ordinary is happening.

Hoots and hollers all around us. And the loudest coming from inside my heart as I know the brother of my blood and of Jennings's soul are applauding the loudest.

When we break apart, Jennings is breathing hard. "What brought this on?"

And I tell him simply, "I felt like flying with the only man I'll ever trust to take me," before I let him go and walk back to my girls knowing his eyes are on me the whole way.

When I reach them, I turn to find him still standing there, a crooked smile on his face.

# JENNINGS

"I don't know how you can eat that." Kevin points to my overflowing plate of chicken-fried steak and eggs.

"What's wrong with what I'm having?" I demand as I fork up another bite. There are few things I miss about living on a farm, but the food my aunt used to make is one of them.

"Nothing," my son reassures me. "I mean, I really don't know where you're going to put it all." He lifts his much more manageable English muffin sandwich to his mouth and takes a large bite.

We both grin at each other with mouths filled with food.

Kara continued to sit at the counter when Kevin announced it was "Man time, Mom. You really don't want to join us." Instead I think I'm the one who crapped in his pants a little.

My first time out with my son. What if I just wasn't as cool without his beloved mom around? Kara must have seen the look of terror on my face because she reassured me, "Just call me if there are any problems. I'll have my cell phone on."

As we pulled away from the Smiths', I caught sight of Kara in the rearview mirror on the front deck waving. It settled my stomach more than anything else could, the knowledge she trusts me completely with our son.

Pulling up at a stop sign, I took my eyes off the road. Kevin was rubbing his wrist the same way I'd seen Kara do a million times—a clear tell there's something he's anxious about. So, casually I asked, "What's up, son? Something the matter?"

"I'm not sure. I just got a funny feeling about leaving Mom at home."

Not moving the car, I asked him, "But you don't feel that way when it's me and your mom out?"

He snorted. "No. I see enough of you two kissing, I think I'll be traumatized if I see any more."

"Then, why don't you text her so she knows we're thinking about her?" I laid my hand across his hand, the way I've done with Kara. His head twisted until our faces were even. There was worry, but something substantially more vulnerable, behind his green eyes. "This way she can be completely jealous we're eating at Donna's."

His brows lowered. "Who's Donna?"

"Not a 'who' but a 'what.' It's a diner not too far from here. They make a great breakfast."

We're currently squished in a little two-top to one side of the bar with my back to the door. Kara's amusing response to our text made Kevin laugh, which is what I was hoping it would do. *I appreciate you letting me know, sweetheart, because now I want a sausage, egg, and cheese muffin. That means moving from the couch.* The emoji with the tongue sticking out emphasized her opinion of us for sending it.

This time with Kevin makes me feel like a superhero, which may be why I ordered like I could eat like one. So, I only groan when Kevin asks, "So, what's our plans for today? What's for lunch?"

"Seriously? You expect me to eat again after this?" I point down to the half a plate of food I've yet to consume.

And I'm delighted when Kevin leans over with his fork and steals a bite of the chicken-fried steak from my plate. "Umm, definitely better than eating at the Crack."

I had just taken a drink of coffee and sputter it back into my cup. "What the hell is the Crack?"

Kevin grins and *wham!* His—my—dimple pops out on the side. His voice is teasing when he says, "You can't tell me you've never eaten at a Cracker Barrel. That's just wrong. They're like *everywhere*," he emphasizes dramatically, before he yoinks another bite of my food.

I burst out laughing. "The Crack," I murmur appreciatively. "Where did you get your sense of humor from, Kevin?"

He chews, takes a drink of soda, and then says, "I don't know. Uncle Dean and Jed for sure. They were both funny. My friends are great too—Brooks especially."

"What about your mom?"

"Yeah, but not as much as the others. Mom's a *mom*, Jennings. I mean, she's the one who tells me to do homework, cooks, does laundry, cleans—"

"And you don't help with any of that?" God, by the time I was his age, I was out in the fields every morning helping feed the stock by 5:00 a.m. before I headed to class.

"Well, sure. But she wants me to focus on school, sports, and friends. She used to say I had plenty of time to grow up. Now, she doesn't say it as much anymore."

He puts his sandwich down and leans his forearms on the table. It's a Jed posture to the extreme, and I'm so glad Kara hasn't corrected it out of him when he asks, "There's actually a reason I wanted to talk to you alone today."

I feel the chicken-fried steak churn in my stomach. But calmly, I place the fork and knife to the side of my plate. "Okay. What's up?"

He swallows hard before opening his mouth. His hand tentatively reaches for mine. I reach across the table and grab his. "Jennings, do you know..."

We're interrupted by Meadow, who happens to be our waitress. "Is there anything else I can get for you guys? Kevin, I know there's some freshly baked..."

"Not right now," I bite out. Kevin's arm slides away from mine. I can literally feel the loss as if the weight of his arm were physically being ripped from my skin. "That all. Thanks, Meadow," I curtly dismiss our friend.

She nods and moves away. Turning my attention back to Kevin, his face is stark white. I reach back across the table, unashamed. "Kevin? What is it? What's wrong?"

"This is impossible to talk about. It was a stupid idea." He tries to brush it off.

"Nothing this important is stupid," I say quietly, not letting go.

Kevin struggles in front of me before finally blurting out, "Winnie the Pooh." Then he bites his lip so hard, I'm afraid he's going to break the skin.

"What about Winnie the Pooh, son?" I prod him.

"There's a quote from Winnie the Pooh that someone gave to me after Uncle Dean died. It's 'If there ever comes a day when we can't be together, keep me in your heart. I'll stay there forever.'" He struggles with his words, and I just wait patiently while he sorts them out in his head. "Uncle Dean was my dad," he declares stoutly.

And as much as that statement causes a hurt deep inside that will never close up, I nod because I know it's the truth.

"Am I letting him go, because I want to call you 'Dad' now?" And right in front of my eyes, the man slips away and I see the little boy who Dean Malone got to raise. I'm being given this terrible burden of childhood vulnerability because another man my son loved with his whole heart died in order to receive it.

What the hell do I say?

"Kevin," I start out slowly, carefully choosing each word. "You're not letting Dean go." I can't call him "Uncle" in this situation. To do so is a disservice to the role Dean played in my son's life. "No matter where you go, he will be right there with you. Always," I emphasize.

"Then how do I make room to love you too?"

"I...don't know, son. I don't know the answer to that." I decide to take a page out of Kara's book and not lie to him.

"I didn't realize how much it was going to hurt, Dad—letting Uncle Dean go and letting you in." My teeth clench with the need to cry over hearing my son say those words to me.

"Why?" I rasp. "Can you tell me that?"

He nods. When he lets go of my hand to reach for a napkin, I feel the loss like someone actually cut off a limb. Then my heart beats faster after he blows his nose and grabs my hand again, the tissue clutched between our clasped hands. With a voice that's completely unstable, I laugh when I tease him gently, "You're such a guy." When he frowns, I nod to our hands.

Sheepishly, he loosens his grip and the tissue drops to the table. "Oops. Let's not tell Mom that one."

"That'll remain a secret between us," I assure him. Meanwhile my heart is careening out of control. My first secret with my son and it's a snot-filled tissue. I want to shove it in my pocket and bronze it. "I love you, Kevin. I hope to God you know that." The words rush out of me.

He nods. "I know." My heart falls when he doesn't say it back. "I couldn't fathom loving someone back the same way. I was terrified after losing Uncle Dean. Then, I wasn't sure how I felt about you, about all of this. But you came along and you were, well. You."

God, he's going to break me before the end of this, I just know it. "What does that mean?"

"You're mine, Dad. No matter where I am, no matter where you are, you're always going to be there, just like Uncle Dean was, right?" His voice warbles. We sit there for a moment, father and son, not saying a word but bonding in a way that's as deep as if I had held him from moment he came into this world.

Because in a sense, maybe we both were just reborn.

"You're damn right I will be." Shoving to my feet, I pull him out of his chair and wrap him in a hug. "I love you, son," I repeat into his hair.

"I..." There's a hesitation. My heart beats fast knowing the internal struggle that's happening inside. I just squeeze him tighter. He relaxes in my hold before sighing out the rest. "Love you too, Dad."

I don't know how long we stand there locked in our embrace before I say gruffly, "What do you say we get out of here?"

Clearing his throat, Kevin ducks his head. "That sounds good."

I reach into my back pocket, pull out my wallet, fish out a couple of twenties, and toss them on the table to cover our bill plus Meadow's tip. Then, pulling out the keys, I hook an arm around my son's shoulders. "Let's figure out what we're doing for the rest of the day, kid."

Just as we reach the entrance, Kevin asks me, "Would—do you think it'd be a problem if we went to visit Uncle Jed and Uncle Dean?"

After stepping outside, I feel the warmth of the summer sky beat down on us. "You know what, son? I think that's a great place to start."

"I've got a lot I want to tell them," he tells me as we make our way to the car."

*So do I*, but I don't share that. I just blip the remote control to unlock the car. But over the hood, I exchange a smile with my son.

My son who just called me Dad for the first time.

"Maybe we'll pick up something on the way home so your mother doesn't have to cook tonight," I decide as I slide into the driver's seat.

Kevin gets in next to me. "That's a good idea, Dad. She deserves a night off."

She deserves the world, but I don't share that either. Instead, I start the car and drive off toward downtown Juneau.

HOURS LATER, I pull into the Smiths'. The minute I do, Kara bursts from the front door as if she's been waiting for us.

Kevin leaps from the barely stopped vehicle. "Hey, Mom! We hope you didn't cook."

"I got your texts. I take it you had a good day?" She slips an arm around his waist, but she shoots a quizzical glance at me as I alight from the vehicle.

"I had a great day," Kevin confirms. He plunks a kiss on her head. "Hey, Dad? Pop the trunk and I'll grab the bags." Kara's eyes widen when she hears Kevin call me the "D" word, but she doesn't say anything.

I hit the button on the remote. "Thanks, son."

"No problem. Mom, I want to call Dr. Alafagonis, okay?" Kevin's already walking toward the front door at a fast clip.

"Sure, sweetheart," she calls faintly. There's only a few feet separating us, but I'm worried it could be insurmountable. That is until the door slams and she's practically leaping into my arms, staggering me back a foot.

"I don't want to know a single thing about what happened today," she declares.

"Wh-what?" And here I thought I'd have to answer a million questions.

"I know everything I need to, Jennings." She pulls back. I growl, which makes her laugh. Lifting her fingers, Kara ticks off her observations. "My son came home with a smile on his face and no pain in his eyes for the first time in months. He's voluntarily calling his therapist. And he called you Dad." She drops her hand to slam against me again. "Whatever you did, keep doing it...Dad."

Racing out of my arms, she hurries after Kevin, yelling, "What did you guys buy for dinner? It'd better not be crap cheeseburgers."

I'm frozen in place as the entire day flashes in front of me. Kevin and I visited Jed and Dean. Then we walked along the water and saw the cruise ships up close. We talked about my time in Ketchikan and growing up on a farm, how much he liked living in Florida. Despite her worries, it turns out my son can't wait for swim season to start. I open my mouth to tell Kara all of that, but she's already inside. Since the windows are open, I can hear her laughter through them.

It's a gift. They both are.

And I'm going to be forever grateful I was loved enough by a lost brother that he fought to rearrange my life for me so I recognized it.

Shaking myself out of my stupor, I yell through the window, "We didn't get you a cheeseburger."

"What did you get me?" Kara calls.

"Your son wanted Subway. Again," I bemoan as I climb the front stoop.

When I open the door, mother and son are both grinning at me. "Why is he my son when he wants Subway?" Kara demands.

"Because I wanted to go to Rainbow Foods and get his mother more brie and prosciutto?" I stroll right up to her and plant a kiss on her lips.

Kevin makes a gagging sound the moment our lips touch. It's a perfect moment I'll treasure for the rest of my life.

Pulling away a few seconds later, Kara regains her composure enough to declare, "You can blame Dean for that. He's the one who treated him to fast food when he was a toddler."

I throw my head back and laugh as I say aloud, "Thanks, Dean. Appreciate it."

And I don't just mean my son's food preference.

# KARA

After Jennings left that night, I pulled out my laptop. I've been so busy living, emailing my brother has completely slipped my mind. Is that a good thing or a bad thing, I wonder as I pull up the email application.

But after today, I need to. There's some very important things he needs to understand as Kevin, Jennings, and I figure out a new future.

And it's that, no matter what, Kevin and I will never forget the past.

Without hesitation, I write.

*Dear Dean.*

*I'm not as haunted as I was when I first boarded the plane for Alaska, but I'm sure you know that wherever you are. Jennings and I have reconnected in a way I'm sure Jed would be saying "I told you so" to, so if you could try to keep his gloating to a minimum, it would be appreciated.*

*Right after you give him a big sloppy kiss from me.*

*At first, it was difficult. You know more than anyone how broken I was as a result of our parents actions. I was devastated when they disowned you, but then when they did the same to me, to my unborn child? I was never the same.*

*Even before that, let's be honest, you were always so much more outgoing than I was. But to open myself up to people after that kind of a betrayal took a near Herculean effort. I'm not going to lie, it was easier to cocoon myself, to remain in stasis. And keeping Jennings on the periphery was a part of that, I guess. But the minute I saw him again, that all began to change. I think you got the idea from my other letters. The more and more I saw him with Kevin, and the more I began to understand the man he is, the wrapping I've held around me has slowly begun to fall away.*

*I'm falling in love with him.*

*I'd be lying if I didn't admit I wasn't terrified because I am. Not just for me, but for Kevin. Today, he had a major breakthrough; he called Jennings 'Dad.' God, I'm sorry. I don't mean to take away from everything you and Jed gave him because you were the best dads a kid could ask for.*

*Did I tell you that often enough? I know I told you I love you. I just hope I told you it enough.*

*So, my fear is awaiting the unknown. Then again, don't we all fear that in some way? Kevin did, and he still took that chance with his father. Maybe I should learn from his experience and let the future take care of itself as it pertains to Jennings.*

*I wish you had a way of answering me back. I'd love to hear you one more time. You stood by me the way no one else ever has. And I miss you with every cell in my body.*

*Kara.*

Pressing Send, I close out of the application and shut down my computer. Just then a text comes in.

*How about a hike with Kevin up Mount Roberts tomorrow? Then we can grab some crab after?* It's Jennings.

My lips curve. *That sounds perfect. I'll ping you after I've prodded the teenage beast.*

A few dots, then: *Sleep well, little Owl.*

*You too, Ace. See you tomorrow.*

And clutching my phone, I whisper, "I look forward to it," before I make my way out of the kitchen, shutting off lights along the way.

# KARA

After that day, things irrevocably changed between all of us. Jennings wasn't simply becoming a part of our lives, he was in them. And all of us shined brighter than the Northern Lights as a result.

With every moment, we began to heal our hearts and our pasts with new memories. Jennings made certain to open up to Kevin about his childhood, creating a bond between father and son that I think healed any remaining uncertainty in Kevin about what he should feel about his newfound parent.

As we're flying to Skagway for a day trip, Kevin brings up my favorite topic: Jennings's days as a Lumberjack. "So, Dad, now that I've seen the show, tell the truth. Was your only job really to attract the tourists by looking good?"

Jennings sputters into his microphone. "Jesus, Kara. What kind of nonsense have you been filling our son's head with?"

"Why, I told him about your impressive log-rolling capability," I say sweetly. Jennings cuts me off with a groan.

"Son, no matter what your mom or Maris says, it was a lot harder than it looked."

Kevin does his best to hide his snicker. "Uh-huh. Did they trust you with the power saw?"

Jennings shoots me a baleful glance. "No, they let Kody and Nick play with those."

"Let me tell you the real story behind the Lumberjacks," I say with relish. Seconds after, I'm squirming in my seat shrieking, "Ten and two, Jennings!"

"Your opinion on what my 'duties' were as a Lumberjack are skewed at best, Owl," he jokes even as he ruffles my hair.

I harrumph, but at least he's not tickling me.

"Why do you call Mom, Owl, Dad?" Kevin asks suddenly.

Jennings stills, before his hand slides over my hair. "That's because she used to be so focused on what she was doing or the people she was talking with, she'd have the stillness of an owl before it took flight. That and owls notoriously are a symbol of wisdom. And as we've talked about, your mom was, and is, the smartest person I know."

"Except Jed. I think he was smarter than all of us," I murmur, leaning into Jennings's hand.

"He was wise," Jennings agrees. "But I'd still put you ahead."

"With Uncle Jed a close second," Kevin pipes up.

Jennings reaches back and slaps his hand against Kevin's. "Exactly that. But back to the topic at hand, one thing your mother is not an expert on is the Lumberjack Show." Jennings's voice carries a note of haughtiness.

I cover my microphone to muffle my laughter. "Right. As if spending the summer in intensive study of all of you wouldn't make me an expert," I retort.

"Who were you studying other than me?" Jennings demands.

I shrug. "Listen, Brad was completely Rainey's, but still, he was Team USA. So was Kody, for that matter." Faking a yawn, I add, "It's hard to root for a rival country."

Suddenly the plane hits a little turbulence. I sit up straight. "What was that?" I screech.

"Just demonstrating to our son some of the talents of Team Canada," Jennings says.

I open and close my mouth several times before I decide to up the ante. Twisting in my seat, I singsong, "Maris has video at the house."

"Crap," Jennings mutters as Kevin hoots and hollers.

"Now which parent do you think he's going to believe? What have I always told you, sweetheart?" I address our son.

"Don't make any claims you can't back up with fact," he parrots dutifully. Then excitement gets to him. "Can we watch it when we get home?"

"We may camp out in Skagway. Permanently," Jennings mutters, as he breaks away from our conversation to speak with the tower. Soon, we're banking to approach.

I turn around but lay a hand on his thigh. Taking his focus away for just a moment, he sends me a smile I'll never forget. It's a smile that sears itself onto my heart.

And I know it's not the landing on the short runway that has my heart pounding inside my chest. It's knowing I am too, despite whatever obstacles we have to work through this time to keep us together.

SOMETIMES, a place exists in the world where you feel you could stay forever and you'd never want for anything. Walking hand in hand with Jennings, with Kevin laughing next to us, I realize that place is Skagway, Alaska. Nestled at the base of steep canyon walls, there's still an excitement that remains within the remnants of this former gold rush town.

Perfectly preserved, I feel like Skagway gives me the hope for the impossible as we wander through the streets up and down the main tourist area. Old and new are woven together seamlessly, preserving the best of the past while moving the tiny town into the future to ensure its existence. Skagway illustrates my fears about Jennings in more ways than one—flooded with love during the summer before the fear of winter months settles in.

Even as I pray with all of my might, Jennings squeezes my hand. I look over and find him intently watching me. "Where did you go?" he asks me quietly.

"Not far," I tell him honestly. The last place I want to be is far from his side.

Checking over his shoulder to see Kevin is engrossed with reading, he faces me. "Stop worrying. We're together. Feel this?" He captures my hand and presses it against the thermal he's wearing against the cooler weather. "Irrevocably, it's changed. That's because of the two of you."

Leaving my hand there, I voice my biggest worry out loud. "How do I survive if you have regrets—"

"Stop." His voice lashes at me in anger.

Dragging my hand down his chest, I whisper, "It wouldn't be the first time." The wind is whipping around us, so I'm certain he can't hear.

I start to pull away, but his arms tighten. "How do I get you to see I'm not the other people who have let you down?"

But I don't get a chance to answer when Kevin comes running up to us. "Mom, Dad! Did you know people used to come through here as part of the gold rush?"

I move out of Jennings arms, not answering him. Turning to our son, I listen to everything he has to tell me about the almost forgotten town that resonates so deeply with me.

After a few minutes, Jennings joins us. "Did you both realize that's not a train? It's a snow plow?" He points to the old steam engine with a cone on the front. His voice is calm as if we hadn't just had words, and I let out a sigh of relief.

"Cool! I'm going to check it out." Kevin dashes off.

I shake my head over his exuberance. "If only half of my students were as enthusiastic as him," I laugh.

"He must get it naturally from his parents," Jennings says smoothly, right before he yanks me toward him.

Eyes smoldering, he lowers his head, pressing his cold lips to mine. His hand shifts to the back of my neck, tipping it back. My mouth opens on a gasp. Then his tongue slips inside for a taste, sweeping through slow and sweet. My mind wants to fight, telling me he's just staking his claim, but my heart? Oh, my heart knows better.

Jennings is telling me I'm his and he's mine and he doesn't plan on letting go now or later.

Breaking our kiss, he lifts his head and then declares, "I'm not going to disappear, Owl. Not if you hold on to me. And if it's within my power, I'll give everything to you." Letting me go, he calls out to Kevin that we should get moving if they want to see the next item recommended by the guide.

I open my mouth and close it several times because I have no comeback. All I can do is follow them down Broadway to the next stop on the map.

JUST BEFORE LUNCH, we wander into a small antiques store. Jennings and Kevin get absorbed by the totems and swords on display. While they're entertained, I wander over to a basket full of smooth jade stones. Quickly reading the dark green stones are the Alaskan state gem and intrigued by the alternative healing powers it claims to supply, I pluck out a few, deciding to bring them back to the girls. "If nothing else, they'll think I've lost my sanity believing holistic medicine over science," I murmur, clenching my fist. But as I turn, my eye catches on something in the case. My heart pounds in my chest as I approach the shiny trinket.

"No," I whisper. "It can't be."

But when I approach, I'm swamped by disappointment realizing it's not my grandmother's bracelet with the pear-shaped sapphire stones in the display case but one where the stones are round. I know in my heart, it's lost to me—like Dean is. If I'd been alone, I'd be emotionally devastated coming to that conclusion. Instead, I squeeze the jades with all my might as Jennings pulls a bear hat on over his head just as Kevin slips a fox cap over his, and I feel a sense of calm wash over me.

To have these two men in my life was worth any price.

Swiping up my stones, I make my way over to the register. When the cashier smiles at me, I ask, "So, tell me the best place you recommend for lunch that can accommodate a teenager and two adults?"

"You have to go to the Skagway Brewing Company. Do you like salmon?"

I nod. "Love it."

"Then make sure you get their Sesame Salmon salad. I've been all over the world and I still can't get it to taste quite like that." Ringing up my purchase, the older woman says, "That will be $22.50."

Handing over my card, I quickly sign the bill before gathering my guys for the next part of our adventure.

"GOD, Mom, tell me Uncle Dean saw this." Kevin's roaring with laughter over Jed directing his friends about the small stage area in Ketchikan in a half-done-up pair of overalls. Kevin pauses the video on a close-up showing Jed's normally wild hair even more outrageous and his smile as wide as the Alaskan sky.

"He did," Maris confirms. "It was my duty as his sister-in-law to show it to him."

"I mean, it was one thing to see the show live, but to see Dad and Uncle Jed in it? That takes it to a whole new level." Kevin's voice is wondrous.

Jennings has a smug smile on his face that quickly evaporates when Kevin asks, "So, I know you said you wore protective gear, but we're all family, Dad. Tell the truth: how many times did you actually incapacitate yourself on the log?"

I fall out of my chair howling. Maris isn't much better, shrieking, "Channel your pain, Kara!" which just sets me off more.

"It wasn't that funny," Jennings grunts, shifting in his chair.

Maris and I can't stop laughing to explain. Kevin's grin gets wider as enlightenment occurs. "Now the story makes sense." He laughs along with us, leaving Jennings bewildered.

Finally getting a handle on my hysterics, I clue him in. "Let's just say, I was very...inventive...on how I cursed you out during Kevin's delivery." I wet my lips and wait for Jennings to piece it together.

It doesn't take him long. Horrified, he yells, "You wished for me to fall on the log?"

Shoving up to my knees, I crawl over to where he's sitting. Resting my hands on his clenched legs, I remind him, "I was pushing an eight-pound human out between mine, the last stage of which lasted for two hours. Let's talk levels of pain, Ace."

Jennings blanches before he reaches down and pulls me onto his lap. "Why don't you rewind that section, son?" he offers.

Even as Maris and Kevin cackle with glee, I lean down and kiss Jennings. Today was about as perfect a day as we could have, but even if we spent it doing just this, I hope he knows I don't take for granted any moment we get to spend together. Every second is precious because our idyllic summer won't last forever.

# JENNINGS

About a week after we went to Skagway, I walk up behind Kara, who's frowning at her laptop. "What are you doing?" I massage her neck gently. If she's writing to her brother—something she hasn't done in a while—I don't want to interrupt her.

"Paying bills. I'm trying to figure out how my electric bill for our apartment went up while we haven't been there," she grouses. Tipping her head back, her lips twist. "You must know how it is. One month the water or heat is up, the next it's the electric or there's some odd bank charge that's never been there before."

"Is it always this bad?"

She shakes her head. "Summers are always a bit tricky," she admits on a small moan when I rub the knot at the base of her neck. "God, I'll give you a million of my nonexistent dollars not to stop."

"How about I exchange it for kisses?" I suggest.

She laughs before turning back to her laptop. "Better currency anyway."

My eyes bug out at the minuscule amount in her checking account. "I've got to ping Reg about the holdup," I mutter aloud.

"Who's that?" she murmurs, distracted.

"I'll tell you later. Jesus, Kara. What bills do you have each month?" I demand.

As Kara details her monthly expenses, she includes a college tuition payment. "Kevin's only taking one course, you said," I interrupt, reminding her of what she told me when I first came back to Alaska.

"True, but I enrolled him into the prepaid college plan, Jennings. I locked in his tuition when he was a baby, so it's affordable and gives him a solid degree with no student loans," she patiently explains, when I'm anything but that. "Look," she urges. A few quick clicks of her fingers pulls up Kevin's payment schedule for a four-year state university including room and board. "I started this months after he was born." Her finger trails alongside the screen reverently. "It was worth everything to give him this start in life," she assures me.

"Even putting your dream of a house on hold?" I ask gruffly. Kara keeps devastating me. Between giving up on being a scientist and what should be a more attainable goal of owning a home, I'm shook to the core once again by her selflessness.

Her hand comes up to rest on mine, giving it a quick squeeze. "Jennings, aspirations can be accomplished no matter the age. Men and women run marathons in their eighties. People who are physically challenged climb mountains. Dreams are meant to shift, and we're meant to adapt along with them. Otherwise"—a wicked expression lights her face—"I'd still be dreaming of boy bands instead of pilots."

I reward her with a kiss to the forehead. "What do you want now?" I ask, and not just because I'm curious but because my world is contingent upon the answer.

"Building a home filled with love. It doesn't matter if it's an apartment or a house," she declares resolutely, shoving her laptop aside. "Now, bill paying always depresses me. I feel like chocolate; you in?"

I nod, even though the last thing I feel like doing is swallowing the silver foil-wrapped drops she places into my hand. That is until she murmurs, "I can't wait to taste your lips after you've eaten those."

Immediately tearing into the foil, I shove the bite between my teeth and chomp down much to Kara's amusement. Standing, she tugs my head down and keeps her promise to taste the candy off my lips.

"Tastes so much better this way," she decides, before walking away calling out to Kevin. "Sweetheart, there's chocolate if you want some!"

"Later, Mom! Brooks and I are...ah, no! Go left!"

"And on that note, I'm going to curl up in front of the TV. Want to join me?"

"In just a minute," I agree. Kara smiles before heading into the living room to command control of the remote.

I want to pick up the laptop and hurl it across the room, my frustration is so great. But I exhale knowing soon, she won't be worried about things like electric bills, I think in disgust. Kevin's college payments will be a thing of the past.

And once Kara understands this isn't because she hasn't done a phenomenal job providing for our son but because I want to protect the family we're building, maybe she'll actually understand why I did it without finishing our conversation. Because the prideful woman who just sat at that table is going to kill me.

But like Reg warned me, once the money hits her account, there's no way to reverse it.

Shoving that thought aside, I lower the lid on her laptop and turn. Then I groan aloud. "No, Kara. Really? We're not watching *Building Alaska* when we're in Alaska, are we?"

"Sure we are. I love watching people who have no clue how to build a house try to put one up on an island with no hardware store nearby." She pats the seat next to her.

Who am I to resist such an offer?

# KARA

The last three days have been nothing but crappy weather, leaving me with a sense of impending doom. I haven't been able to put my finger on why. It must be because we've all been housebound. Maybe it's because we haven't seen Jennings today, I muse. Since the breakthrough between Kevin and Jennings, their bond has grown so much stronger. And every half hour, he keeps asking me when his father is coming by. With an aggravated sigh, I understand now why Jed and Dean encouraged him in sports. "Poor kid. He's trapped without remembering what the sun feels like."

Just then, I get a text from Jennings. *Got caught up with a conference call. How are things?*

I type, *I think Kevin's about to morph into Margaret from Ray Bradbury's poem.*

*All Summer In a Day? God, I haven't thought of that in ages. Do they still teach that in school?*

I'm about to reply when my phone vibrates in my hand with a 904 area code. Frowning, I answer it. "Hello?"

"Hello. I'm trying to reach Kara Malone," an unrecognizable voice says. "This is Amanda with Teachers First Credit Union in Jacksonville. How are you today?"

I grit my teeth and politely answer, "This is she. How are you, Amanda?

"Well, thank you, Ms. Malone. I'm calling today because—"

Suspecting this is likely a telemarketing call, I interrupt. "I'm out of state traveling. Is there a problem with my account?"

"Actually, yes. Before we discuss the specifics, would you mind verifying a few pieces of information for me?"

After jumping through a few hoops, I panic slightly. "I just paid my bills online the other day. Did those go through? Has there been a hack of some sort?"

"I'm sorry, Ms. Malone. Please let me assure you there is nothing negatively wrong with your account. There has been no inappropriate attempts to access your account, nor any funds transferred out without your explicit authorization."

I sag against the island counter. "Well, that's a relief." Even I hear the anxiety drain from my voice.

"Indeed," she agrees. "Normally I'm making these calls for a different reason entirely."

"I can imagine," I reply wryly. We share a laugh that eases the tension. "Then what's the issue?"

"Let me get right to the point. Our bank manager wanted me to give you a courtesy call to inform you we normally don't accept large electronic transfers of this amount without advance notice, but since everyone in the Jacksonville metropolitan area is aware of the circumstances of your brother's passing—"

I stop her polite rambling. "I'm confused. What are you talking about? I wasn't aware of any funds being transferred into my account." Certainly Maris would have told me if she planned on doing so. Wouldn't she?

Her voice becomes cautious. "Ms. Malone, do you have access to a computer?"

"Yes, of course. Give me just a moment." I walk over to the kitchen counter where my laptop has taken up residence. Impatiently waiting for it to connect to the internet, I log in to my banking application. "One more moment, Amanda," I plead.

"Take your time," she reassures me.

And the moment my dashboard appears, I understand why my bank's calling. "Wh-Where did this money come from?" I whisper. There's been a deposit for close to a quarter of a million dollars made into my savings account. My head is spinning with the possibilities, but there's really only two.

"I wouldn't be able to do that unless you want to open up an investigation into the deposit."

I find it difficult to swallow. "If you can't determine the account holder, can you tell me the bank where the money originated from?" That will tell me if it was Maris giving me Kevin's inheritance or Jennings.

And what I need to do.

"Yes. That I can do. If you give me just a moment..." Amanda does this annoying click with her teeth through the phone while she types that makes me want to dive through it. But my frustration is redirected to anger when she says, "It appears the routing number originates from a bank in Seattle, Washington. Do you wish for me to open up an investigation?" she asks me.

"No." I grip the counter behind me, holding myself up. *I can't believe he did this without talking with me first.* "I know who the sender is. Please apologize to the bank manager on my behalf. I can assure you, it will not happen again."

Probably because I'm going to skin Jennings alive the moment I see him.

I'm debating the ways how when Amanda lets out a sigh of relief. "Not a problem at all, Ms. Malone. And again, on behalf of everyone at Teachers First Credit Union in Jacksonville, we're sorry for your recent loss."

"Thank you, Amanda." I disconnect the phone, crushing it between my fingers.

I wonder how Amanda and Teachers First Credit Union in Jacksonville is going to feel when they see I've been brought up on charges, I think fleetingly as I stomp over to the basement door. "Kevin!" I yell at the top of my lungs.

A few seconds later, he edges toward the bottom of the stairs with his "uh-oh" face on. When the first words out of his mouth are "It wasn't me; I swear," I relax slightly.

"I know, sweetheart. Maris ran to the store. She'll be back soon; I have to go see your father."

"Okay. Tell him I said hey." I hear the sounds of things blowing up before he yells, "Oh, yeah! That's how you do it!"

Briefly, I wish I could go downstairs and join him, but sadly, I have to go hurt his father.

Badly.

Closing the door, I pull out my phone and text Jennings. *Is your call done?*

He responds right away. *Just finished. Why? What's up.*

*I'm on my way.*

His concerned *Are you sure you should be driving in this?* doesn't get a response. Neither does the phone call he makes as I'm dashing to my car.

Jennings is just going to have to wait until he can deal with my temper face-to-face.

WHAT'S NORMALLY a ten-minute drive takes thirty in the pouring rain. By then, I'm in a complete state. How dare he do this without talking to me? I throw my car door wide, uncaring my jacket's open, and dash through the rain and up the steps.

Just as I open it, the heavy front door is flung back on its hinges as the wind picks up at just the wrong moment. Expecting to dash up the stairs to his room, I pull up short. There he is—my target for my anger. He's leaning negligently against the counter talking with an older gentleman. As soon as he spots me, the conversation dies abruptly.

He gently mocks as I stalk toward him, "Owl, it helps if you close your coat up so you don't get wet." His fingers toy with the wet zipper as soon as I'm close enough for him to touch it.

I slap his hand away. His brows shoot skyward. I emit a feral sound before hissing, "How dare you?"

"Well, when it's raining, I often take the time to—"

"I don't need your goddamned money!" I shout.

"Ahh," he hums, fanning the flame inside of me. "I see Reg got it done."

"I have no idea who Reg is, nor do I care. Just tell me how to give it back."

Jennings interrupts me to say to the man behind him, "If you'll excuse us, Ron, the things Kara and I need to say to one another are likely not fit for your other guests' ears."

My head barely jerks in the direction of the other man even as Jennings yanks me toward the direction of the stairs leading upstairs. Increasing my stride, I manage to keep pace with his long legs as we hit the landing.

I'm burning up with the intensity of my emotions when he lets go of my fingers to reach for his keys once we reach his door. "Don't you dare move," he snarls, green eyes burning.

I'm about ready to snap by the time he fumbles the key into the lock and shoves the door open. Storming past him without waiting for an invitation, I don't notice a damn thing about the rest of the energy around me until the door slams.

The lock snicks. Immediately, Jennings hurls his keys. "We're not leaving this room until you understand one simple concept," he growls as he approaches me.

"What's that?" I ask. The anger is still pulsating through me, making my voice come out rough as sandpaper, but so is something else.

Desire.

"By the time you walk out that door, you're going to realize I will do anything I damn well please for my family." He's so close I can feel the waves of tension coming off him.

My outrage overrides my urgency to jump him. Hands slamming into his chest, I shout, "Not by dumping a bunch of money I neither want nor need into my account!"

He laughs darkly before hauling me against him. Spinning me to face the wall, he presses me up against it. "By doing anything I feel necessary. Don't you get it, Kara? I would give up the sky, if you asked." His voice cracks when he adds, "My money, my life, what does it matter when you can ask me for my soul and I'd hand it to you?" At that confession, Jennings lays his forehead against the back of my neck.

Our breaths tangle thickly. I quickly lose all the fight inside me as I struggle to stay upright.

Inhale. One hand slides into my hair, yanking my head to the side.

Exhale. There's nothing to lose and everything to gain. Including a love that I never thought I could have.

Tipping my head around, I capture Jennings's lips with mine. He groans, one of his hands wrapping around my chin, pulling my face closer. I tangle my fingers in the hair at the nape of his neck, along the side of his face, anything I can touch so I'm not to be spun into oblivion as his tongue seizes mine. A moan escapes from deep within my throat as Jennings's fingers travel over the collar of my button-down and give it a hard yank.

I gasp. My knees give way. If it weren't for his hard body behind me, I'd be a puddle on the floor.

Every millimeter of my skin is sensitized. I arch my back, which only serves to press my breasts against the wall, but Jennings just grips me tighter.

"You're not going anywhere. I'm not letting you go ever again."

"Then give me that. I don't need your money. All I want is—" I bite back before his mouth silences mine. The kiss sends chills racing through me.

"You. The right way to end that sentence is with the word 'you,'" Jennings finishes when he breaks our kiss. "Because that's the only thing I need."

Following up his words with actions, Jennings slides his hands up to cup my breasts, rolling the already turgid nipples tighter. A long moan escapes. I can feel the anger that drove me here slide into something wild and mysterious, something unknown.

Something we've never shared.

Leaning forward, air whooshes out as Jennings braces his chest against my back, forcing the air from my lungs. He drags both hands down over my stomach, causing my stomach muscles to contract.

Quickly reaching my waistband, his fingers deftly undo the snap and zipper of my jeans.

Panting, Jennings whispers, "Kick off your shoes, Owl," as he drags his bearded chin down the length of my spine while pulling my jeans and panties down.

I shiver uncontrollably, but I do as he asks, my tennis shoes going skidding across the room with a thunk. Soon, I'm naked except for my socks, and my back is still toward him. Jennings is on his knees behind me, smoothing his hands over and over my skin. Tapping my leg, he murmurs, "Part your legs."

"Jennings." I move to spin around, but he grabs my hips.

"Let me, my love." All frustration is gone from his voice, but I'm suddenly trembling. While my heart's trying to assimilate what he said, Jennings parts my the folds between my legs.

The next thing I feel is his lips surround my clit. And I almost explode right then and there. "Jennings!" I gasp.

He smooths his hands up and over the backs of my thighs all the while alternating between lapping at my juices and sucking the little bud over and over again. He flicks it like it's my nipple, then ducks down to lap up the effects of his actions, before starting all over.

Meanwhile I'm clutching the wall, the doorjamb, anything in hopes of staying on my feet especially when he slides his fingers inside me.

I moan in ecstasy as I spread my legs wider to his muted laugh against the inside of my thigh.

"I'm so close," I wheeze, as the tiny little flutters begin deep inside my womb.

Jennings slowly removes his fingers before surging to his feet. "Not without me, Kara. You go over with me."

"With you," I parrot.

I hear a quick swoosh of clothing behind me, then the clinking of his belt buckle before the wide tip of Jennings cock is pressed against my opening. "Tilt your hips, my love," he whispers.

There's those words again: my love. I'm helpless to the directive, but not so far gone to miss the brush of his jeans against my thighs. I grumble, "Too many clothes."

He sinks his cock inside me hard and deep just as his lips trace up my back. "In a minute you won't care."

I refuse to admit he's right. "God, Jennings. Just like that." My head falls back as he slides his hand forward to play with my clit even as he grabs onto my hip to pull me into the force of his thrusts. The combination has sensations crawling all over my skin, dragging me deeper. "Again," I plead as the deep strokes hit a place inside me no one else has ever been able to.

It isn't my body that climaxes but my heart that clenches as my pussy ripples along his dick. My head turns and I capture his lips as he thrusts once, twice, a third time before he gives in to his own pleasure.

As we stand there in the aftermath, we may have come to a détente of sorts, but the war is far from over. Because I'm so terrified Jennings is buried in my soul, I'll never be the same.

It only took me sixteen years to realize it.

# JENNINGS

I hold Kara pressed against the wall. Our hearts are pounding as if we've just run a marathon. Then again, perhaps we have. It's lasted sixteen years—one incredible fight to get back to this. Us. Now.

Catching our reflection in the mirror propped against the opposite wall, I don't think I've ever seen anything so right. Her head's tipped back against mine. Her lips are parted, the remnants of ecstasy illuminated by the lamp I switched on earlier before I went downstairs to meet her.

*God, don't let me mess this up again*, I pray fervently as I lean forward so my nose brushes against hers.

She licks her lips and I feel it, the simple touch sending shock waves through me. "Jennings," she whispers, but I press my lips against hers to stop the words.

I need her to listen, to understand. To believe in me enough to give us a shot because I can't imagine my life without her in it anymore. Closing my eyes, I pray with all my might before I plead, "Kara, we'll talk. I promise. Just give me a moment to come down from flying so high."

"Yes," she agrees.

Pushing my hips forward, I admit, "Never in my life has anyone made me feel what you do." I hold my breath, waiting for her response.

There's silence between us. I can feel her panting as she tries to formulate an answer. And I die a little every time a new flash of air hits my face. My head drops somewhere in the vicinity of my stomach.

Then she speaks and it's like someone destroys my soul. "I spent so much time just living instead of being truly happy. I was afraid when I saw you again because I was still afraid of being let down." I'm confused by the blinding beauty of her smile. Turning in my arms, she clasps my face. "I'm a scientist, Jennings. I should have known the answer to what was missing from my life all along."

I'm terrified to ask because this could be the ultimate abandonment if I'm wrong. "What was it?"

Eyes not leaving mine, our lips touch. I don't hear her say the words as much as I absorb them with every sense. "You."

Within seconds, I'm whirling Kara away from the wall as I stalk us toward the unmade bed in the center of the room. "Say it," I demand as I lower her down. Her hair fans out on the rumpled pillows where only last night I dreamed of her.

"No." She shakes her head back and forth, denying me the words I desperately long to hear. "You say it first. I need to know I'm not alone."

Bracing myself over her, I trail my fingers down the side of her cheek. "I'm afraid," I admit.

Sliding her hand up the back of my neck, Kara grips the hair at the nape of my neck so hard I feel the pinch down my spine. "That's two of us. But choosing this, you, means I'm here despite my fears of what might happen tomorrow, next month, or next year. It just means I..."

"I love you," I blurt out, the words too large to contain inside anymore. "I've never said the words to another woman before. In fact, the only other person I've said them to is—"

"Kevin." Her voice holds a note of reverence. Her eyes glow even as the wet drips from the corners down the side of her temples. "I love you, John Jennings."

I lower my head and capture her lips with a reverence in my heart and a fire in my soul. Her arms pull me down until I'm flush against her. I shift to the side so I don't rest my weight entirely on her frame before I gather her tightly in my arms.

We spend long moments sipping from each other's lips, getting drunk on love. There's never been anything more intoxicating that's ever passed my lips. My head's spinning and my heart's pounding when Kara finally pulls her head back. We're both breathing heavily.

I can't resist plucking another kiss from her lips, causing them to curve. "We need to talk, Jennings."

"I know."

"The money," she protests.

I stroke a hand down her hair. "Kara, based on simple math, if I paid you a ridiculously low amount of child support, that's the amount you would have been owed.'

Frustration crosses her face. "Don't you understand I never wanted that from you?"

"Don't you understand I'm the kind of man who has to give it?" I ask her back simply. Then I pull out the big guns. "If Kevin were Dean's child, Jed's child, they would do the same damn thing and you know it. That's part of taking care of your family—making sure they're financially stable." Rolling into her, I run my thumb over her cheekbone. "I won't watch you struggle with this kind of burden, Kara. That's part of love."

I literally hear her teeth click together. "So is respecting my decisions," she counters quietly.

"You weren't making them," I remind her.

She opens and closes her mouth before the frustrated squawk that only she makes comes out of her mouth. I lean down and press a firm kiss on her lips. "Kara, I love you. I love our son. If you want to invest the money in his future, do that. If you want to use it for living expenses now, do that. There's no stipulation on it."

"Jennings, are you trying to make all our dreams come true?"

"If you'd let me," I tell her honestly.

Her eyes dilate wildly before she curls into my chest. "Then I guess it's a good thing you already made the most important ones come true simply by being you."

I lean forward and brush my lips against hers before a thought occurs to me. "Where's Kevin?"

Kara's lips tip up. "At home with Maris. I got a text on the way here. They're packing. He wants to go see the Lumberjack Show again in Ketchikan again. Apparently, he wants to study it with more depth this time, so they'll be gone for a few days. Since he's been cooped up with this storm, I agreed."

"That will give us plenty of time to talk," I murmur, running a hand down the smoothness of her back.

"Yes, it will." Her voice is unusually serious.

I feel a forbidding in the region of my chest. "I was kidding."

"I'm not, Jennings. There's still a lot to talk about."

My heart lurches in fear. "What do you mean? I love you; you love me."

Kara's body goes stiff before she forces herself to relax. "I don't want to bring this up now, but at the end of the summer, we have to go—"

"No." I refuse to discuss my family leaving me. "Not now, Kara. For God's sake, give us tonight."

A twisted pain crosses her face before she whispers, "All right. But we have to talk; we have no choice."

I nod curtly and wrap her back in the safety of my arms where tonight I can dream there will be no tomorrow to find its way through the crack in the blinds.

Because I suspect this time I'll be the one who will be unable to soar, weighted down by the knowledge both pieces of my heart are three thousand miles away.

# JENNINGS

We're lying on our sides next to each other under the tall tree in the backyard we spent so many summer days lazing under. I'm running my hand rhythmically through Kara's hair, feeling the silken strands pass through my fingers. "I could do this forever," I tell her truthfully.

She giggles a little before reminding me, "That might cause a problem once winter sets in. We don't have the right gear on for you to do that, Jennings."

I smile. Ever logical and oh so practical. And God, my heart races every time she's near. "You're worth freezing to death over," I murmur on another pass of my hand.

Kara laughs and the sound washes over me. "Or we could buy a sleeping bag?" she says sweetly. Her practicality is such a turn-on. I can't not kiss her for that, so I don't even try to hold back. Sliding my fingers around the back of her head, I lift her up and press a lingering kiss on her upturned lips. When we pull back, her lashes flutter open, revealing eyes that have always held me captivated.

Trailing my fingers across her exposed collarbone, I whisper, "Tell me more about them." When her face adopts a quizzical expression, I clarify, "About Jed and Dean. You told me the bad, about what hurt.

Now I want to know about the good. I want to know about your life with them." Rolling onto my back, I stare up at the clear blue sky above us peeking through the branches of the trees. Land, air, the perfect blend of me and Kara. No, that's Kevin, I correct myself as she says softly, "I don't quite know where to start."

I squeeze her close, and it pulls her head on top of my chest. "You mentioned Dean was more outgoing?" I say, trying to get her to start talking. Because something's bothering me about the dynamics in the Smith household. I just can't pinpoint it.

Like why Kara's still talking to her brother instead of about her brother even though she's spending all her time making sure everyone else is honoring their memories.

"God, yes." She laughs, which eases some of the concern I had bringing this up. One of her arms snakes around my chest while the other props up her chin. She grins. "Dean is charming and funny. He can go joke for joke against any comedian and come out beating them. The last is fact as he used to do it when we were old enough to get into clubs, much to our parents' despair." A spasm of pain crosses her face when she mentions her parents, but she forges on. "He's the kind of guy who gives you the shirt off his back and never cares if you ever repay him. He wants to help people." She strums her fingers against my chest, setting off unconscious memories of the heat we've indulged in, but I control it because she needs to let all of this out. "I can't remember a time when Dean didn't want to be in a position to help people. So becoming a firefighter and EMT was a perfect fit. He found a way to do so in so many good situations." She pauses, before a small giggle escapes. "Did he tell you about the first time he asked Jed out?"

"No. What happened?"

"It was a perfect date. And that night, my brother came home to tell me about it."

"You were living together?"

She nods. "Yes, we shared an apartment right up until he and Jed got engaged. The county we live in is a fairly affluent one, and even apartments are costly. We liked the idea of living in the county we work in. Also, this way I didn't have to put Kevin in daycare because he only worked three twenty-four-hour shifts a week. Besides, we're family." She shrugs. "Unconventional, but family."

My arms tighten around her. "Kevin was lucky to have been raised by a man like that," I murmur.

She hums but doesn't say anything for a few. We just listen to the whispering of the leaves overhead. When Kara opens her mouth again, her words shoot an arrow directly in my heart. "Knowing the man you are now, I think you would have done just as amazing a job, Jennings." Then she buries her face in my lap.

When I tip her head back, she's biting her thumbnail. "What are you saying?"

I roll to my back and pull her so her legs are astride mine. Wrapping my arms around her, I pull her hair back so I can see her face.

Kara's body is frozen on top of mine. I begin to panic as her chest moves with such force, her ribs are pressing my back against the hard grass. And then I feel something else. Wetness.

Crap.

"Kara?" I'm worried about her, but her finger slides up my mouth to silence me.

Her expression clears and I see wonder, gratitude, and something more. And my arms pull her tighter, if that's even possible. "With just a few words, you reminded me of a memory that's been inside of me and made it lighter." Leaning forward, she brushes her lips against my jaw. "Thank you."

Rolling her to her back, I remind her, "Jed kept trying to get me to come to Florida."

Instead of being upset, she laughs, her hair flying in all directions as she rolls it back and forth. "You should see him. He does that kind of stuff all the time. My God, the way he plays matchmaker with his..." Her lips tremble before a keening sound escapes.

And there it is. Now, I understand fully. Kara's been responsible for taking care of everyone else around her she hasn't been able to truly let go of her own emotions. Despite admitting she was writing letters to her dead brother, after admitting she sent Kevin to a therapist, even when she cried in my arms the morning after we first made love after telling me how the two men died, she still didn't let go.

I wrap her tight as she bucks beneath me as she sobs. I don't know for how long or what causes the torrent of tears, but the sound tears at my soul. Each one seems to represent an hour, a minute of pain. But since when? Since her brother's death? Since she left Alaska? It doesn't matter, really. Just knowing how much she trusts me to help carry her burden causes my own eyes to burn.

"Why haven't you let go before now?" I ask after her sobs have been reduced to sniffles.

"How could I?" Her voice is hoarse. "I had to take care of Kevin. Maris is overworking—"

"Maris is an adult," I interrupt.

"Maris is lost in more ways than you can imagine," she corrects me. I frown when I hear that. "And my job is to..."

"Protect your family." I interject.

"At whatever the cost," she agrees.

"Nothing is going to harm you, least of all me. That's a promise." My lips brush hers, pride and something much stronger swirling deep inside of me. But even as our lips sip and take from each other, I can't completely lose myself in this kiss. Because I'm worried. Promises mean nothing when they're only words. A woman like Kara needs tangible proof in order to believe, and that's not just because of the past; that's just who she is.

Sitting us up, I bury my neck in her throat, rocking us back and forth. "It's a good thing we have more of the summer for me to show you I mean to support those words with actions."

"Hmm." The sound buzzes against my neck, sending tingles down my spine. "What kind of actions did you have in mind?"

"You're shameless," I declare, pulling back to see a teasing light having chased away the shadows in her eyes.

"Me?" She touches her chest in mock surprise.

"Yes, you."

"This is a first." She's thoughtful. "I kind of like it."

I pluck another kiss from her lips before I tell her, "I do too."

She smiles shyly before wrapping her arms around me tightly but not before I see the sparkle back in her eyes. I feel like racing around the backyard cheering. I did that, I think with pride. I removed a layer of the burden she's been carrying.

I just wish I could remove them all. I'm finding I want to be there for her as much as I want to be there for my son. *I get it now, buddy*, I silently tell Jed, even as I lean back against the tree trunk with Kara in my arms while we talk about Maris bringing Kevin back to Ketchikan. Then I burst out laughing.

"What is it?" Kara asks.

"Do you really think they're still doing the trick where the guy runs on the log in the water and falls on it looking like he crushed his nuts every single show?" I muse rhapsodically.

Kara snickers. "Only if there's a god, Jennings. Because that was the funniest part of the show when you used to..."

Suddenly the back door flies open. Kevin comes running out. Kara tenses and moves to slide off my lap, but I don't let her. "Hey, Mom. Hey, Dad!"

I call back, "Hey, son!" as Kevin races across the grass. "So your mom and I were wondering about the Lumberjack Show. Now that you've seen it twice, what was your favorite part?"

"Totally when the dude lands with his leg spread around the log when he runs on the wet log! Wham! He totally crushed his..."

Kara screeches with delight even as I cut our son off by calling back, "I know what happens." All too well, unfortunately, I think ruefully.

"Right." Kevin drops down next to us. He grins at his mother. "It was way better the second time around."

"Tell us all about it," she encourages. She twists on my lap but doesn't try to vacate it. Another win, I cheer silently. Even if I have to listen to a recap of my son cheering over Team USA beating Team Canada. I pretend Kara's "Aww, poor Jennings. Your team loyalty is noted" does little to assuage my dignity even as I chuckle.

Right now, life couldn't be more perfect. My heart feels filled with joy because the two people who have become everything chatter around me on a perfect day under a tree. I give a quick thanks to Jed for giving me the chance for this perfect moment.

Even though I know Kara and I are the reason we got here.

# KARA

We're at a barbecue at Brad and Rainey's. All of the adults minus Maris are lounging around the picnic table watching Kevin teach the younger kids how to play soccer. Just as Meadow's daughter is about to take a tumble, he swoops her up.

Jennings presses his chin against my shoulder, resting his cold drink against my thigh. "Every day," he murmurs, telling me with those two words he just keeps falling for both me and Kevin. "It's the little things like this, the everyday things."

I twist my head and shiver. His arms tighten, even as his focus remains on our son lining up the kids for drills. His dark hair is wind ruffled, begging me to sink my hands into it, eyes covered by aviator glasses. This—I lean back, letting him take my weight—is heavenly.

Obviously, the gods don't agree.

A ripple under my bare foot causes me to snap to attention. My hand braces on the table, and my heart lurches in my chest as I shout, "Kevin!"

"Mom? What's happening?" He drops to the ground, pulling the others down to sit next to him.

"Earthquake," I call back. "It's not unusual here. Just stay where you are. It will be..."

But Jennings is halfway across the yard at a sprint. God, how many times is it possible to fall in love with one man? I wonder as we all wait for a second rumble.

Long minutes pass before Brad calls, "All clear!"

Jennings brings the kids over to the table, which has barely been disturbed. Kevin immediately announces, "I'll take hurricane season over that," which causes laughter all around.

Jennings grins as he throws an arm around him. "They have them up here all year round," he adds helpfully.

"Alaska's a definite no on my future places to live," Kevin declares definitively.

Thinking back to everything I gained from living here, I counter, "Never say never, sweetheart."

Jennings leans down and brushes a kiss on top of my head in response.

"Hey, Kara, you used to be good at guessing the strength and epicenter. Want to give it a shot?" Brad teases.

I groan, just as Maris comes outside frowning down at her phone. "You do realize it's been sixteen years?"

Kevin's giving me a look like he just found out I'm a cyborg. "For fun?" he shouts. "No, it's beautiful here and I love all of you, but you don't have Zaxby's and now this? Mom—"

One of the benefits of parenthood is freaking out your child. Calmly, I say to Brad, "No more than a 2.0. If I had to guess range, about twelve miles away."

Brad whistles, holding out his phone. "Not bad, Malone."

"A 1.6, nine miles away." My voice is only mildly petulant. "I'm out of practice."

Kevin yells, "Let's not practice, Mom!"

And we all break up laughing. Jennings grins at our son. "Kid, this isn't anything. I bet Maris will tell us not a single thing crashed inside the house. Did it, Mar?"

But Maris is looking distinctly uncomfortable. "Umm, Kara? Can I talk with you for a moment? Privately," she tacks on just as Jennings is about to stand.

My heart is so full, I don't notice the warning on her face. "What is it, Mar? We're all family here."

Her face twists. It's then I notice the phone clenched in her hand. I wonder briefly if she got a message from Nick, when what she tells me is so much worse. "An updated email came in about your flight home. The airline is asking you to call them as soon as possible." Her voice is riddled with pain.

But it doesn't equate to the devastation on Jennings's face.

"Home?" he chokes out. "But, what about...never mind." Shoving to his feet, he strides away from our beautiful family to go God only knows where.

I don't follow him because I feel a trembling hand land on my shoulder before a sweaty body drops down behind me. "Mom?" Kevin's voice is filled with the fear I haven't heard in weeks.

"Damn you," I whisper aloud, but I don't know who I'm cursing. Is it Maris with her piss-poor timing or Jennings?

I shoot a glare at Maris, who merely shrugs. Internally cursing everything, especially wretched timing, I conclude Jennings has to find a way on his own to come to grips with the fact my love for him is strong enough to last across a continent. So is his son's.

He has to come to the conclusion I have—that love can be felt no matter where you are. All that matters are the people who love you, I think fiercely.

Pressing my lips against Kevin's sweaty head, I just hope he does it before it undoes a summer's worth of bonding between father and son. As for me, I've already accepted nothing will change my feelings for Jennings in this lifetime. Not ever again.

HOURS LATER, Jennings comes to the house. I'm drinking wine in the solarium when I hear Maris let him in. I don't call out, despite the increase of my heartbeat. It started raining not long after Jennings ran off, effectively ruining the rest of the afternoon for everyone, not just for me and Kevin.

Because I knew Kevin ate so much at Brad and Rainey's, I'm not overly concerned he said no to food when Maris asked if he was hungry, mumbling, "I think I just want to go online and game for a bit, if that's okay, Mom?"

I gave him a swift hug. "Your dad will be back soon," I promised him. I prayed I wasn't lying.

Now, it seems I wasn't.

Jennings makes his way toward me. I hold up a hand to keep him at bay. "I don't care where you went, but your son very much does."

"Kara," he starts, but I shake my head, still not facing him.

"I lived through his first heartbeats, fear, doubt, and worry every single day wondering if I was going to be enough for that child. We lived and we loved, but it's different with you."

"I know that," he chokes out.

"Do you?" I whirl around. He's drenched and his expression is haggard. Somehow I can't find it in me to care, not when I've spent the last few hours worrying about both of the men in my life. "You're his father, Jennings. I told you when this started he has to come first. Whatever's going through your mind—"

"Is my own insecurity about being left again," he says quietly, shocking me to the core. "Kara, I never told you how I started Northern Star Flights."

"Why does this matter now?" I ask, frustrated. "How can this matter more than what happened today?"

Ignoring me, he continues. "Because I sold my aunt and uncle's farm to do it. I relished doing it. I wanted no memories of that place. After all"—my jaw falls open as he gives me this piece of himself he's held back—"I was abandoned there by parents who didn't want me and raised by two people who essentially treated me like I was free labor."

Even as angry as I am, my heart can't hold itself apart from this knowledge. "Jennings, I knew you weren't happy at home. But this?" I put my glass down and step forward with my hand outstretched. He grabs onto it like it's everything. "Why didn't you say anything?" I ask.

"Because each time I'd see what you gave Kevin as a single mother with nothing, I wanted to kick my own ass over the fact you should have had everything." A lone tear trickles down his cheek before he rasps out, "And I kept trying to figure out a way to give it all to you. Time and again, you kept showing me all you wanted was me. And now, you're leaving."

I can't keep myself back away from him any longer. I crash into him at the same time as he gathers me into his arms. Harsh sobs have his shoulders shaking under my hands. "I've got you," I whisper.

"Don't let me go," he pleads. "No matter what. I can't bear if you let me go."

"I didn't plan on it," I whisper. "That's not how love works, Jennings. We're going to argue, but we will never let go."

He nods, unable to speak, while I hold him, flabbergasted. When he stormed out of Brad and Rainey's, I expected to rip into him for letting us down, and now this? I send up a prayer for help, but as usual, there's no answer except the persistent drops of rain as the storm passes over the house.

I pull back just enough so I can press a kiss to Jennings's ravaged face. Resting my forehead against his lips, each breath links us together in a way distance will never separate. But even as I assimilate all I learned, I realize something else about tonight. Energy takes the form of gravity, motion, light, and so many others. But I don't know why scholars don't account for the most beautiful and harmful force in the world when they write about it.

Love.

Long moments later, Jennings presses his lips against my forehead before pulling away. "I'm sorry, Kara. I love you and I let you down. Can you forgive me for panicking?" His voice is wrecked due to his unshed tears.

I nod, because it seems love will forgive anything. Including, it dawns on me, mistakes made sixteen years ago by a girl who was so wounded she did all she could to survive. "Love forgives many things, Jennings."

He sags in relief. I continue. "But it doesn't change the fact we have to go." Jennings jerks back, his eyes frightened. I rise up and press my lips against his. "I'm not leaving you," I swear to him.

"Kara—" he starts.

But I interrupt. "I have to go because my entire life has revolved around giving that boy downstairs love. And that means giving him everything. I love you, but he represents us. And I love us more."

Jennings shudders in my arms as he pulls me close. "How much time do we have left?"

I don't want to answer, but I have to. "A little over three weeks."

There's so much silence between us, I'm afraid he's not going to say anything else. I should have known what he says is perfect. "Then, let's go get our son and see if he wants Subway. When I drove by earlier, they were still open."

He tangles his fingers in mine. Together we make our way toward the kitchen. I swallow hard before yelling, "Kevin! Your father wants to know if you want Subway for dinner. If you do, get a move on."

Thunderous footsteps follow my announcement. The basement door is flung open and there's Kevin, whose eyes are rimmed with red. "Dad?" His voice quavers.

Jennings drops my hand and strides over to his son, yanking him tightly against him. "I'm sorry, son. I'm so, so sorry."

And if science were to allow me to live for eternity, my heart would still shatter every time I recall the memory of my son breaking down in his father's arms upon realizing our leaving is going to devastate us all.

# JENNINGS

"What do you think of Seattle? Do you think Kevin would like it?" I ask her.

"Jennings, we have a life to get back to," she reminds me. "We can't pick up and move."

*Yes, you can. We can do anything together.* I want to say that, but she continues on before I get the chance. "Kevin starts school in two weeks; I have to be back a few days before that. Our flights were arranged for us to return..."

"Stop talking," I bite out harshly. "Doesn't this, us, change anything? Don't you want to want to hold on to what we found between the three of us?"

"More than anything." I want to roar my triumph aloud, but her next words stop me cold. "But I have responsibilities, enormous ones. And the biggest one has three years of school to finish before he goes off to college." Her eyes well with tears. "Do you think it's easy to walk away from the only man I've ever loved?"

The gravity of what Kara's saying slams into me. "I'm going to eliminate all the barriers between us to merge our lives," I choke out. It's a promise, a vow.

One I intend on keeping.

"It's not going to be easy." Her voice is ridiculously low, but with her body pressed up next to mine, there's no way I can't hear her words. They're like tiny arrows piercing my heart. I don't know of any way to reassure her yet until I'm back in Seattle taking the steps necessary to prove to her I'm serious.

In the meanwhile, I pull her closer and murmur, "There's only air between us, my love. And haven't I proven I know how to navigate that?"

Twining her arms and legs around me, Kara pulls me closer. I rest my weight down on her as she pleads, "Don't leave. Come back to the house with me. Stay with us until we have to go. Maris said she doesn't mind." The desperation in her voice pulls at me.

I slant my head and take her lips in a kiss so thorough Kara's eyes are dilated when they flutter open afterward. "It's a good thing you asked, because I was planning on doing just that."

Relief is chased away by love as she slides her hand into my hair to tug my lips back down to hers. "I wish none of us ever had to," she admits, right before her tongue strokes out to brush against my lower lip. And for a good long while, neither of us are thinking about leaving or our impending goodbye.

Much later, when Kara's sated next to me, I replay our conversation over and over along with a million others I've had in my head. I've spent the last week arguing about this only to come up against a brick wall. Kara's not moving; she won't even entertain the idea. She made a commitment to Kevin when he entered high school she wouldn't move, "unlike all those kids who get yanked around. God it would suck to have to make friends again," Kevin admitted as we munched on cheeseburgers the other night.

Kara didn't say "I told you so," but her look sure did. And that commitment to our son is one of the things I love most about her.

But with each second I feel the beat of Kara's heart knock against mine, I realize I wasted too many years blaming a past I couldn't control, leaving behind everything that could matter except for my friends, who knew better than to dig where their interference wouldn't be appreciated.

All except Jed.

He knew I was missing the something I'd waited my whole damn life for—a love so consuming I searched the land and the sky for it. And it wasn't until I came back to where they seemed to meet each other in one incredibly perfect land did I find both.

Now that I have it, I have to figure out a way to make the adjustments necessary to keep us all level. As the early-morning sun lightens my room, ideas are floating through my head. And as her warm body stirs next to mine, I hope I can make them work without losing a damn thing.

Least of all, the woman curled at my side.

THE NEXT WEEK passes in a blur. I spend every moment with Kara and Kevin, storing up memory on top of memory for the time when we're going to be apart. Even if I intend on it only being temporary.

"Dad, you promise you're going to be able to make it out for Labor Day?" Kevin asks anxiously as he folds clothes and shoves them haphazardly into his suitcase. "Maybe we can go to the beach one of the days I'm off of school?"

Placing my hand on the center of my universe that a few months ago I didn't know existed, I assure him, "I'll be there, son."

The relief that crosses his face is quickly overcome by laughter. "Good. I don't know how you and Mom are going to manage to go that long without locking lips," he teases.

I wince as heartache again tears through me. "Sit down with me, Kevin." I gesture to the open space on the bed. "I want to talk with you about something important."

Anxiously, he drops down on the bed. Curling a leg up, I do the same. "Things are going to be difficult for your mother when she gets back home."

"If you mean with chores and stuff—" I hold up my hand to interrupt him.

"I mean because the last time she left Alaska, she was pregnant with you and, other than your Uncle Dean, no one was there for her. This time, the situation between us is different. My heart, my soul, are completely hers, just like they're yours. But you know her; she's going to overanalyze things that are completely unnecessary when there's nothing for her to be worried about."

Kevin bites his lip. "I do that too," he admits.

"I know. And I'm going to tell you both the same thing: no matter what time day or night, pick up the phone and call me," I tell my son firmly. "Don't let worries fester. This, us, is so much more than we can navigate on our own. Together we can weather any storms, and I promise you, Kevin—" I grab his hand and squeeze it hard. I'm grateful when he returns the pressure just as tightly. "—I'm not going to let either of you down."

"Okay," he says shakily. Then he throws his body across the space between us and wraps his arms around me.

We're holding on to each other when Kara's voice washes over us both. "Come on, guys. I made dinner."

"I'm not feeling very hungry, Mom," Kevin admits from the shelter of my arms.

*Neither am I*, but I don't say it aloud. I know Kara's doing what she has to not only in order to nurture us both now, but to prepare Kevin for what's to come next week.

Her scent envelops me as she sits on the bed pressed to Kevin. But I feel one of her hands grope for mine when she reminds our son, "It isn't forever, sweetheart."

"Sure feels like it," he grumbles, shoving himself to his feet away from both of us.

Kara's face is awash with hurt as Kevin stomps into the bathroom to wash up. "I made him a promise," she whispers. Torment is stamped on every feature and in every line of her body.

I lift her free hand to my lips. "I know. You'll drive yourself crazy if you don't think I understand that."

"Then why does it hurt so much?" Her face contorts with the aching pain that she's not the only one feeling.

"Maybe because last time you were scared." Leaning close, I brush my lips against hers softly. "This time, you're carrying both of our hearts with you. It's not your burden, but you're also taking all my air with you. I'm not going to be able to breathe the same way until we're back together."

"Jesus, Jennings. Make it harder, why don't you?" Her head nestles in the crook of my shoulder.

"If I could figure out a way to make this not happen, I'd make it impossible."

She meets my eyes with a quizzical glance. I shrug my shoulders before admitting, "I'm a selfish bastard, Kara. You know that about me."

"How long is it going to take me to recover from this?" Her fingers dance along the side of my face reverently.

I wrap an arm around her shoulders and tug her closer. Pressing a kiss firmly to her lips, I tell her flat out, "You won't be able to. It may be scary at first, but please, God, trust me. I'll find a way to return to you."

She pulls back a bit, something that causes an ache inside of me. "I'll try."

"Then lean on me when it gets to be too much. There's nothing and no one but time preventing me coming for you," I swear.

Sadly, she rises from the bed. "You forget, Jennings. My mind has a hard time counting on much."

"Then trust your heart. Trust mine," I implore her before I press my mouth to hers.

Her hand drags behind as she pulls away. "Dinner in ten," she calls before she makes her way out of the room.

I scrub my hands over my face. "God, Jed. If you're up there listening, help me out?" I plead aloud. "I need to make them both understand this isn't over." Because in such a short time, I realize I was blessed with the chance to be gifted with love twice.

I'm doomed if I screw this up again. I know it.

And I want a life with the woman I love and our son.

No matter the cost.

# KARA

I'm trying to not let my dejection show as the days move as swiftly as Jennings navigates the plane on a good crosswind.

Am I doing the right thing for us? I question my decisions every second of the day when I'm not actively engaged in a conversation with Jennings or Kevin or being loved by Jennings at night. But it's those quiet moments before I curl up in his arms and sleep that are the worst.

I don't question my love for him. What I question is the wisdom of falling head over heels in love with a man who has a life on the completely opposite side of the country from me.

This is the pain I set up Kevin for—life without both of his parents every day.

If I let myself go back to the woman I was before my heart was indelibly changed, I'd be a shell. But that shell I was living in might be less painful than the heartbreak I know I'm setting myself up for when we board the jet to carry us back to Jacksonville in just three days.

As we bank over the White Pass Railroad chugging along below, Jennings points out Dead Horse Gulch, an immense steel cantilever bridge. As he enlightens us to the history behind the bridge, I think about the men who bravely hung over the sides to build it clinging to nothing but a rope. I realize when I first came to Alaska I was much the same way. Maybe my dream wasn't to work on Mendenhall, it was to find meaning, a purpose. Twisting slightly in my seat, I catch sight of Kevin, who's eagerly listening to his father give a historical perspective of the land below us.

I can't shield him from this, I think painfully. Another loss, and I can't protect him from it no more than I could Dean or Jed. What I want is for life to not to be so riddled with responsibilities so I could just pick up our lives and move to Seattle. But I can't do that to Kevin. Tears of anguish fill my eyes when I wonder if knowing my reasons are because of his son will be enough to ask Jennings to wait.

But what do I have to offer him in three years except being forty-one? An aching bitterness sets in when I realize that despite the fact we've both professed our love, Alaska is going to return me to Florida in much the same condition I was before.

Alone.

As the chatter between Jennings and Kevin continues, which involves them making plans for winter and summer breaks, I absorb the memories, storing them in my heart for when I need to pull them out in years to come.

With a jerk, I realize Jennings is calling my name over the headset. "Yes?" I answer.

"Are you okay?" he asks, concerned.

"I'm fine." I stretch the truth so thin you could see through it. Then I add on immediately behind it, "I was just enjoying listening to you both make plans."

Jennings doesn't say anything for a moment. Then his hand reaches over and grabs mine. He gives it a firm squeeze.

I don't know what that means. Is it reassurance, comfort? I want to ask, but I hold myself back.

This isn't the time. The problem is, with so few days left, will there be a right one?

❄

THE DAY before we're due to depart Juneau is riotous at Maris's. Brad, Rainey, and their family have joined Maris, Jennings, Kevin, and me for a farewell barbecue. As much as I love the camaraderie Kevin and I have built here, I want nothing more than to throw everyone out so I can drag Jennings to my room and alternate between making love to him and crying.

We're not down to days now, but down to hours.

Our flight takes off at seven in the morning in order to get us back to Florida late tomorrow evening. That means we're due at the airport at an ungodly hour to check in a summer's worth of bags. I'm torn between making mental lists and being so utterly morose I want to curl into a corner with a bottle of wine to just forget.

But the reality is, I'm being engaged in too much conversation for any of that to occur.

"You have to be looking forward to getting back to some warmer weather," Meadow teases me, before she takes a bite of one of the brownies she brought with her.

"You'd be surprised," I chuckle ruefully. "It rarely stays this temperate in Florida. It's been a nice reprieve." I'm about to say more when I feel a set of strong arms wrap around me. Jennings's beard brushes up against the side of my cheek. I close my eyes to memorize the sensation of the bristles as they scrape across my skin, the woodsy scent of his cologne mingling with the outdoor air, the strength of his jaw as he rubs it back and forth against me.

And my heart aches because I could be in Antarctica or in the sweltering heat so long as I had my son and this man with me. The air might be uncomfortable, but I'd be whole.

Meadow smiles at me with understanding. "I think I hear Rainey calling for me. Since you're in such great hands, I'll be right back."

I don't respond as I nestle back into Jennings. He obviously feels the same way when he mutters, "If I didn't know everyone was going to miss Kevin, I'd blast Maris for suggesting this. All I want is a quiet night with my family before..." He can't even complete the sentence.

And I give him some of the most honest words I've said in the last few days as I've held up a front for our son. "It hurts," I whimper softly.

He growls behind me, before spinning me around. I gasp softly as he hauls me up against him so closely our bodies are aligned as perfectly as they are when he's thrusting inside of me. One arm is banded around my hips while the other is threaded through my hair, pulling it back slightly. "Look me in the eye and say that again," he demands.

Helpless, I comply. "Of course it hurts, Jennings. It's slipping away again, and the wounds are starting to open. But I'd rather have had this time with you than nothing at all. I..." I don't get a chance to tell him how much I'll always love him because he slams his mouth down on mine.

Voraciously, he kisses me in front of the people that matter to both of us across a continent of living. It isn't until a moan starts to build in the back of my throat he pulls back.

Words almost don't seem necessary, but Jennings gives them to me anyway. And when he does, they're perfect and painful because they give me hope. Damn him.

"Understand me, Kara. We're going to be together in the end. I just have to deal with the how."

My hand lifts from where it rests lightly on his shoulder to drag down the plane of his cheek until I can smooth it over the scruff of his beard. "I want you to know I'll never be sorry." At his questioning look, I expand, "For either summer I spent loving you."

A slow smile spreads across his handsome face. "That's good to know because I'll never be sorry for falling in love with you." Before I can respond, he loosens the grip on my hair. "Let's see what we can do to end this party before dawn. I need to have tonight to hold you."

Woodenly, I nod, incapable of speaking. I always wondered what it would feel like to have all of John Jennings. Now that I do, I'm sorry I don't know what to do or what to say.

And I'm more sorry I have no time to find out.

Slipping an arm around his waist, we head in the direction where our son is laughing with Brad and Rainey's kids. We stand there absorbing the sound since it might be the last time either of us hears it for a while.

THE HOUSE IS FINALLY QUIET. Jennings's hands are running up and down my back after I've collapsed on top of him a limp mess. The words start to form before I know they're coming. "I could talk to..."

"Shh, Kara. Not tonight. Let tonight be about just us." His vivid green eyes meet mine. "Right now, I need to just memorize everything before the air shifts and drags you away from me. We'll figure out our tomorrows then. Tonight, until the sun comes up, I want to put us first."

"How can I possibly refuse that?" Even though my words are the same ones I teased him with when I said yes to our first date over sixteen years ago, there is nothing joking about them now.

"I thank God every day you can't." Unlike the first time, there's no arrogant smile accompanying his words. And the next ones would have melted me if he hadn't already performed that feat with his lovemaking earlier. "Did I ever say thank you? For Kevin, for staying, for being so courageous when you were young, and even more perfect now that we're older?" Jennings's eyes burn into mine.

I shake my head. "You gave me the greatest gift of my life. It's me who should be thanking you," I counter.

"I've spent so much of my life in the air because there was nothing I wanted on the ground. Now that I found you and Kevin, well, I know what he meant."

"What who meant?" I lean down and press a brief kiss to his lips.

"Love and family. They're the secrets that give you a shot at the stars. Funny, Jed told me that on the flight we took when he told me about your brother."

Tears slip from my eyes and fall heedlessly to his chest as I lean down and press my lips to his. Over and over, our lips slide over one another. Our tongues duel back and forth until we're again entwined in each other's arms seeking heights, needing solace, not caring about true sleep because all too soon, the sun will come and with it, the flight that will take me and Kevin away.

We doze intermittently in between long bouts of lovemaking and even longer sessions of talking. For the last few hours, we continue to live a lie that nothing's changing. But all too soon, both of our cell phone alarms start to sound.

I have eleven hours of flights to make up for it or cry. And I'd rather not let Kevin see me in this condition.

Not yet anyway.

# KARA

"I think I want my epidural back," I mutter.

"What was that?" Jennings pants as he hefts another set of bags out of the SUV he borrowed from Maris.

"Nothing," I answer him. But between the shooting pain every time I see another piece of luggage being removed, knowing it's taking another piece of us away from Jennings and remembering the baggage fees from our flight here, I debate the merits of drinking heavily to subdue the agony.

Honestly, if Kevin wasn't with me, nothing would prevent me from getting completely annihilated during the first part of the flight. "I don't want to think," I mutter, softly enough so only I can hear it.

Or so I think.

Kevin drapes his arm around my waist from behind and puts his chin on my shoulder. "Can I sum up our trip?"

Laying my hand on top of his, I watch as Jennings talks to the porter before slamming the trunk closed. We're down to minutes, I think wildly. "Sure, baby," I manage to get out. Anything to distract me from walking into that airport for the second time in my life with my heart feeling like it will never be the same.

Because I'm positive this time is going to be worse than the last.

"We arrived and I thought I would never heal from the pain. Then Dad came into our lives." I jerk a little in his hold unintentionally.

Trying to restore a semblance of calm, I ask, "And you..."

"Fell in love with my father as much as you did," my son tells me bluntly. "Mom." He turns me a bit so I'm facing him. "I know why we're going home. You keep forgetting I'm not a kid anymore."

I open my mouth to start babbling, but Kevin hushes me. "I loved every minute of it, but I'm looking forward to going home. I told Dad the same thing."

Instead of the words wanting to pour out, I find I can't get them out. "When did you tell him that?"

"Yesterday at the party. So, in case I forget to tell you later—" My son leans down and kisses me on the cheek before whispering in my ear. "—thanks for being the greatest mom in the world. Your whole life you've giving me everything."

There's no way I can stop the tears at that point. I try to surreptitiously swipe them from my eyes before Jennings locks the car and comes over. "What's wrong?" he demands, missing nothing.

"Nothing, Dad. I was just telling Mom how great she is. You know she just can't take a compliment."

I reach out and jab him in the stomach with my fingers. "I can so," I protest.

"When it comes to your brain, Owl, yes. Otherwise, Kevin's got you dead to rights." Jennings wraps his arm around my shoulders. He sucks in a breath, and I swear I gasp as I feel the pain swirl between the three of us.

Jennings guides us toward the porter so we can make our way to the airport terminal. Each step we take is physically shredding my soul.

I feel like shouting in the cool morning air, but my voice is trapped inside me. Over my head, Jennings and Kevin murmur to each other about connections and what time we're expected to land back in Florida. I know it's not the concerned lover talking to me but the pilot talking when Jennings says sternly, "I want you calling in between each flight, Kara. Unless you're too close on time. Then text me."

Jolting me from my agonized stupor, I whisper, "All right." But my voice breaks.

Jennings stops moving. "Kevin, give me just a minute with your mom," he orders our son. "We'll meet you inside by the ticket counter. We're less than a minute behind you."

"Sure, Dad," Kevin says. But he's hurting too. I can hear it. I whimper at my weakness and start to go after him, but Jennings holds me fast against his side before turning me to face him directly.

Then he's kissing me as if we've got all night instead of mere moments before Kevin and I slip into the security line. "You've got this. You'll be fine," he reassures me.

I shake my head, but before I can speak, his words stop me. "You have to, because otherwise, how will I? 'I need to know you're going to be okay because my heart aches so damn bad, I feel like I'm going to die."

"Jennings," I whisper his name. I reach up and stroke the softness of his beard. Memorizing it, him.

"I promise you'll get through this. And soon we'll be together again. You have everything you need to make it through, Kara," he whispers harshly.

"What's that?" I ask, because right now, I need to know.

"My whole world. I need you to take care of it for both of us."

"And who's going to take care of you?" I ask wonderingly, finally finding my voice.

He shakes his head, the movement making his beard brush back and forth against my palm. It sends shivers racing up my body, warming me when I'd begun to think I might die from the cold seeping inside me from the thoughts of leaving him. "I'll have you and Kevin looking out for me. It might be long distance, but that doesn't mean you're going to love me any less. Does it?" A hint of vulnerability crosses his face.

"Never." Realizing Jennings's pain is as close to the surface as my own, I pull his head down and tell him the final truth I never shared. "Last time I left Alaska, I was in so much pain because I was scared and alone. What was I going home to? When we came back, Kevin and I were empty from the loss of Dean and Jed. Now, I'm getting on a plane to go home, and I don't want to leave because my heart's finally stopped hurting." I try to make him understand in the final seconds we have. "Jennings, it's you who flung our souls back up into the air." Pressing my lips against his shocked ones a final time, I whisper against them. "That's because of your love. Now, I don't want to leave, but…"

"But the sooner you get home, the sooner I can do what I need to in order to be with you." He turns me forward, and we move again.

"Yes." The word is a single statement that encompasses my willingness to believe in John Jennings as a father and as the man I love. Spotting Kevin, I break away from Jennings.

The porter sees me head for check-in. After a few moments, and wincing painfully at the luggage fees hitting my card, I quickly give the man a tip.

Jennings refuses to let us handle our carry-ons until we reach the security checkpoint. Tipping his head back, he swallows before he grates out, "This is it for me." His head whips around, torment stamped on every feature of his face. I'm about to panic until I feel Kevin's hand settle at my shoulder. "Son, you take care of your mother like we talked about?"

"I will, Dad." Kevin lets me go and steps forward. If it wasn't for the clothes and the beard, I almost wouldn't be able to tell where one began and one ended in their embrace. "Love you, Dad," Kevin mumbles.

"Love you too, son. Always, forever. I'll be there sooner than you think. And use that phone often. Just not while you're in class," he says sternly.

My lips twitch despite themselves.

"Yes, sir," Kevin mutters as he steps back to give me and Jennings as much privacy as he can.

"I'm not sure I can do this," I cry softly. I may be the most practical person in the world but not when it comes to Jennings.

"Yes, you can," he murmurs, as he slides his strong arms around me. I lean into his strength for the last time for God only knows how long. "We both can, because there's no flying away from this, Kara. We're only going to get our old lives sorted so we can determine where we're going together."

I hear the pounding of his heart under my ear. "Don't think just because you haven't been to our apartment you haven't lived there." I pull back to look in Jennings's eyes. "I've been looking in your eyes every single day since the moment Kevin took on your coloring. Genetics be damned. You've been with me for fifteen years. Now hurry up and come home." Rising to the balls of my feet, I press my lips against his while I whisper something I said over and over throughout the night. "I love you, Ace."

"I love you too, Owl. Now, take Kevin and go. I won't leave until you're both through security." The rasp of his beard against my chin gets moist. Pulling back, I'm shocked by the wetness in his eyes. But beyond the same love, the sadness at our separation, there's an absolute certainty in us that gives me the strength to let go.

My fingers clench in at his chest one last time before I step back and let Jennings go. Turning toward Kevin, I move away so father and son can embrace tightly one final time. Kevin's as reluctant to let his father go as I am. *Oh Jennings, you're right. We're going to be fine but only once we're all together again.* And with that thought, it's time for us to begin the journey to head home. "Kevin, it's time," I say softly.

He shakes his head back and forth in the crook of Jennings's shoulder. I step forward and lay my hand on his back. "Come on, sweetheart. It's time to go home. The sooner we do—" I swallow hard as Jennings's damp eyes lock with mine. I have to clear my throat again. "The sooner your dad will come."

The two separate. Kevin moves reluctantly to my side. Reaching over, I grip his arm. I'm about to speak when Jennings beats me to it. "Call. Text. But as much as I want to prolong this"—he glances at his watch—"it's time."

"Right." The three of us shuffle over to the agent on duty. Handing over our IDs and tickets, Kevin and I enter the line. Jennings walks along side of us until we're about to make the first turn.

I open my mouth to tell him one last time how much I love him, but he presses his lips against mine. "I just want to breathe you in one last time," he sighs.

I don't waste words when the molecules of air between us transmit everything I want to say better than I can. Once, twice. On the third breath, I press my mouth to his hard and turn away not because I want to but because I have to. I grab Kevin's hand, and we quickly approach the TSA agent, hand over our tickets and IDs, and walk up to have our bags scanned.

I don't turn around.

Only once we collect our bags and make our way out of the security area do I glance back.

I can't see Jennings. I didn't expect to, but somehow my heart still aches.

Kevin tugs on my arm. "Come on, Mom. I see our gate up ahead." He steers me to the left.

I start to shove away all of my emotions inside a vault I might dare to open when I'm back in our home in Ponte Vedra—when I know it's really over. "So, what's the first thing you're going to do when you get home? Set up your gaming system? Maybe see if any of your friends are around?" I ask.

He stares at me as if I've suddenly grown two heads in the last ten minutes. "Call Dad. Let him know we're home. Tomorrow is soon enough to deal with everything else."

"Right." We reach our gate and plop into two empty chairs. Kevin whips out his earbuds and shoves them in his ears. As for me, I stare out into the light that's beginning to edge its way across the morning sky, another indicator this is real. As if I needed another, I think bitterly.

Occasionally, I check my phone to see if Jennings has texted, but I hope he's headed back to Maris's to find some sleep. He has to pack up himself before he heads back to his life in Seattle and whatever is waiting for him there. But I still clench the phone in my fist, because it's the only thing I've got left tying me to him, this place. I'm willing it to do something before I board the plane.

About thirty minutes later, boarding commences. Kevin and I stand as our boarding group is called. It's just like the last time I left. No, this is different, I remind myself. This time I don't just have Kevin; I have Jennings's heart. That's not going to change. Like he said, there's nothing between us but air.

I cling to that as I wait on the jetway for passengers to make their way to their seats. Kevin lifts our bags into the overhead compartment before allowing me to slip past him into the window seat. We both quickly sort out headphones as people walk past us.

"Ladies and gentlemen, we're almost ready to close the cabin door. Please shut down any laptops and small electronic devices and stow them beneath your seat," the flight attendant drones.

I reach for my cell phone and flip over to Settings. Just as I'm about to flip it to Airplane Mode, a text comes in. My heart lurches as I open it. It's a screenshot of a countdown calendar titled "Number of Days Until My Heart Beats Again."

And it's already ticking down from thirty-two.

A hiccupping sob escapes. I quickly type back. *We're on the plane. And I miss you already. I love you.*

Before Jennings can respond, I flip my phone to the required safety mode, stow it in my purse, and reach for my son's hand. "You know what makes me feel better, Kev? About everything?"

"What's that, Mom?"

"Knowing Uncle Jed instigated this. That somewhere up there"—I tip my chin upward—"he and your uncle Dean are likely sitting on barstools with drinks in hand toasting each other on a job well done."

Kevin's eyes fill, but the tears don't spill over. "I'll always miss them."

I reach up and stroke the scruff he didn't bother shaving this morning. "You loved them; I expect no less."

"But Mom?"

"Yes, sweetheart?"

"Is it crazy to say I feel so close to them after talking about them with all of you all summer? Especially Dad?" His face looks worried as if I'm going to immediately call his grief counselor the minute we touch down in Seattle for our layover.

"What I think, honey—" We taxi away from our gate. We both jerk in our seats a bit. I continue. "—is that you got to know them better than before as you were telling stories about them. That's not a bad thing. That's called love."

He looks thoughtful but doesn't respond. Our flight attendants quickly run through safety procedures before taking their seats. We line up for takeoff.

The engines roar to life. I close my eyes and remember when Jennings took me flying around Mendenhall. Many of the emotions coursing through me are similar to the ones I felt that day: fear, anxiety, nerves. Ironically, they're the same ones I felt when I left Alaska the last time.

*Trust me,* he said. And I do.

We race down the runway, and just as the wheels lift off, Kevin leans over to ask, "Do you think you would have fallen back in love with Dad when you were telling me stories about him? Even if we hadn't come to Alaska?"

I don't answer him right away. Instead, I study Juneau as we swoop up and over her beauty. I've been a scholar, a teacher, and the most important job ever, a mother. And over the course of my lifetime, I've fallen in love with both a boy and man. How fortunate for me they both happen to be Jennings.

Calmly, I turn from the dusky rose sky and tell my son what the evidence points to. "It's entirely possible, Kevin. I'm just grateful we both got to fall in love with who he is now without having to wonder."

His smile, so like his father's, tells me it was the right answer.

"Now, try to get some sleep. We've got a ridiculous trip ahead of us."

"You too, Mom." He puts on his headset and closes his eyes. Within minutes, Kevin's dozing.

I stay awake for a while as memories of past and present collide. We hit a pocket of air, and the plane dips but corrects itself quickly. What once might have thrown me off doesn't faze me.

And that's because of the man who once again settled my heart.

Leaning forward, I grab my phone from my purse. I pull up the last text from Jennings and smile when I think, *We'll be waiting for you with open arms, Jennings. Time stands between us too. Not just air. But hopefully, not for long.*

Then I slide my phone back into my purse again before I put in my own earbuds and drift off to memories of the night I spent loving Jennings the night before.

Later, I'll send him an email. This time, I know he'll get it.

# JENNINGS

I have a whole new appreciation for the idiom "Home is where the heart is," since mine is beating three thousand miles away.

If it wasn't for work, I'd be going mad with the intensity of how much I miss Kara and Kevin. Even though we FaceTime daily, it's not the same. I miss them constantly.

When I first left for Alaska, I was devastated over Jed. I've come back as someone my employees don't recognize. I'm polite and sociable, but more often than not, my door is closed to outside distractions. I'm driven to get through flights and paperwork, because each day I do means I'm one night closer to happiness.

Whether the people I work with miss the old me, I frankly don't care. I don't miss who I was; I just miss the family I made.

"What am I going to do?" I mutter, shoving my hands through my overlong, unruly hair. My office is lit only by the glow of my monitors.

A ping of an incoming email comes in. I sigh, knowing because of the late hour, it's not going to be Kara. She and I talked earlier before she crawled into bed. She spent the night grading tests and making me laugh with the creative answers she read aloud by her students who "feel they're too good to read a textbook. Jennings, I swear, if they think I'm tough, wait until they go to college." She was fuming.

I chuckled, leaning back in my office chair. "So, what you're saying is that I shouldn't take Ms. Malone's AP Physics class?"

Her voice dropped to a seductive purr. "I'm sure we could figure out a way for some after-school tutoring, Mr. Jennings. Since you are much older than my average student, I don't have to play by the same rules."

"Jesus, Kara," I growled as I shifted my hardened cock behind the zipper of my pants. "The minute we're alone again, we're totally role-playing that shit."

"Nineteen days, Ace. And whatever you want, since all I care about is holding you."

She slays me when she says things like that and I'm not fucking there. I closed my eyes and leaned back in my chair. "God, I love you," I said gutturally.

"I love you too. Now, go get some rest." Shortly after, we hung up, and here I am hours later trying to clear my board so nothing can stop me from leaving in nineteen days.

Nothing.

With a heavy sigh, I look at the email. Then I frown. "When did we bid on..." My voice trailing off, I pull up our bid proposal system. And there it is from just under three years ago.

A multiyear charter contract Jed dared me to bid on as a "long shot to expand your business in the southeast. I mean, what's the worst that happens, Jennings? You win and you actually have to come visit me in Florida?"

"I promise, I'll come to Florida if I win," I joked with him over the phone, as I was pressing Submit on the proposal. "Just don't hold your breath. I'm sure they're going to go with someone local. That's how it normally works."

"Hey, you never know. Miracles happen. But you're buying first round at my bar for everyone in the place when you win."

"That's a deal," I laughed as I ended the call.

Now, I can't move.

Fingers trembling, I move the mouse over and double-click on the file attachment. The top-sheet summary acknowledgment of an award of a contract for a billion-dollar company whose corporate headquarters is mere minutes from Kara. The screen blurs as I scan it.

*I told you, miracles happen*, I can hear Jed's voice in my ear. "They damn sure do, buddy. Thank you for mine. And I don't just mean this. I don't know how you realized we were perfect for each other. But because of you, I have everything. There will never be another like you," I whisper aloud.

Excitement churns the blood into my veins and through my heart. I shove to my feet and bellow, "Lou!"

The door to my office flies open. "What's wrong?" she asks anxiously. With my mood over the last several weeks, it could be anything from "I want lunch" to a major part to an engine is missing.

Coming around my desk, I grab my assistant into a massive hug. "I'll be leaving for Florida. As soon as possible."

"What?" she screeches, shoving me back a good three feet. "You weren't planning to head out to Kara for almost three more weeks..."

I just laugh. "This is business."

"Business?" she scoffs.

I walk behind my desk and turn my monitor around. "Business," I reiterate firmly. But damned if I can prevent the grin from twitching at my lips.

Her mouth falls open when she reads. "My God. Jennings, this was... You said there was no way..."

Seeing Lou speechless just broadens the smile on my face, the first real one I've sported since Juneau. It's in my voice when I tease, "Now, about my flight schedule?"

"I assume I should cancel all of your flights. Permanently," she returns dryly.

"That's a safe bet," I agree. My mind is whirling in a million different directions.

Just as she's about to leave, I call out, "Lou?"

"Yes?" She stops and faces me.

"Who do you think is best qualified to run the office here? I need someone I can trust explicitly." I know damn well who it should be, but I'm anticipating her reaction. After all, this is her chance to give me the mouthful I deserve for keeping my shit together since I left for

Jed's funeral and even after I came back. Lord knows, my head hasn't been in the game.

Lou doesn't disappoint me when she storms back up to me, finger outstretched. Poking it in my chest, she barks, "I want a thirty percent pay raise and two additional weeks of vacation. If this works out and I don't kill you after the first year, we'll discuss my buying a percentage of the company." Disdainfully, she somehow manages to look down her nose at me from her diminutive height. "You know you won't get a better offer anywhere else."

I want to burst out laughing. Instead, I swallow my mirth when I hold out my hand. "Then you have three tasks left as my office manager."

Her eyes sparkle, even as she says, "I'm not taking that hand until I know what they are."

God, this is why she's so feared and revered at the same time. And why I know when I print out and sign these contracts that will change all of our lives, things are going to be just fine when I eliminate the final barriers between me and Kara. The northwest division of Northern Star Flights will be in excellent hands. "First, call the lawyers. We need them here not only to witness me signing these, but to draw up your offer letter so it will take effect immediately with back pay to June 1."

Her belligerence fades as her eyes start to shimmer. "Jennings, you don't have to..."

I keep going as if she hasn't spoken because I do. She deserves so much more than compensation for her making this possible. I go on. "Second, get someone qualified in here you think can handle your job. There's things we need to go over, and we don't have much time."

A smile breaks across her face. "That's two. What's third?"

Dropping down into my chair, I pull my tablet into my lap muttering, "I need to find office space." Thank God for Jed sending me all those articles over the years. I pull up the file I saved and go into a zone.

"Jennings! Get your head out of the clouds and answer me, damnit. What's the third thing you need?"

Blankly, I lift my head and stare at her. Then I remember. "I need you find out what's taking so long with that jeweler in Jacksonville. I want to know where the hell that bracelet is."

There's silence between us. A rare smile breaks out across Lou's face. "How long do you think you'll need to get the legal stuff done?"

"I don't know." I frown thoughtfully. "Why?"

"Because the jeweler called me back yesterday. He tracked down the sale, though God knows how. After the Malones sold it—and might I add, I hate them?"

"Lou," I prompt her, though her sentiment matches my own.

"Well, the person who bought it was on vacation from Montana. *That* owner passed away, and the bracelet is back up for sale at an estate sale in Montana this weekend. If I were you I'd reconsider..."

"Tell Reg if he can't get in here tomorrow, I'm going to find someone else to get those papers drawn up. I'll pack what I need when I get back with that bracelet." I shove to my feet and walk to Lou. Pulling her into my arms, I press a smacking kiss on her forehead. "And we're telling the lawyers to give you a huge bonus."

"Screw that. I'm adding a clause to our contract I get to attend your wedding," she warns.

I smile faintly before reminding her, "She has to say yes."

"Jennings, Kara fell in love with you," Lou reminds me. "That hasn't changed in a matter of days."

"I know, but..." My voice trails off in a rare show of insecurity.

Lou pulls out of my arms to lean against my desk. Her next statement shows me exactly why she's been so invaluable to me for so many years. "You have a love that resuscitated itself after so much heartache. Do you know the only thing it needs now?" When I shake my head, she leans into my space and whispers, "Air. Now, set things in motion so you can give it that." She marches out of the office.

And I get back to work. Within moments, there's a second ping. It's the contact information for the auction in Montana.

FOR DAYS, I've been dodging Kara's FaceTime calls, though I've talked to her every chance I've had. It's been pure torture not to shout the news about the business and the bracelet to her, but I've been determined to surprise her.

Now, five days after the darkness never seemed like it was going to lift, I'm about to touch down in the land of the sun.

Twelve hours after I took off from Seattle, I'm impatiently waiting for the tower in St. Augustine to clear me when my headset crackles with, "Cleared to land, runway 2, Juliette Sierra Foxtrot 206."

"Affirmative," I acknowledge the tower's response before I turn in the direction of the runway gleaming in the Florida sunshine. All I want is to do is get out of this plane, get a car, and try to make it to Kara's school before she leaves for the day. I want to hold my woman in my arms more than I want air. And then I want to hold my son so I can breathe. Then I'll feel whole again.

Without much fanfare, I taxi the plane to the hangar. Then, after shutting down, I send Kevin a text.

*Are you and Mom still at school?*

Almost immediately, I get a reply. *Hey Dad. Why, are you sending Mom flowers or something?*

I answer, *Something like that.*

*Yes, we'll be here for about another hour.*

*Would it be possible to get to her classroom if you don't have an appointment?*

*Not without a pass, Dad. Why?*

Deciding to take him into confidence, I type, *Because I just landed at the airport. How do I get in?*

Frustration eats at me when I don't immediately see little blue dots appear. While waiting, I pull suitcase after suitcase down. My phone starts to ring. Seeing a picture of me and Kevin appear, I warn him, "Son, it's supposed to be a surprise."

"I'm going to the front office to have you added to the list of people to come up and see Mom. I told her I left a book in my locker. You're really *here*?" His emphasis on the last word causes me to pinch my nose. He's out of breath, but he sounds so happy.

"Just wait until you hear what I have to tell you both." My voice is choked.

Kevin's yell might be able to be heard in Kara's classroom. "It's a surprise, son," I remind him, as I fling bags over my shoulder.

"I'm on a different floor, Dad." I smile at the excitement in his voice.

"Make sure she doesn't leave. I've already checked; my rental is waiting right outside. I should be there in about twenty minutes."

"You got it. Hey, Dad?"

"Yeah, son."

"I can't wait to hug you." Kevin hangs up the phone.

But I freeze with mine to my ear. Slipping it into my pocket, I stack my bags and make my way into the blistering August summer heat. Unperturbed by it, I quickly locate my rental and throw my bags in before I answer my son aloud. "And I'm so glad to be home, I'm afraid how hard I'm going to hug you both."

Pulling up my GPS so I can navigate to the school, I'm thankful I'm not in Seattle traffic. It's time to go to grab hold of my family. And once I do, I'm never going to let them out of my arms.

All the way there, I can hear Jed cheering inside my head.

# KARA

"Did you find your book, sweetheart?" I ask Kevin when he comes back to my room.

"Uh, no. I guess I put it in my bag after all." He digs through his bag in the back of my classroom before pulling out a book thicker than an encyclopedia volume. He sighs, "I don't know how I missed it."

"I don't either considering you gripe to me daily about my classroom not being closer to your locker," I reply dryly. "But alas, we all have those days." Something twitches near the region of my heart. I ignore it. Now is not the time to be thinking about the way Jennings has seemed to have pulled back in the last few days.

Sure he's said the right things, including "I love you," but I haven't seen his face in five days. And I feel like I'm moving in a fog. Frantically, I try to concentrate on the planner in front of me, but all I want to remember is the feel of Jennings's lips on mine. "Why does this have to be so hard?" I say out loud.

Then everything stills: my body, my heart, certainly time and space. Because there's no way Jennings answers me, "I don't know. What kind of ridiculous torture are you dreaming up for your students over there, Owl?"

And I don't just mean Jennings appearing in front of me wearing a

T-shirt clinging lovingly to his body and a pair of worn jeans. I mean the fact I'm obviously hallucinating and I'm still standing. "How is this possible?" I wonder aloud.

"Dad!" Kevin shouts. Seconds later, my son is crashing into his father with such force, he knocks Jennings back a step. "You made it!"

*You made it.* Kevin's words ricochet inside my head, fueling my legs to move. "You're here. You're really here." My voice is breaking, but I don't care. All I care about is becoming a part of the circle of love Jennings is opening his arm to welcome me to.

I crash into them both with the same amount of force, feeling everything wrong slide out of me the minute Jennings's arm wraps around my waist. But everything perfect happens the moment Kevin's arm slides over his and squeezes me tighter into both of them.

"I can't believe you're here. How did you get into the building?" I babble. Laying my head on Jennings's chest, there's nothing but peace when I hear the perfect cadence of his heart. I hear him chuckle, and the first real smile I've had in days lifts my lips. Tipping my head back, I wait for his answer.

I'm shocked when he nods to our son. "I had a little inside help."

I gently accuse, "A missing textbook?" I'm confused about why Jennings is here weeks early, but in no way am I upset.

Kevin shrugs but gives me an unrepentant grin. "It was a good surprise though, right?"

Squeezing my guys, I answer, "The best. The absolute best."

Jennings clears his throat. "Actually, I think I have one that's going to top it." Pulling back, he reaches for his back pocket before pulling something out. "Son, how about giving your mom and me a little space?"

Kevin quickly scoots a few feet away. Jennings wraps his arms around me fully and pulls my body flush against him. "What's with the big eyes, Owl?"

"I can't believe you're here in front of me." I touch his chest, his jaw, his hair to make sure he's still real.

He chuckles. "I'd have been here days ago, but I had to fly to Montana over the weekend, and that delayed me getting here."

"I don't understand."

"I'll explain everything when we get home." I shiver when he says that word. I know it doesn't go unnoticed when his arms tighten around me. But instead of kissing me like I'm aching for him to do, he continues. "After all—" He reaches up behind his neck and pulls my right wrist down. "—I wasn't coming here without it. No matter what it cost me."

His head bends as something warm from the heat of his body is wrapped over my wrist. Something impossibly familiar. My other hand drops from his shoulder and rises to my mouth to muffle a sob. "No. It's impossible," I manage to get out.

Jennings finishes clasping my grandmother's bracelet back on before he gathers me close to his body again. "Now, everything's the way it should be. Oh, except for this." Jennings lowers his head and captures my lips with his.

I absorb the pure emotion that Jennings sends through every brush of his lips against mine. My trembling arms slide back up his chest and around his neck as his head slants, his tongue briefly licking at mine before he pulls back. "Kevin," he mutters, regret and amusement in those two syllables.

But if the fire in his eyes and the hitch in his breathing is any indication, I can expect more later. Rising up, I brush a kiss on the underside of his jaw. "How do I thank you?"

"Do you love me?"

"Always." And his eyes flare as I vow that to him in front of the most important audience in the world—our son.

"Then take me home. I'll tell you both the rest there."

Stepping back, I hold out an arm to our son, who rushes back in, for once not giving us any grief about our PDA. I don't imagine he would considering his own eyes are damp. "Why don't you head home with your father and order dinner from Napoli's to be delivered?" I suggest.

Kevin lets out a war whoop. "They have the best pizza, Dad."

Jennings frowns. I cede his silent point and tack on, "In this area, Jennings. Remember, you're in the land of humidity. You take what you can get."

His full lips break out into a smile before he leans down and brushes a quick kiss against mine. "Sounds perfect."

Now, Kevin gripes, "Are you two going to be doing that your entire visit?"

Giving me a wink, Jennings says, "I think we'll be doing that a lot longer than you think. How long will you be?"

Twisting until I can see the wall clock, I'm now more determined than ever to finish up the lesson plan and test prep for the rest of the week. "Maybe another hour? But Jennings, Kevin has homework," I warn him.

Kevin deflates right in front of our eyes. Jennings chuckles. "Grab your stuff and let's get going. The sooner you both are done, the sooner I'll explain everything. Deal?"

"Deal!" Kevin proclaims. He sprints over to his bag and shoves in the stuff he needs. "We have to stop by my locker on the way out."

"Maybe you can get him to clean it?" I tip my head back with a smile.

Jennings presses his lips against mine. Hard. "I'll see what I can do. Call when you leave?"

"Will do." The next thing I know I'm being spun around by Jennings, who's laughing.

"God, I can't believe I'm holding you." Putting me down, he grabs Kevin in a bear hug. "Both of you."

"We feel the same way, Dad." Kevin hugs him back just as hard. "Mom, we'll see you at home."

"Yeah, Mom." Jennings eyes are sparkling. "See you at home." They both turn to leave.

"Text me when you get in!" I shout out. After they clear my view, I lift my wrist to the light to stare at the bracelet I haven't worn in more than sixteen years. Clasping my hand over it, I whisper, "God, Dean. Jennings is here and he brought Gran's bracelet to me." I close my eyes. "I don't know what to do with this much happy."

"I do." My eyes snap open when I see Jennings lounging in the doorway. His smile is lazy and full of heat. But his eyes, God, they're lit with love. "So, get behind that desk and get to work so I can show you when you get home."

Instead of throwing a smart comment back at him, I let my lips curve and my hips sway as I do what he asks. But by the time I turn around to see his reaction, he's already gone.

That's when I sit down in my spinning stool and push off in circles until my head's as dizzy as my heart. My hands are raised in the air the entire time in sheer happiness. When the stool stops, my head's still spinning. Better yet, so is my heart, I think, picking up my pen with a smile.

Now, I hurry to get done with my work so I can get home. I need to know every last detail of what happened..

I DROP my pizza on my plate with a splat. "You've got to be kidding?" I sputter.

When I saw the amount of luggage in my bedroom, I joked to Jennings, "Planning on moving in?" He laughed before pressing me up against the wall out of Kevin's line of sight and showed me without words how much he missed me before he muttered, "The plans for your new house are too small. We need to do something about that."

After, I went to the bathroom and yep, whisker burns and a dreamy smile on my face. I didn't bother to hide either from Kevin.

Jennings saved the big news for over dinner. "Not kidding at all." Standing, he walks into the living room a few steps away to pull out a folder. Bringing it back to the table, he hands it to me. "It was Jed." His voice is raspier than it was a moment earlier. "He dared me to bid on the work."

I flip through the file, but there's too many pages and my own eyes are hazing over. Flinging it next to my plate, I beg him, "Just tell us what it means, Jennings."

Reaching over, he takes Kevin's hand before he reaches for mine. As if I needed another reason to love him. "It means, that"—he nods at the folder—"it's a big enough contract to open up the southeast division of Northern Star Flights. I'll be transferring some guys, but I need to hire pilots. For the next five years, we have an exclusive contract with the hotel to fly executives and VIPs from St. Augustine to the Caribbean, St. Simons, well, pretty much anywhere they ask within a day-trip radius."

"Jennings?" I say it at the exact same time Kevin pleads, "Dad?" The word is a hope, a wish, a prayer from us both.

"It means, we're going to need a bigger house. I looked up your model online, and there's no way—umpphh." Kevin and I tackle Jennings out of his chair at the exact same moment.

We're laughing and talking over one another, making plans and celebrating. What we're not doing is letting go. According to Jennings, we never have to do that again.

For long moments we lie on the kitchen floor a tangled heap of family. My head is on Jennings's chest. Kevin has a grip of his dad's hand, but he's rolled off to the side. Amused, I know there's nothing that's going to be able to wipe the smile from his face for a long time. And that's because one of the two men who would do anything for me, did. Squeezing my eyes tight, I pray he can hear me.

*Thank you, Jed.*

I'm surprised when Jennings leans over to whisper in my ear, "I said almost the exact same thing when I got the email," before he presses a kiss on the edge. Lifting us both into a sitting position with an ab curl that makes my toes tingle, he announces, "Now, let's finish eating. Kara, you have to work tomorrow, and I'm taking over your kitchen while you're there. I need to make some calls to some real estate agents for office space."

"Mom, Dad can come to my swim meet tomorrow night," Kevin says with excitement, scrambling to his feet. "Can I call Brooks to let him know?"

"Quickly. Then you have to finish dinner and studying for your history test," I warn him.

"On it." He starts to dash away but freezes. Turning, he jogs back and captures both of us in a hug. Summarizing everything we're all feeling, Kevin chokes out, "I'll always miss Uncle Dean and Uncle Jed, but now I feel like I have everything." Then he dashes away calling, "Save me some pepperoni," over his shoulder.

Jennings and I don't move from our position on the floor. Still cradled in his lap, I whisper to him, "This exact moment was worth waiting my life for."

Groaning, Jennings drops his head and nips my lips, demanding entrance. His tongue seeks and finds mine, licking and twining against it. I don't give him passive; I give him everything in that kiss. My tongue strokes over his, seeking the warm recesses of his mouth, relearning the taste I've been so long denied due to distance. What had been merely dormant since that last night in Alaska only began to flame out of control between us.

That was until we heard, "Come on. Am I going to have to put ground rules in place?" Kevin stomps back into the kitchen. But as aggrieved as he sounds, his face is shining with joy.

Jennings gets to his feet before lifting me to mine. Then he turns a wicked grin to our son. "Get used to it, kid. Who knows, if I can convince your mother, maybe we'll give you a little brother or sister yet."

My womb convulses at the idea of carrying John Jennings's child while he'd be with me the whole pregnancy. But we've had enough excitement for tonight. So, all I say is a mild "We'll see. Now, what do you mean the new house is too small? It's perfectly lovely."

And just like a normal family, we begin bickering about things like three-car garages around the kitchen table. Because that's what we are —a family.

Finally.

# EPILOGUE

## Kara

"What do you mean there's no time for an epidural?" I shriek in the face of the anesthesiologist. I reach out and grab his lab coat and yank him as close to my face as I can. "This is complete and utter..."

"Kara." Jennings comes up on the other side of me and smooths my matted hair away from my face with an ice-cold cloth. My husband says soothingly, "Your contractions are too close together. They expect you to deliver in the next thirty minutes."

Frantically, I reach up and grab Jennings's face. "No, that's not possible. Jennings, I was in labor with Kevin for-ev-er!" I screech the last word as another contraction slams through me. I quite possibly also loosen a few of his teeth, but he doesn't complain at all. In fact, he's grinning when it passes, and I release him. "Oops," I mutter.

"I'm here every step of the way." His voice is husky. "Whatever you need." And damn if that doesn't bring on the waterworks that have flooded both of our eyes every time he's said those words since we found out I've been carrying his second child.

Eighteen years after the first.

Kevin is waiting in the hallway with Brad, Rainey, and their brood. I'm so grateful they're here on vacation, but— "Where's Maris? She missed Kevin's birth. The baby's two weeks early. And now it's coming way too fast. How is she going to get here?"

"Shh." Jennings props me up from behind and rocks me.

It temporarily distracts me from my distress as the pain in my lower back eases. "Oh, that feels nice."

His beard brushes against the side of my damp cheek. "In a few weeks, I'll give you a few more things that feel nice."

"Stop. That's what got us here in the first place," I admonish.

"Yeah," Jennings hums next to my ear.

I giggle as his whiskers tickle my ear like they do every single morning we wake up together.

"I'm just shy of forty-one years old and I'm about to be a mother for the second time," I announce.

"Sexy. You forgot to mention that part. For shame, Dr. Malone."

I sigh. "I haven't earned my doctorate yet, Jennings. I have a feeling this little one might put that on a hiatus."

Jennings shifts a little bit so he's able to meet my eyes. "No, Kara. If I need to shift my responsibilities at the office, I will. But your dreams got put on hold long enough. You will be Dr. Malone by spring, even with our little one."

I'm about to argue with him when another contraction hits. "We'll...see," I gasp out.

He smirks and I want to simultaneously punch him and kiss him. Instead, I decide to derail him entirely. "What," I pant, because that last contraction was awful, "if I want to become Dr. Jennings? You keep saying Dr. Malone as if that's still my dream. Didn't we learn dreams change?" Then I groan as another contraction hits. "Damn, this hurts."

Jennings stills, whether at my pain or my words, I'm not certain. "Go into my overnight bag," I order.

Woodenly, he stands, makes sure I'm settled, before going over to the overnight bag. "Manila envelope inside," I hiss, just as another contraction is about to start.

Jennings grabs it. Inside is copy of court-notarized paperwork Kevin and I gave Jennings for Father's Day last year having his name reordered to be Kevin Malone Jennings. "Hearing...few weeks ago...you were...in Atlanta. Lawyer sent those over." I pant out a few breaths while Jennings fails as a labor and delivery coach but completely rocks it as a father as tears drip from his eyes. "Surprise. Now we'll all be Jennings. And it will be Dr. *Jennings* when it happens," I groan.

"Have I told you how much I love you today?" His voice is quiet.

"Absolutely," I grit out through my teeth.

"Have I thanked Jed and Dean for their help in bringing us back together?" God, if I could, I'd run across the room and throw myself in his arms. Because if there's one thing I've learned over the years, Jennings doesn't take anything about the life we've forged together for granted.

"Not sure. But I am certain they're watching. Mind putting those away before I start making threats about the log again?" I only partially joke, as the pain recedes.

Placing the envelope on top of the bag, Jennings crosses the room. He places his hand on my protruding stomach. Brushing his lips across mine, he says, "You, Kevin, this baby, you're the only air I need."

I open my mouth to tell him how much I love him when the door bounds open behind him. Jennings whirls around. But it's a surprise.

One of the best in the world.

"Did you really think you were going to have this baby without me?" Maris drawls.

"Oh, my God! How did you get here so quick?" I shove my husband away and open my arms to my best friend.

"Don't worry about that. How are you?"

"They won't give me an epidural," I wail.

"Jesus, Jennings. Why don't you take a break and go hit Nick or something?" Maris suggests.

Jennings barks out a laugh but—wisely, in my opinion—doesn't leave my side.

"Nick's here?" I ask, confused.

"Just got here," Maris says breezily. "But that's for later. Right now, let's focus on getting this tiny human out of you. I still can't believe you didn't find out what the sex is."

Shyly, I glance up at my husband, who's shaking his head, and finally admit why I wouldn't. "I couldn't afford to the first time."

Jennings stills. "So, I wanted Jennings to have the same feeling of anticipation I had of waiting to know whether this baby was a boy or a girl."

Jennings mutters, "My Owl," before he scoots me up in bed. Sitting down behind me, he buries his head in my neck just as I let out a piercing yell.

"Christ, Kara! What the hell was that?" He jerks back.

"If I remember from being on the phone the last time, Jennings—" Maris picks up the nurse's button and presses it. "—that's Kara's signal for it's 'go time.' Lucky for you, this one went by much faster than the last one did."

My mind, already in that twisted place of agony and joy mothers go when they're about to birth their children, still has enough sanity to snap, "There is no mathematical way you could have made it here on time."

Leaning down, she drawls, "Not unless I was here already. Think about that while you're pushing out the newest member of our family. Okay?"

"I wanted to be thinking about Jennings falling on a log, damnit!" I shout at the top of my lungs just as the doctor and nurses push the door open.

"Well, that's certainly a more inventive way of cursing out the father-to-be than I've ever heard before," the doctor laughs.

"She can say whatever she wants. Just make sure she's safe." Jennings's voice is terrified.

"First-time father?" the doctor guesses. Before we can correct him or go into our long or complicated history, he asks the nurses to move a lamp over and a tray of surgical implements in place. Jennings holds back a growl as he lifts the lower sheet.

The doctor's head whips to mine. "Mrs. Jennings, did you know you're at ten centimeters?"

I puff out of my mouth. "Can I push?" The pressure in my lower stomach is almost overwhelming.

The nurses lower my bed back to get me in position as the doctor says, "Let me burst the embryonic fluid and then...yes, here we go. Mr. Jennings and...?"

"Just call them Jennings and Maris," I snap. I'm already lifting my legs into position. Jennings pales while Maris cackles like a hen.

"Right. Jennings, Maris, each of you grab one of Mrs. Jennings's legs and brace them while she pushes. It's entirely possible we're going to meet this little one very shortly," the doctor announces before he ducks down beneath my legs.

"Fuck, Owl. I love you." Before he grabs my leg, Jennings leans down and presses his lips all over my face. "Try to remember that as you're cursing me to death."

"Ace?" My hand grips his arm with the strength of a thousand men or a single mother in labor. "I don't think I can curse you. You're here, and soon he or she will be with us too."

Jennings's chest is rising with the force of his emotion. I knee him in the chest with my leg, reminding him of his job. "Right," he says sheepishly, grabbing hold and pushing my leg back.

Maris, who has a death grip on the other, grins. "I think we're ready."

"Mrs. Jennings, on three, push. One, two, three," the doctor counts.

When I hear the magic number, I grab behind my thighs with all my might and let out a banshee cry. "Get this baby out of me!" I strain and hold until the doctor says, "Relax."

I drop back on the bed with a thunk. Within seconds, Jennings's lips are mopping up the sweat on my brow. "Amazing. You're simply amazing."

"Save your compliments, Ace," I tell him on a shaky laugh. "This could take a while."

He grins, before pressing his lips against mine.

I push and ease up seven more times before the doctor says, "The head's crowning. I think one more big push will get the head out!"

It's then I hear him, and the tears roll unchecked down my face. *Do you remember the last time we did this? God, you were so brave and strong then, Kara, even if you wanted to emasculate Jennings. Now? Getting to watch you do this with him at your side? Just know I'm so proud of you, my beautiful sister. And I'll always love you.* Sobbing, I reach for Jennings's hand beneath my thigh and grip it. "If it's a boy, it's Jedidiah Dean. If it's a girl, it's Deana

Smith. Deal?" We hadn't talked about names, but hearing my brother in my head in this precious moment solidified what I instinctively knew.

They'd live on in the child Jennings and I made together.

Jennings bends down and whispers, "Deal. Now push so we can find out which one it is."

My eyes flicker to Maris to find hers wet. "I love you, sister. Find your happy."

"Damnit, Kara, will you push the baby out so I can?" she cries.

And with a push that gets the head out, I listen to the incredible beauty of a cry that started years ago in the Alaskan wild. Another push gets the shoulders out, a final one has the baby landing in the doctor's arms. I lie back as the doctor murmurs. Nurses scurry around as Jennings strokes my hair, his eyes locked on our baby. Then, finally, words I've waited forever to hear are spoken.

The doctor turns to Jennings and says, "Would you like to hold your daughter?"

Jennings is a wreck when he accepts the tiny bundle against his chest. Tears streak down his face as he looks down at the wrinkled face that will grow into a combination of all of us. "Welcome to the world, Deana. I'm your daddy."

The air that was just sucked out of my lungs may be lost forever hearing the man I love saying that. But who needs it anyway? I'd rather live on the love pumping through my heart.

The love John Jennings gives to me every day.

I turn to Maris and weakly smile. "Now, will you go tell Kevin we just added a daughter to our family?"

"With pleasure." Leaning over to press a kiss to my still-damp fore-head, she whispers, "Remember when I asked if you'd ever really got over what you felt for Jennings?"

I think back to that early night in Alaska after we all arrived so close to Dean and Jed's passings. Jennings had just kissed me again for the first time, and I was confused—no, terrified—of falling for the only man who ever truly made my heart soar. "Of course I remember."

"I don't think that will ever change, do you?" She nods to where

Jennings is cooing at our daughter despite the nurses' attempts to corral him to have her weighed and fingerprinted.

A huge smile bursts across my face. "No. Nothing about the feelings I have for Jennings will change. Of that, I'm certain."

And while Maris leaves to go let everyone know the news, I sit back to indulge in watching the new addition of our family wrap her father around her tiny finger. After all, it took exactly the same amount of time for her big brother to do the same, and he was much older when he met his dad for the first time.

As fatigue causes my eyes to drift shut, I can only imagine what Jennings is going to be like when Deana is Kevin's age. Giggling at the thought as I drift off, I never know my husband's tender look switches from our daughter to me when I do.

THREE DAYS after the birth of our daughter, I pull up my email. Taking a deep breath, I start a new message. I read it over and over, making sure each word is perfect before I hit Send.

A few moments later, Jennings's phone pings. Pulling it out of his pocket, he opens the message before his head snaps in my direction. "What on earth? Kara?" Confusion is written across his face.

"I told you, Ace. Every step of the way." I cradle Deana to my breast as a dawning understanding crosses Jennings's face as he receives the first of the emails I'll send him as our daughter has the same milestones our son did so Jennings doesn't miss a moment.

I brush my lips across our daughter's head as I recall what I typed.

*Jennings,*

*God, here we go for the second time around.*

*I can't believe we have a little girl. I know you'll never forget it, but after the shortest labor in history, Deana Smith Jennings was born on November 19 at 6:14 PM weighing only 6 pounds, 13.5 ounces.*

*We named her after the two most influential men in our lives — our two brothers who we wish more than anything could hold her. They were there with us in spirit. I could feel Dean in the delivery room, crazy as that sounds. There's no proof, but he was there — I just know it.*

*I'm so glad you love her name, but to be honest, I still would have been the one to choose. After all, I'm the one who was pushing her out with no drugs. Remember that, would you?*

*Oh, Jennings, I'll never forget that moment when you first held her. Much as I will never forget the first time you held our son. Both images are committed to my memory forever.*

*Beyond anything, know I will always love you. The only thing that ever separated us was time and air and we conquered both.*

*I love you. Now. Forever. Always.*

*Kara*

**THE END**

## COMING SOON
### Return by Land

I never expected my life to take the turn it did. I planned to raise my children surrounded by family and love.

But plans, and people, change.

As I began to pick up the pieces of my life, I found myself confronted with a wealth of memories tucked away inside me I'd long buried. Especially when I came face-to-face with the ones of Kody Laurence from summers long ago.

When we land together thousands of miles away from where we first met, can we return to the friendship we once had?

Or is it our time for something more?

Return by Land:
    Order at Amazon.com
    Add to Goodreads

# ALSO BY TRACEY JERALD

**AMARYLLIS SERIES**

FREE TO DREAM

FREE TO RUN

FREE TO REJOICE

FREE TO BREATHE

FREE TO BELIEVE

FREE TO LIVE

FREE TO DANCE (COMING SPRING 2021)

**GLACIER ADVENTURE SERIES**

RETURN BY AIR

RETURN BY LAND

RETURN BY SEA (COMING JANUARY 11, 2021)

**STANDALONES**

CLOSE MATCH

RIPPLE EFFECT

**LADY BOSS PRESS RELEASES**

EASY REUNION

CHALLENGED BY YOU

**1, 001 DARK NIGHT SHORT STORY CHALLENGE**

COMING DECEMBER 2020

# ACKNOWLEDGMENTS

First, to my husband. You held my hand through every adventure in Alaska, as I hope you do until our last breath. I love you more today than yesterday.

To my son, thank you for growing up to be an inquisitive, sensitive boy who is showing a great talent at quick jokes. You are a miracle I'll never take for granted. Love you, baby.

To my Mom, you gave me everything so I could chase my dreams. I love you.

Jen, when all this is done, you can decide where we go next. Trust me, the Lumberjack show is worth seeing twice. I love you.

Tara, I remember the night on the front porch when you finally told me about you with whatever junk we could find and homemade Kahlua, stars overhead on the front porch in Yulee. The strength of the woman you are shone through all the way back then. I love you sister.

To my Meows, we're an indomitable force together. Just don't let anyone hack our Zoom calls. I love you all!

To Sandra Depukat from One Love Editing, thank you for handling all the randomness I ping to you. And thank you for being my friend. Happy (belated) anniversary, love!

To Holly Malgieri, from Holly's Red Hot Reviews, you are and always will be my twin. Thank you for working on RBA, but I am so damn proud of all your accomplishments this year. I love you.

To Gel, at Tempting Illustrations, it constantly eludes me how you can develop such beauty from mere words. You are a true artist. XOXO

To the amazing team at Foreword PR, you are the backbone to making all of us shine. I can't thank each and every one of you enough for your time, your dedication, and your heart.

Linda Russell, remember when I sent you text from 3,400 miles away saying, "So, look where I am?" Look where it lead. LOL. Just to say, I'm more grateful to call you my friend above every other title. So, just deal with the random packages. I love you.

To Susan Henn, Amy Rhodes, and Dawn Hurst, all of you go so far above and beyond each and every day. Thank you for doing what you do.

For the members of Tracey's Tribe, my Facebook home away from home, each of you is amazing!

And for all of the readers and bloggers who take the time to enjoy my books, thank you for your support. Every day, I am humbled and honored by you.

I rarely do this, but I have to do a call out to The Killers for the song "Shot at the Night." After so many years after the loss of my father, who loved their music, I can finally listen to your music again. It's available on the Return by Air playlist on Spotify.

# ABOUT THE AUTHOR

Tracey Jerald knew she was meant to be a writer when she would re-write the ending of books in her head when she was a young girl growing up in southern Connecticut. It wasn't long before she was typing alternate endings and extended epilogues "just for fun".

After college in Florida, where she obtained a degree in Criminal Justice, Tracey traded the world of law and order for IT. Her work for a world-wide internet startup transferred her to Northern Virginia where she met her husband in what many call their own happily ever after. They have one son.

When she's not busy with her family or writing, Tracey can be found in her home in north Florida drinking coffee, reading, training for a runDisney event, or feeding her addiction to HGTV.

Made in the USA
Columbia, SC
17 May 2021